THE MORTALITY OF QUEENS

The Umbra Book 1

by J. L. Dawn

Interact Publishing - www.interactpublishing.com

ASIN : B095GRZTJG
ISBN-13: 979-8507512300

Cover design by: Small Woodland Creatures
Library of Congress Control Number: 2018675309
Printed in the United Kingdom and United States of America

CONTENTS

THE OTHER REALM

The Queen 'Neath the Hedge came from nowhere – from out of reed and nightshade.

She conquered two worlds: Britain and the Other Realm – home of the mysterious Umbra. She bound the worlds together and, 400 years after her death, every Briton is still mortally bound to a shadow self, to an Umbra.

Arthur knows Amorrie will be the death of him. She is his Umbra. If she dies, he will too, and Amorrie is hunted in two worlds.

England 1792: the era of Pride and Prejudice, of balls, coffee-houses and marrying for love. Umbra are part of everyday life: they come when summoned, attend balls, dress fashionably, gossip, suffer jealousies and are illustrated in newspapers and books.

Amorrie doesn't do these things. She survives.

THE UMBRA

Get involved

To find out more about Umbra and sign up for instructions on how to invent one that we can use in a future book in the series, go to

www.Amorrie.com

Feedback?

Yes please. We respond positively to criticism but it's just as helpful to know what you enjoyed – **Contact@interactpublishing.co.uk**. And please let us know if you post any reviews of the book.

www.InteractPublishing.com

1 – DEATH OF THE BORDERER

Arthur

≡

Umbra of note
Amorrie and her human ally Arthur
Brughe and his human ally Hurting
Muscari and her human ally Viscount Exeter
Charon the Borderer and his human ally the Countess of Alnwick

≡

'Amorrie.'

It was his fourth call since he had begun to ready himself. Damn the girl. She never came on his command. 'Amorrie, do not make me summon you here. I warn –'

'Naked.' The word flitted into that portion of his mind she was wont to inhabit.

He did not believe her. 'I do not care if you are at your toilet. If you are not in this room upon the moment –'

Her sound came, a lost breath entering a catacomb. A wrinkle creased the candlelight. He spun away from his dressing table, for she rarely ventured close to his mirror. A misty mouth of darkness swelled upon his crowded drawing desk, a swamp of unwashed pots, pungent scents and oily cloths where wooden brushes rose up like hunting herons. The mist congealed where the shadows congregated, consuming any lingering light, and there she was, half-sitting, half-sprawled on top of his rough sketches for the portrait of Countess Harrington and Scampion.

'By all the Saints, Amo... you are naked.' He threw a crumpled paint rag at her. It landed close but she didn't move to claim it. The velvety dark earth scent of her world had entered with her.

'Cover yourself,' he averted his eyes. 'Get you dressed; in finery, mind. We are out within the hour. Have you your finery?'

'No.'

Though he had quickly turned away from her unsettling female form, the vision of her small exposed body dawdled in his mind. Shocked at what he recalled, his gaze jerked back. Crimson smudges daubed her pale features and its stain ran over her hands. Drops of the taint initialled her naked chest.

'Is that blood? What is the matter with your leg?' It was misshapen, and she nursed it with both hands. 'Gods, you have broke it.'

Not two hours since, he had clutched at his own leg after a violent spasm of pain that he had put down to cramps.

'It mends.' She nurtured it purposefully, concentrating her will and forcing energy into it. 'You will insist on calling me at the most inconvenient of times and from uncommon situations.'

'What is it you do over there to arrive in such a predicament?'

'Survive.'

A tawdry pile of clothes, rags really, had trailed her into his studio. They were strewn about her like entrails; bedraggled, bloody and riddled with sand.

'Oh it will not do, Amorrie,' he almost sobbed. 'We have an invitation, fresh delivered, to one of the most esteemed addresses in all London and you are not even clothed fit for the parish poorhouse. I may as well have a Portsmouth Poll upon my arm. Conjure your showiest garments, here, now.'

'I have not a whit of strength left for conjuring.'

'We have a party to attend.'

'I abhor those. You know it.'

'You must accompany me, and you know it.' He adjusted a

silken blue cravat in the candlelight in front of the mirror.

'Find more agreeable garments if you can and be quick about it. A carriage comes for us within the hour.' He shrugged on his new double-breasted frock-coat. 'Be sure and wash all that blood away.' He stopped, wondering whether it was wise to ask: 'If it is not yours, then who–'

'It is gone, see.' She had smeared it over his painting cloth. 'My leg knits a little.'

He gave his cravat one final plump before turning to find her half standing, using a stick of his charcoal to steady herself. Dressed now in her rags, she dragged a tiny barely-toothed comb through sand-encrusted raven tresses.

'Never have... You...' The vision of her: pathetic, vulnerable and innocent of the world, made his heart brim, so for the merest moment he forgot all the wilful torments she inflicted on him. 'Oh, Amorrie, you will be the death of me.'

'I intend it so,' she said, snapping the spell, and reminding him that his life was mortally entwined with hers. She treated her own survival as if heedless of this fact.

'And you will sink my career far sooner.'

'I'd end it tonight if only I had power here.'

'Truly, you have that power. That entrance was morbid, even for you.'

'Do not be so thistle-ish. I'm here, aren't I? Where's it we must attend?'

'Oh, you will not believe,' his voice a trill now, his anger vented, 'we are both summoned, no yet, commanded, by the noblest lady...'

◆ ◆ ◆

Their carriage joined a queue halfway round Marksfayre. Light, some from the clean-burning lamps of Monsieur Aimé Argand, paraded out from the porches of the stylish five story town-houses that bordered the square. The probing fingers of illumination burnished the sheen on the stamping horses, awoke carved adornments upon the carriages and sparred with the stretching vastnesses of the eight majestic chestnut trees that dominated the centre of the square.

His head lolled out of the carriage window, gawping like some wanton bawd at the splendour of the scene; drinking in the rich promise the evening held for adding to his small list of commissions.

'There's the Lady of Megginch. She arrived on Tuesday's morn tide upon the galleon Salamander of Leith from Highlands. Her Umbra is Rannock. He's striking; a Henkie. Have you ever met one?'

Amorrie scowled from his lap. He wished she would try more. The girl was his handicap and, far too often, his shame.

'Will there be Catholics?' She soothed her hair, which was agitated and thrummed imperceptibly. She'd told him it was restless and had once tried to escape while she slept.

Catholics had held an unfathomable fascination for her since he had told her of the London riots and marches against popery he had witnessed as a child.

'No, Amorrie, that is most unlikely, and you are not to suggest such a thing to another Umbra.'

At last his carriage lurched to a halt in front of a short wide stair before two ornately-glazed doors. One was held ajar by a doorman, a slave captured from the Africas. Another man, similarly spruce in the season's favoured chalk-blue livery, whisked open the door of their carriage.

'Who should we say, sir?'

'Tenebris,' he said, 'Arthur Tenebris.' The doorman cocked his head as if to enquire whether there was any more to Arthur's title. 'Just plain Mr Tenebris.'

'I await your Umbra's name, sir?'

'Oh yes, sorry, and Amorrie.' Arthur popped the girl into a wide pocket on the front of his frock-coat, tailored for her accommodation. She slumped down untidily, grumbling.

The doorman whispered instructions to a small urchin clad in a military style jacket tied by a sash. The boy raced up the stair, all self-important urgency to deliver his message.

The herald boomed out, 'Mr Arthur Tenebris and Amorrie,' as they entered. No heads turned in their direction, no conversations stopped.

Arthur's gaze swung from one famous face to the next. He recognised many of the Umbra from their illustrations in *The Book of Five Hundred*. 'There, that's the Drowned Lady. She attends with the Sailor Prince,' he said. Amorrie yawned from inside his pocket. A small crowd surrounded the Prince, who would be regaling them with tales of sea battles in the Indies and of his especial friend, Captain Nelson.

The Drowned Lady was daringly attired in a sparse mer-battle tunic in grieving green. Arthur knew it as one fashioned from moray skin, for she had worn the same in the illustration by Reynolds in *The Book* two years since. A ceremonial trident swung from her belt as she stood on tiptoe to whisper in the Prince's ear from a perch by his collar-bone.

'The Chancellor of Balliol is with the Prince. He's Master of Umbra Magicks and Linguistic Studies. No longer at his peak but still he writes for *The Book.* His Umbra, Dawn Withheld, will be with him – though I cannot espy her for the moment. They say she is Mistress of all Kernow's Nymphs. Surely, Amorrie, you must know some of these ladies – they are from your world after all.'

'I do not play well with Nymphs.'

'And, there, Hilltop. I think he's a Spriggan warlord. He's Umbra to that notorious courtesan, Bexie Pallister. You'd like her. Gods, Amorrie, a quarter of The Five Hundred must be in this reception room.'

'You 'n your ratted book,' her head briefly surfaced. 'And there are not yet eighty in this room.'

'There are still so many I know by name alone, so many I needs must know better.'

A young gentleman entered the hall and a hush claimed the room. The herald had yet to make any announcement. Faces turned, knots of young ladies moved closer, ceased their prattle and blushed prettily; older ladies nudged one-another and gossiped behind raised fans.

Arthur did not recognise the gentleman from *The Book*, but knew he must be from a pre-eminent family.

'...£8,000 a year,' came a voice close to Arthur.

'Unmarried still?'

'Surprisingly, though some scandal...'

The herald waited until all the company's eyes rested on the newcomer, before: 'The Viscount of Exeter and the Umbra, Muscari.'

Amorrie's head bobbed from his pocket.

The Viscount stooped low in an extravagant bow and a small woman dressed all in blue-black crow feathers burst from a slitted hood in the back of his garment. She thrust forth two limbs so covered in feathers that they may have been arms but could have been wings. Both held their pose a moment as applause rippled through the room.

The hostess, Lady Rochester, sent her stepson, Lord Strathearn, over to greet the new guests.

'So that is Muscari,' said Amorrie.

Arthur stared down. 'You know her?'

'By name alone. She is reputed to be venomous.' Amorrie pointed, 'Look, in her hair.'

Arthur was close enough to see a hair grip and then some imperceptible movement, 'What is that?'

'Her wolf spider.'

'No matter. Viscount Exeter will surely be the next gentleman of quality to rise to The Five Hundred. He is of an age to be elevated. He will want suggestions and sketches in readiness. We must make his acquaintance tonight for I doubt another chance will present itself.'

'Muscari's ally is coiled,' said Amorrie with rare interest, 'primed like a ripe furze seed pod.'

As soon as Strathearn left the Viscount's side, Arthur stepped forward with a deep breath and deeper bow. 'Forgive my disturbance, sir, but I would introduce myself. I am an artist and you, being among the most gracious in the Kingdom, and near twenty-five, must surely find yourself in the next edition of *The Book*. You are thereby in need of...'

As Arthur lifted his head, he saw the Viscount staring over him towards another group. His plea petered out and the Viscount strode away without acknowledgement. Only Muscari, now perched upon her gentleman's shoulder, a feathered limb drawn coquettishly across the lower half of her face, glared back at Arthur, still floundering mid-bow. Amorrie stuck out her tongue at the departing Umbra, adding disgrace to his humiliation.

A man stepped across to help Arthur regain verticality. He was dressed simply, all in black, but with such a shocking length of jet hair that Arthur was surprised his rescuer had gained admittance. A distinctive Umbra sat on his shoulder. It was seven inches tall, with a backwards-tilting curved horn that rose from one side of its crown. Tapered ears shot out at right angles either side of a head with grey wisps freckling its goatish snout. Intelligence swam from its pale flecked pupils. An astringent resiny tang drifted from the Umbra.

Arthur stepped back and held out his hand. 'Arthur Tenebris,' he said, as the man took it. 'Your Umbra is most singular. I have not beheld her like before. Will you introduce us?'

'Young Mr Tenebris, the artist,' the man was all polite reserve. With his black ensemble and hair, he was turned out like a glossy spring rook. 'Three handsome illustrations in the current edition of *The Book* are yours, if memory serves. This is Brughe, a Pooka.' The creature on the man's shoulder, bowed and spoke. Arthur, of course, couldn't hear the words. Amorrie could, he felt her stir in his pocket.

'Sad that she is missing her other horn,' said Arthur, noting the blunted stump, on one side of Brughe's head.

'Missing many a year now, sir, but lost in a noble cause,' said the man, with a shake of his head that set his long hair dancing. 'I should add that Brughe is not a 'she'.'

Arthur was astounded. 'Brughe is male?' As far as he knew,

Umbra allied exclusively with humans of the opposing sex.

'Brughe is the only Pooka as far as we both know, so gender does not signify.'

'Hurting, God-dammit, there you are, man,' Lord Strathearn blustered up on his far side. 'You meld into the herd in a most irritating fashion.'

'Sorry, my lord. It was not my intention.'

'Suppose Lady Hermione ran short of –'

'Champagne milord?' A click of the fingers.

A shrewish serving girl – her doubtless dull and feckless Umbra absent, or hidden, from so lustrous a company – had appeared at Strathearn's elbow, raising a bottle. She deftly filled his glass.

It mollified Strathearn. He raised the glass high and the small elfin woman atop his hat dipped her own tiny glass into the full one, replenishing it. Hermione of Stones was imaginatively coiffured with a lattice of spider web around tear-blue hair, adorned with droplets of wilder-dew.

'You have summoned your creature, I see,' Strathearn indicated Brughe. 'Hermione tells me news was expected two or three hours since. I don't supp –'

'Brughe only knows they are close, milord.' Hurting's eyes flicked pointedly to where Arthur stood, mouth open.

Arthur bowed so low, Amorrie braced in his pocket to avoid tumbling out.

Strathearn noticed him for the first time. He frowned.

Arthur felt like a blue-coated slug who had slimed his way onto a bowl of cherries

Strathearn clicked his fingers. 'I know you, sir. You're the artist fellow. One illustration, the Earl of Hartsford and lovely Willow-Beth, in *The Book*, year afore last, is that right? Tideswell is it?'

Hermione tapped a stick against Strathearn's ear. Having got her bearer's attention, she communicated some thought and he corrected himself. 'Hermione has the right of it, as usual. It was the last edition, and Hereford, not Hartsford. And you are

Mr Tenebris; Tideswell is another fellow entire and unable to join us tonight.'

Arthur beamed and mouthed a thank you to Hermione, who nodded graciously. 'Hereford it was, I am humbled that you remembered, my lady.'

Small retching sounds fluttered into his mind as Amorrie signalled her thoughts on the discourse. Arthur prayed they had not carried to Lady Hermione.

Strathearn swung around almost catching Hurting and Arthur with his swirling cloak. A black grape flew from somewhere upon his Lordship's person. Hurting caught it effortlessly without the gentleman noticing.

'Well, back to the fray,' roared Strathearn. 'Be sure and catch me later, Tideswell, we have yet to commission anyone for the next edition's illustration.'

Arthur swivelled, swathed in smiles, to Hurting. He sobered quickly, 'Sorry, Mr Hurting, I had no notion that you were... working. I hope I haven't caused embarrassment.'

'The fault is mine, sir, I should have properly introduced myself. Quartermain Hurting, I am lent to m'host here tonight as his own man was taken from us just yester-eve.'

'Dear God, due to misfortune in the Umbra world, I take it.'

'Brughe says war and insurrection is a contagion in the Other Realm, sir. And what of your own companion?'

Arthur hesitated and Hurting, thinking he had been misunderstood, added, 'I refer to she who bound your life to hers. Is she with you tonight?'

'She is, but er... unwell and thereby under-dressed. Come you out, Amorrie. Say hello to Mr Hurting and Brughe.'

Amorrie did as she was bid and clambered gracelessly onto the rim of his pocket, where a small seat was embroidered for her to sit. She stared rudely at Brughe, who recoiled, almost falling backwards off Hurting's shoulder.

'Hello,' she said with a soft sweetness that made Arthur's blood creep.

A glance to Hurting revealed his black eyes transfixed on

Amorrie's. After a long moment, his gaze swung to Arthur. 'I am extremely ... uhh honoured to have made the acquaintance of Miss Amorrie, and you, Mr Tenebris,' he added, 'but I must be about my duties. Perhaps we may call upon you both sometime.'

Arthur nodded dumbly.

Hurting and Brughe departed in hushed conversation. Arthur heard Hurting ask, '... tis the Mor?' And, when his Umbra nodded: 'How can she be here? And if she is, then...'

As Arthur watched, Brughe evaporated from Hurting's shoulder leaving glistening wisps of mist in his stead.

Glancing down to where Amorrie sat, Arthur noted a secret smile pass her lips. 'I liked him, but not it,' she said. 'You should know that the hornéd creature is stitched together from forsaken causes, and stuffed with stifled curses and beech mast. And you apologise more than is good for your vapours. I never do.'

There was a commotion at the door and a man in a travelling cloak burst in, ignoring the herald, who still reached to pluck a tall hat from atop the newcomer's head.

'Have any heard?' the man yelled as faces turned at his bustling entrance. 'Countess Alnwick was taken, not three hours since.'

A shocked hush took hold before a fusillade of unbelieving denials and expletives burst around the room. 'Misfortune in our realm or the other?' one cry came loudest.

'In the other, 'tis certain,' said Hurting with half an eye on Arthur.

Amorrie slipped away, like a silverfish, deep into his pocket.

'Are we to believe Charon the Borderer is murdered, then?' Strathearn's voice shook with incredulity.

'That cannot be,' said the Lady of Megginch, 'The Borderer's armour is impervious to arrow or blade. He is all but invulnerable.'

Umbra stared. Arthur saw some turn to Dawn Withheld, who seemed to be shouting instructions.

'Slain by who?' said the Prince.

'It must be the Greynhym,' said the hatless man. 'Are they capable of ambush?'

'That is not the most urgent issue,' said Hurting. 'If Charon lies dead...'

'...who, now, holds the North?' Strathearn's arms were spread in consternation. 'The Greynhym will be on the move.'

'There will be slaughter.'

As Arthur stared around the room, Umbra vanished. Some in sprays of fine dew, others into smoky clouds, or flashes, or sparks, depending on their element. A flurry of mournful whines and scuffling gasps came and went as they sped back to the Other Realm.

Arthur looked for Hurting and saw a sombre figure disappearing by a previously hidden side door.

Seconds later, there was only one Umbra still in attendance. Arthur spoke into his pocket, 'You have not returned, Amorrie?'

'I know what waits for me there.'

2 – MISADVENTURE IN THE OTHER REALM

Stanton

≡

Umbra of note

Keeper Claw and his British ally Penny Midden

≡

The morning light played over the haphazard line of polished glasses that dotted one end of the breakfast table. That was the first clue.

Keeper Claw squatted among the glasses. His practised scowl deepened as he saw Stanton enter. The strength and reach of the scrawny Umbra's stale reek, redolent of dank unlit passages, was the second clue. Its intensity Stanton took for a barometer of Midden's anxiety.

The maid stepped guiltily from the window now and another glass was fetched from her busy cloth. It chinked down next to her Umbra upon the crowded table.

He caught the clandestine glance between Midden and Keeper Claw.

Stanton had been around maids for much of his childhood, although not in a position to order them to undertake tasks; more the butt of their whispered comments, puckish humour and baffling giggles. His wife, Isabella, understood maids and he normally left her to supervise Midden, but an eleven glass agitation should be commented on.

'Is there something worrying you, Midden?'

'Oh, sir, it is the message we received last night when you and my lady were out.'

Stanton had arrived back late from a meeting of Pitt's Cabinet Council. The house had been dark and quiet. He'd known that Isabella intended visiting a ball across the square that night. He'd insisted that his absence on government business should not deprive Isabella of entertainment, so she'd attended with only her Umbra, Twoshrews. She was already abed when Stanton returned.

She had announced in a sleepy chuckle, with a certain wine-stained pride, that she had caused 'quite the stir', by attending without her husband. 'Some ladies commented that I was "uncommon daring", but Lady Rochester chased the suggestion away as "too meek for the age".'

The message Midden referred to awaited Stanton on his plate at the far end of the table. He saw the cause of her turmoil immediately. The envelope was already ripped open. He read its address: 'For Minister Stanton, alone, and to be opened only by his hand.'

The broken seal was the 'His Majesty's Business' one that Stanton used for his own government correspondence. The message was more out than in. He recognised the official Parliament-headed notepaper. It was the same as he kept both in his desk at home and used at the Ministry.

'Who opened it, Midden?' Stanton had already guessed.

'Please, sir,' another glass had already found refuge in her cloth, 'mistress did, last night. She arrived home in gay humour and quite late enough for a lady.'

'I dare say.'

'I handed mistress the letter, saying, "This has been lately delivered, m'lady, by the most dashing and sharply attired post boy you could set eyes upon. And he arrived in a curricle drawn by two, with the initials M.o.R, upon it in gold. The King's own messenger could look no finer."

'Oh sir, mistress snatched up the envelope, ripped off its seal and pulled out the letter.' Midden's hand was a blur of burnishing. 'She read it to me, sir. I protested, mercy on me, I did, saying as it was not fit for ears such as mine to hear.'

'Calm yourself, Midden, the fault here is not yours.'

Isabella poked her unusually tousled head around the door, interrupting her husband. 'Has he been? Please, Sebastian, tell me I have not missed him.'

'I'm quite sure I shouldn't tell you,' he answered. 'You interfere with vital government communiqués and read messages expressly intended for its ministers. It will not do, Izzy.'

'Midden, you tell me. Have I missed any visitors?'

'Only with master's permission, m'lady?' Midden's glance flashed from mistress to master and toast skittered around the plate she was holding. Keeper Claw, a grey-skinned fellow with war-whiskers, stood on the table, at the limit of Midden's aura. He watched the interplay with tight-mouthed scorn.

'Do not drag Midden any further into your misdemeanours, Izzy. She has told me she was your unwilling co-conspirator last night.'

'We would not have opened it, would we Midden, had it not been the most uncommon and cryptic note ever delivered to our home.'

Stanton was absorbing the message: 'Sir, do not come to the office on the morrow. Your first engagement of the morning is to be at your own house in Marksfayre. It is most secret, and my agent requires that you attend this meeting without even your own Umbra present. It is to be stressed, sir, that on no account are you to divulge the constituents of these discussions: not to your Umbra, not even to your own staff at the Ministry for Umbra Affairs. This is an M.o.R. (Ministry of Retaliation) matter. Once you are apprised of the circumstances, you will understand why this message has to remain unsigned.'

'It grieves me to say it, Izzy, but your behaviour has been little short of scandalous,' Stanton waved the note.

The scolding was acknowledged. 'I swore to limit myself to only five scandalous things a day, so now I must be on my guard.'

'Well, get you about your breakfast, Izzy. No emissaries have yet materialised, neither at our door, nor by more mysterious means.'

'It will have to do with the shocking tidings we received at the party last night.' Isabella's words sobered her mood as she studied the smoked mackerel. Still retaining its head, the fish glared back with an unforgiving grimace that was bound to win the morning. She selected, instead, a glass of squeezed orange juice. 'Countess Alnwick is dead, Sebastian. She was taken last night. Her Umbra, Charon, was murdered by Greynhym in the Other Realm. Can you believe it?'

Midden uttered a distraught, 'Oh great Heavens!' and the cup of tea she was pouring chinked alarmingly. Keeper Claw took three steps to the edge of the table and leapt onto Midden's shoulder via her bosom in a fashion that caused Stanton to wince. The Umbra spoke to Midden. Stanton wondered if the taciturn little brute was berating her.

'You may take the fish back to the kitchens, Midden.' Stanton said and waited for the maid to leave. 'You need have a care not to bring on Midden's palpitations, Izzy.'

Isabella turned to the far end of the table. 'Oh my; nine glasses.'

'Eleven, I moved two.'

'I will speak to reassure her...'

'And a twelfth there,' he pointed to Midden's cloth.

'...straight-ways after breakfast.'

'I did know about the Countess's decease, Izzy,' said Stanton, 'for news of it extended our meeting of ministers by a good three hours. Pitt is much agitated about the number of deaths ascribed to "Affray etc. in the Other Realm". I have it here, in the Bills of Mortality.'

He held up a printed sheet of paper he had brought to the table to study.

Bill of Mortality

The diseases and Casualties this year being 1791

Abortive and Stilborn	643	Jaundies	55
Affray etc. in the Other Realm	1,388	Jawfaln	10
Affrighted	1	Impostume	97
Ague	55	Killed by several accidents	93
Apoplex and Meagrom	21	Kings Evil	57
Bit by a mad dog	1	Lethagie	3
Bleeding	4	Livergrown	114
Bloody Flux	556	Lunatique	7
Brused, issues, sores and ulcers	37	Made away themselves	30
Burnt and scalded	9	Measles	105
Burst and rupture	14	Murthured	9
Cancer and wolf	22	Over-laid, and Starved at nurse	9
Canker	1	Palsie	33
Child abed	224	Piles	1
Chrisomes and Infants	2,970	Plague	126
Cold and Cough	72	Plannet	34
Colic, Stone, and Strangury	73	Pleurisie, and Spleen	47
Consumption	2,543	Purples, and Spotted Feaver	50
Convulsion	544	Quinsie	9
Cut of the Stone	7	Rising of the Lights	126
Dead in the street and Starved	16	Sciatica	1
Dropsie, and Swelling	346	Scurvey, and Itch	12
Drowned	45	Suddenly	183
Executed and prest to death	24	Surfet	113
Falling Sickness	9	Swine Pox	8
Fever	1,665	Teeth	639
Fistula	17	Thrush, and Sore mouth	55
Flocks and small Pox	695	Tympany	17
French Pox	15	Tissick	45
Gangrene	7	Vomiting	1
Gout	5	Worms	36
Grief	16	**Buried**	**14,174**

Born in all - 14,142 Whereof Christened - 13,499 Dead with Umbra ally - 7,635 Whereof from Plague - 126 Whereof after events unknown in the Other Realm - 1,388

'It records well over one thousand Englishmen and women, killed in like manner in London alone last year. And, that figure is doubly shocking when you think that only half the deaths recorded here are adults. The other half are children, who would not have had an Umbra. They were christened but did not live to puberty.'

'Half,' Isabella's glass of orange juice clunked onto the table with a splash; 'half of the dead summed in the Bills of Mortality are children?'

'I did not realise until last night, but the searchers who determine and record the cause of death from which the tallies are calculated also log the deceased's age – where it is known or can be estimated – and whether there is any note of the deceased having had an Umbra.'

'And half the dead have not reached puberty. That is unconscionable. What a sheltered thoughtless wife you have, Sebastian, not to have realised.'

'I did not know, either, Izzy. Those details are kept quiet for a reason.'

'I can promise you those in my circle will be told of it. What duty has Pitt put upon you now?'

'To discover whether the deaths caused by misadventure in the Other Realm form part of some pattern. My investigations are to start with the murder of Charon last night.'

'But,' Isabella took a napkin to the escaped orange juice, 'that was surely the Greynhym.'

'Almost certainly. Last night's meeting of Ministers was attended by Jenny M from the Other Realm. She told Pitt that Charon was known to be over the river, on some mission that had taken him into Greynhym lands.'

'Your task is impossible. How can you uncover a murderer in a world you cannot visit?'

'Deaths caused by events in the Other Realm are rising. Someone must investigate.'

'There will be no witnesses beyond Greynhym. No-one can question them. Do those plague-ridden monsters even have speech? Why does it fall to you?'

'Because there are worse creatures wandering London streets who enjoy speeches a deal too much,' Stanton gave his wife a curdled smile.

'Ministers; more stupid creatures, I'll allow.'

'Always loud to call for action.'

'And silent when asked to take responsibility, I know. They take advantage of...'

'...of my low birth.'

'That is not what I meant,' she said too quickly. 'Or perhaps it is. Of your courage to ignore it and strive beyond it.'

'Only permitted thanks to your resolve in marrying a man who was not the son of a gentleman. You are the brave one, Izzy. I daily thank heaven that you were not claimed by Viscount Exeter. No doubt he was at Lady Rochester's soiree last night?'

She dismissed his question about Exeter with a wave. She always did. 'I worry that you have been set up to fail. You are too apt to leap in. Just because others would not volunteer for this challenge, do not, for one moment, think they will be as slow to condemn you if you flounder.'

Stanton laughed, 'I am not as naive as you seem to think me, Izzy.'

'Well that is hardly any sort of test.' She downed her orange juice. 'Charon's death must embolden the Greynhym, I think. Your mysterious visitor from the Ministry of Retaliation may be here to advise on that?'

'The Greynhym are rapacious enough without this stimulus. How long have they thrown their mutilated bodies against Charon and his soldiery only to be hacked down. They will be drunk on this triumph. Pitt fears the plague will daub its stain more liberally over England.'

Midden and Keeper Claw returned; the Umbra's eyes scrambling to the room's every corner and his ears twitching.

Stanton diluted the conversation, for Midden's sake. 'However, I doubt this mysterious appointment bears upon those tidings. The Earl of Grenville attended last night and, proud as he is, he would surely have spoken had he wanted my views on it.'

Grenville was First Lord of the Ministry of Retaliation and

had barely acknowledged Stanton since he had joined the Cabinet Council following his appointment as Minister for Umbra Affairs four months ago.

'Then it must be France,' said Isabella.

'Everything is.'

There was a knock on the front door and Isabella rushed out of the room, shouting, 'My combs and brushes. Twoshrews, get you here.'

'Goldry will get the door,' Stanton informed Midden as she snatched up a previously polished glass and flitted to the window to look upon the street.

'No carriage,' she reported back.

'Midden, what opinion did Keeper Claw give you when my wife mentioned the death of Countess Alnwick?' asked Stanton.

'Why, sir,' the maid flustered, 'only that he heard tell yester-eve about the Borderer being felled by the Greynhym.'

'Claw is speedily informed,' said Stanton, being quite sure that his own Umbra would swear that she had slept through all such news, was ignorant of any deaths but altogether unsurprised. 'Tell me of Claw's post in the Other Realm again.'

'He is Keeper of the Moon Gate in the Citadel of False Sorrows,' Midden's face lit up as she spoke, displaying evident pride that her Umbra had so important a position in such a fine-sounding establishment.

Stanton remembered being told this before and that Isabella had spent half an hour debating whether 'false sorrows' were better or worse than real ones.

'By what means was Claw told?'

The Umbra spoke fervently to Midden before the visibly ruffled maid said, 'He can make no sense of sir's question.'

'Will make none', muttered Stanton, glowering at the pinch-faced creature. He was convinced Midden had misrepresented what her Umbra had said. Keeper Claw had extended scrolls for ears, on top of which crouched a forlorn carmine cap. The Umbra's thin pale arms and booted legs poked from a simple blue tabard displaying a pattern of downward-facing spears, possibly a portcullis.

Keeper Claw, when attending Midden, occupied half of his time by gazing lasciviously at any food on display at table and the other half appearing to take a more than polite interest in the household's comings, goings and conversations. Stanton had no idea which of these halves was an act.

Penny Midden was new in their lives, employed because, though but twenty-one, she had admirable references, a contented (if nervous) disposition and was of an age to his new wife. Isabella's former maid had refused to follow her mistress into this marriage with its attendant loss of title, status and fine country house surroundings. Like many of Isabella's circle, her maid had disapproved of this match.

Midden knew her letters and had, last night, been alone with government secrets. Stanton wondered if he had made enquiries enough about Penny Midden.

He gave an impatient grumble, 'Goldry, come on man, bring your summons.' He had heard the mysterious visitor being shown into the morning room a minute since. He opened the door to stare into the hall; there was no sign of Goldry. A distinctive scent, like meadowsweet, lingered in the hallway.

Curious to meet this secretive gentleman from Grenville's Ministry, Stanton walked down the hall.

Sebastian Stanton was the youngest member of First Lord Pitt's Cabinet Council, being six years younger than Pitt himself. He believed himself a man of rationality to his core, who gave his opinions forthrightly and had a certainty of direction and purpose.

Stanton threw open the door of the morning room and strode in. He stuttered to a halt within two strides at the sight of a tall slim woman, who stood alone in the centre of the room with her back to him.

3 – A COAT OF BEES

Arthur

Arthur's left leg will not move. It protests fiercely and, when he tries to reposition it, fresh agonies gallop up it to dissuade him. He hears the sea somewhere close but he dare not drag his eyes away from the nightmare figures that converge upon him. They rise from a sweep of sand dunes in twos and threes, sniffing the air rapaciously. They are a collection of diverse grotesques but, so raggedy is their dress and so disfiguring their injuries, Arthur can barely recognise what they might once have been. They carry rough weapons, spears and clubs, with which they poke and prod him until satisfied that he is alive. He may be alone in that regard. They mean to cure him of this condition. He is fearful, but he is also possessed of an unfathomable exhilaration and vindication quite at odds with the events unfolding. The creatures' leader lifts a barbaric club...

◆ ◆ ◆

Praise God, Arthur started awake just before the club lashed down. It was no sort of dream for an honest artist. A sigh tickled his breast and he found Amorrie there, in the 'v' of his nightgown, huddled into the hollow of his sternum. She slept, but her repose was fitful and disturbed. Her tiny body tensed as if at some imagined threat. He detected an unsought swell of tenderness for the raven-haired companion with whom he must share his life.

This unaccustomed benevolence was much due to the latter

part of the evening he had enjoyed at the reception held by Lady Rochester and Lord Strathearn. His abandonment by Viscount Exeter, Arthur now told himself, was explained by the man's eagerness to see old acquaintances, especially the enchanting Isabella Stanton – Lord Lisle's daughter. With her, he was most solicitous, though she received his attentions coolly.

The news of Countess Alnwick's death and the swift departure of all Umbra, save the hidden Amorrie, had cast a pall on the evening but, as the wine continued to flow, there grew a determination not to let events in the Other Realm, and their deadly consequences, subdue their spirits.

'Damn it all, Tideswell,' Strathearn approached, trailing a nervous maid who splashed wine into Arthur's glass. 'If they cast our spirits low, then they have won, d'you see? We must not alter our behaviour – not one jot.'

It was the kind of peppery declamation that had made the young Lord the darling of those Tories who felt First Lord Pitt too reformist.

'Hermione and the rest of our brave Umbra will soon discover what fate has befallen Countess Alnwick's warrior and mete out due punishment. I dare say they'll inflict ten-fold casualties on those ravening hordes, just for ruining this party.' Strathearn's bumbling oratory was said to disguise the sharpness of his wits.

'I should say so too, milord,' Arthur was too thrilled that Strathearn had remembered his existence to think of correcting him about mislaying a mere name. 'Those Greynhym will be sorry they ever attacked the Borderer.'

'Da-de-da de-da, milord,' chanted the unseen Amorrie, from Arthur's pocket.

'Quite so. But it's a damn pity you scared off Hurting, Tideswell. I was relying on the man to keep things running smoothly here.'

Strathearn and his vivacious step-mother, Lady Rochester, rallied spirits and took the edge off the horror of the news. Soon fretful conjecture turned into plucky camaraderie. Gossip meandered to other matters: the fluctuating French situation, Pitt's Government's response to the rise in plague deaths, the wars in the Other Realm, and – much to Arthur's delight – the next edition of *The Book of Five Hundred* and who might be elevated to fill the latest vacancies in its pages.

Arthur found himself in demand for his opinion on the illustrations in this year's edition and the artistic talents of the day. Who would fill Sir Joshua's shoes, now the great master was taken? Joseph Wright of Derby was most likely, Arthur told his enquirers, though he was 'no longer at his peak'.

Several commissions were hinted at and Lady Stanton – lately married to a rising young politician – promised she would employ Arthur upon the instant, were her name ever put forward to join The Five Hundred. And that might now be the case, Arthur reflected, given Countess Alnwick's demise on top of other vacancies.

Because all the other Umbra had dashed back to their own world after news of Charon's murder, no one noticed Amorrie hiding in his pocket and Arthur kept quiet about her.

It was rare for Amorrie to stay with Arthur until morning. She seemed exhausted.

He watched her tiny form scrabbling and grunting through the hinterlands of slumber. And wondered if his own demented night-frits had flown into Amorrie's dreams, through the connection they shared. He ventured a calming finger to quieten her tossing head and smooth the black tangle of damp hair away from her shoulders.

'What do you do?' she murmured drowsily.

'Nothing!' his hand snapped back to his side.

Dark eyes bore into him from between slitted lids. 'Well do not do nothing again. It is unseemly.'

He agreed it was and found other uses for his eyes.

He felt two tiny hands push down as she lifted her chest from his. There came the sound like a door clearing its throat and, when he looked again, a diminishing smudge of shadow told him she was gone. The fresh rain on leaf-litter scent, which he barely noticed until it was absent, fled with her.

What had the disquieting Hurting said: 'She, who bound his life to hers.' What a strange way to put it.

Had Amorrie chosen him? He would never have chosen her. She had entered his life when he turned fourteen, and instantly made clear her intention of ruining it. For the first year she refused steadfastly to come when called politely. When forced to appear, by young Arthur's materialisation summons, as she was compelled to do, she arrived spitting and profaning and pummelling at him with insignificant fists, which he could barely feel, but with such ferocity he could not help but flinch.

On the third occasion that she was made to attend, she did so armed with a cudgel, so out of scale with her size and wispy physique, that an alarmed Arthur hoped, and truly believed, it would be beyond her strength to wield it. It wasn't. Amorrie managed five mighty thumps upon his forearm, before collapsing in a heap. The cudgel suffered more damage than Arthur, breaking in two.

His mother, who had supervised the summoning, dashed from the room, hollering for help. His father came running. He told Arthur on no account could he dismiss the spent little Umbra. That, said his father, would mean her antics had succeeded in their aim, which was to so daunt Arthur that he would be dissuaded from summoning her – at least not so often.

His father's Umbra, Ferch y Pwll, who claimed to come from his own native Carmarthen valleys, arrived to scold Amorrie fiercely. His father told Arthur that Ferchie reminded Amorrie of her obligations under the immutable Treaty of the Hedge before threatening the girl with all sorts of rebukes and retributions.

Amorrie responded with curses, using words whose meaning Arthur scarce knew, nor wished to guess at. Words, he dare not repeat to his father. When a little recovered, Amorrie hurled half of her cudgel at the Welsh Umbra, who ducked, avoiding hurt far worse than Arthur had taken. All hope of following his father into the Church flew after that cudgel

Arthur wished to dispatch the tiny tyke back to whichever savage hinterland she had come from, to leave her there to rot, but it was not permitted.

He pleaded with his parents to discover if she could be exchanged at, what he imagined might be, some enchanted market held under a tor-crested hilltop at moon-dark. Or could they bind her with white cross spider silk, a skein of which young Arthur had collected for the purpose, and float her out in a basket onto some enchanted mist-smudged mere. Whatever they found in the retrieved basket must surely be an improvement. But no one, including his parents' Umbra, knew of such a market nor any magical mere. Neither was there any precedence.

All those whose advice was sought, counselled that attempting to swap an Umbra would result in severe misfortune. Ferchie held that such a commission would leave all involved cursed and afflicted by plagues of dire maggots for generations to come.

No-one could imagine how devout, tender-hearted, eager-to-please Arthur had come to be paired with such a vexatious bundle of spit and fire, but it was truly a life sentence.

◆ ◆ ◆

Arthur left his reminiscences to attend the morning's appointment. The Countess of Harrington wished to see the preliminary sketches for her illustration. He ran to his studio in Cowcross Street, close to the livestock market at Smoothfield, and collected his sketches. He elected to walk to the rendezvous.

He would not summon Amorrie. The Countess had yet to meet Amorrie and Arthur intended that she never would.

The Earl of Harrington's London address was on the far side of the bygone village of Loomesbury. The area was newly laid out into squares and fine parks by the Dukes of Bedford to a design inspired by Thistledew, Umbra to the Fourth Duke.

Arthur entered one such park with wide paths set between young saplings and berried bushes. Slate-skirted clouds bustled across a drab sky but from somewhere sunlight found him, bringing with it a pervading thrum of bees. He traced the swarm to a vibrant swirl of purple daisies, which surprised him for it was past Michaelmas. A slight figure was bending over to admire the flowers.

Arthur was about to call out, to ask after the name and provenance of the daisies when the wind whipped-up furiously, ripping leaves from bushes and flinging them into his face. Gusts tugged at the tan satchel containing his sketches as if striving to relieve him of it. Arthur staggered back, pushing the satchel behind his back for protection. Then he felt his frock coat dashed from his shoulders and torn completely off one arm.

Arthur span, gripping his satchel as the whole of his frock coat became a squall-animated adversary, jerking and hauling at the hand that held the satchel until it wrested it free. Arthur dived after it, but the satchel flew into the nearest bush and lodged there, while the frock coat celebrated its freedom by cart-wheeling and somersaulting gaily away towards the daisies.

Another older man, dressed for commerce, with a shocked Umbra clinging to his lapel, ran to Arthur and helped him to his feet. 'I've ne'er seen the like,' he said. 'The most rumbustious squall to have hit the parish, I shouldn't wonder.'

'My satchel,' groaned Arthur.

'The wind fought you for your case, sir. You did well to hang on to it for so long. There was such a gyration of leaves, I quite lost sight of you in the melee. Look, the case is there, salvation by bush.'

The man and his Umbra left to retrieve the satchel while Arthur dusted down his shirt sleeves and set himself to rights. The zephyr had either spent itself or moved on to ambush another. He felt a pat on his hip and saw his frock coat reaching up to him. It was as if the garment was begging forgiveness for its frantic and violent departure. Confused, he pulled up the coat and discovered a small child, dusky as night, beneath it, raising it up.

The child was dressed in scraps and tatters, in this respect resembling most other ragamuffins in the city, but was not from England. Tight curls of short black hair were pulled into braids and Arthur wondered at the flawless mahogany of the child's skin.

'A devil wind,' said the child in a hesitant voice, quieted by shock. 'Sent by Eshu.'

'You are from the Africas?' said Arthur, taking up his coat and searching its pockets for a penny.

'Yes, master. The wind sucked up leaves. They became a dead spirit that fought with you.'

'It certainly felt like it.' Arthur handed over a penny to the child and looked around. 'Do you have a mistress or master nearby?'

'No, master. I was no longer required.'

A laugh came from the businessman behind Arthur, 'Dead spirits indeed. These slaves are full of gloomy portents.' He turned to his pretty Umbra, dainty in a lamentable lilac dress. She stood on his shoulder, quick eyes fixed upon Arthur, 'What say you, m'dear?'

She spoke some words and the man's smile turned brittle, and his expression serious. He thrust the satchel at Arthur. 'Here is your bag. It is quite undamaged.'

'That is more than can be said for my frock coat. It is slashed, here.' Arthur pointed at the front pocket, where Amorrie was oft contained. His pocket had been ripped asunder.

'Unlucky indeed, sir,' said the businessman, now impatient to be away. 'I wish you good morrow, one free of wind-devils.'

His Umbra shook him by his side-whiskers and whispered into his ear. The man took a few stumbling steps off, 'Teasel says not to tarry, sir.' Quick paces sped him away to the park gates.

Arthur noted that the hum of bees had ceased and turned to the daisies. Most lay stripped or flattened by the wind. The figure who had stood before them was gone.

'Did you see a man over there?' Arthur asked.

The child stared where Arthur pointed, turned back and nodded. Black irises expanded in the clear white of expressive eyes. 'Yessir, he wore a coat of bees.'

4 – DARE YOU LAY A QUEEN?

Stanton

≡

Umbra of note

Twoshrews and his human ally Isabella Stanton

Capu and his human ally Lady Rochester

≡

Stanton stared.

The woman's full skirted dress-come-gown was the most handsome he had come upon. It was a midnight purple, which Cook would name aubergine – after the fashionable Spanish vegetable – and extensively embroidered with crimson. It had ruched and puffed three-quarter length sleeves and a generous hood that had been thrown back.

Stanton's knowledge of garments extended only to 'it being very fine,' but his gaze snagged on the tumble of red-black hair flowing in impossible waves into and out of the open hood of her gown, before coiling and surging down the woman's plumbline-straight back beyond her waist. Each convoluted curl ended with such body and vigour that he imagined it capable of disarming a Stepney footpad.

The lady spun at his interruption. The sight of Stanton gawping before her like a trout new-landed at Teddington seemed to surprise and then delight her. She stepped towards him, her hand rising graciously to his unready lips and her steely grey eyes meandering over him.

'Ah you must be the new minister that Pitt was so anxious to seat on his council. Did he not invent a new ministry just for you, Master Stanton, so noteworthy is your advice?'

'My ministry is somewhat new, madam...?' he paused expectantly.

'I had not thought to have to introduce myself to you, sir.'

'No, I know I know you, but all names, and even words, have fled my mind.' He found himself uncertain how to breathe – a be-tailed tadpole emerged too soon from the pond it knew as its entire world, unequipped for this new element it now floundered in. Stanton was unglued by the infinite horizons and unknowable threats arrayed before him.

'Ah, of course,' he tapped his nose, 'you mean that our meeting is utterly clandestine and no word of it can ever emerge.'

Stanton was subconsciously aware that a door had opened somewhere but quite incapable of imagining what might exist beyond it or what being could have entered.

'Even from your wife, sir...'

Stanton was unsure whether this was a question. He chuckled, 'Especially from Lady Stanton, I should say.'

'I'm intrigued of course,' her laugh swirled with a whisper of wickedness, 'but you are already undone.'

'I am?'

'Lady Rochester.' She said it with a flourish of exoticism that entirely beguiled him.

'Of course, Lady Rochester. I had not expected you to be a woman.'

'No really!' her laugh ended abruptly, and she added with a note of utter seriousness. 'What manner of creature do you suspect me of being?'

There was something of a precocious teenage girl about her, coquettishly flirting to discover the boundaries of her power over men, yet threaded with the assurance of an experienced paramour who knew she could unpick any man and reshape him. You have cards in your hand, Minister Stanton, her eyes suggested, and, if you but pick the right one, you might play me. Dare you lay a queen?

She slipped into the space between them. So close that he observed the first flaw in her glamour; her eyebrows were jaggedly wild. So close that he felt he must either retreat a pace for propriety's sake or plunge forward risking all.

'I mean, of course I knew you *were* a lady, a woman, never was any more so...' Stanton had beached upon his own words. He was gabbling himself into unknown depths of social faux pas. He pressed his lips again to her hand desperate to stop his wayward tongue.

A touch upon his other arm moored him back into the morning room, preserving him from the mesmerising maelstrom of swirling red-black hair.

'None more so, indeed,' came Isabella's rescuing voice from behind him, where an agog Goldry still held the door. 'Forgive my husband, Lady R, he is not used to having such female beauty about him.'

Lady Rochester took a half-pace back and studied Stanton. No, naturally, of course he isn't, her expression seemed to imply before she retreated into a smile, 'Nonsense, Isabella, for he has you.'

Stanton wished he could start this encounter afresh but attempted to explain himself. 'We received the note late last night that you would attend me here and, I am ashamed to say, I expected some military phantom to appear at my door.' He showed her to a chair. 'I am intrigued to learn what dangerous mission you must have that requires such a burden of secrecy.'

Lady Rochester quieted her frock into the indicated chair, flowed herself in after it and shook her head. 'Now, Sir, you have quite captivated me. What can you know of my mission here? Can there be more secrets still for us to share?'

'Sebastian,' Isabella took full hold of her husband's arm, bolstering him against the powerful current of his guest's intoxicating proximity. 'Lady R is not your mysterious guest. She has come today to visit me.'

'Ah, oh, yes, of course,' relief swamped Stanton's embarrassment.

'Now I confess, I wish I were your secretive guest,' said Lady Rochester. 'Indeed, I am confounded to find that there exists in all England anyone more mysterious and bewitching than I. There is certainly no-one *plus dangereux*.'

'It was Lady R's party I was at last night, Sebastian. She is a long-time friend to me and is also our neighbour – with her stepson, Lord Strathearn – across the square, remember?' This last with a nudge of steel that set Stanton nodding.

'Quite so. It is upon the untimely demise of Countess Alnwick I wish to touch.' Lady Rochester clasped her hands together, 'It leaves another vacancy in next year's edition of *The Book of Five Hundred*. I feel you are both sure to be on the list of names who might replace her.'

'There must be worthier candidates than I, surely,' Stanton said.

'Not at all, my dear,' said Isabella, 'I can think of none finer; none, who stand likely to do our country better service. If I am privileged enough to be invited, I will directly stand aside for you.' She set down her Umbra, Twoshrews, atop of a sofa of the design made popular by the Earl of Chesterfield.

'You shall do no such thing, Izzy. Your father would never forgive me.'

'I will champion both your causes,' Lady Rochester said, 'and you are to give of it your best. Your former acquaintance Viscount Exeter will be on the list, Isabella, and we can't have that haughty noble entered into the pages of *The Book*, before you, can we? Either of you would be far more worthy and many times more cordial. The youngest English Minister since Pitt, and the charming progressive daughter of Lord Lisle. And Twoshrews would be the giddiest Umbra among its pages. Who could be better?'

Twoshrews executed a sweeping bow on Isabella's shoulder and said something that made Isabella's expression crease in surprise.

There was a knock upon the door and Goldry put his head around it, coughed awkwardly and said that the Minister had another visitor. 'A Mr er...' – Goldry was uncertain – '*Lambswink*, I think he said. Penny has admitted him to the scullery, sir, where he awaits you.'

'The scullery?' Isabella rounded on the servant.

'Penny assures me that was his demand, m'lady,' said Goldry. 'He quite insisted upon it.'

'That is my cue to depart your morning room, I fancy,' said Lady Rochester. 'I must leave you to the intriguing Mr Lampwick. Come Capu!'

Her Umbra, who Stanton had been too preoccupied to notice, was sitting on a small table behind the door, amusing himself with a bowl of almonds and hazelnuts. He took a couple of small steps and launched himself fully five feet from the table and onto the shoulder of Lady Rochester, flattening the material on landing. A fawn skull face peered from beneath a close-fitting hood that formed part of a suit and gown fashioned in the same material and style as his mistress. Overlarge hairy hands emerged from the sleeves. Some sort of goblin, Stanton supposed. Capu was both more lithe yet more heavy than any Umbra he had previously seen.

Stanton bowed low and, when he arose, her Ladyship had gone from the room and he heard her chatting to Isabella in the hall about an up-and-coming artist they had met the previous night, a certain Mr Tenebris.

◆ ◆ ◆

'The French are plotting, Stanton.'

'That's hardly news, Mr...er... Lambswink, is it?'

Stanton had stood aside to let Midden flee through the scullery door, Keeper Claw clinging to her skirts. Four polished glasses remained as glinting evidence to the maid's discomfort at being alone with the visitor, who had his back to the door.

'You have the advantage of me, sir. We have not been properly introduced,' Stanton stepped inside.

'Nor will we be, Minister.' The man spun around, returned a fifth glass to the table and spread his hands in mock apology. 'I have given your servants the name of Larkwing and that will, I am sure, suffice. You will have seen from the ministry memorandum we sent, that secrecy is paramount. I hope your Umbra...'

'It is too early an hour for my Umbra and she takes little interest in our affairs.'

'Hmm, I wonder...'

'This is all very irregular, Larkwing; not at all the way I do business.'

The wiry man was boldly attired, every inch in black, a dark cropped redingote with snug leather breeches extravagantly buttoned and tied at the knee with generous bows. The wear of his long boots was disguised by their sheen of polish. Neat sideburns prospered alongside thick dark eyebrows at odds with his short-cropped greying hair. Stanton struggled to put an age to him, but he looked every buffed button a ministry man.

'I see.' The visitor put his head to one side, one finger to his chin and contemplated Stanton before whipping the air theatrically. 'If you want regular, my dear Stanton, then I fear we have appointed the wrong man to the task.' He reached for his hat and gloves.

'Stay,' said Stanton. 'State your business, sir. How can I be of service to the Ministry of Retaliation?'

'Let me ponder. Have you considered why we now have a Minister of Umbra Affairs when we never had any such before?' The fellow perched beside his hat on the edge of a rough chopping table.

'I know full well why. The Greynhym offensive mu –'

'Because we no longer trust them,' Larkwing spoke over him. 'My own agency impressed on Pitt the need for action regarding Umbra. The First Lord agreed but unfortunately determined that the possibility of an Umbra agent working with the French was such a threat, it must needs answer to the Parliament. So, here you are, Stanton. That is why you exist; such is your genesis.'

'Working with the French? An Umbra? That is not possible – it must surely contradict the terms of the Queen's Treaty.'

'Ah yes, the Treaty. Have you ever read it?'

'Of course not, it was written in Hedge, a lang–'

There was a scuffling outside. Stanton imagined that Midden was dusting or polishing the sheen off some ornaments there, but Larkwing motioned for Stanton to keep speaking and crept to the parlour door.

'... a language that has been neither spoken or written to any great degree for nearly four hundred years.' Stanton rumbled on as best he could. 'Although, I believe that Hedge documents are cultivated rather than writ.'

Larkwing snatched at the scullery door, yanking it open to reveal an empty corridor and an open kitchen door. Stanton imagined he heard a giggle somewhere in the house. Having stared about, Larkwing returned to the table, picked up his hat and gloves and said: 'Perhaps you would honour me with a turn about the square, Minister.'

Marksfayre was not busy. Two carriages trundled between the fine houses there and the weather was brisker than either.

Stanton buttoned the coat Goldry had thrust at him upon leaving. As they entered a gate in the railings around the small park at the square's centre, a raggedy urchin of nine or ten detached himself from a bush under the nearest horse chestnut and ran to Larkwing's side.

'Visitors?' the Ministry of Retaliation agent asked the urchin.

'Just you, mister, and Lady R. She's still in t'ouse.' He stretched out a hand as grubby as his accent.

The boy received a penny. 'Keep watching,' he was ordered.

They walked on towards the square's centre.

'Urchins provide commendable intelligence,' said Larkwing. 'A penny buys you their loyalty and the more beggarly they look, the more invisible they are to gentry. As a source, they are second only to correspondence; for everyone writes, Stanton. They commit their innermost secrets to diaries, to letters; to twice-removed aunts, to confidants, to children, to lost paramours; to the penny-post boys, who let us pillage their content and then return them to their envelopes, seals remade.'

'Waifs and penny-post boys – to these we entrust the preservation of England? I must look again at your Ministry's budgets,' said Stanton. 'To the matter at hand: all talk is of war but surely the new French Republic is too busy with internal frictions to concern itself with us.'

'True, but these events were set in motion at the end of Louis's war in '83. With the Revolution now secured, our support of Brunswick's Prussians at Valmy means the new government in France has declared us their enemy. They no longer intend invasion, but plan to conquer us from within. They aim to inspire rebellion from across The Channel.'

'Naturally, this is spoken of in Government. What has it to do with Umbra?'

'We understand that in the late 1780s the French recruited an Umbra and persuaded him, or, more likely, her, to bring Britannia to its knees.' Larkwing spoke and walked swiftly.

'This is too fantastical, Larkwing. I've yet to meet a Frenchman who believes Umbra even exist, excepting the Marquis de Mont Ferrer, and he has more English mutton in him than côtelettes d'agneau.'

'The Marquis, yes, he is of interest to us. If ever a man sailed under a false flag. Stanton, what do you imagine an Umbra working against us might achieve?'

'Well, there are two areas in which the Umbra could do damage...' Stanton considered further, '...untold damage. If they let the Greynhym escape their borders, we lack any means to push them back let alone corral them again.'

'Catastrophe.' Larkwing swung one riding boot at a conker. It bounced away along the path, scattering a bustling dole of doves. 'Plague, a return of all Englishmen to the tyranny of pestilence.'

'Quite.' Stanton could scarcely imagine the carnage. 'And, with revolution in mind, an Umbra could lay waste to Britain's gentry. By killing off the Umbra of those in power, they could un-man all our institutions: state, army, church, land-owners.'

'They would have to be able to identify our Umbra, match them to our most influential people...' Larkwing goaded Stanton to the answer.

'*The Book of Five Hundred* would be the perfect resource,' Stanton's tinder had caught. 'And Countess Alnwick was taken last night. The means of her taking: the murder of the Borderer, Charon.'

'Alnwick?' Larkwing's march paused, ' another one.'

'Yes although that was the work of the Greynhym, we believe.'

'The Greynhym, yes, but might they have had help?'

'Well,' said Stanton, 'I confess, I have been wondering why was Charon there alone? What could have induced him to remove his famed armour? Do Greynhym have the guile to set such a trap?'

'Or was the Borderer lured onto their spear-points by an Umbra – an Umbra working for the French?'

'Surely,' Stanton aimed a foot at a still intact chestnut case, but missed, 'the Queen's Treaty allows for no such acts against us. The Umbra take the alliance even more seriously than we do.'

'The Countess makes it ten of The Five Hundred dead in as many months,' Larkwing stepped in front of Stanton, halting them both, and took him by the sleeve. 'In the army, we have lost sixteen significant officers to events in the Other Realm in the same period. That is more than lost in good honest warfare. Many ministries are newly shorn of key functionaries and administrators. Slowly, but surely, our great and good are being struck down by events in the Other Realm. I suggest, Mr Stanton, that the Hedge your Treaty is writ in has already been put to the torch.'

'Why did Pitt not warn me of this when he placed me in post?'

'Two reasons suggest themselves. He, like you, is not wholly convinced, quite adamant that the Treaty binds the Umbra. Secondly, we swore him to secrecy. This matter is too important for mere Parliament. You may be unseated from your rotten borough by a goodly bribe at the next by-election, Stanton. Pitt could be voted down by a rash of Whigs. Also, Pitt has insisted this is not spoken about in Parliament or cabinet. Word would get out, and then...' He spread his hands, their width representing the repercussions of such an outcome.

'So, what is it we must do to discover if this threat is real?'

'You need do nothing, Stanton. You are merely for show. We, on the other hand, are busy. We are focussed on The Five Hundred, and those around them, this radical Umbra must be well-connected. We have suspicions about several of them and I have men – well urchins – set to follow their human companions. Mont Ferrer is one such. Today, I undertook *only* to brief you. Leave all skullduggery to the experts.'

Stanton spun around and began striding back to his house. 'You have briefed me well, sir. I thankee for it,' he shouted over his shoulder.

'Wait. Where do you go?' Larkwing ran a few steps after him.

'To my Ministry. I have work to do; real work, at last.'

'Hold, Minister,' Larkwing trotted up to Stanton. 'This is still most secret. What do you propose?'

'I am the man charged with Umbra dealings, and I will not allow this rumour to stand and not investigate it fully. Everyone believes the Greynhym murdered Charon, but if an Umbra was part of their plot, an Umbra whose purpose is to destroy Britain...'

'Perhaps we have underestimated you, Stanton. We thought you adept at looking busy and earnest, sufficiently bustling to have married well. If you are to be our ally in this, and would help us identify this Frenchie traitor, then we must work together.'

'How so?'

'You can move in circles I cannot. As Minister you can legitimately ask questions I would not get answered. Find out all ye can about this other-worldly brood your ministry was named for, but promise me you will guard our secret knowledge and certainly not speak about it to your Umbra.'

'Have no fears on that score.'

'We will talk again when you know more about what you are dealing with.' Larkwing pulled a chequered yellow and scarlet cravat from his pocket. 'If you want us to meet, wear this. My urchins will see it.'

Stanton turned it over with distaste, 'Half of London will see it, I fear; my wife among them.'

'Trust me. There will be still greater trials ahead, Stanton. I wish you good morrow.'

5 – THE CHARM CHAIN

Arthur

≡

Umbra of note

Scampion and his human ally the Countess of Harrington

≡

'You are not dressed for October, Mr Tenebris, and that is a plain fact. Need you borrow a coat?'

Arthur had left his torn frock coat with the Countess's doorman and was anxious that this fine lady would think him too poor to afford a jacket. 'I stumbled in the park and my coat was torn, Countess. Your housekeeper kindly offered to make such amends as she can during our appointment.'

The morning room was set with four portraits of the Countess, all by the most celebrated artist of the age, Sir Joshua Reynolds. These had adorned *The Book of Five Hundred* since 1779 and the Countess, Jane Stanhope, wife of the Third Earl of Harrington, had scarce aged a day since. She was (along with Lady Rochester and Georgina, Duchess of Devonshire) part of the most fashionable trinity in the country, and her depiction was undoubtedly among the first pages to be turned to in any new edition of *The Book*.

Sir Joshua had been taken in February of that year following the evisceration (supposedly by Bogles) of his Umbra, Treesruin, in the Other Realm. The Countess was conversing with three artists to replace him. Arthur was astonished to be one of them. Just being on her Ladyship's list was a considerable spur to his standing in the profession. He didn't expect to be chosen but was determined to give of it his best. He had offered to do some preliminary sketches and the Countess had favoured him with an hour in which to capture the likeness of her and her Umbra, Scampion.

'The light is prettyish, here I think,' The Countess tapped a treatment. She had been three minutes walking around the rough sketches, passing agreeable comments that seemed to demand no response from Arthur, or, if they did, he had yet to summon one.

'This one is the most tolerable. The popinjay serves as a token of my time in Jamaica, I suppose.' She gave a light laugh, 'Yes this depiction would rightly grace *The Book*.'

Without her knowing, the Countess had been led along a path just as surely as any oxen on its way to Smoothfield's livestock market. Arthur had a trick. He would create one good portrayal, the one that he wished to paint and intended to be chosen, and several inferior examples, intended to cast his preferred version in a better light.

'You are too gracious, madam. Your excellent judgement is well known in all things and this proves you have a good eye for art. That, too, would be my choice.'

'However, I strive to be honest in all things and must be critical where I see cause. You have not captured Scampion as I would wish him to be seen.'

Scampion, a mischievous gangly cherub, described as a 'High Piskie' in *The Book*, was now sat on a nearby table alongside a squat pot containing an aspidistra at the limit of the Countess's aura. He was never parted from his oddly misshapen cursing crimson hat.

Scampion didn't intend to be captured, thought Arthur. 'He would not stay still, madam. Indeed, for a good two thirds of our hour together he hid behind the chair or table or beside yon plant.'

'It is a trial. I used to have a locket, which came from my mother, that would keep Scampion at hand. When I spoke its charm, he had to stay close and to be still. Sir Joshua insisted I used it always in a sitting, but it has been missing these three years.'

Arthur knew of these 'charm chains' as they were called. They dated from the Queen's time and were linked to an item of significance, often jewellery. They could be used either to limit an Umbra's range, or, more commonly, to enable them to stray further from their human ally's aura.

'Scampion hated the locket with a will of course, but, on occasion, it was essential to curb him.'

'No matter,' said Arthur looking around the room. 'There are many fine depictions of Scampion here, by Sir Joshua, that, I flatter myself, I can use for reference.'

'No, that is not what I require. There is a trend for Umbra depictions to be more martial of late. Scampion and I have agreed that he will adopt a more combative stance and show more weaponry in our next illustration for *The Book*. He will be attired ready for battle 'gainst those Greynhym divils.'

Arthur nodded, 'Your Ladyship ever leads us to new fashions.' It was a practised phrase and he had hoped to find a use for it.

'Quite so,' she had recognised it for what it was. 'Sadly Scampion, while as brave as they come, does not own a costume that is sufficiently soldierly, so,' she left a significant pause, 'how should I put it...'

'One will have to be invented,' finished Arthur. Flattery and minor deception were as important a part of the society artist's tool-chest as a paintbrush. Arthur often amused himself by inventing elegant compliments to use on his clients.

'You put your opinion bluntly, Mr Tenebris. Nothing dishonest, I am a woman whose integrity is beyond reproach.'

'I have in mind nothing more than is used in many illustrations in *The Book of Five Hundred*, madam, where a gown needs a slightly different hue to match the light in the sky, or a backdrop is imagined instead of using the clutter of the poor artist's studio.'

She smiled. 'Good, it seems we may do business. You are familiar with the illustration of The Drowned Lady from the last few editions, no doubt.'

'Yes, oh yes, I saw her in the same outfit, last night, at Lord Strathearn's party in Marksfayre.' Another phrase Arthur had tried out before his mirror that morning.

'Upon my word, you were at Lady R's petite soiree, were you?' Arthur was sure he detected a note of respect entering the room. 'We were invited, and Charles wished to attend but I was not so inclined.'

'Lady Rochester is a most charming hostess.'

'Lady R's allurements and charms are not in doubt, sir, it is how she deploys them that… I should say no more.'

'Unfortunately, news of the taking of Countess Alnwick and the murder of her Umbra, the Borderer, in the Other Realm, near spoilt the evening.'

'That news was more shocking to me than to most.' The Countess's tone softened, 'I lost a niece in the Anglian borderlands. My poor sister lives beyond the City of Cambridge beside the River Lark. The Greynhym pestilence is now south of the Great Ouse it seems.

'Last year there was a brief incursion over the River Lark and a nearby village succumbed to the contagion that arrives when the Greynhym make an advance. One of my nieces was visiting there at the time. The pestilence overtook her. She died soon after.'

'Your poor sister must have been devastated.'

'Aye, no doubt, though she has daughters aplenty.'

'Do I know this lady?'

'No,' the Countess shook her head, 'my father, the Baronet, washed his hands of her. It is the greatest pity, but she married beneath her station, an artist…' she recognised her faux pas, adding, '…though not as respectable a one as you, Mr Tenebris. Still, I am very fond of my sister and she lives beyond the back of nowhere. It is not to be borne.'

'No indeed, can she not move further south, to safety?'

'She will not. She has three or four other daughters, fine girls but wilder than you can believe. She left them too long without a governess. I never heard of such a thing and acted to provide one. They will soon be of an age to be chosen by their Umbra, but I fear they will not attract the right sort at all. And then the oldest child will be out in society. They are not ready for society; indeed, society is not ready for them. What sort of Umbra will want to ally to children of marsh and fen, from so dangerous a place?'

Arthur was touched she would admit such fears to him. 'I'm sure your Ladyship's connections –'

'Yes, yes... enough.' She cut him off and spun about to beckon Scampion. When she faced him again, the youthful face – not yet twenty when first captured on canvas by Sir Joshua upon her elevation to The Five Hundred in 1779 – was no longer in evidence. Instead, Arthur saw, behind her fresh features, the eyes of the woman who had survived the intrigues of her marriage and the scrutiny of court for thirteen years. Jane Stanhope had written off the debts of the Second Earl of Harrington upon her marriage to the Third Earl. Her marriage contract dictated that she held the purse strings and she had used her wealth and beauty to enhance her husband's standing and influence in the country. Scampion appeared, leering hungrily, upon her shoulder and Arthur felt his new-won confidence crumble under their joint gaze.

'Let us be frank, Mr Tenebris. You are little over twenty, new in your profession, and you cannot expect me to trust my reputation to such as you... yet. However, by letting it be known that your talents are under my consideration, your stock rises daily. You have a ladder to climb, and just by binding my name to yours, I have lifted you several rungs up it.'

'Then why am I here?'

'For reasons I have touched upon. I do have a commission for you and you should accept it as a favour to me. I have decided to ward my nieces into society, as my sister will not, and her station cannot. I require you to travel to the Fens at your earliest convenience and to undertake a commission to illustrate my sister's daughters employing some of the artistic artifice we have spoken of, depicting them as civilised young maids, fit for dinner and ball.'

'You wish me to paint your nieces' portraits?'

'Yes, at Larkenfen.'

'What is at Larkenfen?'

'Gracegirdles; a family of no distinction and primitive heritage. My sister has become one such, by marrying for love. Her husband was born to it and instead of bettering himself, paints savage and ugly things that only he can imagine. And between them they have given birth to four or five – I lose count – more, all girls. It behoves me to help my nieces marry into fortune. Currently they are as untamed as the things upon their father's canvasses.'

'What age are they?'

'The oldest are on the cusp of puberty by my guess. Soon they must be selected by their Umbra. Before that I want them in London, in fine gowns, in good temper and ready for society.'

'Where do I find Larkenfen?' Arthur was playing for time, wondering how best to refuse a commission in the wilds beyond Cambridge.

'North and east, by the River Lark. They say you can see the Great Cathedral of Ely from there on a clear day.'

'But Ely is surrounded by water,' said Arthur, now doubly alarmed. 'And that water is surrounded by pestilence.'

'Just so, it extends from the Fen of Ely to the far bank of the River Lark, which, to date, it has thankfully been unable to cross, well, apart from that one unfortunate occasion.'

The Countess broke off to listen to a short speech from her Umbra.

'Scampion reminds me there is talk that the Montgolfier brothers are encouraged to attempt a balloon flight across to that beleaguered city. But that adventure lies beyond your commission.'

Scampion feigned disappointment. How, wondered Arthur, had it come to this. 'But I have other comm –'

'Do not seek to vex me on this. You are outgunned in every way, Mr Tenebris. But, do this well, make me proud of my nieces, and you will be paid handsomely. You will also advance a few more rungs up the ladder, to a height where I may even see you, should you wave. Build a reputation that permits me to commission you to paint me for future editions of *The Book*.'

Scampion spoke to the Countess.

'Ah yes, Scampion says that we have never yet seen your Umbra. He hears tell she is some kind of Hag. Can it be? Before I despatch you into the wilds, I would see who will accompany you there.'

'Amorrie is not with me. She was exhaust –'

'Now, please, Mr Tenebris.'

Arthur had no way out. He did his best to give Scampion a bitter glance. 'Amorrie, come hither.'

'Can't. Narls.' Her voice sounded shrill and breathless in his mind.

'Amorrie, I will summon you if you make me. Bring what finery you have.'

'Gnaargh,' he heard.

Arthur glanced around to where his shadow concentrated, away from the tall windows. At its centre a familiar misty darkness began to form. Scampion gave skittish jumps on the Countess's shoulder.

The tiny girl arrived, jabbing at the air for invisible enemies with a short spear. She was barely clad at all: a breastplate covered what its name required of it, there was a short skirt of chain, tiny boots and a shield. Something sticky, lurid and greenish glazed her hair and shoulders – Arthur knew it for blood or some other ichor better employed inside a body than out.

Amorrie screamed in frustration, broke her thin spear across her bare thigh and dropped in a vulgar heap.

Arthur all but sank to the floor with her, such was his embarrassment. This was surely worse than anything awaiting him at Larkenfen.

'Heaven and Earth, but she materialises some distance from you. She seems a sprightly little thing, somewhat pugilistic. Was she battling Greynhym?'

'This is the Countess of Harrington, Amorrie. What were you doing?'

'Gutting narls. They will escape me now.'

'She had a misunderstanding with some narls, your Ladyship.'

'What are narls?' The Countess inclined towards Scampion, whose grin extended up both sides of his jaw almost as far as his famously peculiar hat.

'Half bats,' Amorrie spread her hands and spear ends as far apart as she was able. 'Ugly as the malformed imp on that woman's shoulder.'

'They are like bats,' Arthur interpreted.

Scampion laughed and spoke again, causing the Countess to giggle girlishly. 'I understand they are stupid, barely able even to fly and generally considered harmless, Mr Tenebris.'

'You probably have the right of it, madam, I have never seen one, or heard of any such before today.'

Amorrie spoke again, in low guttural tones. It sounded like an oak grunting in a tempest and carried a resonance that felt like a bramble scrambling up Arthur's arteries.

'Oh, she's adorable,' said the Countess, who could not hear Amorrie's noises, but the smile left Scampion's features. He dropped behind the Countess's shoulder and disappeared in a small shower of glistening sparks.

'Scampion, do not you dare...! Pah he is gone. That is inconvenient. I have other guests arriving and Scampion has done his duty for the day. I doubt he will return now. If I had my mother's locket still, I would call him back.'

'What speaks she of?' asked Amorrie.

'The Countess used to keep her Umbra close by means of a charm chain, Amorrie. The charm was in a locket, but it is lost to her these last three years.'

'Does she remember the words that awoke the locket's charm?'

Arthur relayed the question and the Countess, a little puzzled, confirmed she did.

'If she speaks her charm, and the locket is near, the imp must reappear. He will be summoned to wherever the locket is hidden,' said Amorrie, climbing to her feet.

Arthur informed the Countess, who scowled uncertainly. 'I doubt your scrappy Hag understands the workings of such a magick, Mr Tenebris. Still, I had not thought before to do so, and I will try it. Pray, cover your ears.'

He did so, and the Countess spoke a little sing-song charm. No sooner had she finished than there was a rustle of foliage and Scampion was returned wearing a horrified expression, quite glued to the soil where the aspidistra emerged from the pot.

'Well 'pon my soul,' the Countess was equally astonished.

Arthur relayed Amorrie's belief that the Umbra had stolen the locket some years ago and secreted it under the soil in the pot.

'Hmm, I have underestimated you, Mr Tenebris. May I call you Arnold?'

You probably will anyway, thought Arthur, but corrected her use of his name.

'I am glad I chose you for this task. I believe you and I will work well together,' she said. And, seeing a new plea forming on his lips, added, 'Do not think this means you escape your trip to Larkenfen, but your advance is doubled.'

'Surely, you could find another artist, madam. I could recomm –'

'No, I am intent on you, Arnol... Arthur. So much so, I wrote a day or so ago to my sister to tell of your coming. I will ring now for your mended frock coat and ensure that all particulars for your commission are placed in its pockets. Remember, I have all the power over you and you have none over me.

You are commendably obsequious and that will serve you for a time, but there are other skills for you to master if you are to advance.'

'But if the pestilence crosses the river, while I am there, madam...'

'Then you have your spear-toting Hag to defend you. I very much doubt you will succumb to pestilence, Mr Tenebris. However, I dare say my Gracegirdle nieces may do for you.'

6 – THE CASE OF THE NYMPH

Larkenfen

'What have you there?' Tabitha crouched down beside her nine-year-old sister Naomi. The boardwalk creaked as they both leaned out and ripples gyrated into the marshy pool.

'A skeeter hawk. It is fresh out of its water coat, still unready for the world.'

Tabitha reached out an exploratory finger but Naomi tapped it away. 'No, Tabby, it is still between its two selves. You will harm its wings.'

'It glistens so, as if it has not shaken off the watery element,' Tabitha shielded her eyes from the delicate autumn sunshine wriggling between the bent trees to shiver on the water. 'What kind is it?'

'One of the big bruise blue ones, I think. It is not yet showing its true colours.'

'It is surely born too late, in October.'

'They will fly into November, Tabby. Anyway, it was born at least two to three years ago. This is just growing up.'

'Like when we get our Umbra,' Tabitha was eleven; two years older than Naomi, and a year younger than the twins. None of the sisters were yet showing signs of puberty. She adjusted the daisies she had formed into a chain and wound into her bound-up hair. 'I was born too late. I should have been born five hundred years ago when there were knights and…' she pointed at the newly emerged nymph, 'he could have grown up to be a real dragon.'

'When all damsels were sweetly disposed and much distressed.' Cassie hugged her two crouching sisters. She had a capacity for creeping up on anyone and anything – even on the rickety creaking boardwalk – and may have been behind them for a while. Usually the first sign of Cassie's presence was her singular rosemary scent swirling in the air. 'You would make a perfect princess, Tabby, all hooped dresses and dramatic vapours.'

'Is Lavinia not with you?' Tabitha recovered from the surprise and looked around.

'She will come soon. She has astonished the penny-post boy who brought a letter for mother. Lavinia dropped from the trees without skirts or petticoats and demanded to see what he carried, on pain of further assault on his senses.'

'And what was his message?'

'Lavinia will give you its constituents shortly, for she broke the seal to read it before taking it to the house.' Cassie tried to lift the ends of Naomi's long sleek hair – coloured regretful orange like a French pompion vegetable – from the water, and failed.

'Whose seal?'

'Aunt Jane's, I fear. Which is why we had to wrest it from the boy.'

'Instructions for governess Pikestaff, no doubt; endless etiquette for her to teach us,' said Naomi.

'Look, there,' Tabitha pointed to a further stem of iris, lifting out of the marsh. 'There is a baby one.'

'Not a baby, Tabby,' Naomi scolded her older sister, 'another kind entirely. That must be a damsel fly nymph. It is only a case.'

'Oh, I like that much better. Of all things that steep in the marsh, I should be a damsel fly,' said Tabitha.

Cassie laughed, 'Where do you learn these things, Naomi? Not from Pikestaff, I know.'

'Papa, when he has time and is lucid. He knows everything that is to be found in these fens.'

'What would become of the skeeter hawk if we pulled off its wings?' Cassie studied the insect intently.

'You will do nothing so cruel and wicked, Cassie.' Tabitha shook off her sister's embrace.

'You know I could not, of course, but I am allowed to wonder.'

'It would stay here by the pond, forever, living out its short life,' said Naomi.

'That sounds like me,' Cassie hopped about, hands by her sides, 'a wingless dragonfly, doomed to forever wander Larken-fen.'

'Do not be morbid, Cassie,' Naomi turned and put a hand up to the spice-coloured freckles clouding her sister's cheek and forehead.

'There is a version of this creature for each of us,' said Cassie. 'Tabitha you are the damsel. I think I would have to be like this one,' she put a finger onto the dry case that the dragonfly had just emerged from and laughed, 'A crispy husk, all empty-headed.'

'You are not empty-headed, Cassie,' said Tabitha.

'What am I?' asked Naomi.

'You must stay the nymph, Naomi, for we would never coax you out from the marsh. There are too many wriggling gibble-y-bites to engage your study in the water. You would want to write of them all in your book of things.'

'Five hundred things,' said Tabitha. 'We could get Papa to illustrate it.'

'What of Lavinia?'

'Why she would be one of those busy and beautiful emerald and sapphire ones –'

'The demoiselle,' said Naomi.

'A demoiselle,' Cassie smiled as she described her absent twin, 'all in a flap, flying over the village, bossing and beguiling all the boys and not one who could catch or tame her.'

The girls laughed. Naomi stood up and said, 'Let us go to the river. It is such a clear day, we can climb the willow and see the Cathedral.'

Tabitha jumped up too. 'Yes, we should go, but you need not come, Cassie, if it will cause you too much bother and worry.'

'I am far beyond botheration these days,' Cassie rose too, hands pushing at her sisters in front of her along the boardwalk.

Fast steps came from behind them. The boardwalk echoed with their patter. The structure, constructed centuries before, snaked through the fen leading to the river. Its long stakes – driven down three yards, said their father – were secure in the ooze surrounded by sedges and trapped among long-drowned tree roots.

The sisters turned to see Lavinia racing around a corner. She wore only vest and pantaloons.

'What of your petticoats, Lavinia?' Tabitha's laugh trembled with shock.

'I have hung them in the ash tree,' said Lavinia as she slowed to their pace. 'A village girl told me the gypsies believe that if petticoats are hung in a tree, the Old Queen will leave a sign to show how fruitful the wearer will be.'

'Three droppings from the gulls, perhaps,' said Naomi.

Tabitha's giggle broke off into an appalled expression. 'You were not dressed so when you jumped out on the penny-post boy, Livvi!?' She turned the question to Cassie, who laughed and nodded.

'That scandal will be all round Reedston by dinnertime,' said Tabitha. 'And mother; did she see you in just pantaloons?'

'No, I slipped the message into Miss Pikestaff's room and made haste away before she could call me to lessons.'

'Pikestaff will tell mother,' said Naomi.

Lavinia pushed her way to the front and turned to face them walking backwards, steps unerringly centre of the slender wooden structure. 'I have more intriguing news,' she said.

'From Aunt Jane, I suspect,' said Naomi.

'Pray tell us, Livvi,' said Tabitha.

'Our Aunt, the high and mighty Countess of Harrington, has arranged for someone to visit us. We should expect him to follow fast, on the heels of her message,' said Lavinia.

'Who?'

'An artist. He is to illustrate us, so the Countess can show us off to her friends and London gentlemen of high renown.'

'They will laugh at us for being bumpkins,' said Tabitha. 'They will think us raggle-taggle gypsies who eat slugs and hedgepigs. Look at us, look at you, Livvi, without petticoats even! And poor Cassie.'

Cassie, who was ever found with her spice hair in unfashionable plaits, which made her appear younger than she was, and whose dress was stained and streaked with grime, gave a little curtsey at this.

'The Countess's letter says that this is a Society artist and he will display us in the smartest clothes and stylish designs, hair in bows or bonnets and not a one out of place. All Umbra, she writes, will be agog to ally with us.'

'Who is he?'

'He is a Mr Arnold Tenebris.'

7 – WAR, FOLLY AND POLITICKING

Stanton

'Izzy,' Stanton called from his study, pushing papers into a leather satchel.

His wife arrived promptly, hands wet from helping Cook and Midden. He was thankful to see that her Umbra, Twoshrews, had returned to the Other Realm.

'Izzy, I have a suspicion that you and Lady Rochester, snuck up to the scullery to listen to my visitor and myself conduct Ministry business. What have you to say?'

'That your hunches are as sharp as ever, Sebastian.'

'It is a serious matter, Izzy. It's bad eno –'

'You are right, I know, but Lady R is such a corrupting influence. She just wanted to hear your mysterious visitor's voice that's all.'

Stanton contained his frustration at the careless way Isabella was treating Ministry affairs. It was unlike her. 'I imagine Capu and Twoshrews were present too, privy to state secrets that they can relay across the Other Realm. Really, Isabella, it was the explicit orders of the missive..'

The use of her full name was unconscious but it dispelled her frivolity.

'We learnt nothing of consequence, Sebastian, truly. But, Lady R heard enough to pass on a warning.'

'She did what?'

'You are to be careful of Mr Lampwick, she says.'

'Larkwing...' retorted Stanton, before biting his lip.

Isabella smiled at his slip. 'Well, she said Lampwick. She may not have mastered his name, but she is more certain of his character.'

'Which is?'

'A low sort, a skulker.'

'Lady Rochester may have her own reasons for blackening the man in my eyes, Izzy. I know her reputation for shallowness but she wields power, and her son, Strathearn, is no friend to Pitt.'

'Step-son.'

'Even so, but let us drop it. As a Minister of the Crown there must always be a part of my work that remains hidden from you.'

'Yes, my dear, but please do not spurn her warning out of hand. Sometimes, Lady R's head seems as empty of sensible thought as Signor Torricelli's vacuum but, since Marie Antoinette's downfall, she is the most influential person of my sex in all Europe. She is capable of intrigues, survives adversity and twists powerful men around her finger. I doubt she works to a strategy but she has sharp instincts.'

Stanton enjoyed it when Isabella expounded earnestly. 'I suspect, Izzy, it is far more to do with the effect her plunging necklines, full lips, slim waist and handsome features have upon weak men. I included. She ravaged me mercilessly with those grey eyes of hers and I fell under her spell. My tongue has never before behaved so traitorously.'

'I give you leave to be agreeable to her. I forgot that you had not met Lady R before,' Isabella gave a forgiving smile. 'Had I known of her visit, I should have taken better precautions.'

'To prepare me for what, exactly?'

'Of what she is unconsciously capable of. We saw her at balls when we were growing. As young girls we'd follow her around rooms with our gaze, remarking at her ability to strew wreckage in her wake. If she bestowed a glance upon you, it imbued you with a magical wonder. If she spoke to you for two minutes, it was gold-dust. We used to stroke her picture in The Book, believing it brought us good luck.

'Men – young and old, servants and lords – women, Umbra; all were disturbed by the churn of her passing. She imparted greater damage if she stopped to converse. Lady R was married to the Duke then, but it wasn't her title, it was... well, it was her.

'I once saw my father exactly as you were in our morning room. A proud man of honour, as you well know, a respected officer and capable in his business affairs, yet reduced to gabbling and pleading as the goose might on feast's eve.'

Stanton tried to imagine Isabella's father, the domineering Lord Lisle, so corrupted. He could not.

'I and my cousin, Connie, recognising his malady for a Lady R funk, ran to him to pull his attention away from her. As I led him off, she smiled at me as if to say, "well done; just in time." My mother never let him close to Lady R again. I have been a little in love with Lady R since that time, for her refusal to be intimidated by men, I think. She was in her pomp then. Of course, she is scarce changed now. The most riveting company, flighty, but there is some mad alchemy about her.'

'Yet her Umbra is nearly as taciturn and ugly as my own Maraziel,' Stanton said.

'Capu has always been such a mean-spirited little thing. But, you know what they say, the Umbra you summon will always be your opposite. I have never seen Capu speak to Lady R. They say her aura is so far-reaching he can wander out of her sight or hearing.'

'Her aura, yes, it left me floundering, I confess.'

'You are as susceptible to her alchemy as all the rest, then.'

'It is good of you not to scold me for it, Izzy.'

'You have fallen for stupider people. And you never reproached me for my childish infatuation with Viscount Exeter.'

'It was over before we met, you said.'

'It wasn't over, Sebastian, for it never started. Exeter had no interest in me.'

'Then he never had a chance with you...' Stanton allowed Isabella's surprise to assemble before adding, 'for he is clearly a fool. Although, I have never met him, so have little right to an opinion.'

'Proud, certainly, cold some say, but not foolish. The fault was mine. I mistook his reserve for consideration, and his pride for discretion. I was too gauche, he, too mannerly. He attended Lady R's party last night; changed I think, more cordial, but also more awkward.'

'In Lady Rochester's presence, I understand his awkwardness all too readily.'

'Yes, it was perhaps Lady R,' Isabella's wondering turned into a laugh. 'I had already seen Goldry arrive upstairs like a moon-struck loon. I don't know why I imagined you should be immune. I thought you to be too good for her, I suppose.'

'Lady Rochester seduced the King before she was 18, married the third most powerful man in the country, and now has visiting heads of state from half the Prussian provinces grovelling to replace the Duke of Cumberland in her bed, Izzy. Perhaps you think me finer than I am.'

'No, Sebastian, that I could never do,' she said, and he took it for a compliment. Later, he wondered.

'At least I shall be fore-armed next time I meet her.'

'Oh, innocent Sebastian, how little you know of the world,' said the woman, who was some six years his junior. 'That is not the way it works at all.'

Stanton lifted his satchel. 'I must to the Ministry, I have at last discovered my true purpose there. But, before I leave, tell me what Twoshrews said to Lady R?'

'Nought of significance, only... he addressed her in French. "Vous êtes trop gentile, ma Reine," he said. I would swear she gave a little nod of appreciation at his comment, though, of course she could not have heard it.'

'Has he ever spoken French before?' Stanton tried to imbue his question with a lightness he did not feel.

'No, never.'

'Did he say anything else?'

'Nothing that could be said aloud without propelling me to the court of slander.'

'As you know, Maraziel tells me nothing, Izzy. Could you note down for me, anything that Twoshrews tells you about the world of the Umbra. I have decided my Ministry understands too little about what happens in their kingdom.'

'War, folly and politicking,' said Isabella, 'the same as here. Sebastian, if I wrote down but a tenth of the dizzying lore and flighty foolishness that pours from Twoshrews' mouth, you must needs send for more gall nuts lest the country run short of ink. Give me your questions tonight, and I will try to keep him to the point.'

◆ ◆ ◆

'Cotteridge,' called Stanton as he sat at his desk in the Ministry for Umbra Affairs. The charcoal-coated clerk stepped into the room, an old-fashioned grey-white wig and a flash of white lace at his wrists the only variety in his attire.

'Cotteridge, what is your understanding of what we do here?'

'We conduct the Ministry's business, sir, to the best of our ability.'

'But do we have a definition of what that business is?'

'I doubt we need one, sir. We answer such correspondence as we deem important, we attend the many meetings in our own Ministry and through other parts of the government, we write reports of those meetings, and we ensure those reports are filed conscientiously.'

'Do we know enough about Umbra?' Stanton had never met Cotteridge's Umbra but imagined her an ill-fed thing with lifeless hair, whose costume would be unadorned afflicted grey.

'Too much, I fear.'

'What in Britain would change if First Lord Pitt closed our Ministry down on the morrow?'

'Little, sir.'

'My thoughts concur, Cotteridge.'

'That is disconcerting, sir. We are told never to agree with our ministers.'

'Things are going to change, Cotteridge.'

'Oh dear.'

'Take notes.'

The clerk sat at his desk and prepared quill and paper.

'We need to know what languages are used in the Other Realm,' said Stanton. 'I also want dossiers compiled on the following: casualties we have noted due to violence in their realm, say in the last five years; a full understanding of the Queen's Treaty; any Umbra we suspect may have radical sympathies; have there been any reports of undue magicks; list the main experts in Umbra er... doings, people we can speak to at short notice.'

'Doings, sir,' Cotteridge's tone underlined the word somehow.

'Do we have a good record of the Bills of Mortality? From when were London's deaths first registered?'

'From memory, consistently in all London parishes since 1603, Minister. I can order in copies.'

'Do so. Also events in the Other Realm, how things work, their politics. The Chancellor of Balliol should top our list of experts. He's in town at present, according to Lady Stanton. Am I right in thinking the Umbra retain allegiances to various tribes or powers?'

'I couldn't say, sir.'

'And that is the problem. We summon our Umbra daily, we admire them, we converse with them, share our secrets, we present them to society, but we know nothing about what they do when they return to their own world.'

'Do we really want to know more than we do?' Cotteridge raised his head from the paper. 'They are rash and chaotic creatures.'

'Just so, yet our lives are linked entirely to theirs, Cotteridge. I intend that we become the font of all Umbra knowledge.'

‘Yes, sir, only… won’t this get in the way of our real work?’

8 – IN THE POOKA'S EYES

Arthur

With Amorrie returned to her deep, now neatly sewn, pocket, Arthur reclaimed his sketches and made his leave of the building. He had given his promise to travel to Larkenfen at the first opportunity.

'Must you scrap with narls?' he said to Amorrie as he hurried away.

'They had been sent against me.'

'But that frightful Piskie reported them harmless.'

'They are not "harmless", their wings are clawed. There's two teeth like stakes.'

'Stakes, you say. Amorrie, do you not realise that if harm befalls you...'

'I know.'

Arthur imagined the cruelly innocent smile upon her lips as she said this. He shook his head, 'And what did you say to Scampion to make him disappear so?'

'That I would rip off his bulging hat and show your world that beneath it, his head is the self-same obscene shape.'

'You used such a harrowing language.'

'It was Hedge.'

'You...' the words caught in Arthur's throat, 'you spoke Hedge in one of the finest morning rooms in all London?'

Amorrie popped out her head. 'He is a Hedge Imp. He understood me well enough.'

'No, *The Book of Five Hundred* has him for a High Piskie.'

'Your book,' Amorrie said, 'is wrong.'

Perhaps, realised Arthur, he did have some power over the Countess after all.

He skirted the park on his return. Amorrie's head bobbed out of the pocket. She sniffed the air and then climbed up on Arthur's shoulder.

'Get down. You have embarrassed me enough.'

She ignored him. 'You are followed.'

Arthur turned in time to see a small ragged figure step behind a tree-trunk. Walking back, he stopped a yard from the tree. 'Come you out.'

It was the child from the Africas.

'You cannot follow me, child,' said Arthur.

The little ragamuffin sniffed and wrung its hands.

'We're you perhaps employed as a page boy in a house?'

The child nodded.

'What is your name?'

'My mistress named me Norman.'

'What did your mother name you?'

'Nouhou.'

'Where in the Africas do you come from, Nouhou?'

'I do not know, Master. I was hidden still inside my mother on the ship, and born here, in England.'

'Oh, I see.' It was not a small point, born on British soil, Arthur knew, the child would ultimately have an Umbra. 'Then you are an English boy.'

The child was a study in uncertainty.

'Please, follow me no longer.'

'I must, master,' the child shuffled forth a penny from somewhere and showed it to Arthur. 'I have been paid a penny to do so.'

◆ ◆ ◆

Arthur agreed that Nouhou could follow him to the studio at Cowcross Street as he had shadowed Arthur from there that morning, but that was to be an end to it.

The little child took his duties so seriously that he would not walk by Arthur, instead keeping some three chains length behind him, skipping behind trees, hiding around corners.

'Why let it follow you when it is in the service of your enemies?' Amorrie observed the charade from Arthur's shoulder.

'People are not creatures or "it"s, Amorrie. You must name them or assign them a proper gender.'

'Well I do not like her or trust her.'

'Nouhou is a little boy, Amorrie; a former page boy, he says.'

'I like him even less. You could kill it.'

'I certainly could not.'

'It smells wrong. Why does it look different? Is it Catholic?'

'He is from the Africas is all. African boys are not Catholic.'

'I could kill it for you.'

'You cannot, at least I think you cannot. Can you?'

'I could try and then we would know.'

Amorrie did not favour children. When first summoned from the Other Realm, her fury was visited upon anyone within distance of her fists or feet or using any projectile she could reach, lift and hurl. Children, she would submit to worse.

Arthur's little sister was only three when Amorrie first appeared to Arthur. The tot had the misfortune to have been christened 'Gwragedd Annwn' by her Welsh father. No-one could pronounce it, and few tried. To Arthur and the servants, she was 'Gwennie'. A sweet-natured child, she soon learned to steer clear of her brother's combative Umbra. Even so, Amorrie prepared snares and frights in the expectation that Gwennie might stumble into them. Such was Amorrie's ambushing instincts that (even though she was constrained within Arthur's aura or shadow) she enjoyed an unlikely success rate.

To preserve the sanity of Gwennie and other members of the household, Arthur's father had purchased an austere first floor studio for his fifteen-year-old son. There, to practice his art, on the understanding that Arthur would only summon Amorrie in the studio and nevermore in the home.

At the door of that studio, Arthur waited for Nouhou and encouraged the child to approach, inviting him in for a pot of beer and some bread.

'You have earned your penny, Nouhou, but I cannot permit you to follow me more,' Arthur said as the child nervously eyed the bread.

'No master.'

'What spirit did you say sent the wind?'

'The devil wind is sent by Eshu, a demon, my mother told me of. Eshu is not known in England, only Africa.'

'What devil wind?' Amorrie's interest stirred.

'A squall that blew up from nowhere and tried to steal my sketches,' Arthur removed these same from his satchel and wondered if the sketches now served any purpose.

'No master, the devil wind wanted your coat. It wanted it so badly it made your coat fight you.'

Amorrie climbed onto the coat, now discarded on a chair, and studied the previously slashed and now mended pocket.

'Can you describe the man who paid you to follow me?' asked Arthur.

'He was dressed all in black, master.'

'Hurting,' Amorrie said, settling into the folds in the coat. 'That villain in black from your hateful party.'

'I hardly know Hurting,' Arthur said.

'Hurting would do this. His creature recognised me. I saw it in the Pooka's eyes. It means me dead.'

'Amorrie, you live in a warlike and wicked world. Do not imagine this one is the same.'

'They slashed my pocket. If I had been in there...'

'Hurting does not want you dead, I guarantee it.'

Amorrie made a show of pondering the situation before saying, 'Catholics, do you think?'

'No, of course not. Well, it is true that Catholics dislike Umbra, but they must suffer them... as we all must do. No-one wants you dead.'

'I know that to be untrue. Firstly, you are followed. I hear a devil wind attacks you. My pocket has been slashed. Something or someone wishes one of us dead. And if they kill one of us, then...'

There came a knock at the front door below. Arthur and Amorrie shared a look. Arthur turned to Nouhou, who was nowhere to be seen, but a small covered table had grown an extra leg.

A window was open, and Arthur took Amorrie over to its sill and encouraged her to look down on the door of the studio.

'Can you see? Who is it?'

'Hurting.'

9 – ONE HUNDRED MICE IN WHEELS

Stanton

≡

Umbra of note
Maraziel and her human ally Sebastian Stanton
Jenny Moonshine (Jenny M) and her human ally First Lord Pitt (the Younger)

≡

'Twoshrews has agreed to attend us here upon your business, Minister.' Isabella was all formality when Stanton returned home. She had set out the parlour with ink and quill at the desk, so Stanton could record the interview.

'He will answer five questions, or he will give five answers to your first question. I'm not truly sure where that discussion ended. He is brimming with tales of misbegotten liaisons, forbidden trysts, licentiousness of every hue that will doubtless be essential in the forth-coming wars with France.'

'You must take it more seriously, Izzy,' said Stanton. 'And, if Twoshrews tells us aught that I determine is of significance, you must swear that it will not be repeated outside this parlour.'

'If Twoshrews tells you anything that you can make sense of, or that doesn't portray love-gorged Umbra under bed-linen we will all be much astonished.' Isabella pointed to the quill, 'Pray write down your questions.'

Stanton had mentally composed one hundred such questions during the day and remembering those of most significance now was a task beyond him. Still, he reasoned, given his absence of surety about almost any aspect of 'Umbra Affairs', anything he discovered would be useful.

'I've told Twoshrews that you are a personage of much import in the lordly dealings of our realm,' said Isabella as he scribbled. 'It transpires he had always assumed you were a servant...' she coughed, 'assigned to deal with my more personal needs.'

Stanton determined he did not possess any expression pertinent to such a statement, so declined to satisfy Isabella's obvious desire to catch his eye. Twoshrews swished out his cape, sat on the table edge and gave Stanton a preternatural level of attention.

'Question One, Twoshrews' Stanton said, 'How are affairs organised in The Other Realm?'

Twoshrews heard and understood the question without any involvement from Isabella. He had the appearance of a slim handsome youth with an uncombed straggle of dark auburn hair. His high-collared rune-embroidered cape hung long over a plain white shirt, dark breeches and boots. He stood again, adopted a pompously serious pout and paced a little before proceeding to gush forth an answer.

Isabella smiled her delight as it unfolded, before relaying it on to Stanton. 'Everyone knows there are fourteen different versions of England with twelve of these in the Umbra Realm. Each is a distinct and separate world organised around a unique dance. These Englands are powered by one hundred racing mice in wheels that generate sunlight, moontide, wind, rock-fire and earthdark.'

'What in heaven's name is earthdark?'

'Do you really wish me to waste a question on that, Sebastian?'

But it was too late; Twoshrews paced the table to the limits imposed by Isabella's aura, and offered some extravagantly wiggle-some hand movements. Isabella interpreted with a growing expression of surprise: 'Earthdark is the goodness that is found below the land and in wood-litter that plants and trees hunt down to feed on. No Umbra has ever seen it but how else would they grow, and why else would they send down roots if not to search it out.

'I never knew,' she added her own thought with a suppressed twinkle. 'Oh, and Twoshrews is surprised anyone who claims to be of import, hasn't heard of it.'

Stanton finished writing and stared doubtfully at the sentences.

'I warned you,' said his wife.

Undeterred, Stanton tried again. 'Question two: when Izzy calls you how do you get here, Twoshrews?'

Back came his answer: 'He says Bella (for so he calls me), Bella's voice tinkles in his mind like a bell to say, "Come hither," and with it appears a door made of a thin material that shivers like frosting on an autumn web. He says that this door is neither one thing or another, neither hither nor thither, both there and here, but he has only to step through it, and his Bella is there. Don't you think that is sweet, Sebastian?'

Sebastian knew his wife well enough to know she thought it common poppycock, but kept his own counsel.

'Three: what compels him to come?'

'Sleep, for most Umbra agree that such a thing as the human realm is mostly impossible; it is, therefore, a thing of delusion and trance. They may travel here only when they sleep, and you cannot defend against dreams.

'You,' Isabella waved an encompassing hand, 'by which he means us... humanity, only exist in Umbra dreams – we are all sleep-chaff and if ever they cease to dream or sleep then we will all stop existing.'

'That is going to upset Pitt,' said Stanton.

Isabella gave him a look and suppressed a giggle.

'Four: who rules in The Other Realm?'

'The Elven King rules over everything in the light,' relayed

Isabella.

Stanton wrote earnestly, saying, 'Now, at last, we have something germane.'

'There is more,' said Isabella. 'The Over Goblin is Lord underground, Helliconian, Lady of the Lake, is Empress of the Rains and everything that follows from it – streams, springs, waterfalls; Ca-bjorn the Spriggan controls the moors and high-passes in England, while McTaw the Henkie is master in Highland...' the stream of translation bubbled from Isabella's tongue, but Stanton could see that Twoshrews was still spouting forth.

'Enough, Izzy, do we know any of these Umbra?' Midden knocked and entered and Stanton motioned her to wait by the door as Isabella answered.

'None are names I'm familiar with. I would swear that not one of these important Umbra is allied to any of The Five Hundred... Oh, and he says Ceretide the Selkie is titled Daughter of the Waves; Seigine and his terns have command of the Air; Gorgomon the Dead is Lord of –'

'Stop, I beseech you,' Stanton let drop his quill. 'This is not government, it is chaos. There must be one thousand situations each day in which one lord's law countermands another's rule. I just wanted to know who is in charge.'

Twoshrews had stopped his pacing and now spoke again. Isabella passed on the message: 'Of course, all of these lords historically owe fealty to the Queen.'

'A particular Queen?'

'The Queen 'Neath the Hedge.'

'But she's been dead for what, over four hundred years.'

'Twoshrews says that her rules still bind them.'

'Does the Queen rule there to this day?'

'Yes, though she has not been seen in the Other Realm for many centuries, he says. Even now, it seems, it is forbidden for any Umbra to use the title "queen" there.'

'None of these powerful Nymphs, Sprites and Merrows are queens then?'

Twoshrews shook his head, then another thought struck him. Isabella spoke, 'He says he is friends with one Umbra who claims to be a queen. She once showed him a picture of herself wearing a crown, with a fierce creature like a yellow weasel on one side and a horned steed on the other, but everyone thinks her crazed. She calls herself "The Mad Queen".'

'But the Queen 'Neath the Hedge still rules?'

Twoshrews nodded nervously.

'How,' wondered Stanton in a whisper, seeing Keeper Claw taking his usual interest from behind Midden's skirts, 'do you rule from the grave?'

Twoshrews peered to all corners, pulled his long cloak to him, said something and span until he was just a swish of cape and runes vanishing in a flamboyant whirlwind of vapour.

Stanton stared at his wife.

'Through fear,' she said.

◆ ◆ ◆

Stanton ran a troubled eye over the sheet of scribbled notes after Twoshrews had left. Isabella prescribed brandy and returned with a bottle and two glasses.

'I'm sorry,' said Isabella, 'it's not that he dissembles deliberately, but he is overly keen to impress. I think his mind plans an answer only to find that his mouth has already made a start. Then, in attempting to get from that which he has already spoken to the truth before the answer is done, his stories become ever more fantastical.'

'Four fifths of it a maddening confusion.'

'But the last fifth…?'

'Utter earthdark.'

Isabella studied Stanton's paper, 'What about Umbra still keeping to the Queen's laws, is that not of use?'

'I only know of the Queen's Treaty. And all detail of that is much fogged by time. No one in my Ministry can lay hand on a copy.'

'Think you that the Umbra are still governed by her?'

'I think I know a little about government, Izzy, and being alive is a requirement.'

'Can you not ask Maraziel about some of these eminent lords and ladies?'

Stanton shook his head, imagining his Umbra's response. 'She is lazy and so steadfastly determined not to be of use, she turns everything to a jest. In this instance, she would deride me for awakening her on so trivial a matter, deny interest in the politics of her world, claim them all to be self-important nobodies and scare our servants to boot.'

'She is a fright,' Isabella pictured the perpetually drowsy witch, with wild hair that resembled a shocked burr, burrowed inside which was a face fringed with rooty growths and – Stanton assured her – horns. 'But did not Pitt's Umbra, Jenny M, approve Maraziel before you were considered for a Ministry? She must be sound, I think, not flighty like Twoshrews.'

'Oh she has wits aplenty, but hidden below a thick bark of slovenliness and indifference. I wonder if her tenacious neglect and conspicuous disinterest wasn't the making of me.

'My father drove me to accomplishments, then along came Maraziel to show me how easily they would be disregarded if you had an unsightly Umbra and, of course, no gentlemanly connections. She saved me from arrogance perhaps.'

'I owe her some debt for making you such an admirable husband then,' Isabella stroked a curl of dark hair from his forehead. 'Though there is still much work to be done in that regard.'

'Maraziel says Jenny Moonshine proffered her blessing only because she wished to consult her on how to style her hair.' Stanton's chuckle died on his lips. 'I cannot engage Maraziel on this issue. I was specifically warned not to speak to any Umbra on the particulars.'

10 – THE ACE OF MOONS

Larkenfen

≡

Umbra of note
Galt and his human ally Miss Pikestaff
Hellekin and her human ally George Gracegirdle (Papa)

≡

'What kind of Umbra will you have, Lavinia?' Tabitha was head down studying *The Book of Five Hundred* on Governess Pikestaff's desk as closely as Mr John Harrison might the innards of a marine chronometer. It was not six inches from her nose, her head clamped between hands that twisted in her chestnut hair, her elbows spread over the desk.

The Book lay open on Tabitha's favourite spread. It wasn't a current edition, but the one from 1788, the first to be printed with colour illustrations. It was much thumbed and even missing a page, long since torn out. Tabitha viewed an illustration displaying the late Sir Joshua Reynolds's most recent rendering of Aunt Jane and her Umbra.

'Scampion looks so shrewd in his little jacket with silver buttons. He would give good counsel, I think.'

'He should counsel himself to procure a better hat,' said Naomi, who sat at the long sturdy table that served as a school desk for the sisters. Cassie was perched upon the table while Lavinia prowled the room studying her father's prints on the walls.

'My Umbra will be more comely and of better disposition than Pikestaff's performing bear.' Lavinia was garnering her grievances, arming for an argument.

Miss Pikestaff had hunted them down in their favourite spot, the trees above the lane that led to the village of Reedston and from there to Eely Bridge. She was angry that they had scared a messenger, sent to Larkenfen from Reedston.

'It will not do, girls,' she shouted up into the branches, 'if you are not in the schoolroom, properly attired and with no sign of rabblement within five minutes, I shall take up quill to your aunt.'

They were now present and presentable, but Miss Pikestaff was still elsewhere in the house, learning the messenger's news.

'Papa should sack Pikestaff,' said Lavinia, 'What use is she to us? She cannot draw a quarter as well as he, learning to crochet and doing needlepoint with her is a torment, and why bother to teach us French, for if we go there now, we would be locked away like Marie Antoinette.'

'Miss Pikestaff is not Papa's to sack,' Cassie reminded her twin. 'Aunt Jane pays for her to attend us, and you know mother would not allow it.'

'She is to turn us into ladies,' Tabitha left the desk and performed a twirl, 'so we can ally with the most gallant Umbra and are fit to be seen in London dancing at balls and conversing at the table.'

'Why would anyone care if I use a spoon or a fork to eat my potted beef?' said Naomi, who often sided with Lavinia and provided her older sister with better arguments. 'I wonder at a woman who can take so much time to teach us nothing of import. She is the worst of them so far.'

The sisters had seen off three governesses. The first had lasted five months before denouncing them as little better than vagabonds. In her letter to Aunt Jane, the second governess had named them 'barbarous rakehells'. She had written this from the sanctuary of the Lamprey Inn at Reedston, having fled within a week. The third, Miss Bell – the only one to have been given Papa's blessing – had fared better. The sisters, and Cassie in particular, had taken both to her and her Umbra, Partridge – a Drus thought Tabitha, who spent most time studying such things. Lamentably, Miss Bell had been taken by an outbreak of the pestilence whilst on a visit to Eely Bridge.

Strident steps approached down the hallway and Tabitha leapt up from *The Book* and back to her place at the school table. Miss Pikestaff had no problem with the girls reading the copy of *The Book* (the Countess had insisted upon there being one in the house. it was a condition of her continuing to employ their governess) but their father detested it and the sisters, Tabitha included, took their lead from his opinion in most things.

Miss Pikestaff entered the schoolroom, which also served as parlour to the household. Her Umbra, Galt, stalked from one of her shoulders to the other on all fours, crossing behind Miss Pikestaff's neck. The governess surveyed her charges. 'Will you sit please, Lavinia?'

'There is no call to.'

'The messenger tells me he was much affrighted by your calls, hoots and rustles from the trees.'

'It certainly sped him on his way,' said Cassie.

'He set off at quite a lick,' said Naomi.

'He has been stood a glass of ale in the kitchen, to settle his agitation before his return. You are savages to tease and torment a boy so.'

'Hardly a boy,' said Lavinia, 'almost a man full grown. The penny-post boy is not so timid.'

'The post boy knows you and expects you to be uncivilised, Lavinia, but even he was offended by the method you employed to steal the letter yesterday,' said Miss Pikestaff.

Galt whispered to Miss Pikestaff. It was a needless guardedness, for the girls could not perceive his words and there were no other Umbra present, but he always did it. Galt wore a small metal helmet, an open leatherish jerkin too small for him and a cudgel at his belt. His skin had a bruise blue sheen and his arms and legs were hairy and thickly muscled. He was brutish and seldom still.

Galt's presence always unnerved their cat, Rushie. The Larkenfen mouser would scoot from any room Galt appeared in and, if no escape was possible, would adhere to the door and scratch constantly, until liberated. The girls speculated that Rushie must have ended up on the thicker end of Galt's cudgel upon occasion.

'And, he was naturally offended to see a young lady, from one of the oldest families in the region,' Miss Pikestaff continued, 'in such a state of undress. Yes, word has reached me of that detail. To think, there have been Gracegirdles at Larkenfen since 1267, and never any so disobedient.

'Mr Tenebris, the artist, will be attending you shortly. At the very least, he must find you in clean clothes, with washed and well-brushed hair – yes, Tabitha, I know you set a better example in this regard – civil and well countenanced. What is that you have around your neck, Naomi?'

'A lapwing skull and mummified Weasel's parts.'

'Which parts I will not ask and with a knife in your belt, too. You are two-thirds feral cat.'

'Galt carries a cudgel,' said Naomi.

'When in the Other Realm, Galt is a brave warrior, defending high passes, you are an English maiden of quality and breeding. It is no sort of comparison.'

'Papa will not receive Mr Tenebris.' Lavinia did not disguise her disdain. Their father had been indignant since the borrowed letter was found, then read by Miss Pikestaff, and its contents shown to the girls' parents. He retreated to his studio. Mother was angry with her sister, the Countess, for the high-handed manner of her action and had 'gone visiting' around the parish. Neither parent was in the house and this was a common state of affairs. 'Papa considers that all paintings in *The Book* are frivolous and empty of meaning.'

Miss Pikestaff took a pause to stare around the room at the

many illustrations on its walls. 'Your father is an excellent draftsman, inventive and with a good eye for detail. His skill far exceeds my own, but his austere landscapes filled with empty skies, lonely plains, impenetrable woods, and wretched or raging creatures do not attract admirers. Mr Tenebris, whose talents I only know from less than a handful illustrations in the most recent edition of *The Book*, is the better artist for the task the Countess has in mind.'

'Papa is the artist,' venom coated Lavinia's words, 'This Tenebris is no better than a tradesperson.'

◆ ◆ ◆

Lavinia left the room with her remark still bouncing off the walls. She would go eel-babbing. Galt vanished to the sound of three clashes of flints, as he ever did, and the scent of wild heather tinged the air for a few moments after his departure. The other three sisters stayed put and bore the grim-faced governess for another hour.

With Miss Pikestaff gone and the schoolroom returned to a plain parlour, Tabitha hovered by the walls, studying her father's paintings by the shafts of low afternoon sun. His art and topics were provoked by nightmares and visions. He could no more choose other subjects than he could control these disturbances of his mind. The canvases depicted a drab barely hued world, whose only charm was found in the occasional daubing of a pale sun picking its way through threatening clouds to glint on a barren hillside, or a gaunt spectral tower reflected in a still, sombre, reedy lake.

Mistletoe was oft a component of his work, either in the patterned borders that framed his scenes or borne on the jerkins of creatures and characters that stared out from them. It was the emblem on the Gracegirdle's family crest and etched into many windows in the house.

'Are Papa's creatures Umbra, do you think?' Tabitha asked as Cassie appeared at her shoulder.

'That is never how they are depicted in *The Book* or in other portraits we have studied,' said Cassie.

'And Papa has never said they are any more than the phantoms left after fractious dreams.'

'Perhaps Hellekin whispers these visions to him when she attends him in the afternoons,' Cassie's tone was hushed. Hellekin was their father's Umbra. She visited little in company, wore long shawls patterned in black webbing over gowns dyed harrowing holly and their father said she constantly muttered, 'Everything is fluxed; nothing is as it seems', whenever she appeared.

Some characters and landscapes appeared more than once in different paintings. A scene would be redrawn from a further viewpoint or under altered weather conditions. A character or creature might reappear injured or dead, or with more or less brutal weaponry on its person. Demented things whose rags trailed behind them becoming wisps of night, flew at the artist, as if angry at his observation and disturbance.

'Papa's mind is a sombre place, full of sorrows,' said Cassie. 'It is little wonder he can be driven half out of his wits by his time there.'

'There are some I like,' said Tabitha, 'The Ace of Moons for one.'

Some years before, urged on by his wife, their father had turned his illustrations into a set of playing cards. Rather than spades, hearts, diamonds and clubs, their father's suits were: Tides, Storms, Dreams and Flies.

The full pack was still to be finished, but among the illustrations prepared for it, was a close-up portrait painting of a fierce girl whose irises rose up – half-moons of impregnable darkness – from eyes set in shadow. Blood speckled her neck and drips of it fell onto the start of her chest. Her face was set in a challenge with a web of jet hair crawling around the top of the canvas. She was assigned to the suit of Storms and the top left corner of the card bore her title, 'The Ace of Moons'.

11 – HURTING'S HAT

Arthur

Below Arthur's studio window stood a man wearing one of the new tall circular broad-brimmed hats. Arthur had only seen them before in illustrations and could not imagine they would ever replace the tricorn. Like the rest of his ensemble, it was black. Arthur had every reason to believe Amorrie's assertion that this was Mr Quartermain Hurting.

As he dithered, the hat lifted, and Hurting's face materialised, staring directly up at Arthur.

'Mr Tenebris, good day. I asked if we could call, I hope now is agreeable.'

'Amorrie is not here,' Arthur shouted down, pushing her back away from the window.

'It is you I hoped to speak with, sir. Perhaps you could open the door.'

'I'll attend you in a moment, Mr Hurting.' Arthur turned to Amorrie, 'You must go.'

'No, I stay.'

'You are never happy to come when I summon you,' Arthur was exasperated, 'and now, when you say you are in danger, you will not leave.'

'I like danger,' said Amorrie, with a moue of petulance. 'But he should not see me. Was the Pooka with him?'

'I saw no sign of his Umbra, but that is far from the point. Since you must remain in my aura, he will certainly see you when I go down to let him in.'

'Wear your white frock,' Amorrie pointed at Arthur's painting smock, 'I can hide beneath that.'

◆ ◆ ◆

Hurting stepped into the studio.

'This is a superior work space, sir.' He was a plain faced man, long of chin with grim shadows under his eyes and pupils nearly as black as Amorrie's. He appeared even swarthier than on the previous evening, having not shaved since. His tall hat was off his head – clutched to one side – freeing long vulgar whips of black hair.

'Would you like some tea?' asked Arthur. 'I recently sampled it with some sugar, it is –'

'No, sir, I thank you. I have a duty to perform and it is not a pleasant one. I fear it may cause you to choke on any tea.'

Under his smock, Amorrie pinched him as fiercely as her small hand would allow. Arthur would have preferred it if she had just spoken her warning; after all Hurting couldn't hear her. It was not as if Arthur had any means of defence; he never carried a blade for the very good reason that he had not the merest idea how to use one.

'Then I must press you to be brief, Mr Hurting, for there is work to do,' Arthur said. 'I have today won a commission from one of London's most prestigious houses. What business do you have with me?'

'Ah yes, your new commission, it is that I have come about. You are speaking about the Countess of Harrington, if I'm not mistook.'

'How the deuce could you know that?' Arthur felt Amorrie tap her 'told you so', under his smock. 'You are having me followed, sir.'

'No indeed, but I do know of the Countess's commission. Two other artists turned her down before she called upon you.'

'Oh,' Arthur hadn't wanted the commission at all, but would have preferred not to be the third choice for it. 'The Countess did not say.'

'William Bell was to have undertook it but his health is too poor for the journey from Newcastle. Mr Wright could not be persuaded. You are in good company.'

Arthur determined he should make a study of Hurting's polite deference. Arthur knew that he came across as simpering and over-eager to ingratiate himself, while Hurting's courtesy was unobtrusive and underlined by capability. Something about him suggested he would do whatever duty was required, but also the petit morceau more that was necessary to fulfil the task beyond what was expected. If Hurting was here to kill him, or Amorrie (effectively both of them, whichever was the case), Arthur was confident that the man would do it well and thoroughly and leave him little complaint in the matter.

'Before I say more, Mr Tenebris; I need to be sure we are alone.'

'Quite alone,' said Arthur, wondering if it was a wise thing to admit to and never more aware of Amorrie clinging beneath his smock.

'You do know there is a young child under your table, sir.'

'Ah yes, so there is. It is only Nouhou, a boy from the Africas. He's shy. Come out Nouhou and say hello to Mr Hurting.'

The child emerged nervously but offered no greeting.

'Does the lad work for you?' asked Hurting, his stare laden with suspicion.

'I thought he worked for you.'

'Hardly.'

'Is this the man who gave you your penny, Nouhou?' Arthur encouraged the small child but Nouhou shook a downcast head.

'Then, who? Was it the man with a coat of bees?'

'What's this?' Hurting turned his eyes from Nouhou to Arthur.

Nouhou's head shook again and a small voice came from it, 'No, master, for his coat was all golds and browns. My penny came from a man all in black, but not this man.'

'Then why did you hide when Mr Hurting came to my door?'

'Because he means to kill you, master.'

Hurting's stare ran from the child to Arthur, whose embarrassed laugh revealed too much. 'You think I mean you harm, Mr Tenebris?'

'You say you have a duty that will make me choke. This boy was paid a penny to follow me. I have been attacked this morning and my good frock coat slashed –'

'By a devil wind,' added Nouhou in a soft aside.

'Sent by a man with a coat of bees…' finished Hurting and indicated a stool, sitting down at Arthur's nod.

'Nouhou may not have all the details correct,' said Arthur, who could feel Amorrie's punch and hear her cursed exclamation. 'There were just a lot of bees on some handsome flowers in the square.'

Nouhou's head dropped a little lower.

'Really, describe to me the weather you experienced today, Mr Tenebris,' said Hurting.

'Dry,' Arthur's confusion was growing, 'not cold for the season. Dark clouds when I left my studio, and then sunshine and warmth, almost a summery note, as I approached Bedford's squares and parks. Then a fierce squall…'

'A devil wind,' put in the dogged Nouhou.

'I think the child has the gist of it, Mr Tenebris,' Hurting placed his own hat on his thigh, so that it's top faced Arthur. 'The weather for most of us in London was unremitting cloud and a steady breeze. Yet sunshine found you and then you were attacked by a devil wind.'

'What of it?'

'There is a name, I have heard mention of recently. I had not at first believed the rumour, but this same character carries the breath of summer with it. Perhaps that is what the child saw.'

'Character?'

'An entity. Oh, it is in human guise, I do not doubt. I understand little of it but believe it has some small control of the local weather, preferring sunshine. It was written bees would flock to it when the seasons turned. If I am right, its visits are exceeding rare, and its purpose is death.'

'Death?' Arthur slumped down upon a chair, causing Amorrie to squeak. 'My death?'

'Well, we only have the child's word. I do not intend you harm...' there came a pause. '...for now. Indeed, I have need of your service.'

'What is it you do, Mr Hurting – for your profession I mean?'

'Barely a profession, Mr Tenebris, I work for gentlemen and, occasionally, for gentlewomen. They seek me out to undertake tasks they consider beneath them but that are beyond the trust and scope of those that usually serve them. They value my opinion on certain matters. I bear a reputation I did not seek and do not advertise, but it brings me a modest living.'

'Whose work are you on today?'

'No small part of my reputation rests on my discretion, Mr Tenebris. I do not divulge who my employers are. However, you may rest assured that none of them...' again the careful qualification, '...at this moment, want you dead or harmed. But it seems another may do so. Perhaps they are on the trail of your Miss Amorrie.'

'Why say you so?'

'Do you know anything of the killing of Charon at all?'

'I? No, nothing.'

'Hmm,' Hurting scratched his long chin. 'Until last night, I was unaware of your Umbra's identity. Others may also have noted her presence at Lady Rochester's party; others, whose interest will be piqued.'

'That is ridiculous,' said Arthur. 'Amorrie is a singular Umbra, I confess, but who would wish her harm? She is barely ever here.'

'No, she is in the other place,' Hurting kneaded his long chin. 'Perhaps it is for the best that you are to travel away to Larkenfen for this commission.'

'I may not. I have not decided.'

'Oh, you will. Do not doubt it.'

'Yet Wright of Derby turned it down, you say.' Arthur grew a shell of stubbornness.

'Joseph Wright is a much sought-after artist. Since his scientific depiction of An Experiment on an Umbra in an Air Pump graced the National Gallery, many think him a genius on a par with the late Sir Joshua. His mastery of light... but I digress. The Countess of Harrington cannot so readily ruin his career. Yours, sir, is barely begun and all too easily ended. You will travel to Larkenfen because you have no choice. But, take care; if I have guessed at your commission, others will have too.'

Arthur groaned. 'What has any of this to do with you, Mr Hurting?'

'I, also, have a task for you in the Fens. It is not one I would give to anyone lightly, and you perhaps least of all. I don't doubt it will cause you a deal of distress but there is no-one else I can task with it. Only you have cause to be admitted to the home of the Gracegirdles and are now expected there.'

'What do you require of me?' Arthur could tell this would be worse than anything demanded of him by the Countess.

'It concerns one of the daughters of George Gracegirdle.'

'Which one?' asked Arthur, trying to remember the names on the note he had been given by the Countess.

'That is just it, Mr Tenebris; we have no idea.' His fingers ran around the brim of his strange hat. 'None of us do.'

◆ ◆ ◆

'The Pooka was in the hat,' said Amorrie, emerging after Hurting had left. He had first outlined the task Arthur was to perform at Larkenfen but promised that two rewarding and reputation-enhancing commissions would follow its successful completion.

'How do you know he was in the hat?' asked Arthur.

'Because when I cursed you for not mentioning the man in the coat of bees, it heard me and reported to Hurting that I hid beneath your frock.'

Arthur's hands flew to his head with an accompanying groan. 'Oh no. Hurting knows I was deceiving him, that I lied when I said you were not here.'

'He deceived you, similar-wise.'

'Hurting is a bad enemy to have, Amorrie. It seems he is capable of dark deeds, and moves in sinister circles. I believe reputable gentlefolk use him to undertake fell tasks, like the one he has forced upon me.'

'You're right. We must kill him.'

At this, Nouhou scampered back under the table.

'Please, no more talk of killing. I have had my fill.' Arthur slumped to his chair.

Amorrie, who had been pacing the floor by his feet, climbed up onto his lap. 'And this man in a coat of bees has tried to kill me,' she said, causing Arthur to cover his face with his hands. 'And this place we travel to, it seems, this too, will be full of death and danger.'

'I said, enough.'

'After all these years...' she said.

Arthur peered out from between his fingers and saw his Umbra studying him with a new expression on her tiny face. '...when I thought you only good for balls, and making your scrawl on canvases, and grovelling... you are in danger of becoming interesting. That was never part of our pact'

'We have no pact. You are a fiend sent from your vile world to torment me, and you do your duty too well.'

Arthur dwelt now, upon the duty he had promised to perform in the Fens and became morose.

12 – IN THE QUEEN'S HALLS

Stanton

≡

Umbra of note

Dawn Withheld and her human ally The Chancellor of Balliol

≡

'There is a depiction of your Treaty, Minister.' The Chancellor of Balliol had arranged their meeting in The Queen's Halls near Crutched Friars. The imposing early 14th Century building was kept as the Queen had left it, part shrine and part-museum. It acted as home for many artefacts, paintings, other depictions and a little-visited archive on her rule and various queendoms. On this Monday morning only three other visitors were present, scattered around the stately vastness of the main hall. Silence reigned where once the Queen had ruled.

Remote ceilings reflected the reticent light, which crept in from high small windows, with little enough slithering down to where Stanton stood with the Chancellor.

The Oxford College don held up a lantern to better illuminate the picture, which he informed Stanton was 'too lifelike' to have been painted by Walter of Durham, and therefore, was probably, 'by one of the Italians'. In it the Queen did indeed sit 'Neath the Hedge, cross-legged in a manly leather jerkin and hose. The remnants of a gown, shredded to rags, draped over her thighs to the knee. Behind her was a stretch of hedge, which Stanton estimated at six yards in length.

Upon the hedge, above and beside the Queen at its left-hand end, sat, stood or swung seven Umbra, diverse and battle-clad, gazing straight out at the observer. At the other end of the hedge stood King Edward Longshanks, bent by the tribulations of his reign and age. He was attended by three knights of the realm, a bishop and a herald. These faces too were stern. The artist had done his job too well in capturing the lines on the King's face, the notches and contortions of the knights' weapons and shields, their stained armour and frayed robes.

Stanton studied the stretch of vegetation that dominated the painting between the two groups. The only message he took from the depiction was that defeat was clear in the slumped demeanour of the King's contingent. The Umbra and the Queen were yet more sombre, showing none of the triumph that was their due. There was nothing amicable in their fellowship.

'What does it say? Can you decipher its contents?' asked Stanton.

The painting displayed the constraints of its time, which the Chancellor gave as barely into the 1300s. It was simple and muted in colour, dark hues masked their secrets from the lantern light.

The Chancellor was a corpulent and jovial man, more often seen at dinners and party gatherings than at Oxford College halls. Umbra Studies were of passing interest to everyone (and accounted conspicuously for the popularity of the one hundred and fifty newspapers of the day) but they were considered of little practical value. They attracted students with inherited wealth and more attractively flamboyant or socially inclined Umbra – the very opposite of Stanton and Maraziel.

'Decipher its contents.' The Chancellor studied the painting hard, until a smile interrupted, '...elder, may, reed, buckthorn and bramble with rose briar accents, bindweed and honeysuckle running through it.'

Stanton coughed his disappointment, 'I meant...'

'Forgive me, it was my jest. I know what you meant, however, the skills of the artist do not extend to capturing the script within the hedge. Like you, Minister, I know the broad scope of the Treaty, but as for the exact terms written into it, I have no information to give you.'

'But you are Master of Umbra Magicks and Linguistic Studies,' said Stanton. 'This is surely the most important document relating to the Other Realm.'

'Hedge is barely read, even by most Umbra, these days. It is still sometimes spoken, but few understand the seasons' portents sufficiently to write... haha should I say, to grow, a solitary sentence of Hedge, let alone a tract of legislation.'

Seated on his chain of office and swinging gently, whenever the Chancellor's posture and stomach allowed, his Umbra, Dawn Withheld, spoke to her ally. She was immaculate in flowing robes of bruise blue, the colour favoured by Umbra with a connection to water.

Stanton had not intended to have Umbra present at the meeting, but when the Chancellor confirmed the venue, he also let it be known that the Nymph, Dawn Withheld, would be in attendance. Custom and courtesy prevailed on Stanton to summon Maraziel to the Queen's Halls. The two Umbra could hardly have contrasted more: Dawn Withheld was beautiful, reputed to give wise counsel, a power in her own realm; her charming company a sought-after boon to any occasion. Maraziel was none of these things.

At the introductions, Dawn Withheld had studied the drowsy, inscrutable presence of Maraziel, slumped cross-legged on Stanton's shoulder, for a long moment. She made to deliver a comment to the Chancellor, decided it lay beneath her dignity and instead turned her penetrating teal-eyed gaze on Stanton.

Now the Chancellor listened to his Umbra, nodded enthusiastically and swung to Stanton, murmuring, 'Yes, yes, an excellent point indeed. Dawn Withheld reminds me that Hedge is a more versatile language than our own, Minister. While our documents, once written, are enshrined in the moment, points captured and nailed down, unchanging; a document writ in Hedge evolves with the passing years.'

His Umbra lifted her head to add new thoughts, also relayed. 'Clauses extend with the seasons, flourishing passages endure the trim of winter, new appendices flower forth on summer's quill, redundant points wilt in the autumn cull. In short, whatever was writ in the Queen's Treaty is now modified and reshaped by events. It no longer says what it did, no longer binds what was bound.'

Stanton was witnessing a performance that could have been reserved for Oxford's lecterns. Maraziel snuffled her disinterest.

'Do you know these Umbra depicted with the Queen?'

The Chancellor pointed at a slim woman, whose hair gushed from a circlet of stone on her head, cascaded over a bruise blue gown (shaded as was Dawn Withheld's own) and pooled in places below the hedge. She held a spear wrapped in cloth. 'Here is Helliconian, Lady of the Lake, you can find her likeness in other illustrations from more recent times.'

He pushed the lantern forward to illuminate other sombre countenances. 'This, is the Elven King. He was the last of the Umbra lords to be defeated by the Queen. Haha this one is so grim-faced, he can only be the emissary of the Over Goblin, and this, here, must be a lordly Spriggan, a hulking specimen, but I do not think his name was reliably recorded.' He chuckled again, 'I doubt any Englishman present could have converted his name into letters; not even Langtoft.'

Stanton addressed his next question to Dawn Withheld, holding the Chancellor's eye for any show of affront at this trespass. 'Are these Umbra still living today?'

The Chancellor returned his Umbra's answer with gusto. 'Dawn does not know about the emissary, of course, but the Lady still rules o'er the Lake, the Elven King sits still on his throne. The Spriggan probably rules some of his tribe although is no longer Chief of their kind. Unless they have met with death in warfare or other mishap, they all still live.'

'Over nearly five hundred years.' It was more wonderment than question.

'As indeed may we all, thanks to the regenerative energies supplied by our Umbra, Minister.'

'Yes, but we English folk fall constantly to war and pestilence, still.'

Dawn Withheld spoke and was translated for Stanton's benefit. 'Here is Timberlene, from the Council of Dryads; peaceful creatures, hard to believe they were involved in her wars.'

'That was the Queen's great talent.' The voice by his ear caused Stanton to start in surprise at Maraziel's engagement. 'Only she could unite the Umbra.'

'Through fear?' asked Stanton.

'Through hatred.'

The Chancellor spoke again. 'This separate shaded figure, I understand, is Shait'n, Captain of the Greynhym.'

Maraziel stirred on Stanton's shoulder. 'What was he doing there? Why was he present?'

Dawn Withheld's gaze settled on the burr-haired witch.

Stanton studied the faded figure indicated, his open wounds, ragged clothing and filmy white eyes. 'I didn't realise that a Lord of the Dead was actually party to the Treaty. I thought it merely bound the Umbra to contain the Greynhym to the territories the Queen had confined them in and allocated to them.'

'The Greynhym fought against the Queen, of course. They battle against everything. She conquered them, as much as you can ever vanquish such creatures. The dead could not then fight for her, as the Umbra did, but the mere notion that she held sway over the Greynhym – over the plague – was enough to end any resistance to her in England and Wales. Highlands too, surrendered to her two years later in 1304. She was then thought to be just twenty-two.'

'At little more than the same age as Izzy, she had conquered two Britains.' Stanton pulled the Chancellor's lantern closer to the young woman who stared back from deep-set eyes. Thick black hair lifted from her shoulders, held back by some unseen clip behind, but thick tendrils burst from its constraints. She was proportioned like an English maid, yet her presence and something disquieting in her gaze favoured the Umbra. As his lantern illuminated her eyes, the stone chill in the halls seemed to permeate his garments. Maraziel shifted again on his shoulder.

'The fear of pestilence wore her colours into battle,' said the Chancellor, his voice lowered in harmony with the austere surroundings at last. Stanton wondered if the original jauntiness had been a ploy to fight against the oppressive scrutiny of the building. 'At the turning of the 14th Century fear of plague was all-consuming.'

'How did she know that every Greynhym invasion and expansion in the Other Realm, brought plague to our world, to England and the Welsh borders?'

'She was one of a handful of English men or women in history who could travel to the Other Realm. She saw the correlation between skirmishes the Greynhym won there against the Umbra – also against her – and the spread of pestilence to new villages or towns in England or Powys. Where the Greynhym expanded, our men, women and youths took sick and died, to be added to the Greynhym's number.'

The Chancellor turned to a chest covered in glass and set at waist height. In it were a number of articles. 'Here we have The Queen's Effects, some of the possessions that defined her reign.'

Stanton had never seen them before. He brushed an unseasonal bee from the glass, where it had landed.

'Here is her Ruby Darter,' said the Chancellor pointing to the bejewelled dagger sunk into a sheet of discolouring pale fabric that lined the chest. 'She wears it in the illustration we have just seen. Here, a belted silver girdle she supposedly wore in the Swarm of Witches battle.'

Maraziel harrumphed at this. Dawn Withheld said something, obviously directed at Maraziel, for the Chancellor did not bother to repeat it to Stanton.

'A cloak of doubtful provenance,' he pointed at some regretful orange rags, much admired by moths. Next, a hilt and shattered sword: 'The Water Spear, broken when Helliconian whistled up an ice Elemental to join battle at Aberdulais.'

'Typical Nymph,' came Maraziel's husky growl, 'even their tunes are cold, wet and bothersome.'

Dawn Withheld said something and stood in her chain, staring at Maraziel.

'Oh, this is unexpected,' said the Chancellor. 'Do not rise to it, m'dear.' But his Umbra vaporised in a burst of fine evaporating spray.

'Oh dear. Two wolves cannot share one rock it seems. It is these halls, it was a misstep to meet here. The place affects us all,' he said.

'I'm sorry for any offence caused,' said Stanton, unnerved by Maraziel's unprecedented involvement.

'Let us hurry along.' The Chancellor was truly cured of jauntiness now. 'Here, the Crown of Dream Fragments, here Ceretide's Abyssal Trident; you know that we are missing the true treasure.'

'The Queen's Sprig.'

'Yes,' the Chancellor swung around and pointed to another portrait of the Queen on the nearby wall. It showed her hair streaming down in an endless black 'V' over bare shoulders, 'as displayed in this portrait by Duccio di Buoninsegna.'

Around her neck was strung a tight black choker holding a silver casting in the shape of a stem and leaves.

'Mistletoe, is it not,' said Stanton.

'Mistletoe was her sigil, indeed. A pagan symbol, it steals its strength from others, eventually overcoming them. This treasure was thought to be the source of her power by many Umbra. It vanished with her. If I had a penny for every time someone had asked me what I thought happened to it, or where it might be found…'

'I take it you have no answer, Chancellor.'

'If I knew that answer, Minister, I would be wearing a Mistletoe Sprig 'pon my lapel, and ruling England instead of King George and your Pitt the Younger.'

'So, you believe that her magick powers come from the jewellery – it was the sorcery of the Sprig and not her will and abilities?'

'Many believe it. The theory is a little supported by one legend. Before her death, she said: "When Britain hath need of my power hence, you must look to my Sprig to return it to you." The saying of it is not in doubt for she made sure it was competently recorded, but the interpretation is, as always, less certain.'

'No wonder so many seek it out.'

'Have I answered all, Minister? I have other duties to return to. I understood it was the Treaty you were most interested in.' He waved away the returning bee, which buzzed its annoyance.

'Maraziel wonders at Shait'n at the signing of the Treaty.'

'He is mentioned in Trevet's account and no-one has had sight of Langtoft's original chronicle for over a century.'

'How do I get a better understanding of the Treaty's exact form of words.'

'Impossible Minister, as my Nymph explained, the Treaty has swelled and thickened beyond its original meaning. It was devised to bind two worlds as intricately as Old Man's Beard binds a young hawthorn. Cultivated in haste during war it now falls into dilapidation and decay. They say many clauses relating to the Greynhym were consumed by a spawning of wolf's head caterpillars many years ago.'

'Are Umbra still bound by it?'

'Most consider themselves so. They fear that if they disregard it, the Queen 'Neath the Hedge will return, and no-one wants that.'

'But if she can control the spread of the Greynhym – the spread of pestilence – then surely…'

'Does King George want to hand control of our new Britain to a medieval warrior who fights with magicks and is closely allied to fell creatures in the Other Realm – does Pitt, or Helliconian? No, Minister, they all would like her powerful Sprig, but no-one wants the Queen back.'

'Can Umbra harm people?'

The change of tack and directness of the question, caused the Chancellor to consider a moment. 'Before the Treaty, they took up arms with the Queen against us, yes. But now, what would be their purpose? They have every reason to dread death, any death – and all that follows from it – more than even we do. Death strengthens their fiercest enemy.'

'But they have constant wars, do they not?'

'Because they are unstable creatures and swift to temper, but they have fewer battles and generate endless treaties. Now, Minister, I really must go.'

Stanton watched the Chancellor turn towards the doors. He had one final question: 'Do you believe, Chancellor, that a renegade Umbra might be persuaded to kill a fellow Umbra in the Other Realm in order to destroy a human, say, a prominent Englishman or woman?'

'Of course it is possible. I can think of Umbra who would do so.'

The Chancellor turned around with a doubtful expression, but he had not spoken, the answer had come from beside Stanton's ear.

13 – THE UMBRA IN THE VACUUM

Larkenfen

'Girls, here is Mr Tenebris.'

Miss Pikestaff herded them before her into the schoolroom. Tabitha stopped shyly at the sight of the visitor, Naomi bumped into her and Cassie and Lavinia, thronged behind looking over and past their sisters' heads.

They had been given most of the morning off lessons, so Miss Pikestaff could take the carriage to Reedston and collect the artist. Here he was, standing by the governess's desk, no Umbra in attendance, trying out a flustered smile, adequately attired in a fusty frock coat with lace at collar and cuff and – as Lavinia whispered – 'nothing especial and nothing like Papa'.

Their father knew of the man's arrival, so had retired to his studio. Mother knew he came from the patronising benevolence of her sister, so had 'gone visiting' around the parish. Left to their own affairs in the morning, Lavinia had led them into the fen beyond the range of the maid.

On her return Miss Pikestaff promptly tracked them down, rounded them up and returned them to her sanctum with a satisfied smile.

Standing, with the artist, before her sturdy desk, Miss Pikestaff introduced her charges: Tabitha first, curtsying and earning an acknowledgement from both governess and artist; Lavinia last, a dry nod with accompanying scowl.

Miss Pikestaff was in her newest gown, never before seen outside of a Sunday. It fitted close to her body and was of lamentable lilac with a small pimpernel pattern repeat and white lace around the bodice – cut too plainly and tightly, said Tabitha, too modern for a governess, complained Lavinia, uncommonly fetching, thought Cassie.

The artist waited as Miss Pikestaff picked up the letter from her desk, unfolded it with a snap and held it before her as if it were a proclamation and she in Reedston market square. 'Girls,' she glanced past the letter to check their attention, 'as you know all too well, we received this letter from your aunt two days ago. In it, she says that she has arranged for you to begin your introduction to London society, so that you may one day take your place there as her much adored –' here Lavinia snorted, the artist turned apprehensively at the sound, '...nieces.

'Most of my time in Larkenfen is spent preparing you for that day and I am delighted that the Countess has procured the services of so fine an artist as Mr...' she consulted the letter, 'Mr Arnold Tenebris, who has already had three illustrations in *The Book of Five Hundred*.

'He has travelled here in haste from his studio in London to capture your likenesses in such a way that society can only be impressed by you and fine young gentlemen of good family will anxiously await your attendance in person at your aunt's side.

'I will leave it to Mr Tenebris to set out his plan, but,' and this came weighted with firmness, 'we will do all we can to be charming to him, so your aunt gets good report of you, and we will in every way accommodate his ideas to allow the best result. Mr Tenebris...'

She took a long pace back and the artist was now the full focus of their attention. He was young, but at least twice Lavinia and Cassie's age, tall and – Naomi thought – had a good physiology. For all that, Naomi imagined he quailed slightly. Aunt has warned him of us, was her thought.

'Good day, ladies,' he conquered his hesitancy. He had the advantage of the thin October sunlight that played on the window behind him and lit his audience. 'Your aunt, the most noble Countess, whom I have recently had the honour of meeting – and her adorable Umbra too – in her elegant drawing room, has bestowed upon me the task of displaying your prettiness, charm and accomplishments to those of her acquaintance she considers worthy.

'She insists that I am prompt in my commission and your excellent governess assures me that schoolwork will be put aside so my time with you is prioritised. Miss Pikestaff has appraised me of your characters and interests and we have agreed on how they can be shown to best effect.

'I am overjoyed to find you so amiable to my eyes. You are not attired for town, I know, but I have brought costumes in my baggage that your aunt has approved as suitable for your good impression, even on society's most discerning young gentlemen. Please sit. Do you have any questions of me?'

Tabitha raised her hand and received a nod. 'Where is your Umbra, Mr Tenebris?'

'Ah,' he hesitated, before saying, 'she has visited me already this day and is now busy in her own world.'

'He is ashamed of her,' Cassie confided to Naomi.

'Will we meet her later?' Tabitha again.

'Surely.'

'Where are your brushes?' asked Naomi.

'To hand and they are the finest ones, ready to do you all justice.' He gestured to two bags of baggage with what looked a brand-new H-frame easel tied roughly to one of them.

'Should we call you "Arnold"?' asked Tabitha.

He turned to Miss Pikestaff and his uncertain stare took in the letter of introduction on the desk. She stepped forward, 'No girls, Mr Tenebris would not expect you to address him so. He is here on an assignment of work, you are ladies with connection to the highest in the land. He remains Mr Tenebris.'

She picked up a book from her desk. 'He has brought with him the latest edition of *The Book of Five Hundred*, which contains three of his fine depictions, including one of the Earl of Hereford.' She laid it open on the table in front of Lavinia, Cassie bent forward, too. 'See what an outstanding artist your aunt has found for you.'

The illustration displayed was credited to: 'Mr A Tenebris, Smoothfield, London'.

'Papa is better,' Lavinia said with barely a glance, gesturing at the paintings that clothed the schoolroom walls.

'Your father is not a Society artist, Lavinia. He does not undertake commissions.'

'Though these are capable works,' said Mr Tenebris stepping to the nearest wall to make a study. 'Most affecting.'

'He does not do commissions, because he is a real artist,' said Lavinia, 'he paints what is in his head.'

'Hush Livvi,' Cassie admonished her twin, 'Mr Tenebris deserves his chance.'

'Let us get on,' said Miss Pikestaff. 'Mr Tenebris, please explain your idea.'

'Yes girls, I have heard of your interest in the workings of the world. I also heard tell that you saw a painting by the celebrated artist Mr Joseph Wright of Derby that was on public display in Cambridge last summer I believe, and that you visited it there.'

'Oh, not the one with the poor little Umbra,' said Tabitha.

'It was very interesting, though,' said Naomi. 'Very scientific'.

'Please, Mr Tenebris, do not put your Umbra in a vacuum on our account,' said Tabitha.

'No little one, believe me, I would not and woe betide me if I tried. But Miss Pikestaff thought that we could combine a picture of you all at your study and include your interests. You like discoveries I think, Naomi, and there are some classical costumes from history that Tabitha will delight in.'

'An experiment,' said Naomi, clapping her hand and earning a glare from Lavinia.

'A study,' insisted Miss Pikestaff, 'being attentive to some interesting flowers, perhaps... or well, an insect if you must, Naomi, but make it a tame one. It is not to be loosed. And we will most particularly not allow weasel parts.'

'We will dress you up,' said the artist, 'costumes that will win you admirers in sheer silks and chiffons. Tabitha, what kind of costume would you like?'

He had chosen his subject well. 'Oh, can I be anything? If you have chiffon, can I be a princess of Arabia?'

'The benevolence of the esteemed Countess has provided just such a costume. Naomi, you too?'

'May I be a scientist, Mr Tenebris?'

'No, Naomi,' said Miss Pikestaff, 'you cannot be a lady scientist. No one would understand.'

'Be a princess, Naomi,' pleaded Tabitha, 'you are so pretty.'

'I want to be an explorer,' said Cassie, 'and see the world.'

The artist did not seem to hear, instead, turning to Lavinia, 'And you little miss?'

'Do not call any of us "little miss" again, sir, not ever,' said Lavinia. 'This is a sham, you have brought the costumes our aunt has prescribed and will force us into them whatever we wish for.'

There was a sound like three flints being struck and Galt appeared, cudgel in hand, on the desk beside Miss Pikestaff. Within moments the scent of wild heather stirred through the room.

'You will be accommodating girls,' said Miss Pikestaff. Galt's stare imbued her words with extra menace. His cudgel twirled in his fists. 'Your aunt's letter impresses upon us all the import she attaches to this request. Your mother is aware that the Countess's support for Larkenfen depends upon it. She has instructed your father of its urgency and he has understood its necessity.

'It happens, Lavinia, and it happens this afternoon. Now, I must take up my other duties as your mother's companion. I am to take the carriage to your mother at the Hunsfords and take her to her next appointment. Mr Tenebris will let you choose your costumes before dinner, which is being served at 1 o'clock. I will help him set up in the dining room, where there is better light. I will then help dress you and ensure each of you is presented as a young gentlewoman of accomplishment.'

She unpinned her simple brooch, a silver pick set with garnets and placed it in the centre of her desk. 'And, while I am gone, Galt will attend you.'

The brooch acted as Miss Pikestaff's 'charm chain' for Galt. It had a simple elegance when seen above her breast – expensive for a governess, thought Naomi – but it meant, she could leave them under Galt's eye while she pursued her business in other places. When she spoke her private charm, her aura was projected from the charm chain. The sisters marvelled that Galt could prowl to every corner of the desk despite Miss Pikestaff's absence.

'He is contrived from earth and stone, I think,' Tabitha had once advised her sisters, 'so can roam as far as Miss Pikestaff can pitch a rock.'

'How came a governess by such a treasure?' wondered Cassie.

'How large a rock,' pondered Lavinia.

Galt could not admonish them, but he could give a report on any misdeeds and the violence imbued in his stare was deterrent enough.

'Select your costumes, be civil to Mr Tenebris, then you are to go to luncheon.' Miss Pikestaff said as she departed.

Mr Tenebris made busy with his luggage and soon, classical gowns in pale satins and chiffons were brought out onto the desk, requiring Galt to jump to a chair seat and climb onto its back to continue his vigil.

'They will need some pinning and adjustment, which I shall leave for Miss Pikestaff,' said Mr Tenebris.

'These are too sheer,' complained Lavinia. 'We will be all on display.'

'Your aunt thinks a classical and romantic appearance will excite most esteem. I flatter myself that my skills can preserve your modesty but display all your perfections.'

Naomi said, 'Papa has a glass exhibition case. We could use that to contain the objects of our study.'

'Just like real scientists would,' Cassie said with an indulgent chuckle.

'We could have your Umbra in it, Mr Tenebris,' said Tabitha, 'and all study her as they did the Umbra in Mr Wright's picture.'

'But not use an air pump to take all her air,' added Naomi.

'No,' said Tabitha, 'that was too wretched. Do you think the Umbra died in the vacuum, Mr Tenebris?'

'Assuredly, for so Mr Wright, himself, informed me, when we met at the Academie. "That Umbra was only some trollkin of the most perverse kind, Arnold," said he, in confidence, "And belonged to an orphan girl, who had a handicap most cruel."'

'But they would both have died.'

'It was truly nothing of consequence, little one. I have seen the same trick performed with birds and small spiders.' He gave an involuntary shiver.

Naomi didn't waste time on small spiders. She preferred the big raft spiders that skated out on the fen to hunt fish. Her gaze wandered to Galt, but she saw nought beyond his silent churning fierceness.

14 – M IS FOR MARAZIEL

Stanton

Cotteridge looked up when his Minister entered the offices with an Umbra asleep on his shoulder. Cotteridge had seen Maraziel rarely in person. Stanton suspected there was a secret file on her, compiled with the help of Jenny Moonshine and others. He had expected Maraziel to return to the Other Realm once the business with the Chancellor of Balliol concluded, but she had offered a trade.

'Sir has forgotten something, I fear.' Cotteridge's eye fixed upon Stanton's shoulder.

Stanton was momentarily at a loss but rallied. 'Clear desks, Cotteridge. Maraziel attends me with good reason. We have made a discovery, I think, and must now pursue it.'

'Indeed, sir, so your meeting with the Chancellor; it went well?'

Uncertainty clouded Stanton's features, 'Of some help, I think, but mainly he has engaged Maraziel's interest and she is here – mayhap briefly – to help, in return for information on the signing of the Queen's Treaty.'

The delicate delay before Cotteridge's 'Just so, Minister,' was enough to inform Stanton that this was not any kind of way for business to be conducted in a Ministry.

'Bring maps of England and Wales. Do we have maps of the Other Realm?'

'We have diverse sketches with holes in them that appear, coagulate and recede, sir. I would not call them maps.' Cotteridge left the room to discover them.

'What nonsense would you have me do?' Maraziel yawned and displayed her customary lassitude as he set her carefully on the desktop and began clearing it in readiness for charts.

'Ministry business.'

'You are aware that I have made my required appointment for the day and can return to my bed at any time?'

'I'm surprised you have not already done so.'

'Does this task require more parley with Jenny Moonshine and her Englishman, who is one of the silliest creatures in all Albion?'

'Rest assured, Lord Pitt will not be attending. I want us to work together, Maraziel. Firstly, on my business and then on who was and wasn't present at the Treaty signing. I would know about this Umbra who murders others, possibly to kill their English, Highlands or Welsh allies.'

'The first I thought of… well, I only know that she can set out a plan with the aim of killing a particular Umbra. This is of itself unusual, as she kills to a design; most slay by mistake, for gain or because they are unduly bored.'

'She? This is a member of the fairer sex?'

'If you mean my sex, then yes, and it is well that you believe me fair. It reflects on you creditably.'

'And her name?'

'I am reluctant to betray her. I rather admire her, and she is no friend to Nymphs. Give me your other demands first and we will see?'

'I wish to understand the working of your realm. Twoshrews has given me some answers.'

Maraziel's head raised and she twisted some of the madness of hair away from her face. Through its hazy entanglement he found a formidable violet eye claiming him.

That eye took him back. He was thirteen again, sitting upon his bed reading when he first became aware of a presence beside him, first beheld those transfixing violet orbs. He had flinched away from the intensity of their scrutiny. Whereupon they had blinked and the creature beholding him had yawned and apologised for arriving late. Only then did he deduce the dark nightmare that dwelt beneath the eruption of hair, the hint of horns, the glimpse of the disfiguring rooty growths around the jawline.

He knew that somewhere inside the ball of stiff fluff was a small woman and she must be his Umbra. He had set his heart on an Elven warrior maid or a sharp-witted and beautiful Nymph. Here was a Hag, he was sure of it.

'I made a point of being delayed,' she said, 'for I did not wish to disturb you discovering what young boys are wont to discover upon erupting into puberty. I thought my appearance might put you off your stroke. Well, in truth, I o'erslept.'

The husky voice emerging from the hair also made a show of disappointment: 'Oh, you are scrawny. I hope you are not overly active or prone to study. You should know my name. It is Maraziel.'

Young Stanton's manners fired, 'I am Sebastian Stanton, pleased to meet you.'

'Let us not begin this with a lie,' she said. 'You will do tolerably well, I think. I require but two things of you: do not interrupt my day more than need be and do not die unless it is entirely necessary.' Hair had swirled back in front of her gaze as clouds might to obscure the scrutiny of the sun.

Here, nearly 14 years later, that violet gaze held him again. The voice was every bit as withering. 'You asked Twoscrews? You wanted the Piskie to explain the working of my world… what demonstrable foolishness.'

Stanton sighed in agreement.

'And now you wish me to fill in any small gaps he may have left in your enlightenment. This is too diverting. How, pray, did Twoscrews explain our realm?'

'Not well,' said Stanton. 'He told me it is ruled by a dead – or was it a mad – Queen, he spoke of a hundred mice in wheels, and said that humankind exists only in Umbra dreams.'

Maraziel took her moment to consider this.

'And he expounded on earthdark,' Stanton finished.

'He understands earthdark! More insightful than I expected. Do not misunderstand me, I like the Piskie; he has talents, but you have not put your finger on them.'

'Twoshrews has talents?'

'All Piskies are exceeding stealthy and Twoscrews,' she persisted in mis-naming him, 'enjoys truthsense.'

Stanton was incredulous, 'You can't mean he tells the truth?'

'No, indeed, that is a power beyond any of us. I mean he has the rare ability to know if the speaker believes what they say to be true,' said Maraziel. 'Charmingly, it follows that he will repeat no lies he has not been told by someone who believes it to be truth.'

Stanton's confusion was evident, so she continued: 'He speaks what others believe to be true, so ends up the honest mouthpiece of all those who have been deceived.'

'I am told he spoke French.'

'Good for him. He has mastered something of no use in his world. Who to, pray?'

'Lady Rochester.'

She smiled. 'Twoshrews' charm is so boundless, it is little wonder his wits remain confined.'

'Think you he works for France?'

'Jenny M tells us things are bad in France, but not that bad, surely. More likely the Piskie attended French lessons with your lady, Isabella, when she was growing.'

'If Twoshrews has unwittingly misled me, you tell me: how is your realm ruled?'

'Badly. Those born to command possess the least aptitude for it.'

'The Elven King?'

'And the rest.' Cotteridge re-entered the room, peering over armfuls of charts and files.'

'Let us begin with maps,' said Stanton. 'The Queen learnt

about the Greynhym by seeing where plague struck. Can we do likewise?'

Soon the desk was covered with charts.

Maraziel professed herself uninterested in places as she never stirred from 'Cernyw'. This turned out to share the space reserved for Cornwall on English maps. She gave a doubtful account of recent Umbra battles with the Greynhym, but Cotteridge thought he found some on the Umbra 'maps'. Eely Bridge on the River Lark, for example, he thought to be 'Babbing Ford' on an Umbra map. The Greynhym had burst their confines there early in the spring, said Maraziel. The date approximated to a devastating outbreak of plague in the English village.

A few crosses, quilled meticulously by Cotteridge, onto an Umbra chart showed Greynhym offensives recalled by Maraziel where pestilence had hit English and Welsh localities. Parts of the Umbra map named 'Albion', bore some resemblance to England in shape. Stanton realised that the shaded area Cotteridge had labelled 'Pestilence' on his maps, conformed to a region called 'Mierce' on one Umbra chart, the drawing of which dated from the 13th Century.

'It is similar in shape to north Mercia in some old maps from Viking times,' said Cotteridge, pointing to how it bordered Welsh Powys.

'Danes and Norse,' Maraziel smoked the words in distaste. 'We advised they return home, lest, through absence, they ran the risk of offending their gods. And their horns were not hard-won like mine.'

Satisfied that some progress had been made, Stanton returned his enquiries to the rule of the Other Realm.

'You have done unduly well out of me,' Maraziel refused to be drawn. 'Let your fellow exhibit what he has on who negotiated the Treaty. Was Shait'n truly there and what about Gorgomon?'

Stanton asked Cotteridge. 'Do we know who was at the signing of the Queen's treaty?'

Cotteridge shuffled other files and reached for a book. 'The best source is Nicholas Trevet, who is especially strong on the reign of his contemporary Edward I – Longshanks.'

Maraziel stared at the book. 'Gorgomon and Longshanks are both bound together in there? Gloomy company for one-another. Gorgomon should not have to endure that.' Maraziel watched as Cotteridge opened the old book at a pre-marked page. 'Your book is unusual. Is that English?'

Stanton passed on her comment.

'Trevet was a man of Somerset, but first published in French,' said Cotteridge.

'Send for the Piskie,' said Maraziel.

The clerk ran a finger through the text: 'Trevet writes plainly and finds fault even with kings, and especially with Longshanks, who he says, "fought on too long and obliged his subjects to endure pestilence and hostilities over-much".'

'Were any Lords of the Dead at the signing?' Stanton asked, sensing Maraziel's impatience.

'The Queen insisted on the attendance of all the warring parties,' Cotteridge translated. 'Longshanks wanted the Lords of the Dead bound to the Treaty for the longest time. The King and the Umbra agreed an area where the Dead would stay confined.'

'North Mercia?'

'Not stated here, but likely so, for that is a region with meaning to the Umbra.' Cotteridge read on: 'Trevet is succinct but offers little detail on the Umbra present as his concentration is on Longshanks. Shait'n is mentioned but not Gorgomon. Trevet refers much to Langtoft. That's another chronicler, Peter of Langtoft, from Yorkshire, one more in thrall to Umbra. He witnessed the signing but was killed by royal decree soon after he had written his account of it.'

'The King's decree?'

'It is thought the Queen's.'

'Why...' began Stanton.

'Do not play the innocent, Sebastian, I schooled you better

than that,' said Maraziel.

'You schooled me...?' said Stanton, partly astonished at her calling him Sebastian. He caught the look Cotteridge gave him, and rather than pursue his surprise, said, 'Because Langtoft understood too much.'

'Because he understood more than the King had,' said Maraziel.

'Do we have Langtoft's report?'

Cotteridge consulted a ledger. 'We have it included in Thomas Hearn's republishing of Langtoft's chronicle in 1725, but that is almost certainly shorter and much altered.'

Maraziel's burr of hair quivered suggesting the smallest shake of her head.

'Where is the original, Cotteridge?' asked Stanton.

'I will discover, sir.'

'Perhaps it would be helpful if we knew who this Gorgomon was,' said Stanton.

'Knowing who Gorgomon was never helped anyone,' said Maraziel.

'I will endeavour to find out, sir,' said Cotteridge.

Something had changed in the clerk's mood. Stanton wondered if his clerk had discovered urgency. That was the power of plague, he thought, it commanded your attention. It also broke governments and claimed kings.

'We will get there,' Stanton promised Maraziel. 'You owe me a name.'

'Not yet, in truth, but still, here are two. Firstly, look to The Mor, she has killed... no I will not tell you who she has killed, but when she did, it was artfully done.'

Stanton wrote the name down. 'Would she act against the Queen's Treaty?'

'Not against clauses that still bound her, but she bends the knee to no-one,' Maraziel said. 'The other, Muscari, I only know by her notoriety. She is more mischievous and malicious. If she kills, she will do it out of rage or amusement.'

Stanton showed both names to his clerk, who knew nothing

of what was going on. 'Are either of these in *The Book of Five Hundred*?'

'No, Minister.'

'Who are they bonded to in my realm, Maraziel?'

Her bony shoulders shrugged into her hair.

'Then, who are their allies in yours?'

'Creatures, such as these, do not have allies…' beneath the obscuring hair Stanton imagined her smile as she added, '…for long.'

'What would be their motivation for malevolence, or for murder?'

'In my world, it can almost always be traced back to being crossed in love.' She yawned, 'I have told you rather more than I intended, but remain confident it will be of little use. Summon me when you have this original account of the Treaty.' She stood unsteadily.

'Wait, why have you named these two?'

'For murder? Because their names begin with a "muh". You can never trust any Umbra whose name begins with "muh".' She dropped from the table and evaporated into Stanton's shadow before she had gone a foot.'

Cotteridge looked from the departing Umbra to his Minister, 'Is there anything more you need to know, sir?'

'Not today thank you, Cotteridge. I must act on what we have learned. Oh, Cotteridge, what is the name of your Umbra?'

The clerk turned, uncomfortable, 'Meg Mantis, sir.'

15 – THE BUTTERFLY MAGICK

Larkenfen

Miss Pikestaff had not returned by luncheon. Their father had not stirred from his studio. Mr Tenebris picked at his meats and pate and was quiet, deflecting the few questions that came his way. Instead he focussed much attention on the windows and, most particularly, on the mistletoe motif to be found there. He was likely ill-at-ease to be eating with his commission subjects, was Naomi's conjecture, while Tabitha thought him unused to the company of young ladies.

When, at last, she strode in, Miss Pikestaff said, 'Your mother it seems had other appointments, and I must attend her later at Withie Witton. She knows Mr Tenebris has arrived, but there you have it.'

She went to the schoolroom for her brooch – and to cast Galt free with her spoken charm – and returned with ribbons. These, she took in turn to each girl's hair and fussed with them trying colour and style. They were relieved when the maid brought in her food and they could escape.

'We are behind in our plan now, girls. It is vexing so do not go far. When I finish my dinner, I expect to see you in the garden and for you to come promptly at my call.'

As they opened the door, Rushie the cat pushed in, then changed his mind and slipped back out.

'Poor Rushie,' said Tabitha, 'he never feels safe around Miss

Pikestaff.'

'Usually it is Galt that scares him.' Lavinia reached down to pick up the cat, but he gave a plaintive meow and slipped away.

'Miss Pikestaff has never before shown such resolve,' said Cassie as they walked to the boardwalk, leaving the artist to discuss his ideas and preparations with the governess.

'Never has she dressed so spruce before, excepting for church.'

'Her hair was just so, and she was near handsome,' admitted Lavinia.

'Perhaps she is sweet on Mr Tenebris,' said Tabitha.

'Tabby, you will bake-up a romance from the most unpromising ingredients,' said Naomi.

'Mr Tenebris tries to be more mannerly than truly he is,' persisted Tabitha. 'His refinement is an act I think, perhaps so that Miss Pikestaff will think him genteel.'

'Cassie should go back and spy upon them, to see if it is true,' Lavinia suggested to her twin.

'Oh do, Cassie, you are the most quiet and secret,' Tabitha's entreaty was both earnest and playful.

Cassie laughed, 'I do not believe it for a moment, Tabby, but I will go back and report any tender feelings to you in the garden, as soon as I may.'

The other three walked on until Naomi bid them sit by the boardwalk's edge. 'Here is the first part of our study,' she announced, showing two flag iris leaves where three empty dragonfly nymph cases clustered and one more such that had burst open at the back of the head with the skeeter hawk inside, just pushing its way through.

'This is a ruby darter, I think, it will not fly for hours yet.'

She gently folded and cut both leaves and gave one to Tabitha, who said, 'We will put them in Papa's exhibition glass. Do you think the Umbra in the painting died as Mr Tenebris said, Naomi? It did not look at all like a Trollkin; a Nymph I thought.'

'The painting was an imagination, Tabby,' said Naomi. 'While it would be quite the fascination to discover such things about

Umbra, it would not be permissible, nor possible – how could you stop it just vanishing back to its own world?'

'It would be a cruel use of a charm chain,' said Lavinia.

'Mr Wright's painting is a fiction; it said so in the pamphlets we read,' said Naomi. 'I do not believe Mr Tenebris has ever met Mr Wright of Derby. Nor do I think he has seen that painting, he was confused on its proper title. He is not at all as well-to-do as he pretends. When he forgets himself, there is a lilt to his accent.'

'He is young to be a member of Sir Joshua's Acadamie, too,' Lavinia leapt on the claim. 'I think he is a charlatan. We will let him paint us, for we must, but we must not trust him.'

'His easel is new and has not been used,' said Naomi. 'Think on the state of Papa's. Would Mr Tenebris not bring his favourite easel to paint us?'

They collected two more specimens, dead creatures, saved in jam-jars Naomi had secreted along the boardwalk and they returned to the garden and sat among the hydrangea bushes, new from Japan, whose flopping cushions of bracts and blossoms still carried colour.

They did not have to tarry long before Cassie returned to them. She raced back, pigtails sailing in her wake, for her hair alone had survived Miss Pikestaff's attentions. Her exertion deepened her swarms of freckles to a mahogany colour, conspicuous against skin two shades paler than when she left. 'Something abominable is afoot,' she said. 'Mr Tenebris and Miss Pikestaff are plotting. They know each other in some way, I think.'

'Tell us everything exactly,' said Lavinia.

'The first mystery is that the copy of *The Book of Five Hundred* Tenebris bought was lying open on Miss Pikestaff's desk. One page has already been torn out of it'

'Just like in our old edition,' said Tabitha. 'Perhaps it was an illustration Mr Tenebris was not proud of.'

'Then I heard Mr Tenebris saying, "You have been here six months and you do not know which of them has it." Miss Pikestaff said, "I am tasked only with watching them as they approach puberty. It was hoped I would find out which of them has it – if any – but my duties are in the school room. I can hardly search them. At least, I have not been able to construct a reason to do so, until now. When I am helping them into these costumes, I may be able to search better," or something of the sort.'

'What are we supposed to have secreted, Cassie?' said Naomi.

'That is by no means clear. She told Tenebris that she was unable to examine our rooms closely for fear that Larkenfen is haunted. Galt has warned her of this often.'

Cassie's audience shared a look and a laugh.

'Oh it is the age of the house,' said Naomi, 'much given to hauntings.'

'And governesses are markedly superstitious,' said Lavinia.

More serious, Cassie went on: 'Mr Tenebris then said, "You must have an idea from your time here. Who do you suspect?" And Miss Pikestaff replied, "It is almost certain to be Lavinia" – you, Livvi – "She is their natural leader, has a knack for open sedition and is most like to have it. She has a kind of wild courage too." And so it went on.'

'Was only Livvi spoken of?' asked Naomi.

'No, Naomi, you were too; they thought you the cleverest. And Tabby, they said you knew most about Umbra and had Elven features and the darkest hair, though what is that to do with anything I hardly know?'

'You were right about Mr Tenebris, Naomi,' Lavinia kicked out at an overhanging hydrangea bloom.

'Mr Tenebris also said that they would not have long, perhaps a day to find this thing we conceal – the word he used sounded like "spring". Miss Pikestaff noted that things were becoming more urgent.'

'Then, just before I slipped away, it got darker, shockingly so. Mr Tenebris said to her, "We will discover who has it, if we can. Then, my instruction is to kill that one, but only if we are certain. Otherwise, all of them must die. I have no stomach for it but if we leave the wrong one alive, we would be subject to the most horrible vengeance."'

'Kill one of us?' Tabitha's mouth gaped open. 'Mr Tenebris is here to murder us?'

'What did Pikestaff say?' Naomi's voice was barely audible.

'I did not wait to find out,' said Cassie, 'but raced here.'

'Is it possible?' Naomi appealed to the twins, 'Why would anyone want us dead? It can't be the Countess's instruction, surely.'

'Cassie would not make it up, dear-heart,' Lavinia said. 'When we return to the house you must be ready to run, Tabby. Naomi, you and I must have our blades. At least they do not know we are prepared.'

'We must tell Papa,' Tabitha was struggling to keep the tremor from her voice.

'Papa knows my objection to these illustrations and would not believe we could have overheard such a horror. Be sure, I will not let Tenebris kill any of us.'

'Oh Cassie, what do you think?' said Tabitha.

'I used to think that some secret magic kept us safe, Tabby. We got into and out of such scrapes and survived all adventures, but now we have been served proof that it is not so; any of us can be killed.'

'Oh, Cassie.'

Miss Pikestaff appeared, at this moment, by the back door of the once impressive building now gilded with age and garlanded with untidy drifts of rambling roses.

'Come now girls,' she called to them, beckoned and returned inside.

'We cannot go.'

'We must, Tabby,' said Lavinia. 'We have to discover more and remember, they do not suspect that we know.'

'Mr Tenebris did not appear to be a good artist,' said Naomi, 'but neither did I think him a murderer.'

'Perhaps his Umbra is very fierce,' said Tabitha.

'Fiercer than Galt?'

Her eye was seized by two dishevelled gatekeeper butterflies, twirling so tightly together it was as if a thread of spider's yarn were tangled between the two. They tumbled around each other in a tryst that neither dare leave. Each time one danced even a little slower, a little further away, it remembered this was the last of the meagre autumn sun and their gyrations became more furious. Her gaze followed this blur of entanglement into the hydrangea, as though under a spell. Then she realised that a magick was exactly what it was, for their dance led her to a presence deep within the bush's billowing darkness.

Only now did the scent of wild heather identify in her mind and she sprang up. 'Galt! Galt is here among us. He has heard all.'

He came rushing at them from the hydrangea and launched himself at Lavinia.

16 – ASTIR IN THE COFFEEHOUSE

Stanton

≡

Umbra of note

Hannah Lightfoot and her human ally King George III

≡

The gaggle outside Pickadills Coffeehouse was several bodies deep. They thronged all around the curve of the main window, causing an obstruction to Jermyn Street. Stanton had to force his way through to Pickadills' entrance.

He had learnt of his wife's whereabouts from Midden. On hearing the maid's answer, he asked again more volubly, 'She is *where*?'

He had dashed inside and re-emerged from his home a short moment later sporting new neckwear and headed to the coffeehouse.

Outside it, ladies in wide frocks and small hats, gentlemen and waifs and strays, high-born and low, moved reluctantly aside as Stanton entered their heave. Umbra gawped and grumbled into nearby ears. Stanton was a subscriber to the Pickadills Coffeehouse at twenty-eight shillings a year and visited it often for its enlightened selection of London papers and journals, with two more from Edinburgh, plus Hunts Weekly Examiner.

Pickadills' heavy door opened with its customary complaint

and he stepped into the lamp-lit interior, noting the unusually low-pitched hum. Older gentlemen edged the room in conventional, somewhat crusty, attire. They stared out from beneath long wigs, tricorn hats and knitted brows, behind slender pipes and affronted expressions.

There was none of the prevailing rowdy debate on war and battles – either in our world or the other – nor any bellicose arguments over the Rights of Man as set out by Tom Paine, defended by Mary Wollstonecraft and nourished by events in France. Instead, the gentlemen shifted uneasily behind wide-open journals, decked with headlines on the abolishment of the French monarchy. Papers notwithstanding, most gazes slid, instead, onto the central table in the room.

It was there that Stanton strode, to be greeted by his wife with warmth and Lady Rochester with a complicit smile. A coffee pot sat on the bare table between them and several stained shallow white cups testified to the time they had already spent there. Neither Capu or Twoshrews had joined them in the excursion.

'What is that vulgarity about your neck, Sebastian?' Isabella turned to Lady R. 'It was not there when he left me this morning, madam, I assure you.'

Stanton fingered the hurriedly tied cravat, 'It is... of no importance.'

'There is mention of us in *Lloyds Evening Post*, Sebastian,' Isabella, pointed to a newspaper in Lady R's lap. 'It is in relation to the death of Countess Alnwick and the fact that there now exist ten vacancies for elevation to The Five Hundred. Lady R thinks we may make *The Book*'s next edition and recommends that we should politic a little to add energy to our cause.'

'I politic more than enough already, Isabella.'

His wife turned to Lady Rochester and said, 'You see, I told you I would be in trouble for venturing here. Now I am "Isabella" for my trespass on space reserved for gentlemen. It is a scolding.'

'Not for my sake, Isabella,' said Stanton, pulling a seat up close so he could speak softly, 'but these gentlemen pay a high sum each year to sit quietly in this coffeehouse to study their papers. Your appearance here, so admirably and formidably gowned, is causing a commotion.'

'On the contrary, Sebastian, there was noise aplenty before we entered; a clamour of argument. Since we have sat here to make a quiet study of the papers, everything has been much hushed.'

'I am a subscriber, here, Mr Stanton,' said Lady Rochester, 'and asked Isabella to join me as my guest. If there is fault, then I am wholly to blame and not at all sorry. I suspect when we depart our presence here will add much to general discourse.'

'You subscribe to Pickadills?'

'Just one of my petit vices, sir. The proprietor's wife, over there, assures me subscriptions increase each time I visit – now near twelve hundred, she says. If you must take anyone away to chastise or beat, Minister, it will have to be me.'

Stanton felt he had himself been chastised and knew when he was beaten. 'Such was never my intention, Lady Rochester. You come to study the headlines?'

'And distressing they are too, Minister. The Jacobins have declared war on my kind.'

'The aristocracy?'

'Women; especially mistresses. We were a potent and cogent force under Louis's regime.'

'Mistresses were?'

'More so than wives. As my countrywoman Olympe said, "As mistresses we used to be despised and powerful; now we must be respected yet excluded".'

'Many a French aristocrat suffers worse.'

'Quite so, dear Louis is dethroned, his eldest, Louis Joseph is dead and little Louis Charles incarcerated with his father, both to be executed before Christmas if the journals can be believed. If these headlines came true, I would then be regent of France,' she turned her grey eyes on Stanton, challenging him to find fault with her claim '...had I been born a boy, as I briefly was.'

'Who was your father again, madame?' He tried to navigate his way through her extraordinary claims but every time she turned her gaze on him, Stanton was lost in a grey sea.

'These things are never certain,' she waved a dismissive hand, 'but Maria Josepha was my birth mother.'

Stanton was not well-versed on either the French royal line or midwifery but before he could stumble further, Isabella swept the conversation past him with: 'It is this story we have been discussing, Sebastian.' She pushed *The Post* in front of him. 'Sixteen names are being discussed for ten vacancies to The Five Hundred. Seven men have been advanced for four male vacancies and nine ladies for the six female vacancies that exist now Countess Alnwick has been taken.'

'You are named, sir, as is Viscount Exeter, now he has reached twenty-five years and is thus deemed eligible. We ladies, as you are aware, can be elevated younger,' said Lady Rochester.

'You will remember Lady R is thought the youngest ever to feature in *The Book of Five Hundred* when elevated aged just seventeen years,' Isabella prompted her husband.

'Only because the King was so besotted with me then,' Lady Rochester said. 'When you had a dalliance with Exeter many thought you would be chosen for The Five Hundred at little more than that age, Isabella.'

'It turned out it never was a dalliance,' said Isabella. 'I lay too far beneath his notice.'

'He set himself at such a rarefied height then, few dared speak to him and he spoke to less,' said Lady Rochester. 'From memory he favoured you far more than most. Something has recently chipped away at his conceit though. You found him more civil at my gathering, I think. I so much prefer him when Muscari is not in his ear.' Then, seeing Stanton's expression and fearing she was being indelicate, she reached out and reordered his cravat, 'But this elegant gentleman recognised your worth, Isabella, and here, see, he models a new fashion.'

'You said "Muscari". Muscari is the Viscount's Umbra?' Stanton was unsure he had heard properly. The ramifications of this morsel were enough for him to forget to be discomfited by Lady R's grappling with his neckwear and the scrutiny this provoked around the room.

'Yes, dear,' Isabella was watching her husband with amusement, and to Lady Rochester, she confided, 'Sebastian has never met the Viscount and loiters little in the society pages.'

'Hmm, he needs come to a ball, so we can show him off, more. There,' Lady Rochester released the cravat but stared at it still, not satisfied that it had been properly subdued.

'He may come,' said Isabella, 'but the cravat is not to be invited.'

'What ball?'

'The Countess of Harrington has a private ball organised for this Saturday next. We had not been invited, Sebastian, but now we are among the likely candidates for The Five Hundred we can expect more hospitality to be proffered in our direction. Lady R helped too, I know.'

'Will Viscount Exeter be there?'

'He will most assuredly be invited, sir, for Jane Stanhope claims him as some distant cousin and would be most offended if he did not show himself. The Countess is forever in competition with the Duchess of Devonshire to be London's supreme hostess. It is like some interminable game of quadrille and Exeter is one of Jane's trump cards – she plays him often. This ball is just her latest deal of the cards.'

'And Umbra will be there too, I imagine.'

'Of course, my darling. What society ball would be complete without them? You have been too long in darkened rooms in Westminster. Say, we may go.'

'We may go.'

'You must look to portraiture,' said Lady R. 'Do you have an artist in mind?'

'What about Mr Tenebris?' said Isabella.

'He is not currently in London,' said Lady R, 'but commissioned to paint the Countess of Harrington's nieces and has sped hot-foot to the Fens.'

'Jane has nieces in the Fens. Surely that must be dangerous.'

'People say they are the most dangerous girls in the Kingdom. Jane wants them civilised and has fed poor Mr Tenebris to them. I doubt he will return the same man. If he returns at all.'

There was a tug on Stanton's elbow, and he turned around to find a small dark child there, a slave perhaps from the Africas but in the rags of an urchin. It was unusual to see one in rags, for page boys from Africa were still much in fashion. He did not know how the child had been allowed into Pickadills but guessed why he was there.

'Have you been paid a penny?'

The tight black curls danced as the child nodded, picked a penny from about its person and showed it to Stanton. A grubby finger pointed to the garish cravat.

'I'll come now,' Stanton rose, shrugged an apology to his astonished wife, bowed to Lady Rochester, ignored the shocked glances of his fellow subscribers and allowed himself to be led out of Pickadills' door.

Outside the child pointed in the direction of St James's Park, and then ran off.

An ominously dark figure emerged from the shadows of a doorway and shuffled into step with Stanton for the short walk to the park, tapping him playfully on the shoulder with a cane. 'Splendid cravat, Minister, you cut quite the dash. How did it fare in Pickadills?'

'Quieter than expected, Mr Larkwing. My wife and Lady R preside over it.'

'Have a care with Lady R. She claims French lineage you know.'

'Yes, an absurd impossible one. Forget Lady R, I have two names for you.'

'I congratulate you on your alacrity, Minister,' Larkwing steered them to a bench, sat and removed his hat. 'It is not a moment too soon. I too bring news, more shocking than you can imagine. Tell me all.'

Stanton gave him the first name, The Mor. Larkwing had not

heard it, nor had any notion who this Umbra's ally might be. 'The second name given to me is Muscari, and I know who she is bonded to.'

'A radical, like the pamphleteer Tom Paine, I imagine.'

'Far from it, she is bonded to Viscount Exeter.'

'He doesn't sound a likely candidate for the French to subvert.'

'He's the only son of the Duke of Portland, man, loyal to the Parliament, loyal to his core.'

'So, you think this Umbra, Muscari, acts alone?'

'If indeed she is your French spy. I have only heard that she is thought capable of murder. Exeter, alone, can hear her speak, so I cannot see how she would have been recruited in our world. Is it possible that she was persuaded into this in the Other Realm?'

'A hard job becomes yet more devilish difficult. We can hardly involve the Viscount. We must see if we can discover anything from his correspondence.'

'And your news, Larkwing.'

'There is a threat to the Queen.'

'Queen Charlotte?'

'Not that bellowing German mare from Mecklenburg, who has driven poor King George insane, no. I mean, the "People's Queen", Miss Lightfoot.'

'Hannah Lightfoot, the King's Umbra; what of her?' But Stanton's mind charged recklessly ahead and before Larkwing spoke again, he already knew what would come.

'We have discovered that this French Umbra's orders are to seek out Hannah Lightfoot in the Other Realm and to kill her.'

17 – THE RAFT SPIDER

Larkenfen

≡

Umbra of note

Dearbhla and her human ally 'Arnold' Tenebris

≡

Galt's final bound saw him upon Lavinia. She, too, was springing up, but he fastened onto her hip. Claw hands grasped at something on her belt. Lavinia was on her feet now, pushing at the fierce grey-blue goblin. Her hands had no effect on him. He was intent on wresting something from her skirt.

Tabitha and Naomi were also up and instinctively moving to aid their sister. They had no idea what Galt was capable of. Naomi dived on the little warrior but met with no resistance and slipped through him to the ground.

'Away, you blue horror,' Lavinia was partly seething, partly repulsed at having Pikestaff's Umbra on her person but much as she tried to bat him away, he seemed immovable. Galt was now applying claws and mouth to the belt hoops of her skirt.

'Cassie, help her,' Tabitha appealed to her older sister.

Cassie stepped forward, her features a frown of concentration. She clasped Galt in both hands. The shock caused him to lose hold of Lavinia's skirt. For a moment he froze in astonishment before writhing frenziedly, but Cassie wrested him clear and hurled him bodily away. He flew off but caught against some unseen leash mid-air and dropped hard to the ground.

'It's on Livvi's skirt,' shouted Cassie.

'Your skirt, Livvi, now,' Naomi was back on her feet.

Galt had shaken his head to clear it and was already moving.

Lavinia hopped away, slithering out of skirt and belt as Galt ran at her again. As he leapt, Lavinia threw her skirt to Naomi. Galt spun, his attention on the youngest Gracegirdle, as she twisted through the belt hoops of the skirt. Something flashed between her thumb and forefinger. 'It's here,' she cried as Galt bounded onto her.

She freed it and threw Lavinia's skirt at Galt, holding her hand high. As he ducked the skirt and furiously climbed up her frock, she flicked her find away. 'Run Tabby,' she shouted to her sister.

Tabby needed no more urging. She snatched the silver brooch from the air and raced away to the fronds of a tall willow, securing the brooch onto the highest one she could reach. She corralled a curtain of lower fronds and hauled them away from the one on which the brooch danced. Skirt-less, Lavinia stepped beside her sister, pulled out a blade and cut any lower fronds away. Galt jumped but he was built for close combat, not athleticism, he could not get within two feet of where the brooch dangled.

'It's Pikestaff's charm chain pin,' said Tabitha.

'You're very quick-witted, Tabby,' Naomi told her.

'When you stop your dreaming,' added Cassie.

'What was it doing on my belt?' Lavinia was clambering back into her skirt.

'Pikestaff must have secreted it there, when she was fussing earlier,' said Cassie. 'She meant for Galt to spy on you, on us.'

'That was why Rushie ran from me.'

'You saved us, Cassie,' said Tabitha. 'How did you do it?'

'I just focussed all my thought on Galt, pulled him fully into my world, I think. In truth, I hardly know.' Cassie let out a breathless nervous laugh. 'Did you see his fright when I grasped him?'

'He has heard all,' said Naomi. 'He knows that we know.'

'But he has no way to return and tell Pikestaff,' Lavinia ran a comb through her hair and smoothed her skirt. She stuck her knife in the back of her skirt and lifted her top over to hide it. 'He cannot reach the brooch, so is stuck in the range of its charm until Pikestaff comes to find him and release him.'

'When will she miss him?'

'She will think him still secreted, following me.'

'She will wonder,' said Cassie, 'but he is too far here to be heard and cannot be seen from the house. I think we have some time before she searches for him determinedly.'

'Imagine her fury when she learns what we have done,' Lavinia could not keep the relish from her voice. Tabitha shuddered.

'What now?' Naomi's voice was freshly washed in an uncertainty rare to her.

'We are actors in their play,' said Lavinia, 'but we work to a different plot. Seem amenable but be clumsy and slow. Try to discover what they are searching for, but if we just thwart their hunt for whatever it is, Cassie can find out more after.'

'But if they find it...?' Tabitha spoke the fear uppermost in all their minds.

'Then you run to Papa, Tabby, while we three fight.'

◆ ◆ ◆

Miss Pikestaff spent most of the afternoon arranging their costumes in the parlour, while Mr Tenebris waited in the dining room, setting up his easel and materials. Naomi had fetched Papa's tall glass specimen jar from his library room and placed her scientific studies within. She positioned it on Miss Pikestaff's desk and hid her blade inside the jar.

There was much hustle and fluster regarding the costumes with Miss Pikestaff adamant that the girls remove their everyday clothes and Lavinia protesting at the sheerness of the material of the garments provided.

'Nothing indecorous or untoward will be shown in the final painting,' said Miss Pikestaff.

'Mr Tenebris will see more than is proper,' insisted Tabitha.

'Mr Tenebris is an artist; he does not see young ladies, but colour and light and shade.'

'You have lectured Livvi often enough about displaying her under-things to the Reedston post boy, saying it will turn his head and inflame outlandish desires,' Naomi said. 'You cannot mean us to show even more to this stranger.'

'The penny-post boy is at least familiar with Livvi's under garments,' said Cassie, 'so has proved resistant to too much inflammation.'

That set Tabitha and Naomi giggling.

Eventually it was decided that undergarments could remain, but Miss Pikestaff took great care to closely examine each girl before announcing herself satisfied. She then took much time to sort out ribbons and fret over their hair.

The afternoon advanced. At half past 4 o'clock, Mr Tenebris, knocked and entered and said that the light was now too poor for what he had in mind and that the girls should be put in their costumes again tomorrow. Miss Pikestaff took the news better than they expected and told them to undress again but to keep the costumes neat. As Miss Pikestaff left the room, she picked up Lavinia's skirt, claiming she had seen a stain upon it.

Her shared glance with Mr Tenebris, Cassie noticed, contained his questioning look and her subtle head-shake.

She told her sisters so.

'She has not found it,' said Naomi 'and intends to try again on the morrow. If it were not for the letter from Aunt Jane, I would think it all a sham.'

'Follow them, Cassie,' said Lavinia. 'Let us know when she finds the brooch missing and hunts for Galt.'

Cassie listened at the door until the voices moved to the dining room and then slipped out.

She returned promptly. All but Lavinia were dressed again. 'I know what they are searching for: not a spring, but a sprig.'

'A sprig,' Naomi pointed to the motif, a slender stem of white berries and leaves, set in coloured glass in the parlour window, 'that sprig; mistletoe? We have no jewellery or valuables, like that.'

'And if I did,' said Tabitha, 'I would not keep it in my undergarments.'

'They are at a loss,' said Cassie. 'Pikestaff is complaining that we were not co-operative. I cannot tell if Mr Tenebris is angry or relieved.'

'They will be angry when she finds Galt,' said Lavinia. 'Pikestaff will guess we have led her a merry chase.'

'She is searching for him now. She thinks the brooch must have come unpinned on the boardwalk and fallen into the fen.'

'Come, we should go to Papa,' said Lavinia. 'This charade has played out. We'll see if he can make sense of it.'

She opened the door and found the way blocked by a hesitant Mr Tenebris. Lavinia retreated, and her sisters likewise, as the man entered the room. An Umbra was on his shoulder, a bony woman with skeletal hands ending in long claws. Her wilderness of grey-black hair was restrained by a lattice head-piece made of horn. There was a mad hunger to her grin. Her small intense eyes pursued them through every backwards step. Galt was fierce; this Umbra was savage.

'Tabitha, you said you wanted to meet my Umbra,' Mr Tenebris offered an unsettling smile before closing the door behind him.

'She's... is she a Banshee?' Tabitha took a tentative step forward, horrified and fascinated in equal measure.

'We need to see our father, Mr Tenebris,' said Naomi.

'Arnold, please; Miss Pikestaff is not here. Perhaps you can answer one question for me first.'

'What question?'

'I have been told, Naomi, that you or one of your sisters has a sprig,' he pointed to the family sigil in the window, 'like that. Please, I need to know which of you has it.'

'No-one has it, Tenebris,' said Lavinia, the assurance in her voice undermined by the fact that she was once again reduced to petticoats.

'I know one of you has it, and I suspect it is you, Lavinia,' any act of shyness was gone from him. His lilting accent roamed a good deal further west and dropped an equal measure south in station.

'Leave or I will call our maid.'

'She is out, running an errand for Miss Pikestaff. She's gone to fetch your mother, I believe. So, your mother and maid are at least thirty minutes distant, your father locked away in his studio…' there was a banging elsewhere in the house. 'And that I suspect is Miss Pikestaff returning.'

He made a sudden lunge and grabbed Tabitha, who screamed a shrill cry that was quickly cut off by Mr Tenebris. His Umbra also screamed, busy eyes scrunched tight and her face contorted. Although the girls could not hear it, they felt it, a jagged thing, pulsing through the air in the room. Mr Tenebris stiffened, grimaced and shook uncontrollably at the sound. When it ceased, he said, 'Now you have upset Dearbhla.'

Cassie was not to be seen. She had ducked behind the desk when first he entered.

Tabitha was quiet now, trying to be brave and not wanting to provoke the Umbra again. Dearbhla was climbing down Mr Tenebris' waistcoat in jerky unnatural movements. She stretched out clawed fingers to stroke at Tabitha's hair.

'Your blade?' mouthed Lavinia to Naomi, who glanced at the specimen jar, now behind Mr Tenebris.

He caught the look, stepped to the jar and reached his free hand inside through plants and dead creatures with an expression of disgust on his face to pull the blade out and drop it in a pocket. 'Miss Pikestaff is right; you girls are more whetted wolves than young ladies.' A longer blade was pulled from his pocket. 'I found this among your skirts, Lavinia,' he held it to the side of Tabitha's cheek.

'Do not worry, I will not kill your sister, but she is too comely do you not think, perhaps a scar or two might return her to the common herd.' Dearbhla threw her head back and gave another serrated shriek. The girls cowered away even though they heard nothing.

Mr Tenebris covered one ear and waited, face distorted by its effect, until the scream ended, then said, 'Who has the sprig? Next time I ask, there will be blood running down Tabby's cheeks.'

'Please don't, Mr Tenebris, we will –'

Cassie crept forward from behind the desk. She held the large dead raft spider from the specimen jar. She reached up to slap it against Mr Tenebris's neck. It landed with a splat and stuck by his ear as he recoiled and spun in shock. Dearbhla leapt onto the table. Mr Tenebris writhed like a tortured thing, desperate to remove the dead creature that adhered by his collar. He dropped the blade as he tore the corpse away, stared at it in horror a moment, perhaps thinking it still alive, then hurled it to the wall.

Tabitha was forgotten and both she and Cassie ran to join their sisters. The table lay between them and Mr Tenebris. Naomi and Cassie hugged Tabitha. Lavinia darted forward and grabbed the dropped blade.

Mr Tenebris stepped between them and the door. He had not recovered entirely, and the experience left him mystified, but he had wit enough to find Naomi's blade in his pocket. He faced the four of them.

'Put it down, Arnold,' said Lavinia. 'You will not beat us in our own home.'

He spluttered out something between a yelp and a cackle, 'My dear, Lavinia, when they ask why I cut you and treated you all so cruelly, tell them it was because of your brazen impudence.'

Dearbhla snaked towards them across the long table that served as their desk. Mr Tenebris approached on the other side, the small blade now a natural extension of his hand.

It was hard to know which carried the greater menace, such was the bestial glint in the Umbra's eyes.

'Last chance. Remove your clothes girls, or must I kill you to find what I seek.'

Eyes wide, Tabitha began to unfasten her blouse. Cassie noticed the door opening behind Mr Tenebris.

Please, let it be anyone but Miss Pikestaff.

It swung open to reveal a young gentleman in a frock coat with a black-haired Umbra upon his lapel and a small shabby child from the Africas.

18 – THE UMBRA ABOMINABLE

Stanton

'Black-hearted murder of the Borderer by Greynhym and evil Umbra' called out a young girl on the corner of Marksfayre Square. She was selling one of the 'Umbra Abominables', salacious scandal sheets that were produced weekly and read out by literate folk on street corners, in ale saloons and bawdy houses.

Others of her kind shouted their competing news from publications of the same ilk. Stanton had never been disposed to buy them but dug out his halfpenny for the girl, who was doing brisk trade.

'Monstrous business, sir,' she informed him, curtsying. 'There'll be no stopping those Greynhym horrors now – there's not one of us safe from plague.'

Dusk was mustering in the city and the street lamps were already being lit in the square as he entered his house, hoping that Isabella might have followed him out from Pickadills; she hadn't.

Stanton had already purchased a copy of *Lloyds Evening Pos*t on his way back from Pickadills. He sat in the parlour and opened the paper on the story of the 'Death macabre of the Umbra Charon and thereby Countess Alnwick'.

It was relegated to the smallest section of the front page, owing to the urgency of the news of events in France, which included the de-establishment of Christianity on the Friday just past.

The Post report on Charon was much focussed on the Countess and reports of her early life and elevation to The Five Hundred. Details of the death of her Umbra were scant:

'Umbra were called to arms on the news of the sinister death of Charon, the Borderer, doubtless by a band of Greynhym. Charon, known as "the scourge of the Greynhym", led his forces to many victories holding the line near the Rivers of Witham and Trent and keeping the pestilential horde at bay.

'The Countess of Alnwick, now taken from us, readily told of the courageous deeds of her Umbra and his efforts to keep the north safe from the evil that is the Greynhym and the plague they carry into our world. Charon fletched his arrows with white feathers, dipped in blood and bore a sword and dagger made of argentium. His armour was said to be impervious to blade or arrow point. The Countess was quoted in the latest edition of *The Book of Five Hundred* as saying: "Never have I any fears for my own life as Charon is so brutal and cruel in battle, 'tis the Greynhym I fear for."'

The paper spoke of the Borderer and 'his brave Umbra band of Spriggans and Wood Elves as they dashed to push back against any breach'. The paper also named several towns and villages 'to the north of the Province of Pestilence, that should carry themselves wary for any sign of swellings or tumours in the groin or armpit, or of black spots or livid in the arm, thigh or elsewhere.'

Stanton's eyes ran, though, to the bottom of the column where he saw the word 'disquieting'.

'There are several disquieting aspects to the murder of the Borderer. Not least among these are that a small band of Greynhym spawn would be able to withstand such a resolute and accomplished warrior whose armour they could not breach. Also that they might attack on the strand line of a beach.'

Stanton's mind went to Larkwing's suspicion. Could it be that

Viscount Exeter's Umbra had been turned by the French and tricked the Borderer into an ambush? He inked his quill and applied himself to some notes:

- Is Exeter's Muscari the undercover Umbra?

- Could she have access to the King's Umbra, Hannah Lightfoot?

- The 'People's Queen' may not be guarded in the Other Realm.

- George the Third is well protected here, but Miss Lightfoot's death there, would decapitate this world's most powerful empire.

Larkwing had spoken about uncovering the Viscount's closest confidants and studying his movements. Urchins must be organised, discrete correspondence found and studied. Stanton, still reeling from the discovery of the threat to the King, had agreed that all knowledge of the Viscount at his Ministry would be sought out and passed on. But, if it was Muscari, she must be acting without the Viscount's knowledge.

As for this other creature, The Mor, they had no intelligence and therefore, no plan. What motive could anyone, human or Umbra, have for abetting the incursions of the dread Greynhym? Stanton still found it all but impossible to believe.

He turned to the half-penny Umbra Abominable scandal sheet. Normally he considered such publications wild fictions, fit only for such common folk as delight in any titillating gossip about their betters and their fae companions. Commoners suspected the gentry of having more lewd and diverse associations than they had themselves. Stanton imagined the Abominables to be full of the kind of salacious gossip that Twoshrews fed Isabella. Every other headline dwelt upon 'Umbra Gold'.

'Other Realm in bedlam as Borderer is betrayed by evil Umbra,' he read. 'The famed Borderer, Charon, has been beaten down by a perfidious act, which will strike fear into all honourable and proud Englishmen and especially those in the north.

'While it is not in dispute that a band of Greynhym laid the Borderer low, what we contend is that they had help from a scurrilous creature: an Umbra who acts against all interests. With the Borderer dead and his band of warriors leaderless, Umbra lands will be claimed by the dead. The north of England lies open to incursion from the pestilence-spread by ghouls.

'Our Other Realm correspondent reports that the Borderer was lured to an empty strand by this betrayer and there set upon by concealed Greynhym, who, despite being poor and cowardly warriors, so outnumbered the Borderer that he was eventually overcome.

'The Greynhym have a known aversion to water – and salt water above all, as its touch is as poisonous as nightshade to them – so The Borderer would have had little occasion to patrol there.

'The trap that was set by this villainous underhand Umbra, whose motivations are his or her own and about whom little is known, except that this traitor must be hunted down, for by their actions they seek to betray those of their own kin and all good Englishmen.'

'What do you study so intently, Sebastian?' said a soft voice at his shoulder, 'a scandal sheet, I declare. And what have you writ here, "Muscari? Hannah Lightfoot? Undercover Umbra?"'

It was Isabella, returned from Pickadills, who had crept close to him. 'What have you to do with the King's Umbra?'

'As Minister of Umbra Affairs, Izzy, I am looking into the unfortunate situation of the death of Countess Alnwick and her Borderer, as you know.' He turned over his sheet of notes.

'How can that involve Hannah Lightfoot?'

'It doesn't; in fact, the opposite. Never you mind, it is ministry business. In what temper did you and Lady Rochester leave Pickadills?'

'Better temper than you did, for there was uproar when you departed, with many cries of "shame".'

'Because of my association with a street waif, no doubt?'

'That you brought a raggamuffin into the establishment was cause for outcry, worse still, the child was from the Africas, and yet the vilest insult, the urchin was female. For many older gentlemen that is the worst outrage.'

Stanton shook his head, 'Was she a girl? I took the child for a page-boy fallen from favour.'

'You are right, but also wrong. Lady R confirmed it so. The family was told by the girl's mother that her child was a boy. They employed mother and son, believing they would have a fashionable page boy. When, after the mother deceased they discovered her to be a girl, they put her out on the streets. Lady Rochester suspects that she runs errands for your secretive acquaintance. She says he oft set urchins to spy on her and believes that he tried to intercept her correspondence.'

'Well, I'm sorry the child's appearance caused a clamour.'

'Don't be. Those gentlemen are content enough to discuss the liberties of the common man in France,' she said, 'but will suffer small boys and girls, to be stolen out of the Africas and shipped in every kind of distressing circumstances to Britain, the Caribbean and the New World without rights or succour. And they were much put out to see Lady R and myself in their establishment.'

'They subscribe to Pickadills in order to read their journals there without such beautiful distractions,' ventured Stanton.

'It was little to do with our disturbance and everything to do with our gender.' Her tone had turned angry.

She grabbed the half-penny abominable from the desk-top, took a lamp to it and read before exclaiming. 'You cannot take note of this, Sebastian. It is all titillation and prejudice. Twoshrews is more to be believed. Is this what you and Lampwick –'

'Larkwing.'

'Whichever.' Her fingers whipped the corner of the provoking sheet. 'Umbra traitor indeed; is this the subject of your clandestine conferences?'

'You are being uncivil without cause, Izzy. These are things I cannot discuss.'

'You are happy enough to indulge me when you want Twoshrews' service. This is why you grew so animated on the likelihood of Exeter's attendance at the Countess of Harrington's ball. Do you propose to have Muscari arrested there?'

'Hush, Izzy, I plan no such thing.'

'You cannot think that Exeter, of all gentlemen, has instructed his Umbra to murder Hannah Lightfoot. God knows I have much cause to think ill of him, but even I would never believe that.' She strode to the parlour door, the Umbra Abominable dismissed with a flick to flutter in her wake. 'I thought you over all jealousies with regard to the Viscount.'

19 – DEARBHLA'S SCREAM

Larkenfen

The creatures' leader lifts a barbaric club... His compatriots inch closer; their injuries, ailments and stink fill his senses. Arthur's mind quails before the impact yet his head lifts against all fear, to stare defiance into the leader's dull lifeless eyes. They remind him of the eyes of the huge shark that fishermen caught in the Thames and put on display five years before. The assailant is about to lash down... then grunts to stare at where an arrow tip has sprouted rudely from its chest. Apart from juddering forward a little at the impact, the monster seems unaffected at being pierced by the arrow but turns around, curious to see from where it came. Arthur sees the answer as it does; between its legs he spies a distant figure racing toward them, flying boots raising puffs of sand.

◆ ◆ ◆

Arthur came roughly awake with a grunt. The coach wheel had stumbled into a rut. Fellow passengers on the coach had been similarly discomfited and one stared across at Arthur and Amorrie, who slept still on his shoulder grumbling softly into his neck. Arthur wondered if his dream had caused him to mutter too. He wiped his chin, suspicious that drool had escaped the corner of his mouth.

'I hardly see you all day and when you arrive, straight-ways you fall asleep,' Arthur said when Amorrie came awake later.

'Tis this blasted 'traption,' she responded, 'it rocks and creaks and afore I know it…'

'I think you attend me just for respite.'

'There is such hullabaloo in my world, I get no rest there.'

After Hurting had left his studio, Arthur had packed and made enquiries before booking himself onto the next morning's coach on the Cambridge Road. He had not intended to take up the Countess's commission so quickly. It was testimony to the anxiety induced in him by Hurting's visit that he now felt himself safer close to the borders of pestilence than in Smoothfield.

Nouhou must have endured similar terrors for Arthur found the small child waiting on his doorstep on the morrow, with a woeful collection of belongings and a pleading look that Arthur could not ignore. He allowed the child to travel with them, paying threepence for a place up top of the coach.

There was no Royal Mail coach to be had and Cambridge was a day and a half's journey from London. They ambled along the Great North Road to the coaching township of Puckeridge, in which Arthur spent the night at an inn. Nouhou bedded in the stable; Arthur's willingness to share his bed, being prohibited when the landlord saw the state and origins of the child.

The following day the coach reached Cambridge in the afternoon, from where Arthur's enquiries led him to a cart and driver who had brought fish and eels into Cambridge from the fens that morning. He was returning and agreed – readily at the sight of Arthur's sixpence – to take them to Larkenfen. The man was a caustic fellow who smelt as stale and pungent as his cart, but offered his opinions readily. He was by turns jovial and sinister and Arthur felt cowed by his accent. The man kept sneaking glances at Nouhou, who mainly slept in the back of the cart.

'S'over eight miles Cambridge to Reedston, master. We's deep in Fenland, with the causeway rare passable at this time of year. S'lucky, weather's unus'al fair. We be s'picious folk, but hardy n' abidin'. When rains come the causeway is lost to we.

In drought, we be for'ver on our guard 'gainst the Greynhym's forays. If 'n marshes dries up or streams stop their runnin', the plague is 'pon folk, quicker'n a heron'd gulp down a frog.

'That's Fenland for 'e; everythin' ends in witchery 'n eels.'

Occasional unearthly cries, which the Carter blamed upon 'perfidious waterfowl that'd ruin the fisherfolk's livin', rose up from the marsh upon either side.

They made steady progress and Arthur's artistic spirits lifted at the swathes of sepia reeds, which undulated to an unknowable rhythm, as if the small elephants proposed by Georges Buffon scurried beneath their swaying tops. The low sun gambolled among their tassels, lingering here and there as though to do mischief.

They arrived at the historic mansion house at close to 5 o'clock. 'Tarry not, master,' advised the Carter as he turned back to spend his night at Reedston, 'un autumn blow is all it'll take to make yon causeway impassable.'

Amorrie had not yet been with Arthur this day, so he summoned her, and she arrived with a ready scowl for Nouhou.

Arthur banged at the door but received no answer. Instead there came a soft stifled cry from within.

Amorrie's listlessness abruptly vanished and she leapt up, eyes clenched tight, covering both ears with her hands. 'Some vileness is abroad.' She grabbed at Arthur's ear, 'the scream, did you not hear it?'

'There was something. I felt it.'

Amorrie had drawn a tiny knife from somewhere on her person. 'May you break down this door?'

Arthur stared from the heavy arched oak door to his Umbra. 'No, and that would not be a good way to begin our commission.' He knocked again. Nouhou was behind him, clutching both his legs tight. The child had barely spoken for two days and his tiny frame quaked alarmingly.

Amorrie had climbed around to the front of Arthur's coat. She grabbed part of his shirt ruff in one hand, 'We must discover another entra –' She stopped, eyes shut and body quivering as if beset by needles. Nouhou gripped Arthur tighter. '... trance. All haste.'

Her urgency transmitted itself to Arthur. Leaving his bags, he ran around two sides of the house, finding an open door into a dining room at its back. They followed the sound of voices and stopped outside a closed door. A male voice spoke inside, its simmering anger more apparent than the words. Arthur glanced to Amorrie, who nodded, and he opened the door.

It swung wide to reveal a man with a knife in his hand and his back to them. A bristling Umbra, prowling upon a long table, turned to leer at them, and a confusion of young red and ginger-haired girls stared at him in much astonishment beyond the far end of the table.

The man turned. 'What is this? A-hah you are expected, sir, but not today. It's mightily inconvenient. A gentleman would surely send word that he was in the area and sought an audience with the family before arriving in person. Perhaps you could go back to Reedston and spend a night at the Inn there.'

Arthur had stepped into the room but now stalled, 'Mr Gracegirdle?'

The man wagged his knife, 'Now, sir, if you please.'

Nouhou ran from the room. Amorrie leapt from Arthur's shoulder onto the table. Arthur stood transfixed. 'What goings-on are these?' he asked generally. Then, more specifically, 'Are you girls, Gracegirdles?'

'We are, sir,' said the tallest, who also wielded a blade, pointed towards the man, 'and who are you?'

'Mr Tenebris, I have a comm –'

'Another one?' said the smallest of them. 'Are you brother to this villain?'

'No, not at all.' Arthur wasn't sure whether his bewilderment was bettering his fear but still wished he had not opened the door at all.

The man bowed low. 'Arnold Tenebris, at your service, sir. Now pray excuse us, your arrival is provokingly bothersome.'

'Arnold?' Arthur's bafflement increased.

'Kill him,' said Amorrie, 'I will do likewise to his she-welp here.'

Arthur tore his eyes away from the knives on display to see Amorrie and the feral spirit closing towards each other. He thought on a cock-fight he had reluctantly witnessed in Limehouse, where the participants lined each other up beak-to-beak and waited for some sign of wavering before bounding upon their opponent. The largest cock with the longest talons always won. In both particulars here, Amorrie was outmatched.

The man stepped forwards. Arthur's instincts said run but he remembered that Amorrie was still there and his life was every bit as at risk if she was killed by the talon-festooned creature before her. 'Go, Amorrie. Leave me now,' he said.

Her eyes did not leave her adversary. Nor did she vanish or speak. Arthur stepped closer to her, 'Please Amorrie, I wish you gone, return,' he pleaded.

'No,' she said. A clawed hand raked towards her. She swayed back and, to Arthur's astonishment, tucked her knife into her belt.

The man giggled, 'Well, Dearbhla, we have a competition, it seems. Let us see which of us can kill which of them first.

'Perhaps they will all kill each other,' whispered a pretty girl, who had not previously spoken. She seemed to think this the best solution.

'Who do we help?' hissed the smallest, then paused before adding, 'Cassie's right; look, Livvi, this new one's Umbra is...'

'The Ace of Moons,' said the prettiest one with a gasp.

A knife lunged towards Arthur, who skipped away, putting the table between himself and the man. One of the girls squealed and they ran the other way.

The two Umbra were now fully engaged in skirmish. Amorrie was ducking and blocking blows. Arthur's cheek stung and he saw talons rake Amorrie's intense face, leaving reddening streaks.

The man rushed around the table and Arthur yelped and ran,

the girls scampering ahead of him. A figure of a handsome well-presented gentlewoman, hair neatly tied, appeared in the doorway.

'Madam,' yelled Arthur from the far end of the table, 'run, get help.'

The woman looked too much stunned at the tableau to obey, but her Umbra, a fierce blue-skinned brute of a Goblin, leapt from her shoulder onto the table. At least he can help Amorrie, thought Arthur. Still he feared that this Dearbhla would win out.

'Who is this?' gasped the woman.

The man ran back the other way, as if to grab one of the Gracegirdle girls. 'A Tenebris too many,' he said with a laugh. Arthur now raced ahead of the girls as they all strove to keep the table between them and the man's blade. One of the girls tripped and fell.

'Ah, I have you now, little one,' but as the man ran forward, the tallest girl stepped over her fallen sister, pushing her own blade towards him.

'You have nothing, Arnold,' she said, too calmly.

On the table the Goblin swung a large cudgel into the fray. It was a clumsy stroke, for he might have hit Amorrie as much as Dearbhla.

'Finish it, Galt,' said the woman from the door.

Amorrie leapt through the weaving talons and took Dearbhla in her chest, knocking her backwards. The club whooshed over both their heads.

The man feinted with his knife but used the trick to knock the blade out of the girl's grasp with his other hand. It fell against the wall. Below the taller girl, the younger sister screamed.

'Too easy, Lavinia,' said the man, as she crouched before him, her stance altered but still unwilling to give ground.

'You really should have been better schooled.' The man's blade drew back.

Dearbhla had pushed Amorrie back a little. Now she opened

her mouth and – though Arthur heard nothing – the air in the room came alive and his skin prickled. Amorrie fell backwards as if struck, rolling and holding her ears. Galt dropped his club and all but slipped from the table. Dearbhla rose, lifted a taloned claw in readiness to plunge it through Amorrie's neck. Arthur had no time even to yell.

He saw the man's hands clutched to his ears. His eyes screwed briefly tight.

The girl, Lavinia, dived onto the floor, picked up her dropped blade and stabbed the man in his stockinged calf. He cried out and dropped onto all fours, clutching at the injury. Dearbhla also stumbled back, her hands seizing upon her own leg.

Amorrie jumped to her feet, grabbing the Goblin's dropped club and smashing it into the she-demon's head. Dearbhla fell unconscious to the edge of the table.

Turning, Amorrie threatened the Goblin, Galt, with his own club. He leapt off the table and vanished before he reached the floor. A flintish sound echoed after him. His club fled with him. Amorrie drew her blade and held it to Dearbhla's neck.

'May I,' she said a little breathlessly to Arthur, 'slice through this screeching succubus's throat and despatch her and yon counterfeit Tenebris to join the Greynhym throng?'

20 – A HUBBUB OF FURIES

Larkenfen

'I have explained to the other Mr Tenebris what has befallen and asked for his good behaviour,' said the second Mr Tenebris. He was addressing his Umbra. 'His thoughts are mostly upon his bloodied leg, so I have extracted no promise, but I do not think he will trouble us.'

Lavinia had taken the first Mr Tenebris' knife from his unprotesting fingers and now held the point of it against the back of his neck.

'Can we trust you, sir,' Naomi asked the newcomer, 'or do you also seek some treasure here?'

'I am here only to paint,' he said. He was a thin gentleman, barely over twenty, and perhaps the most nervous of all in the room. 'I have no skill with blades or skirmishing and truly seek no treasures.'

Tabitha brushed past him with a short length of cord brought from the outhouse. 'Pikestaff is fled,' she told her sisters.

'Cassie is looking out for her,' Lavinia said and then to her captive, 'Hands behind your back, Arnold, or your Umbra's life is forfeit.'

Naomi tied his hands using knots she'd learnt for boating. Tabitha brought a kitchen cloth to bind his profusely bleeding calf. The new Mr Tenebris slumped into a school seat too small for him and faced away from the bloody scene.

Tabitha finished her repairs on 'Arnold' and approached the new Mr Tenebris. 'Do you have credentials you can show us, sir? We have been misused and deceived once already.'

The new Mr Tenebris produced a letter from his pocket that bore their Aunt Jane's seal. Naomi broke the seal, opened and read it. 'What is your Christian name Mr Tenebris?' she asked him as she handed it to Tabitha.

'It is Arthur, there was some misunderstanding with the Countess about my name, but she had it right before she despatched me.'

'Then who is this "Arnold"?' Lavinia stroked the knife along the man's neck.

'An imposter,' said Tabitha.

Cassie slipped back in, 'Papa is coming,' she said.

Two silhouettes filled the doorway; Miss Pikestaff and the tall, broad-shouldered outline of their father. Three of the girls rushed to hug his waist and had their fiery hair ruffled.

'We must send to Reedston for the constable, Papa,' said Naomi. 'Both for this counterfeit fellow but also for Miss Pikestaff, who has abetted him.'

There began a row both furious and bewildering. During it Dearbhla came to and was persuaded to stay by Lavinia's blade's proximity to Arnold's neck

Miss Pikestaff had one version of events that quite contradicted the story told by Lavinia. Annoyingly, she was endorsed by the genuine Arthur Tenebris, who haltingly congratulated her on her Umbra's courage, 'In fighting to subdue the villain's hell-wench. He was only undone by the Banshee's scream, else he would surely have clubbed off her head.'

Lavinia's story was also refuted by her captive, who claimed he had acted alone, that he had heard of Mr Tenebris's commission and believed there would be spoils to be had if he presented himself at Larkenfen under the guise of being the artist.

Their mother and the maid returned during this confession. All had to be explained again so their mother could hear the main constituents of the story.

'This man's confession is a nonsense, Papa,' said Lavinia. 'Miss Pikestaff had sight of the message about a Mr Tenebris coming and plotted with this villain in his deception. How else could he have known of it?'

'Ah,' said Arthur Tenebris, 'I fear my commission was not as secret as perhaps it should have been. I know others have found out about it. I doubt the scoundrel heard anything from this gentlewoman.' Miss Pikestaff inclined her head in thanks.

Their mother was quick to add her support to the governess and companion selected and paid for by her sister, the Countess.

'But we heard them plotting to find a treasure, a sprig, they said,' Tabitha pointed to the motif in the window. 'Whichever one of us had it secreted away, was to be killed and this sprig treasure stolen away, no doubt.'

'You could not have overheard such nonsense,' said Miss Pikestaff rounding on the girls, 'which of you claims to have heard this? Was it you, Tabitha?'

'No Miss Pikestaff, it was –'

'It's no use, Tabby,' said Cassie, 'no-one would believe me.'

Miss Pikestaff made much of the way that her charges had teased and constrained Galt. 'I must consider if I can continue in my position. I have a mind to write to the Countess, so cruelly was Galt tormented.'

'He should have yet more credit then, for fighting for the girls so valiantly,' said Arthur Tenebris.

The four girls stared at each other in disbelief, was it possible he had understood so little.

'He was over-gallant to Miss Pikestaff,' said Cassie later, 'too quick to demure to Papa and excessively apprehensive around us. Were it not for his Umbra's valiant defying of the Banshee, I would suggest he be sent packing back to Aunt Jane.'

Eventually a halt was called. Papa and Arthur Tenebris would take the carriage to Reedston and ask the constable to detain the fraudulent Arnold there. Lavinia volunteered to go with them to help keep guard upon the prisoner. She did not trust the new Tenebris to keep a blade close enough to the villain's throat and she wanted to ensure a proper account of the affair was given to the constable. Hearing this, Amorrie dismissed the Banshee back to the Other Realm.

'See, this gentleman's Umbra, Papa,' Naomi pointed at the small dark-eyed girl sitting sour-faced, and determinedly unimpressed by events; 'she is surely your Ace of Moons.'

All eyes turned to study the Umbra, whereupon she abruptly vanished into a shadowy darkness.

'I'm sorry, Mr Gracegirdle' said Arthur Tenebris. 'Amorrie is unused to receiving attention. She lacks even a guttersnipe's manners.'

'Manners be damned,' said Naomi, earning a shocked look from her mother and Miss Pikestaff. 'I believe we owe our lives to her bravery and Lavinia's.'

There was a scream from the kitchen. The maid had found a small child from the Africas hiding under a table.

◆ ◆ ◆

While mother, Miss Pikestaff and the maid, set about preparing a supper of cold meats and eel pie, Naomi, Cassie and Tabitha, ran to their refuge at the end of the boardwalk. They settled on the jetty to try to make sense of the afternoon.

'He is genuine,' Cassie said of the new Mr Tenebris. 'His easel passes Naomi's test and paint spots soil his cuffs. I think him a man that arrived with much to say, who has been struck all but dumb by events.'

'Papa was strong, do you not think,' said Tabitha. 'The calamity made him so much more engaged. I think he looked in your direction with special affection, Cassie.'

'Hardly,' said Cassie.

They watched as the sun cloaked itself in a nightgown of velvet clouds while the pinprick lights of Ely congregated and coalesced to the north-west. The moment the sun's last ray fled the sky, slithering serpents of breeze sped in to harry the vegetation on the far bank of the Lark.

'Cassie?' Tabitha huddled close to her sister.

'I am all right,' Cassie's eyes were fixed beyond the swirling water. 'I will survive it.'

They heard rapid steps coming towards them, light and purposeful. Lavinia arrived carrying a lamp and raced onto the jetty before stopping behind them.

'I am to fetch you for supper,' she said. 'But first there is news. The constable says he will keep Arnold for tonight only, as there is no more likelihood of magistrates or assizes this side of spring. Tomorrow, he'll put Arnold on a cart for Cambridge, but doubts they will know what to make of the story there.

'Papa told me that shortly before Miss Pikestaff went to him with tales of ruffians with knives doing battle in the school room, Hellekin came to him. She was most distraught and told Papa that three of the most vicious and viperous creatures from the Other Realm were this afternoon assembled at Larkenfen. She added that, "Everything was fluxed, and nothing was as it seemed," and disappeared. For once, she was right.'

'I recognise Galt and Dearbhla in that description,' said Naomi, 'but not Amorrie.'

'I'm surprised at Galt being described so,' said Cassie. 'Tabby bettered him only this afternoon.'

There were smiles but the cold searching breeze whipped away any laughter.

'And Miss Pikestaff is still among us,' said Naomi.

'Mr Tenebris is convinced of her innocence,' said Lavinia. 'He and Papa spoke of it on the carriage. Papa named our clamorous recall of events "a veritable hubbub of furies".'

Lavinia's voice dropped to a compelling whisper as she pulled her three sisters to her, 'The new Mr Tenebris had a message for Papa. He had been sent on his commission, he said, with a warning. It did not come from the Countess, but from some other fellow. A troubling scoundrel, who pretends to be a gentleman's gentleman, but has all the appearance of a dark-hearted rogue. The man dresses ever in black and wears his hair long as a gypsy's, as no gentleman would.'

'Mr Tenebris has taken offence against this man mainly because his hair is unfashionable I think,' Cassie's attention turned from the rushes.

'Mr Tenebris had been ordered by this man to take Papa and our mother aside and warn them that there was a plot afoot. Someone, Mr Tenebris had been told, was out to kill one of us but this London ruffian said no one knew which of us was wanted dead.'

The girls had one hundred questions, but Lavinia said they must wait until after supper, they had to return. They started back along the boardwalk, but Cassie lingered a moment on the jetty.

She gave a final look to the far bank, where she saw gathered one thousand or more grey figures crowding upon every inch of dry land. They were silent and watchful and hemmed tight against each other. Of many ages, of both sexes, and without Umbra, they were clad in ragged and rent clothing. Their collective gaze – eyes neither sharp or lifeless, but with a hungry quality – was fixed upon Cassie. Some, she saw, carried weapons, others everyday implements: a woman with a blackened pan, a fisher with a slashed net, a girl – no older than Cassie – with a doll composed of scraps. Most had visible injuries or marks of affliction on their person.

The girl, whose arm hung uselessly by her side, had unsightly tumorous swellings on her neck and face. She held Cassie's eye and beckoned to her.

21 – ALL HALLOW'S BY THE TOWER

Stanton

≡

Umbra of note

Wissendene and her human ally Feargod Chislett (Archbishop)

Meg Mantis and her human ally Cotteridge

≡

Four days had passed since the disagreement with Isabella. While his wife was one to hold a grudge, she would not do so against logic or nature, so they were again on good terms and making plans for the Countess of Harrington's forthcoming ball.

There was progress too at the Ministry. Cotteridge's enquiries were bearing fruit. Bundles of documents were aligned on the table in the corner of Stanton's office in the Ministry. The clerk entered with the Minister's diary. 'Will you be calling Mistress Maraziel today, sir?'

'Busy sleeping I fear. What does your Umbra…'

'Meg Mantis, sir.'

'Of course. What does Meg do in the Other Realm?'

'I have taught her script, sir. She uses it at her place of residence.'

'Well done indeed, Cotteridge. I have taught Maraziel nothing I fear. Where does Meg dwell?'

'A desolate and labyrinthine structure, falling into disrepair and largely abandoned. She is making a record of it for me. It is called the Citadel of False Sorrows. '

'Truly? So it does exist. Does she know a Keeper Claw?'

'I will enquire, sir.'

'Please do. Maraziel is withholding help. She says I owe her Peter of Langtoft's original account of the signing of the Queen's Treaty, to repay her for her help with the identity of the murderous Umbra.'

'There may be progress in that regard.' Cotteridge opened the diary.

'The Archbishop of Canterbury?' Stanton tapped the proffered entry. 'Today? Why would His Grace wish to see me?'

'I have scant detail, Minister, only that it pertains to our quest to discover more about Umbra.'

'How can he know of our enquiries?'

'Everyone in Government has noticed our…' Cotteridge gave a discreet cough, '…bustle, Minister. To fulfil your orders, and answer your demands for information, your colleagues have been chasing hither and there. We make demands of other Ministries, we secure records held by the Church, ransack our universities and send to those in Highlands, we seek out Umbra experts across the country.'

'We do no more than is our business,' said Stanton, 'and this attracts the interest of the Church?'

'With respect, Minister, our application is unique in my experience of Whitehall. It is commented upon everywhere. Take the records on that table, there. They were left to rot in the lowest vaults of the Ministry of Guardianship until they heard of our interest. They have been dusted off, bundled up, checked against a ledger and deposited here into the light of day.'

'What do they contain?'

'The record of magicks you requested. They form all reports from the last seven years.'

Stanton studied the mountain of documents, 'Why seven years?'

'Few magicks were uncovered or reported until the last decade, Minister, but there were then sufficient coming to the ears of Government that it was decided a record should be kept.'

Stanton went over to the table and checked the labels on the largest pile. 'This is the present year? Can there really be so many reports?'

'Reports of magicks double every year I am told. It is a tendency unlike any other they monitor in the Guardianship Ministry.'

Stanton took a handful of the most recent. 'This is from Cleeve Abbey, a disestablished monastery in north Somerset. "The Diocese of Bath and Wells has been inundated with accounts from those responsible for the old Abbey's upkeep and prolongation. They claim that every night the carved wooden figures set in the angel roof can be heard whispering to each other."' Stanton glanced up from the note, 'Do we really believe this?'

'It is a record of a report, Minister. No-one would trouble to determine its veracity. It is merely the official note of the Ministry being informed by the Diocese.'

Stanton already held another report, '"A congregation was attacked on leaving their church in the Huntingdonshire village of Hemingford Fae. Tall trees hurled small balls of foliage down upon them, causing much consternation and talk of the end of days." Surely the trees were just old, and the gales strong that day.'

'As you say, Minister.'

'"An outcrop of rock on the clifftop upon Bolt Head beyond Queensbridge in Devonshire, changes its shape each year and increasingly resembles a young woman or girl." A magick, or perhaps this is merely the work of an apprentice mason in the locality?

'"A fusilier from Bickerton, who had no words but English ones, awoke one morning speaking in a foul groaning language such that all his comrades refused his company. But birds would appear and follow him."' Stanton chuckled and plucked another from the pile.

'Here is one from this last week. "A respected man of business reported that a young gentleman was attacked in Bedford Square in London, by a fierce squall of wind, conjured up by a man wearing a coat of bees." Surely this nonsense is beyond the remit of Government?'

'And so it was, Minister, until we announced our interest. However, while each individual report can be questioned over its authenticity and perhaps ridiculed, there's a fact that cannot be disputed: over the last nine to twelve years reports of magicks have escalated at a formidable rate. Before this time, reports were much rarer.'

Cotteridge received the sheet from Stanton's hand and read it himself.

Stanton shuffled through the reports before him. 'But the Chancellor of Balliol assured me, only last week, that whatever magicks Umbra enjoy in their own realm, he has found scant evidence of them here – not since the Queen's time.'

'He does not have access to our archive,' said Cotteridge.

'Find out if he is still situated in London. I would discuss some of these cases with him.'

'Yes, sir, and reading on from your Bedford Square report; the man of business claimed he was at first sceptical, "but his Umbra whispered to him that such a creature as might attract a coat of bees was there present in the park."'

'Listen here. "A landowner in Bettws Asrai keeps finding the same cracked chess piece. First it lay hidden in his bed, then his habitual chair, his calving barn, upon his dining table. Each day it appears again despite him having the offending piece buried, dropped into a mine, thrown into the River Usk and locked away in a chest."' Stanton dropped another sheet.

He idly picked at another report. 'This is cut from yesterday's *Umbra Enquirer*: "The Cambridge Constable says that a gentleman artist was split into two halves, one evil and desirous of murder, the other genteel but cowardly. The evil one is deemed dangerous and has been incarcerated until magistrates discover how to reunite the two halves." I declare.'

'That one is at least partly true, sir,' said Cotteridge, 'for he was sent down from Cambridge to Baynard Castle Prison on the Thames yesterday.'

'It says here: "He was intent on stealing the Queen's Sprig from a family in the Fens. And that this man, one Arnold Tenebris, has an Umbra so grievous and murderous that none other can abide her company." I have heard of Mr Tenebris.'

◆ ◆ ◆

Twin footsteps invaded the gloomy church. Their echoes violated the silence that lodged between the rough pink Saxon stone walls. It was midday outside but little evidence of it bled into the confined interior. Stanton was in the company of a young curate, whose white surplice hung loosely on his gaunt frame. The fair-haired young man would have been handsome indeed had his features not been so skeletal.

They turned a corner and saw a robed figure waiting in the chancel at the far end of the narrow nave. Lines of two-seated pews lay either side of the uneven and time-worn tiled floor. Stanton moved to continue but the fresh-faced pastor restrained him with a touch.

'Ah the Minister,' a bitter rasp rattled along the walls. Feargod Chislett – the eighty-ninth Archbishop of Canterbury in a line stretching back to the Sixth Century – was new in post but had not the appearance of it. Stanton could think of no-one in Parliament or in any seat of power in the realm who was more ancient in feature or stooped in body.

The old man was dressed more as a beggar than a clergyman. His robes were dark and plain, and Stanton could see stains upon them even from this distance, even in the hunted light and predatory shadows invoked by the torches flickering from venerable wall sconces.

'Is he unarmed?' the Archbishop spoke to the curate.

'I searched him myself.'

The Archbishop leant forward at an alarming pitch until his

legs must either pump into action or he would fall to the floor. They did the former, propelling him towards his visitor. Stanton had seen ducklings exhibiting the same gait at Hyde Park. The Archbishop lurched to a halt before Stanton.

He dismissed the curate with a flick of a gaunt head, covered in wisps of white hair. He was a gnarled gnome of a man, all bent nose and busy white eyebrows, but Stanton also noted his left eye was milky and useless.

'Welcome, Minister, to All Hallows by the Tower, London's oldest church. It has survived the ravages of the Queen's wars, it persisted when plague turned the people against God and when fire licked at its holy walls.'

'Perhaps the coldest church also, Your Grace.' Stanton bowed, 'You requested this meeting, yet you search me like a common vagabond and give poor welcome in a sorry venue. Why are we met?'

'Why did I drag you across London at such little notice, you mean? I think you will find it worth your time. You are looking for a rare historical document I believe.'

'How could you know?'

'How could I not? If you seek something you must enquire of those who have it. Peter of Langtoft's account of the signing of the Queen's Treaty fell into the Church's hands after his unfortunate end. My long-ago predecessor, Archbishop Winchelsey was present at the signing, even though he and Longshanks were not on good terms.'

'You have the original document?'

'As God is my witness, my son.' The old cleric hacked out what may have been a laugh.

'Then you can do your country a fine service, by letting me take it for examination, sir.'

'No, sir, I cannot. It is the most significant legible document on a Treaty that sets down the rules and circumstances by which not just our lives are governed, but our deaths too. Rightly is the Church its custodian. I will not give any sight of it lightly to any functionary.'

'Functionary? I am here representing Parliament and your King, sir,' Stanton's vehemence was fuelled by the insult but undermined by the hoarse whisper he found himself adopting in the old church.

'I represent God.'

'Do not those two interests usually align?'

'Let us hope so. You may have sight of it, if,' the pause was measured, 'I feel that might serve both our plans.'

'Why guard it so resolutely?' asked Stanton.

'Because the Queen was no friend to the Church. The Roman Catholics barely survived her rule, or her wars. Edward Longshanks won the concession to found the English Church, but the world she put in place after, so undermined all religious beliefs, that our Church walked a different path from our Catholic forebears. She undermined God's purpose when she conspired with the Umbra to bind our two realms.'

'She won that right by arms and, remember, she all but ended the spread of plague.'

The Archbishop's face pushed up and forward into Stanton's, his one rheumy grey eye watering with passion, phlegm burst from between brown misaligned teeth. 'She took that right by unholy magicks and wicked design, aided by creatures from outside God's Kingdom, sir.' He subsided back, 'As you'd know if you studied your Bible. I refer to the King James edition, of course.'

'I have not come down the river to trade scriptures with you, Your Grace.'

The old man shook his head. 'She began the dissolution of the monasteries, if you remember your history. I cannot fathom why she would fear us, so believe she must fear God. Nor did she cure the plague, my son, she confined it to a region that besmirches our green land, splits England in half and flies in the face of what God intended.'

'Hell.'

'Literally Hell on Earth, filled with poor souls who become pestilential fiends.' The Archbishop pointed to a rood screen with a primitive doom painting on a wooden tympanum above the chancel arch. It depicted a grey multitude riven by infirmity, crammed into a dull landscape with small fierce warriors with spears and swords threatening any who dared try to escape.

'That doesn't explain why you skulk here rather than receive me in finer surroundings, or why you have your visitors searched.'

The old man dropped into a plain wooden pew and indicated one across the aisle for Stanton.

'My need for that caution is where I suspect our plans coincide.'

'How do you know my plans? My business is quite secret, and I may not share it.'

'We have no secrets from the Lord, my son. I know you seek out an assassin in the Other Realm.'

'Who told you?' Stanton started and knew he gave himself away.

'Your face just did. I added my predicament to recent rumours, multiplied by your Ministry's enquiries and activity and hoped it might sum to a common foe.'

'Your predicament?'

'When John Moore was appointed Archbishop in '83, I was not considered for the post. Nor did I expect to be, I was too old, many others were favoured before me. I was a forgotten man in the Church of England; too ingrained in antiquated views, espousing the wrong doctrines, fonder than I ought to be of Catholic texts, too strong a whiff of brimstone in my sermons, wrapped in old-fashioned robes, buttering up the wrong cheeks.' The Archbishop gave what Stanton hoped wasn't a lascivious brown-toothed leer.

'So, how is it that I now occupy this most holy post? Because, before Archbishop Moore was taken from us (and I doubt it was by God), at least eight other high-ranking men of the cloth had already been killed. The few Bishops who remained volunteered me for the post, so daunted were they by the coincidence. Not since the Queen's time has the Church fallen victim to such a heinous conspiracy. Someone in the Other Realm is murdering the Umbra of clergymen.'

'How is it I was not aware of this?' asked Stanton.

'Because the Church is out of fashion. Only the Archbishop ever finds his way into *The Book of Five Hundred* – I am not there yet. Our Umbra must be pious, so excite no interest from common folk. None believe in Heaven, as all know exactly what depravity and deterioration awaits us should we be unfortunate enough to die. Everyone knows where Hell is located, and the path to everlasting life is now forged without reference to the Church.'

'Even so.'

The Archbishop shrugged. 'Murders in the Other Realm go unreported, but I know ecclesiastical Umbra are being eliminated.'

'Why would the French want to disrupt the Church?'

'The French? Who said anything about the French? This is a plot born in the Other Realm.'

'You fear your life is in danger?'

'I fear more for Wissendene's life.' A twisting white cloud materialised next to the Archbishop and, when it evaporated, a pale, pretty Sprite sat in its midst. She had long straight white hair, which matched her simple tunic. As pretty as her ally was ugly, she was a picture of piety, but when she turned her face to Stanton and flicked her hair away from her face, he saw a white patch on her left eye with a scar running top and bottom of it.

'I have no love for Umbra, save one, who has been my lifelong companion. She has the countenance of an angel and has never been a tribulation to me. I would not be the cause of her death.'

'Who did that?' Stanton pointed towards the scar.

'She does not know; a blade in the night that was meant to do more damage. She says my colleagues' Umbra are all under threat.'

'Is this campaign recent?'

'Perhaps over the last seven or so years.'

22 – THE EEL FAYRE

Larkenfen

Everyone agreed the flying fish was a wondrous apparatus. Lavinia wore the front end of the construction and used internal levers by its gills to flap its short silver wings. Naomi wiggled around behind her older sister, pulling on two strings to cause the tail to flex most realistically, just like the quick fawn trout at Scatrush Shallows. Naomi had come up with the idea of the flying fish costume and she and Lavinia wore it at their waists from straps suspended over their shoulders.

Tabitha was dressed as a mermaid in a costume they had made for her two years since, and which now cinched too tightly. Its thick padded tail wobbled high off the ground behind her, where before it had swished a trail through the grass. Her chestnut hair was swept back and held by a tiara woven simply from willow withies decorated by sprays of hawthorn and rowan berries with clusters of russet briar hips.

It was the afternoon of the Reedston Eel Fayre, which coincided with the harvest and was a joyful occasion. The small village was plumped up by refugees from the outbreak of plague in Eely Bridge, supposedly caused by a Greynhym incursion in the Other Realm after the river had run low. Other folk from nearby Fenland communities had thronged to the fayre.

At the last, Cassie had decided not to go; she had much to think on, she said.

The girls were popular in Reedston. Their father was admired for staying at Larkenfen when he would surely have the means to move his family out of danger to Cambridge, or so the villagers believed. The crowd were, in the main, dressed in their Sunday threads, and many had summoned their Umbra for the event. Children wore felt hats and scarves in most of the twelve Umbra colours but there was nothing to match the flying fish. George Gracegirdle had made it to Naomi's design and painted the stretched canvas of the fish with lifelike scales.

The girls were much praised and commented upon as they promenaded through the market, but the greater spectacle was Nouhou, who had joined them at the fayre. Out of his rags and dressed in an over-sized hand-me-down tunic and simple breeches stitched by Miss Pikestaff, he drew all eyes. The villagers were agog with curiosity; the child was too large to be an Umbra but beyond the learning and experience of any present, bar one.

'He'n a black-a-moor,' the Carter walked along the edge of the crowd, keeping pace with the girls, 'I brought un in my cart from Cambridge. They come from o'er the sea in ships, from somewhere 'ot I heard; hell most like. He was no trouble in my cart, mind, but I know there's some deviltry and wickedness in 'im.'

'There is not,' Naomi spoke from the tail end of the fish, 'he's just a commonplace little boy from the Africas, who's been treated poorly by people in London and has no harm in him.'

'Not another word, Dob Carter,' Lavinia turned the fish's head towards him, 'or folk will think you unchristian.'

Tabitha held tightly onto the hand of Nouhou, into whose stiff black curls, she and Naomi had twined new-fallen leaves in many of autumn's colours: scarlet spindle, coppery beech, and yellow fingers of ash.

The African child had won the girls' hearts when the new Mr Tenebris told them that Nouhou had been a page boy, who had been brought to England by his enslaved mother but thrown onto the streets when he was no longer wanted. They had been impressed that he knew his letters and shared their books with him. All had shown him kindness, even the maid (despite still being scared of him) and Miss Pikestaff, but he had barely spoken, not managed a smile and God alone knew when he ate.

Stalls were set up in the market space between Reedston's straggling Lamprey Inn and the tiny squat chapel. A crusty man stood by a table of dried pike fillets. He had a netted bag of still moving eels. His Umbra, who had scales on her arms, sat on his table entranced by a large bowl of bustling pink craycrabs, whose long delicate feelers emerged from the water as they clambered clumsily over each-other. A trio of tiny children stared at the man's Umbra with as much intensity.

Two gypsy women, dressed in matching mourning red aprons and frocks, were peddling talismans to keep away the dead. These included loose-woven bags into which one woman's red-capped Umbra would place a lump of musky Ambergris having first hummed some magick enchantment over it. They had bracelets, brooches and necklaces that supposedly contained some argentium, crude hanging crosses made from decorated bones and tiny stoppered jars threaded on cord that contained sea water, known to deter Greynhym.

Most affecting were some tuppeny dolls: a throng of feathers threaded together for a torso with protruding reed-stem limbs. They only suggested a body because painted ovals of white shell with girlish features and curls scrawled in black, sat atop them. Of the three dolls on display, one had open eyes; one, no eyes; and one, sullen eyes that leaked red blood. As the girls passed, they heard one of the women tell a customer that the dolls contained Umbra spirits and no dead could suffer them.

Around fifteen traders were selling wares in the market, surplus rye flour and peas from the harvest, or drink, or livestock – mainly ducks and chickens. It was another fine fall day and the crowd were in good spirits.

The girls had arrived at the market in the Gracegirdles' carriage, tight-packed with Mr Tenebris and their mother. The flying fish was light enough to lay across their laps. Mother had gone off on errands, leaving Mr Tenebris to escort the girls and he followed their procession at a discrete distance.

Little had been said to them about the threat to their lives or any imagined sprig treasure, although they were sure their parents must have discussed it with Mr Tenebris when they were safe abed.

As for Miss Pikestaff, she had received such good account of her actions and her Umbra's courage from their new guest that the girls would not be believed about her involvement in any plotting. The governess had suspended lessons since the incident (neither side was yet willing to reunite in the parlour) to punish the girls, she said, for their cruel treatment of Galt. Neither of their parents challenged this.

Instead of lessons, the girls spent time having their likenesses sketched by Mr Tenebris and talking through ideas for the final illustrations. It did not begin well. Lavinia was angry with him because he would persist in defending Miss Pikestaff, but Cassie said she should be agreeable because his feisty little Umbra had probably saved her life and was 'such a close likeness to The Ace of Moons that she must have appeared to Papa in a dream and her coming could only be providence.'

Naomi found his constant over-indulgence of them and simpering way of complimenting them, their parents and, especially, Miss Pikestaff, wearing. It was just his nervousness, said Cassie.

Tabitha worried that this new Mr Tenebris thought too little of himself and compared his talents unfavourably to those of their father, although it was clear from the first rough sketches that he was a skilled artist.

'He has spent too much time around lords and ladies who demean him,' was Cassie's interpretation, 'and must offer up so much praise of them, he has become overly aware of his own lowly station and his reliance on their good opinion.'

'I think he has filled his head so full of little compliments for others that he has none left for himself,' said Naomi.

Only Cassie had seen even glimpses of his pugnacious Umbra in the four intervening days since her dramatic entrance into their lives. Amorrie must visit him daily, but she did not tarry.

After some days' acquaintance with Mr Tenebris, he had won

some entries on the other side of the ledger. He had rescued Nouhou, who Mr Tenebris suspected of being in danger from the ruffian with long black hair in London. This man – the girls had gleaned – knew something ('too much,' thought Lavinia) about the wicked attack on them.

Mr Tenebris at least listened to their ideas for the portraits, although they had to be reminded that the illustrations must serve both their own sentiments and the uses that their aunt, the Countess, had in mind. They had agreed to have one portrait of each of them as they would like to be imagined and one larger canvas, more pleasing for Aunt Jane, of them all together.

The London artist claimed to be enchanted by their father's paintings, which proliferated throughout the house, although it was hard to be sure how genuine his praise was, since Mr Tenebris had only good words for everything. Even Papa could not explain the likeness between his Umbra and the Ace of Moons.

On their arrival at the fayre, with the whites of Nouhou's eloquent eyes wide with wonder at the clamour, Mr Tenebris produced two pennies from his pocket and pushed them into the child's tiny fist, inviting him to find something to buy in the market.

Tabitha diligently took Nouhou around the stalls. The flying fish and Mr Tenebris joined them both at a small table set with beautifully illustrated cards. It was common practise for games to be based on, and linked to, Umbra. Chess pieces were carved with the best-known Umbra of the day, lined up facing each-other across the board. They could only be afforded by those likely to have a witchy bishop or warlike knight in play, but the best sets travelled the country on exhibit and were much-admired.

Packs of cards showing king, queen and knave as Umbra were popular. Whipping tops were illustrated with valiant Elf warriors to impress street boys, huzzlecap sets made with the penny-like disks stamped with Nymphs or Piskies, which could be captured and collected.

The cards on display at the fayre showed famous Umbra imagined in appropriate settings, dressed in finery, showing off items associated with them or their allies.

'This unusual one dressed in a costume both French and English is Capu,' said Mr Tenebris, pointing to a card. 'I have seen him, he is Umbra to Lady Rochester, the most captivating woman in all England.'

'Her illustration is always so handsome in *The Book*,' Tabitha stroked the card. 'Look Nouhou, you could buy two of these cards with your two pennies.

'Here is Jenny M, Umbra to First Lord Pitt, more stern of feature, perhaps, but her wits are esteemed by the Parliament.' The card showed a severe, slim, shrewish, silvery madam, whose hair climbed into a nest of twigs. She was set before the Palace of Westminster, holding a ceremonial mace. A shining crescent moon appeared over one bare shoulder, Saint George's shield and lance decorated one corner of the card.

The same symbol adorned another card showing a willowy fae woman with a private smile. There was also a white on blue saltire and a small red dragon. She was set before Kew Palace and held hands with a lion on one side and a unicorn upon the other. 'This is Hannah Lightfoot,' said Tabitha to Nouhou, 'she is Umbra to the King. The card maker has written her a sweet ditty:

> 'When the King suffers from sadness
> Call up the Umbra rarely seen
> Only she can o'ercome his madness
> For Hannah truly is our Queen.'

'The commons call her "the True Queen" of Britain. She is thought to share the King's madness and is more popular than Queen Charlotte,' said Mr Tenebris, bringing forth a penny. 'I will buy this card, Nouhou, for it has given me a notion.'

The former page boy stared down at the pictures. He picked up a fourth card, it showed a brave warrior, clad in bright armour and helm with a slim sword and bow. Dead and decaying creatures were strewn around his feet.

'That's Charon, the Borderer,' Mr Tenebris's voice faltered, 'he's a hero... he was er...'

Tabitha read out the verse on the card:

> 'Brave Charon in his armour bright,
> That turns each arrowhead and blade,
> Sends Greynhym into lasting night,
> And makes them wish that they had prayed.'

Nouhou was hunting for a penny.

'No,' came a voice. It was Lavinia. 'That is not the card for you, Nouhou. We'll find something else for your two pennies.' She took the card from him and returned it to the table.

A voice came from behind them, 'You have brought pleasing weather with 'ee, master.' It was the Carter, there with his horse. He thrust forward an eel with two heads, 'Av you e'er seen the like? I bough' 'im for a penny.'

Mr Tenebris stumbled back with a cry from the gaping mouths of the proffered aberration. The Carter's horse gave a wild whinny and reared up. Being such a heavy creature all were fearful about where its fore-hooves would land. It seemed Nouhou was most in danger and Tabitha pushed him away. Lavinia and Naomi fell sideways in the unwieldy fish costume knocking over the table. The nag came to earth, pulled its rein clear of the Carter's hold and careered away. Nouhou ran in the opposite direction. Tabitha tried to run after him but was undone by her cumbersome tail.

People leapt clear of the startled horse and then ran forward to help or gawp at the confusion. By the time the girls were righted and fussed over, Nouhou was gone.

'Tha's your black-a-moor's doin', master,' the Carter said, handing Mr Tenebris the milky-eyed eel. 'His pagan looks were too much for my God-fearin' Mossop.' He clomped away after his horse.

Lavinia and Naomi clambered from their costume and they all set about looking for Nouhou but he was nowhere to be seen. The villagers had been watching the horse or the spectacle provided by the upended table and Gracegirdle girls, so no-one could say where he had run to.

They paired-up and searched: Tabitha with Mr Tenebris, Naomi with Lavinia. They called, but he would not answer. The afternoon wore towards dusk and their mother had returned to them before they saw Nouhou.

He was in the company of Miss Pikestaff, who, it transpired, had walked into Reedston to see the fayre. She had found him as she began her return, she said, 'on a field edge, up to his chin in all manner of flowers and more insects than even Naomi might collect'. The girls fussed over Nouhou, while Mr Tenebris was fawning in his appreciation for Miss Pikestaff and offered up his place in the carriage to her, to save her the walk back.

The governess let her eye linger on each of her charges in turn, then smiled gratefully at Mr Tenebris. 'Thank you, sir, you are indeed the gentleman. I am unused to such kindness, but no, the walk will be better for my disposition.'

'May I not join you, then, Miss Pikestaff, as it will be after dusk, before you are returned.'

The governess's eye, this time, strayed to the girls' mother. 'I thank you for the thought, but that would not be proper. I walk briskly and will be back soon after you.'

Mr Tenebris bowed low and took his place in the carriage. Lavinia stared hotly at him, from over the bent form of the flying fish that lay across their laps, but he did not notice.

'I have an idea,' he declared as they returned. He fished out the card of Hannah Lightfoot he had purchased, showing her with the lion and unicorn. 'Your father has begun a set of illustrations in the style of playing cards. We could make your portraits like the cards we saw today, choosing backgrounds from your father's pictures and including emblems of things that are important to you. Your family's sigil, the mistletoe sprig, could be in each.'

Tabitha clapped her hands, 'That is a clever idea; I will think on which emblem I desire in my illustration.'

'I will have a skeeter hawk,' said Naomi.

As the last of the sun dropped from the sky, the sudden breeze brought a distant tolling of bells from across field and fen. The girls paled and looks passed between them. Their disturbance was caught by Mr Tenebris, who asked what ailed them. Naomi saw that their mother was too upset to answer, so she began. 'The bells are tolling at St Lucia's in Eely Bridge,' she told him.

'Do they so every dusk?'

'Yes, but we cannot hear them from Larkenfen.'

'Why do you quail so?'

'No-one has lived at Eely Bridge for over a year,' said Lavinia. 'Its situation was overrun in the Other Realm by the Greynhym. It is a plague village now, sir, quite empty.'

'Then how is… who is…' began Mr Tenebris but stopped as if he had answered his own question, while their mother gave a tight sob in the seat next to him.

When the sound of the bells was stolen away on the wind, the artist attempted to change the mood. 'And you Nouhou, did you buy aught with your two pennies?'

The African child reached into the capacious tunic and pulled something out. It dangled from his tiny hand. It was made of feathers and reed-stems and topped by a shell, upon which was painted the face of a girl with curls of hair at its edge. Her eyes were downcast and leaked painted drops of blood.

23 – A TINY GLASS OF SANCERRE

Stanton

≡

Umbra of note
Agnieszka (of Pomerania) and her human ally the Earl of Grenville

≡

'What uncharted reef have you beached your runtish ministry on now, sir.' Was Grenville's bellow across the dignified hush of Whites dining room.

Whites was the gentleman's club Stanton wasn't gentleman enough to be allowed into. It wasn't a question of money or rank, but ermine and grounds. Yet, here he was; surprised on two counts: firstly, that the Earl of Grenville would have anything to do with him at all; secondly, that the Earl was prepared to be seen in Whites (of all places) with anyone whose grandfather hadn't thrashed Grenville's ancestors for being impudent fags at Eton or Winchester.

His maritime insult was made worse by the fact that, although Grenville was six years older than Stanton, he appeared, if anything, younger. None of the other diners bothered to raise their heads to stare at the object of Grenville's ire. Stanton was beneath even their momentary curiosity.

'Tacking hither and yon in a squall of your own making.' Grenville conversation was awash with nautical expressions.

It was his way to remind others that his youngest brother was already climbing high in the rigging of the Royal Navy, with a hand clawing towards the admiralty. After the heir and the spare, a third son was a superfluous distraction, unlikely to marry well, liable to sully the family crest with indiscretions or gambling debts, perhaps even to cause estates to be subdivided. The Navy carried them out of sight. Naval recruits were taken young, aged six to ten, they sailed away before puberty to be spared their Umbra arriving only to depart on their first voyage – even Selkies and Merrows rarely strayed far beyond British waters.

'We merely fulfil our brief, your lordship.' Stanton hadn't been invited to sit. There was no second chair at Grenville's circular table, just a large oval plate, with an even larger salmon flopping beyond both ends, and a barely touched bottle of Sancerre. There were two wine glasses; one was miniscule, designed for an Umbra.

'Oh there's a brief?' Grenville's attempted laugh was undone by a salmon bone and he made Stanton wait until it had been retrieved from his gums.

'To fully understand Umbra and their influences upon us, sir.'

'That could be done in five minutes, and Cotteridge was appointed to make sure it took five years. Didn't you understand, you idiot, your Ministry was invented to give you a place to sit, not something to do. It only exists because Pitt was trying to save Lord Lisle's face after allowing his daughter to marry such a finless sprat.' The Minister for Retaliation was, at least, embodying his office's brief.

Without a seat, Stanton found himself standing to attention opposite the Earl's salmon. His eye alighted on a spare chair at a nearby table but, seeing this, a vigilant waiter claimed it and spirited it away.

'You weren't supposed to be heard, Stanton, let alone seen. The role was to allow the charming Isabella to inform her admirers at the many balls and dinners you will never be invited to, "My husband… oh d'ya know, I think he may be something or other in the Parliament".' This last was delivered in a disturbing falsetto that should not have been attempted mid-salmon.

'Are you finished, sir?' asked Stanton, realising it made him sound like a waiter who had come to claim the Earl's fish.

'No, damn you, man. I've barely started. I told Pitt that a new ministry was a waste of resources when the tide of war was breaking over us. I said you wouldn't be able to stop yourself exercising power you will never have. A worrisome tendency to seduce impressionable young gals does not make you a fit member of the club.' He meant the Parliament, which was less a club and more of a family; a quarter of MPs were married to daughters of other members, near all were sons of peers. Grenville himself was a cousin to Pitt.

Stanton was about to turn on his heel and leave, but the next sentence made that impossible. It was more chilling for being delivered in an undertone and being immediately preceded by the arrival of an Umbra, Agnieszka, on Grenville's shoulder in a shower of glistening dew, much of which caught and sparkled in the Earl's wig.

'And now you have tripped, Stanton; misused your Ministry for personal advantage. Pitt will throw you out on your ear when told. Avoid the scandal, resign now for the Parliament's sake and try to be a gentleman about it for heaven's sake.'

'To what do you refer, your lordship?'

'If you resign now, I will burn this.' Grenville took a sheet of thick paper from an inside pocket and placed it beside his salmon. It had an official look to it. Stanton reached out a hand.

'Do not touch it, sir. You know its content well enough. It bears your signature.' Agnieszka flowed down onto the table and knelt upon the document. Her arresting bi-colour eyes dared him to venture closer, the bow slung across her back, behind a fall of honeyed hair that ended in a froth of curls, added substance to her challenge. She gave the merest shake of her head.

He had seen Grenville's Umbra before in Cabinet Council.

Pitt's ally, Jenny Moonshine, liked her kinsfolk present to run a parallel debate at least once a month. Maraziel complained the resulting cacophony made her horns ache.

The Book of Five Hundred placed Agnieszka as a Sibyl Empress who owned half a mountain and four clouds in Pomerania – a country of which Stanton knew little, beyond it being a besieged state beyond Prussia. It seemed a romantification too far as Umbra had not been discovered in France, Prussia, the Americas or any other foreign shore, as far as he knew. Still, it was easier to believe than Maraziel's assertion that Agnieszka had been fashioned from drowned voles and the screams of lost children and amused herself firing arrows at travellers from behind a waterfall in western Dyfnaint.

A waiter drifted over to pour some Sancerre into a small mouse-shaped decanter before dripping three drops of the liquid out of the decanter's tail and into the tiny glass. He put it beside Agnieszka.

Stanton returned his eyes to Grenville, 'I really have no id–'

'It is this evidence of abuse of position that compelled me to summon you.'

'You had best explain, my lord.' Stanton felt he had strayed into a trap and now been stupid enough to trigger it.

'I'm informed that your Ministry, acting on your orders, has requested sight of all intelligence relating to one of our finest young nobles, Viscount Exeter. I insist that all dealings with your Ministry are brought to my attention, and 'tis well I do so. On receiving sight of this, I now understand that all the unjustified toing-and-froing you have set in motion is so much smoke, sir. Here,' Agnieszka's hand tapped the document, 'is the true cannonade. The rest is a ruse, under which you would slip this requisition for Exeter's correspondence.'

'The request is made on government business. Why would you feel I have any improper motive?'

'That is obvious, sir; because of the contemptible rumours about your lady wife.'

'What rumours?' Stanton asked before he could stop himself.

A pink forkful of dripping salmon paused on the way to Grenville's mouth. Agnieszka made some comment. The Earl returned the salmon to the plate, sat back in his chair and stared at Stanton, as if it was he who had just materialised in the room.

'You have the right of it, Aga, I don't believe he does; not an inkling,' Grenville said to his Umbra. Then to Stanton, 'You are like the Sargasso Sea, Stanton, a long way from anything significant, oblivious to the currents that swirl around you and with a thickness that impedes progress.'

He poured himself a half glass of the Sancerre. 'Now your presence is spoiling this fine Loire wine we had promised ourselves. Ignorance is of no consequence; your request still manifests as an ill-conceived plot against the good Viscount, and that is how it shall be presented to Pitt. I bid you good day, sir.'

'Ah-ha,' said Stanton, 'I see the problem.'

'There is no problem.'

'Pitt has not seen fit to inform you of the grave situation we face.'

'Pitt and I share everything.'

'Not this, it seems, my lord, for all that the source of it is one of your own Ministry's agents.'

Grenville waved a waiter over to dispose of the salmon's remains. His smile was wafer thin, 'This had better be good, Stanton.'

'I was told in strictest confidence,' Stanton dropped to a whisper and was satisfied to see both listeners strain forward, 'but since I am instructed by the Ministry of Retaliation...'

'Get on.'

'I am told you are helpless to prevent an attempt on the King's life.' Stanton saw a newly vacated chair and claimed it. A waiter attempted to wrest it from him but desisted at a shake of Grenville's head.

Sitting, finally, Stanton resumed. 'I know nothing of rumours regarding Isabella, and would not believe them if I heard them. It was your agent Larkwing who requested I requisition anything you have discovered regarding Exeter. I only did his bidding because he has convinced me of the existence of a French plot. My Ministry is currently engaged to only one end, to preserve his Majesty's life.'

'This is utter bilge, sir. Exeter is as loyal as they come and as honourable a gentleman as Britain can muster. Pitt knows he would never countenance such treachery. You had best leave here, close up your Ministry, oh, and you may take Cotteridge with you.'

Stanton made to rise, 'And do you also vouch for his Umbra?'

'Muscari? Course I do, she –'

Agnieszka leapt up and pounced back onto the Earl's lapel. She spoke urgently to him.

24 – THE FOURTH GIRL

Arthur

Arthur watches the running figure discard a bow as it races towards the group. His would-be assailants are turning now to face the archer, shuffling uncertainly. Only the leader steps towards the threat and its bedraggled followers parade out upon each side, clubs and spears to the fore. The leader is little discomfited by the arrow shaft protruding from his back. It is fletched with three white feathers, tipped with crimson. Arthur feels he should know those colours.

The approaching warrior unsheathes a slim sword. Somehow Arthur knows it for an argentium blade. He hopes and believes it will be deadly to the fifteen or so creatures now ranged before him.

The leader extends his club to engage the warrior, but the sword lashes down to disarm him – literally – the club flies away with half a forearm attached. The creature screams but the cry is cut irrevocably short as its borrowed body topples onto the sand.

◆ ◆ ◆

Amorrie mumbled something indistinct, but it was enough to bring Arthur awake. He had fallen asleep in a chair after the visit to the Reedston Eel Fayre. Nouhou running off, the two-headed eel, the church bells ringing from the empty plague village, Miss Pikestaff's late return on her walk back, causing Arthur to set out to meet her with a lamp, quaking at every unnatural cry from the reed beds; all these had unsettled him, so that when he retired early to his room he called for Amorrie. She had no obligation to attend him, as she had already visited briefly in the morning, but she did, and he declared his disquiet to her. She offered no counsel but fell asleep in his lap and he drew strange comfort from it.

The next day he met with the Gracegirdle girls as they gathered by his easel and canvasses in the schoolroom. They had begun the week suspicious of him and he could find no blame for them in that. The tallest, Lavinia, had particularly wanted nothing to do with his commission.

He had won them around through his admiration for their father's pictures, which, though melancholy, displayed vision and inventiveness; and by his suggestion that these sombre landscapes could form backgrounds to their portraits. They had been curious too about Amorrie and how much she resembled their father's imagined character, the Ace of Moons.

Tabitha had shown much sympathy for Nouhou's plight and said it had been kind of Arthur to remove the child from the reach of the long-haired ruffian, who scared the former page-boy so.

Finally, Arthur's sketching talent convinced them that he was a real artist who wanted nothing more than to paint them as they wished to be portrayed, in clothes they were comfortable with and that he would be faithful to their ideas.

On the Saturday morn, Tabitha arrived first. She had been the most patient with him and he was happy that his several sketches had caught her delicacy and graciousness. She was already in her costume, a russet silk scarf that set off her chestnut hair, a makeshift tiara as might be worn by an Arabian princess and long blue skirts over which the enterprising Miss Pikestaff had fashioned embellishments to turn the chiffon into something that passed for exotic. Arthur had added an imagined peacock tail design onto the chiffon.

He put up Tabitha's still unfinished canvas.

'Oh, I am Scheherazade, Mr Tenebris,' she said, her fingers

almost drawn to touch the canvas. 'And the white bird with the curly beak is perfect, every bit as good as a white peahen.'

'An avocet,' he said. In the illustration, it dabbled behind her. The background was of one of her father's reedy desolations.

'I have chosen a swallowtail as my emblem, but could the av-o-cet,' she pronounced it cautiously, 'be part of my face pattern too?'

Arthur had told the girls that many prominent ladies set out a style guide for their illustrations so that they were instantly recognisable: the tilt and angle of their head, the style of hair, particular Umbra colours, dress and adornments. These distinctive details were known as their 'face pattern' and every authorised artist must be bound by them.

They had jointly agreed the previous evening, on common elements that would appear in all their depictions: the family sigil, the mistletoe sprig, would be displayed as their card 'suit', like spades or hearts; a colour, regretful orange, would run the elaborate borders, and reeds, copied from their father's paintings, would the feature in the backgrounds.

Now the swallowtail butterfly would be added to Tabitha's illustration. Arthur would get a good reference for them back in his studio. His method was to quickly capture in sketches the likenesses of his subjects – most of whom would not suffer to model for long – and take them away to paint the finished canvas in his studio. He was fortunate that his memory was a picture book that faithfully recorded every detail of face, hair and pose and presented it back to him when he came to paint.

Naomi arrived next. Her portrait sketches captured the quick intelligence of her eyes, which confronted the viewer directly, and showed some of her seriousness without any severity. She was in a black dress patterned with silver sprigs. Her long straight regretful orange hair flowed over both shoulders. A specimen glass sat before her.

'You are both sensible and beautiful, Naomi,' said Tabitha. 'Isn't she Mr Tenebris.'

'Indeed, she reminds me of mine own sister, Gwennie, who

is of a similar age and disposition, ever with a book or some study in her hands.'

'Tell us of her.'

'The most remarkable thing about her is her name. My father, a man much given to history and tradition, named her Gwragedd Annwn, which no-one can pronounce, so the maids and I call her Gwennie.'

'You are lucky to be named Arthur.' The sisters chuckled.

'Named for a long-ago king, Naomi, who had a mythical sword and was served by an enchanter. He defeated invaders and my father has him as Welsh.' He committed their bright mirth to his memory as he lifted a wide rough canvas to his easel. He supposed the girls thought him unlikely to capture any invaders, saving with a paintbrush.

'Is Gwennie a good friend to Amorrie?' asked Tabitha.

'I wish it were so, but no, they do not get on. When Amorrie first arrived, she was in no mood to be a friend to anyone. Gwennie was only small, just two or three and easily scared. Amorrie would shout such things at her. She could not touch or hurt her but would arrange strange traps and pretend monsters to lie in wait for her. Gwennie is a little afraid of her still, I think. Amorrie is too fierce for friends.'

Naomi had brought a jar with a dragonfly in it for her emblem, a ruby darter. Once Arthur had drawn it and noted its colouration, she let it fly.

'Lavinia wants her emblem to be the hawk of the Fens,' said Naomi. 'She means a harrier.'

Later, Miss Pikestaff arrived in the schoolroom to send the girls to the kitchen for refreshment. Nouhou, who had formed an attachment to the governess, trailed in her shadow. She had brought a tray of tea for Arthur. Nouhou tarried as if to chaperone, but the attractions of the kitchen must have been too much, for the child made off.

'I wished to thank you for your kindness, sir, supporting me against Lavinia's cruel allegations and hunting me out in the gloom last night. And you a fine gentleman, while I, a mere governess.'

'I could do no less, madam, after you saved Nouhou yester-eve.'

'That poor child. I understand some dark-haired devil threatens you both in London.'

'Quartermain Hurting, I first met him at a party given by Lord Strathearn and Lady Rochester in their home at Marks-fayre.'

'You move in such exalted circles, Mr Tenebris. I wonder now how I ever mistook that rough imposter as an illustrator for *The Book*. I only knew a Mr Tenebris was sent by the Countess and when he presented himself in Reedston as such, I did not think to check his credentials.'

'You were not to know, madam. Your nature leads you to be kind. It is one of your many perfections.'

'And Mrs Gracegirdle tells me this Hurting knew of the villain's designs beforehand. I fear poor Nouhou will never be safe in that city with such scoundrels as Hurting there. I hear his hair alone is an assault upon the spirit.'

'Yes, but Lord Strathearn himself told me how much he values the man. I wonder at it. His Umbra is most singular, too.'

'Promise me you will avoid him utterly on your return. Now we are met I would not wish to hear harm has befallen you.'

'Could we correspond, madam? At some future time, you may seek a position in London. My connections grow and I could vouch that you are amiable and admirable in your duties.'

'Mr Tenebris, I should like nothing more, though this situation does not suit the mail out of season. But surely there is a gentlewoman of your association who would object to you corresponding with a single lady.'

'There is none such, though, I confess, I feel my situation in life could be exceedingly improved if there were a Mrs Tenebris to attend grand gatherings in London upon my arm.'

'And you no doubt seek her among the finest in society,' a pause as Miss Pikestaff's head lowered and her eyes slipped away, 'not a governess, I daresay.'

'Not so, my dearest lady, not if she were as sweet in temperament, as fair of countenance and as modest as you.'

'You are –' she began.

'May I –' said he; but at that moment steps were heard in the hall, the door burst open and Gracegirdles raced in, breathless, as if they had been fetched to some likely alarum.

Arthur found Miss Pikestaff's hand in his and set it free hastily.

◆ ◆ ◆

'Do you have affairs of the heart?' Arthur asked Amorrie when she joined him in the schoolroom after all had left.

'If anything beats inside me, it is the opposite of love.'

Amorrie had been behaving contrarily at Larkenfen, emerging mostly when Arthur was alone and constantly peering around whichever room she visited him in. He had even seen her spying in mirrors – rare, for she had no love of reflections. When pressed as to why, she told Arthur, they revealed too much.

She walked to the edge of the long table and stared at the Ace of Moons illustration. 'Do I look so sour and angry? How is it I am imprisoned upon a wall.'

'How is a mystery. The illustration comes from the imagination of the girls' father.'

'It does not, for I also recognise that lake and tower,' she had turned to face another painting. 'Though it is altered somewhat. Here the trees are impossibly bent, the lake over-dark, the tower writhes like a live thing.'

'"Nothing is as it seems," I hear their father say, 'and "everything is fluxed".'

'That's Hellekin?'

'She is Umbra to the girls' father. You know her?'

'I know to avoid her. She lives by the Whipped Woods. She is a starer.'

'Perhaps Hellekin torments George Gracegirdle with her dreams, as you do me.'

'You plunder mine without my permission. He may do likewise. I have a notion,' she studied the large canvas which portrayed a trio of George Gracegirdle's daughters. 'You have only three, here.'

'What?'

'You should add the fourth girl.'

'What fourth girl?'

'That one,' Amorrie's finger pointed to the window, then abruptly to the brass scuttle where it hesitated and wavered as her eyes flitted around.

'That is a coal bucket.'

'She is in here somewhere. She spies on you, often.'

'Who does?'

'The fourth.'

Arthur had hardly been at ease since he arrived at Larkenfen and disquiet stole up on him now. 'You tease me,' he said, and when she shook her head, 'There are but three daughters.'

'The fourth is different, though a little like the angry one in size and feature. She retreats promptly when she knows I look for her.'

'Can you see her now?' Arthur's gaze joined Amorrie's, casting around the room. He felt cold and unnerved.

'No, I see her fleetingly in shiny ornaments, sometimes in dark windows, twice outside I caught sight of her in water, twice more clearly in mirrors. It is to do with angles. She is careful if she sees me watching.'

An unfelt draught caught the door, swaying it gently.

'She is gone,' said Amorrie. 'She will not speak to me, but her sisters talk often to her, they call her Cassie.'

Arthur's breath stumbled. 'Cassie is dead. She was taken by plague, last year. Why, pray, would she haunt me?'

'You insist that I must haunt you.'

'Is she vengeful... malevolent?'

'Less so than I.'

'What must I do?'

'Put her in your illustration.'

'I cannot.'

'There is space here,' Amorrie pointed to an area of canvas next to Tabitha.

'The Countess...'

''...cannot count nieces; she only knows there are more than two.'

'I cannot paint her because I cannot see her, Amorrie.' Arthur's voice had become a threadbare hunted whisper.

'That is my notion. I will show you.'

'Gods! How?!'

'Tonight.'

◆ ◆ ◆

She appears to Arthur in pigtails, her hair the colour of spice, a herd of dark freckles graze her cheeks and range over her nose. The shy half-smile is enough kindling to set sparks in her deep mahogany eyes. In his mind he sees her stand and sit and move. Her guileless grace keeps him from noticing her stained and tattered garments. Before all ends, her eyes surge into him, flooding his unconscious mind with her understanding. The wisdom discerned here has not come, like Naomi's, from books. It is innate. 'I know you Arthur Tenebris,' says her gaze, 'too well to judge you harshly.'

25 – IT MUST BE THE BENDITH

Stanton

The intervention from Agnieszka – Stanton could only imagine what she had said – gave Grenville pause and made Stanton suspect he was not alone in thinking Muscari capable of mischief.

Maraziel had informed him that Agnieszka uttered little beyond one pronouncement each Cabinet Council meeting, which Jenny M would make efforts to record, but which noone – perhaps not even the Sibyl herself – could make sense of. Then at some later time, an event would happen, or situation arise, that Jenny M would argue gave meaning to Agnieszka's words.

When pressed for examples Maraziel had come up only with: 'In the last of these interminable gatherings she declared: "In France, a cockerel has awoken who will crow over two-thirds of Europe." It came in the midst of a heated discussion about whether Pitt had ordered beef or fowl for the ministers' dinner.'

If Grenville's Umbra's declarations came with a seasoning of prophecy, Stanton wondered if she had warned her ally that the King's life was indeed forfeit. The immediate result of her words was a grudging agreement that Grenville would pass on any of the Viscount's correspondence the Ministry of Retaliation had 'inadvertently intercepted and copied'.

Stanton imposed further and asked if a pass could be arranged for him to visit a prisoner in Baynard Castle Gaol, who was allied to an Umbra that had fallen under suspicion.

Grenville agreed and asked if Stanton would be attending the Countess of Harrington's ball on the morrow's eve. When told 'yes', Grenville shook his head at the declining standards in London society but said he would arrange for the pass and bring it with him to the ball.

Stanton worked late in Westminster and the lamplighters had already been about their duties when he made for home. Much occupied his mind, so he walked back along the river, watching the sparse lights from the deserted wharves of Southwark reflect and shimmer on the black tide. Some rowboats traversed the Thames still, but the stubborn drizzle and over-eager night meant that passengers were few. One or two low-riding, dark-sailed wherries pursued their trade, announcing their presence only when distant lamplight reflections became tangled in their wakes.

One week into his investigations, Stanton felt he was more mired in mystery than before he started. Every discovery produced more questions than answers. The England he thought he knew and helped govern was being replaced by a cryptic serpentine concoction he barely recognised.

'Flee fornication,' a bearded beggarly preacher railed at him from his position by the river. 'Renounce depravity. Save your Umbra from licentiousness and lewdness that ye both may live forever.' A delicate Umbra maiden, simply pretty in a damp pale gown sat at the man's feet. She raised her head to stare at Stanton as he crossed the road.

The preacher's words unfairly spurred Stanton's thoughts to what rumours Isabella might be subject to. He turned at last up one of the many cramped streets and alleyways that climbed from Embankment towards Strand. This one seemed empty and ill-lit. Shadows swarmed its boundaries and ahead of him one such eased back ominously against a doorway. As Stanton's steps slowed, soft padding came from behind him. The luminescence of Strand beckoned but from too far away.

As he stalled a small icy hand grasped his finger and he looked down to find a darker shadow standing beside him. The little urchin from the Africas raised a sombre face towards him and tugged him to return down the alley.

As he retraced his steps to the river a silhouette stepped out into the gap at the end of the alley and stood in a wide-legged stance staring towards him. Stanton recognised the spry figure of Larkwing.

'You do not wear your dandy cravat, Minister,' the agent greeted him as the silent black guttersnipe merged back into night.

'No, Lady Stanton has threatened to take the poker to it, if she finds it again around my neck.'

'She is a caution.'

◆ ◆ ◆

Larkwing chose the bustling bar-room of The Sailor's Curse over the crypt-like silence of The Darkling Queen.

'What is the sailor's curse?' asked Larkwing as he returned with two small beers from the scrum at the bar to Stanton's hard-won corner of a table.

'To be Umbra-less.'

'Of course,' Larkwing laughed and clapped Stanton's arm. 'I had suspected something altogether more salacious.'

Stanton stared around, hemmed in by lusty inebriation and rumbustious banter. 'Is this a fit place?'

'None have entered since we. We are not followed. Have you found out more about either of our suspects?'

'I make progress, but you needs brief your Minister better.'

'It is true then,' Larkwing found Stanton's eyes over his glass, 'you were in the company of the Earl of Grenville?'

'Yes, I assumed as Minister of your department, he was aware of your investigations. He is not and caused a near fatal obstruction to our enquiries.'

'Ah, we work on the basis of a requirement to know, Minister. Grenville is the political wing, not the service.'

'Well he thinks he runs the service. I should warn you that you are likely to be hauled before him.'

Larkwing took a rueful sip. 'You gave him my name?'

'I had to, man. It was the price of his assistance.'

'No matter. Any more news?'

'The affair is more serious than I realised. I have stumbled upon a plot by the Umbra against the Clergy.'

'Our Umbra?'

'How many can there be? It seems someone's Umbra does murder in the Other Realm to disable the running of England – even the Church falls prey to them.'

Larkwing looked rightly astonished.

'Grenville has agreed to show me copies of correspondence between Exeter and his closest confidante. He will also grant me a pass to Baynard Castle Gaol.'

'Why so?'

'I may have uncovered another murdering Umbra and that is where her ally is currently imprisoned.'

Larkwing's eyes gleamed, 'Marvellous, I mean, good work Minister. I will accompany you if I may.'

'If you must. There is no connection to the French affair, as far as I know.'

'My Ministry believes all murderous Umbra are potential suspects.'

'Very well, the pass should be ready by Monday. I will need some time with the prisoner alone to discuss other matters, but we will see if we can induce him to summon his Umbra – she is thought a Banshee.'

'What is that?'

'A screaming hell-hag by best accounts.'

◆ ◆ ◆

The ball came as an unwanted distraction for Stanton but he endeavoured, for Isabella's sake, to attempt a smile and speak charmingly. Jane, Countess of Harrington did likewise when she was introduced to Maraziel and he. Her Umbra, Scampion, frowned and refused to doff his hat. Stanton wondered if the slight was because the Countess disapproved of his lowly birth or because they had arrived with her rival, Lady R, sharing her carriage from Marksfayre.

Both, confided Isabella, adding that Scampion never removed his hat for anyone. She said that he should not be cast down for he was, 'a match for any man in the room in charm, style and graciousness and Maraziel more formidable than any woman – human or Umbra.'

There were around fifty guests in the room, all with their Umbra and no sign yet of Viscount Exeter.

Stanton saw the Earl of Grenville with Agnieszka and tarried nearby until he was without company, setting Isabella and Lady R free to promenade the room.

Grenville glowered at him before handing over a sheaf of papers. He said softly, 'I give you this only because the King's life may be at stake. If this falls upon the wrong ears or is misused in any way, Stanton, I'll see you drummed out of Westminster or hung, whichever can be soonest arranged. Exeter will be here shortly, but you will not cause a scene at Jane's home.'

'Of course not, milord,' Stanton hid the documents in an inside pocket. 'And the pass to Baynard Castle Gaol?'

'Also in the papers. Do not let any murderous fellows escape if you can help it.'

Agnieszka had left her quiver and bow elsewhere and wore a grey dress, exhibiting depths of bruise blue within it. It swirled tightly about her figure as if wringing with damp but left no stain on Grenville's shoulder. Her arms were bare, and the dress held in place by a tiny mussel shell. Her honey hair billowed above her head in such a fashion that Stanton wondered if she had been summoned while plummeting through a lake.

She had so far spent the encounter playing with a necklace formed of bubbles of air trapped within a sheen of water, now her bi-colour grey and blue irises pinned Stanton with the previous afternoon's intensity, and she spoke.

Grenville listened, nodded at Stanton and Maraziel, and said: 'Not this one, then?' His Umbra shook her head before he continued. 'Now we are engaged on this together, Stanton, I expect reports as soon as aught is discovered.'

'Do we tell the King?'

'What? To keep Miss Lightfoot close; not to let her tarry in the Other Realm close to treacherous Umbra? I think not, sir. I half believe this plot is born from your delusions and have no wish to join you – or, indeed, the King – in the madhouse.

'Now I think I will pay my regards to your delightful lady wife.' His eyes lit upon Maraziel, 'Do not let him stray too far in this world alone, madam. It is no place for innocents.' He stepped away.

Agnieszka's eyes lingered on Stanton a moment longer.

'He thinks me your keeper,' said Maraziel. 'While the wet thing on his shoulder thinks there is something in your concerns.'

'That's useful.'

'It is not. Her head is two-thirds full of fish. I cannot think upon what they feed.'

'What did she say when she stared at me. Those bi-colour eyes of hers are unnerving.'

'She said, we "must beware the Umbra-less man." I would not worry about it for a week or so, then one may turn up. Agnieszka possesses the happy talent of making the inscrutable incomprehensible.'

Her head swivelled, following Stanton's gaze as Grenville took Isabella's hand. 'Observe Twoscrews,' she said, deliberately mispronouncing his name, 'dressed like a gallant huntsman in his runed cape, twittering incessantly to his ally. Your woman has the goodness of heart not to confide that 'tis balderdash and scandal, so all Englishmen and women assume him amiable and shrewd. Perhaps he is; after all, he was wily enough to speak French to Lady Rochester?'

Stanton grunted.

'Look, there are your friends from the Queen's Halls.'

Stanton saw the Chancellor of Balliol with Dawn Withheld and exclaimed, 'The Chancellor, blast him. He told Cotteridge he would return to Oxford today.'

'Sadly not.'

'I have reports of magicks I would discuss with him.'

'I am prodigiously fond of magicks. Discuss them with me.'

Stanton took out his examples and read them to Maraziel, finishing with, 'Do not imagine I think any of these could be true?'

'I like the one about the chess-piece, ever-returning to places it is not wanted. I have known Piskies with similar inclinations. And how old is the roof in the church with whispering wooden angels in it?'

'At least five hundred years, I should think,' said Stanton.

'Well, it seems unlikely they would have anything left to say to each other.'

'I wish you would be serious.'

'I wish you would find this chronicler's account of the Treaty signing as you pledged to.'

'The Archbishop has sent for it, but it is yet to arrive.'

'Religion ever promises more than it can deliver.' Maraziel peered at him through her corona of hair, 'Have you investigated these accounts of magicks?'

'Not yet.'

'Do so. Magicks take immense energy, there will be a purpose, a pattern; discover it.'

'There are many hundreds.'

'Start with these eight. Oh no, they are coming to talk to us.'

The Chancellor was stepping across the room.

'His Nymph has the stormiest glare in Cernyw. She must make a practice of it in every pool she passes.'

'Her glare is reserved purely for you, I think,' said Stanton. 'You better leave me, Maraziel. I needs speak to them.'

'You are sure? She looks fierce. Well, I do not complain if it frees me to return to my bed.'

'You have done your duty and I thank you for it. I will not call upon you again this night.'

'And I had my hair done just so. Take care with Muscari, if she materialises.' Maraziel stood, shook her grizzled swarm of hair, stepped into Stanton's shadow and was gone.

The Chancellor's pout was wry as he greeted Stanton, 'Ahem, Minister, you have ferreted me out.'

The Chancellor's moon face was already flushed with drink. Dawn Withheld made a show of being gay, but the way she eyed Stanton for any lingering scrap of Maraziel, suggested her wits could be called upon at any time.

'Your man told me that you wished for another meeting.'

'And you told him you were travelling to Oxford.'

'On the morrow. After all, one cannot say no to the Countess of Harrington, especially for an evening of such captivating company. You find me in merry spirits and your man's description of reports of so many magicks did intrigue me, I must confess.'

'I have a few examples with me.'

'Ah, so you thought to find me here. You are like the Burford Highwayman, sir, hunting me out before I am home and requiring me to stand and deliver my knowledge. Ask me what you will.'

'Well, there is a report from Baynard Castle Gaol. It claims that a single personage was split into two, one dangerous and intent upon theft or worse; the other half weak, quiet and cowardly. They have the brutal specimen incarcerated until the pair can be reformed into one person. Can you make anything of it?'

'It is almost certainly nonsense but if your description calls anything to mind, it is the Bendith. Its visits are rare indeed but have been recorded in our past.'

'What is the Bendith?'

'It is as you described; a spirit creature sent from the Other

Realm. It takes over a human's life, by making a twin of it.'

'Like a changeling, at birth?'

'There is a connection, but changelings are a swap; this is an occupation. The Bendith divides the person in two and takes control of one of the pair. That self retains all memories and is imbued with vigour and life force. That half is set upon its mission. The lesser self, the original, continues its life, but as a spiritless shell, capable of simple errands under instruction, but little more.'

'Is the Bendith capable of murder?'

'Assuredly so, assassination is its purpose. Its last known resurrection came when it was brought unto life to kill the Queen 'Neath the Hedge. Bent on her end, it divided and took control of one of her close lieutenants, killed two more and would have likely done for the Queen, but that she was warned of the creature's presence by one of the Dead lords.'

'Shait'n?'

'Another I think. If the story is to be believed. Thomas Hearn wrote of it in 1725, but I have never seen the contemporary account.'

'By Peter of Langtoft?'

The Chancellor chuckled too loudly, 'Oh very good, Minister. You are on your game.'

'Who sent the Bendith against the Queen?'

'The El –', Dawn Withheld jumped up to impede the Chancellor's mouth, berating him ferociously. He was momentarily shocked but recovered. 'Yes, you are right, m'dear. Dawn points out that it was never discovered who resurrected the creature, or if the story is even true. It would be wrong for me to suggest I knew. Haha, and I doubt your prisoner is the Bendith.'

'Nor, in truth, do I, Chancellor. Why do you not believe it?'

'For one thing, we are not far from Baynard Castle here, yet we are beset by rain and cloud. The Bendith cloaks itself in sunlight. It can control weather, the windy element, to some extent and keeps it fine. It blesses its locality with sunny weather. Bendith is Welsh for "blessing". Any scrap of moonlight shows it in its true form. Also, in the 14th century, Britain was very different, Minister. Magick flowed between the realms. All kinds of creatures slipped through. The Queen opened doors that should have stayed closed. When she died, magick speedily drained from our world.'

There was excitement at the door as Viscount Exeter made his entry into the room. The Countess of Harrington swept across to greet him. Stanton could see no sign of his Umbra and there was no repeat of the performance Isabella had described, when Exeter and Muscari arrived at Lady R's party. Two young women arrived in Exeter's wake.

'Then, what do you make of my reports that magicks are increasing in Britain?' said Stanton.

'Magicks are bursting out all over; every hedgerow, copse and pond, or so your man Cotteridge has it. However, people will rush to apportion any occurrence, no matter its banality, to Umbra and imagined magicks. The common folk require illusion to make reality bearable.'

'Can you tell me why the Church and the Queen were so at odds?' Stanton's eyes and thoughts had travelled over to the sight of Exeter, who had left the Countess and was now in gay conversation with Grenville, Isabella and Lady Rochester. Isabella had been singled out for an especially warm greeting.

'Obvious, Minister; she had defeated the King and ruled our land in his stead. The Catholic Church saw a challenge in everything she stood for; everything she proved. To them, she was an archetypal devil – a fiend who unleashed pagan creatures and magick phenomena upon the land; who not only threw open the doors of Hell but ruled there for a time; and, perhaps worst of all, a woman – only the hated Empress Maude ever attempted to rule as Queen before her.'

'That explains only why the Church feared her.'

'She abominated the Church because Longshanks told her common folk needed a God. If she must abolish Catholicism, he pleaded, she should allow him an Anglican religion. But it was still God, and still required faith. She began to believe it was Him or her. She determined He must be forsaken. The monasteries were suppressed, but she under-estimated the influence of the Church, I think. Eventually, of course, God outlasted her.'

'So even the Anglicans...'

'She would destroy them, if she could.'

The Chancellor turned to go and Stanton, half his attention on Isabella, let him, but then the Oxford don paused. 'What was your Bendith's mission?'

'To discover the Queen's Sprig.'

'Truly,' the plump man spun back, 'that is improba... er... curious. Who from pray?'

'One of the few reputable families left in the Fens.'

'Good Lord, the Gracegirdles.' The Chancellor and Dawn Withheld shared a look and words passed between them. Stanton felt the Chancellor had again been warned to give away no more.

'Minister, I hope my assistance has earned some reward. If this woman incarcerated in Baynard Castle is indeed the Bend –'

'It isn't a woman. It's a man, did I not say?'

'A man? Then it is surely not the Bendith. For she is female and must seek out a woman as host.'

26 – THE GREY BRETHREN

Larkenfen

The artist's whistling intruded into her contemplation. He was awake early, walking outside and the whistle, though unmelodic, was fat with satisfaction.

She heard Naomi say her name and discovered her sister in the schoolroom.

'Look at what Mr Tenebris has done,' said Naomi. 'He must have been working since before first light.'

The large canvas roughed out for all the Gracegirdle girls, which had numbered just three when Amorrie's hunting gaze had driven her out of the room last night, now had a fourth completing the composition. Cassie gawped at her likeness, beyond astonishment.

'It is not finished,' said Naomi. 'He says we must choose you an emblem to add to the picture, like my ruby darter, or Livvi's fen-hawk. Perhaps, also, something for you to hold.'

'How is this possible? He has never seen me? He cannot see me.'

'You came to him in a dream he says.'

'I did no such thing.'

'But then he changed his thought and said it was Amorrie's dream?'

'It makes no sense. I have not learned that trick yet. Would that I could. If it were possible, I would visit you always in your dreams, Naomi.'

'You do already, Cassie. Most every night.'

'Like this?' Cassie held up her pigtails and stared down at her fraying garments.

'I don't know, I never notice how your hair is done or what fashions you wear.'

'What then?'

'I memorise your smile and hold fast to your eyes and feel your clear thinking and sense your breath, and...' Naomi's voice had slipped into a well of emotion.

'Would you dream of me still, if I did not visit you here?'

'Most certainly.' Naomi grew concerned, 'why?'

'It is good to know. That is all.'

Naomi studied her sister closely.

'He has made my clothes new again.' Cassie took up the pictured pose and tried out the smile. 'Is it a good likeness, do you think?'

'It is a miracle,' said Naomi. 'The painting is raw yet, but already it is manifestly you.'

'What will Mother and Papa make of it?'

'Mother will cry for a day,' said a voice behind them, 'and we will get nothing out of Papa for at least a week.' It was Lavinia. The tear had already fallen from her chin and was now soaking into her sleeve, but its track on her cheek bore testimony to it. 'And then his first words will still choke him.'

A movement behind her and Nouhou entered the room with Tabitha. The former page-boy stared at the painting, first in bewilderment before slipping into understanding and finally, wonder.

'It's Cassie, Nouhou,' Tabitha's words fought for air in her throat before she took a sobbing breath. 'Our dearest sister. Your Mr Tenebris has somehow captured her likeness.'

'Mr Tenebris started his assault on Larkenfen in cowardly retreat, but with this he will conquer us all,' said Naomi.

'I have made a decision about Mr Tenebris,' said Lavinia.

'What?'

'We cannot allow Pikestaff to have him.'

◆ ◆ ◆

'Are they there?' Tabitha sat in the small flat-bottomed boat, tied to the jetty at the end of the boardwalk. She looked out across the lazing sun-stroked river to the far bank.

'I think they only come at dusk, or that is when they are observable, and I distinguish the murmur of them above the sigh of the river. Or, if they are there all the time, then the sunlight shines through them and makes them invisible.' Cassie sat upon the jetty, above the bobbing Tabitha.

'Do they call across to you?'

'No, but I feel they want to.'

'Do they still distress you?'

'Not as much as they distress themselves.'

'Are...' Tabitha's voice dropped, 'are they Greynhym?'

'They do not appear warlike.'

'Do not go over there, Cassie.'

'I cannot, for I cannot cross the river.'

'You cannot because you belong here with us.'

'I have been trapped on the wrong side of the river by events and cannot find my way over. If a way over is shown to me, then I will have to decide.'

'It is not Heaven, you know.'

'It is most surely hell.'

'If you go over there...what then?'

'Once there, I do not think I am allowed back.'

Tabitha pulled herself up on the thick ropes, which kept the boat tight to the jetty and sprawled over the boards in serpentine loops beyond the post. Near the top she held a hand out to Cassie for aid and the older girl laughed, 'You are on your own, Tabby, my hands are no use to you.'

A footfall of steps brought Naomi out from the shadowed boardwalk where slender alder, birch and willow struggled clear of the marsh to scratch at the sky.

'Nouhou is with me,' she warned. 'We've been watching pool creatures. I could hear you both. Nouhou will imagine you are talking to yourself, Tabby.'

'Where is he?'

'He was with me until we came in sight of you, but he stopped. I think he saw something in a pool.'

'Will he be alright? He is such a timid child.'

'Miss Pikestaff has it that he has been threatened by this black-haired ruffian in Smoothfield, for so he has confided in her,' said Naomi.

'Mr Tenebris says the same. I do not think we should let him return to London with Mr Tenebris until it is safer for him there,' said Tabitha.

'Let us talk to mother about it.' Naomi had climbed a small way up a tree and now shaded her eyes to make out Ely Cathedral rising up beyond the reeds, distant marshes and fields. She could only just make it out for grey clouds hung above it, as if tethered there, an unwilling congregation.

'Cassie has chosen the swallow as her emblem,' said Tabitha.

'I am surprised she did not decide on the raft spider, after her instructive use of it against Arnold.'

'It was the first thing I found that I could pick up, and then only because it was dead, I think.' Cassie gave a shiver, 'I have no love for them, truly.'

'First Galt, who we could not grab because he is bonded to Miss Pikestaff, now you can hold dead things, Cassie, perhaps you are becoming alive again.' There was a yearning need within Naomi's thought.

'Hardly; that is not possible.'

'Cassie wanted something explorish and every winter swallows fly south,' said Tabitha.

'Across France, over the sentinel Pyrenees, and Moorish Spain and right down to the Africas,' said Cassie. 'My emblem travels where I cannot.'

'And we will ask Mr Tenebris if Cassie may hold an ornament or sculpture in the shape of an angel in the painting.'

‘To symbolise death?’ Naomi made a face, ‘It may be apt, Cassie, but it is morbid.’

‘Angels represent faith, hope, trust and love, too,’ said Tabitha.

‘When, one day, you follow our painting down to London and Aunt Jane introduces you to hordes of young gallants, they may ask, “where is this fourth sister?” The angel makes it clear which of us was taken by the pestilence,’ Cassie said.

‘We will find a way to take you with us.’

‘I will be long gone by then.’ Cassie laughed, ‘I cannot be expected to look after you three for ever. I have my death to lead.’

‘Tell her she is not to go over the river, Naomi.’

‘You are nev –’ started Naomi but stopped as Nouhou ran out from the trees. He opened his hands and a small repentant yellow frog leapt from it, flew straight through Cassie and landed with a plop in the Lark.

27 – BLIND UMBRA HUNT

Stanton

'I see Exeter fawns over Lord Lisle's daughter.'

'That is the least he can do, given that he is the cause of her ruination.'

Stanton had slipped onto a balcony moments before, intending to check on the documents the Earl of Grenville had passed to him. The two young female voices came from the other side of the drape he had half-closed behind him, causing him to return the sheaf of papers to his pocket. He edged closer to the gap in the curtain. The two young women who had entered with Viscount Exeter were close by, conversing in low tones while they watched the dancing.

From the darkness between the drapes Stanton could see they were uncommonly pretty, one dressed in a shiny gown that had begun as lamentable lilac but veered close to black. The gown left her shoulders bare. Stanton couldn't imagine how it clung to her bust and arms. Her confidant was gowned in white with puffed sleeves. Both had their hair pulled back and tamed into ringlets in the fashionable style. They were speaking of Isabella.

'So I heard. For a daughter of a Lord to give herself too freely before wedlock; what could she have been thinking?'

The dark-gowned woman turned mischievous. 'Why, Clo, that Exeter's fortune outstripped her father's of course, and, if he were honourable, he must marry her after.'

'Few men are ever that honourable.'

'My guardian says as much, but she was young at the time and has paid a hard price for it, marrying so far below her station.'

'Lucky to have married at all.'

'Is she pretty do you think, Clo?'

'Tolerable.'

The music ended and the women clapped perfunctorily and moved away to secure partners for the next dance.

Stanton slipped back in from the balcony and watched as Grenville led Isabella onto the floor. The 'contemptible rumours' the Earl had mentioned yesterday, had found their way to Stanton's ears soon enough.

While he watched Isabella, Viscount Exeter veered into his vision. 'Minister Stanton,' he gave a stiff bow. 'Izzy pointed you out. We seem to be the only two Umbra-less men in the room.'

'Viscount,' Stanton was taken by surprise, and Agnieszka's counsel or premonition to beware the Umbra-less man, clanged in his mind. Was she warning the Earl about Exeter? He was also shocked to hear anyone other than himself, or close family, call Isabella by her pet name.

'Maraziel was with me earlier, but she takes no particular enjoyment from balls and begged leave to return to the Other Realm. What of your Umbra?'

'Muscari is on other duties tonight,' said Exeter.

'Back in the Other Realm. Where does she hail from?'

Exeter was taken aback by the question. 'I hardly know, somewhere west I daresay. Are not they all dwellers of mountain and moor, forest stream or lonely strand?

'I came over because I see that we are in competition for the vacancies among The Five Hundred and I wanted to introduce myself and wish you every fortune in securing elevation. I would see Izzy – forgive me, I mean Lady Stanton; we have been close since childhood – in *The Book* too. She would unquestionably grace its pages.'

'I thank you, sir.' Every part of this was unexpected. Stanton had only heard of Exeter's pride and reserve. He shelved the two questions he wanted to ask: What did you do to my wife? And, Is your Umbra away killing Hannah Lightfoot? Instead, he said, 'Though I'm sure your place in *The Book* is guaranteed.'

'Perhaps so, but less deserved. I hear your new Ministry causes quite the stir.'

'If, by "stir" you mean taking action to secure the realm, then yes, sir, I stir for England.' Stanton's anger took horse, spurred not by Exeter's innocent remark but by all that had come before.

Exeter caught the animosity. 'The thing about stirs, Minister, is that they require good outcomes. Take care you sweeten the pot, for if it is thought poisoned thereafter, then you will be made to drink it.'

'You have been talking to Grenville, I see.'

'Yes, but he is always sparing in praise for any man, saving his cousin, Pitt.'

'And his brother in the Navy.'

'It is a close community, the Parliament, Mr Stanton. More ties exist between family and fortune than between Whigs and Tories. I worry you are disadvantaged by your lack of these connections. Now, forgive me, I am promised in this next dance.' He took heel and strode away.

As Stanton wondered what had just befallen, the music dropped and couples bowed. The young woman in the near-black dress was walking directly towards him, a dare running ahead on her gaze. He saw the train of her ball gown was pinned up, ready for the dance. The Umbra on her shoulder was her opposite: white-haired where she was dark, stooped where she was tall, head and gaze lowered humbly where hers were proud. The Umbra was near-naked, with pale runes decorating the dark sinewy limbs on show. The mystery of her gown was solved for the Umbra hauled at threads that kept her modesty intact.

'That is at least two dances you have missed, sir,' she said.

'May I claim you for the next one? I saw you dance with Lord Lisle's daughter before. You seem to have mastered the basics.'

This was scant praise. Stanton had been assiduous in his dance lessons, just as he had hoarded all Latin that came his way, gleaned every scrap of etiquette, worried the grooms to better his horsemanship and borrowed and polished his way of speech. His father had been but a steward, but Stanton was schooled with the two sons of his employer's family in gentlemanly fashion. He took his father's words to heart, 'Others will be judged on their fortunes, estates and ancestry, Sebastian; you will be judged on your flaws.'

Refusing dance offers from society ladies would be a flaw – poor etiquette. He bowed his ascent to the dance, and she forgot her curtsey. 'Do I know you? You must be at least a baronet to be at Jane's function,' she said. 'Are you too young for *The Book*?'

'No, madam, too new.'

'Let me guess, a Parliament man then?'

'You have me, madam, and you are?'

'Let us preserve our anonymity, for now. We can be frigates adrift on the night swell with just the suspicion of something flickering…' she took his hand as they approached the floor, '… below decks.'

As the dance began and they met to clasp hands in the middle of the floor, she said, 'You must give more to the dance, sir, your head is still in Whitehall.'

'I fear you are correct, my –' he managed before they sprang back to skip behind another couple.

'You are aware of the function of the dance, sir?'

'Remembering the steps,' said Stanton as the jaunty swirl of the frenetic dance again brought them close.

'No, that is the poorest reading of it,' she said, as they tripped down a corridor of dancers. 'It is little to do with feet, everything to do with the eyes.' Hers batted demurely at him as they faced each other again. 'For we single ladies, this is courtship, or as close as we are allowed to it. The room may be full, but your eyes must be mine alone. They should evoke every kind of...' she was gone again.

'Impropriety,' she murmured as they stepped together again.

'Even if...' Stanton's voice had become a little lower and breathless.

'...especially if.'

At the next meeting of four dancers, Stanton found himself facing Isabella, who gave him a wondering and stern stare as they stepped around each-other.

A twirl, and his partner had him to herself again. 'By now, sir, if I have any arts or grace, Countess Harrington's ballroom will have dissolved to shifting shadows. Through my eyes you are transported to an alluring harem in far-off Samarkand.'

'Your imagination, madam is –' he started, but a finger flaring towards her lips quietened him.

'Your gaze sees through my gown. You leave me in only my shift, sir. Do you not see?'

Stanton was starting to think he could. Was her Umbra loosening the threads he had previously grasped so resolutely?

'Now, I see your eyes insist that I let it fall...' the rhythm of her whispers matched the swell of the dance. Stanton's feet found their steps by rote. As they came together again, with a lewd hiss, '...you have reduced me to this. I am your wanton...'

The music ended, the couples faced one-another, and Stanton just remembered to bow. To his dismay his partner let out an animal whoop, leapt a little in the air and applauded wildly. All eyes turned.

'I should have said, madam, that I am married,' confided Stanton, flushed and breathless as they made to part.

'I knew that, of course, Minister Stanton, to my friend Isabella. I noticed you earlier, retreating behind the balcony curtain.' She turned and ran to where her friend waited.

He discovered Isabella's arm in his, and she guided him off the dance floor.

Her face was set in a smile. 'Well danced, indeed, Sebastian,' she passed him a handkerchief for he was sweating.

'She… who?'

Isabella shook her head, her smile relaxed into something more natural. 'I am prepared to forgive you your infatuation with Lady R, Sebastian' she said 'We all endure that; and even your passing passion for secret spies of names various, but I draw the line when it comes to Desi Fitzroy… the less-than-honourable.' She stifled a laugh. Twoshrews smiled knowingly.

'Isn't she…?'

'Grenville's ward, yes.'

'He is so severe and strict with his colleagues, I wonder he hasn't taken her in hand.'

'She can do little wrong in his eyes,' said Isabella, 'whereas you…'

Stanton groaned.

◆ ◆ ◆

'Take care not to let yourself be played by artful women, sir, for I have noticed that you are susceptible to our imagined charms.' Lady Rochester had him for the next dance.

Dancing was like horses, Isabella said, when you have had a tumble, you must return to the saddle as quickly as you may. Lady R had reneged on a promise to some lord or princeling, in order to escort Stanton back onto the floor.

'Beauty is seductive, a black-sailed galleon to pursue across a breathless ocean, drifting away whenever you think it may be boarded, then just as you reach for its booty…' the dance swirled Lady R away from him, then she reeled him in again, '… a storm breaks over you.'

'A storm of…?' Stanton said as his slim, yet imposing partner sashayed close again, whorls of red-black hair and every glance in the room frothing in her wake.

'Innuendo, in my experience. Once tainted by that sort of reputation it hangs upon you like an exhausted albatross. Such is how I recently described it to young Mr Coleridge.'

'I hardly think I was to blame, on this occasion, Lady R.'

'Do not seek to blame Desdemona's stratagems, she is in the invidious position of being a still single woman,'

'She is young, beautiful, wealthy and spirited, madam, she will have no shortage of suitors,' Stanton made his point through the comings and goings of the dance.

'Dearest sir, how little you appreciate the rigours of maidenhood. Desdemona reminds me a little of my younger self.'

'I cannot believe you were ever so desperate, Lady Rochester.'

'It is the abundance of suitors that is our quandary. Do any men look beyond beauty and fortune in their cravings? No woman can be sure her beau loves her for herself, if she is both comely and of good family.'

They went two more rounds of the dance before she added '... saving Isabella, of course.'

The dance ended but Lady Rochester kept his hand. 'No, Desdemona is not for you. If you must stray, choose a married lover. The Countess perhaps... Jane is supposed the epitome of virtue but Charles is away often and she is desperate for daughters.'

'Madam, you jest; I would be beneath her.'

She gave him a sharp glance. 'A maid then. Have you a pretty maid?'

He laughed uncertainly, unable to read whether she was in earnest. 'Midden's looks are less evident than her nerves.'

'Oh dear, that sounds the worst combination. She must go.'

'I must go, madam.'

Her next words held him. 'You seek a spy, I hear.'

'Did Isabe –?'

'No, your wife is too shrewd for that, but Parliament brims with over-eager men who mistake gossip for news.'

'Who?'

'One is much like another and all know I am too featherbrained to employ their reports, let alone remember their names. I daresay they think I may bestow favours on them in return for the latest French intrigue.' She attempted an innocent look. 'What favours, I cannot guess.'

'Do you have information, madam?'

She was watching Isabella and Twoshrews chat with Exeter. 'On French infiltration...? I do.' She turned away. 'Look closer to home.'

◆ ◆ ◆

Carriages came and went, couples departed first, soon only the Countess and fourteen of her guests remained. Among them: Isabella, Stanton and Lady R; also, Desi Fitzroy and her friend, Exeter and Grenville too.

The Countess scolded Exeter and (by association of his omission) Stanton too, for being without their Umbra. She had intended to play the party game Blind Umbra Hunt at the end of the evening, she said, but that would now be impossible.

Lady Rochester stepped forward. 'Capu also has returned to his own realm,' she said, 'and there is one woman too many. I can play the parts of Viscount Exeter's and Minister Stanton's Umbra for the operation of the game.'

'There, Jane,' said Desi Fitzroy to the Countess: 'fetch the cards and blindfolds; tell servants to prepare rooms, we shall have our entertainment after all.'

Stanton would have preferred to be back home – he had much to think on – but Isabella was enjoying the evening and the attention she received.

He had never before played Blind Umbra Hunt but understood the mechanics, and could guess the motivation, of the game. Cards were picked secretively by Umbra to pair off one man and one woman and decide which of the two were 'Hunter' and which 'Prey'. All were then blindfolded and the Prey led to a room by their Umbra and sat upon a chair.

All players could ask one question of their Umbra to try to guess at the identity of the other half of their pair. The Hunter was led to the room after to undertake one action. The rules suggested that the Hunter should whisper a secret, apply a chaste kiss, or ask an immodest question; women could apply a dab of scent; men could leave a token.

Umbra could report any untoward or unwanted attention, though this was rare and not in the spirit of the game. Convention advocated that Umbra paired off husbands and wives if both were present and couples thought to be soon-engaged or known to be in courtship. Grenville was 'charting a course' for his ward, Desi, to dock in Exeter's harbour, Stanton had learnt. He could not imagine two more poorly-suited dispositions and hesitated to think on what might occur if Desi were the Hunter in this likely pairing.

The blindfolded guests now sat in a circle while the Umbra were handed their cards by Lady Rochester with a whispered 'Prey' or 'Hunter'.

Stanton allowed himself to be led by Lady R into a room – Prey. He could tell the lights were low but felt the heat of a candle as he passed. An upright chair awaited him, and he heard Lady R leave. Outside he heard the giggles and low converse of waiting Hunters. He had forgotten to ask her any oblique question to guess at the identity of his Hunter.

There followed a long wait before the whisper of a door opening and light female steps approached. The candle flared closer and he imagined the Hunter carried it to a nearby table. If it was Isabella, Twoshrews would be guiding her.

The tension built. Some light pressure circled his sleeve. A scent, but it was not Isabella's. The rustle of a gown but no clues there. Hair tickled his cheek, then away. He felt warm breath close to his face; to his lips. He was kissed, there, urgently, a hand coming around to pull his head forward into hers. His resistance fell away and then it was over.

But no. The same lips brushed against his ear. A voice, pitched low and harsh, so he could not recognise it, hissed: 'We are not meant to know too much about Umbra, Minister. For Isabella's sake, desist now.'

He struggled up, heard the whoof of breath, sensed the candle going out. He reached for the woman, but one of his arms had been secured to the chair. She had skipped away. He used his free arm to wrench off the blindfold. He lurched after her in the darkness, the chair came with him and both crashed to the floor. As he lay there entangled, he heard the swish of the door open and close.

He untied his arm in the darkness and ran to the door. Opening it, he saw Desi Fitzroy talking to her friend and two other male guests, all Hunters, he assumed. They caught something of his flush of anger or confusion and Desi burst into laughter. Exeter and Lady Rochester emerged from another corridor a moment later. And then others were surfacing, laughing and with expressions of mock shock upon their faces.

Isabella was tripping towards him, as flushed as he, her smile spreading, turning roguish. She took his arm and whispered in his ear, 'That, Sebastian, was by no means a chaste kiss. By the heavens, your blood runs hot tonight.'

He realised that she believed he had been her Hunter. Isabella laughed and confided, 'If that is what dancing with Desi Fitzroy and Lady R stirs in you, we must attend more balls.'

Twoshrews refused to meet Stanton's eye.

Grenville called over, 'Were you Prey or Huntress, Lady Stanton?'

'I have been most royally Preyed upon, my Lord. Only bones remain.'

Grenville's eyebrow raised to Stanton.

'I do not believe I am at liberty to say more under the rules of the game, my lord,' Stanton found himself bedding in the fiction with his coyness – he did not see what else he could do without mortifying Isabella.

'That is decidedly the most important rule of the game,' the Countess said hurriedly. Fetchingly aglow, she near matched her Umbra's cursing crimson hat.

Stanton wondered if she may be overly enjoying the absence of the Third Earl, who had not been able to attend, being called away to oversee the muster of the 29th Regiment of Foot, of which he was Colonel. Then he put her flush alongside Lady Rochester's comments and role in the game and wondered anew.

Stanton left to call for Lady Rochester's carriage. On re-entering the room, he paused to take in Isabella's laughing discourse with Lady R and the Countess. If she was not quite their match in beauty, she outdid them in charm. Across the room he noticed Exeter studying Isabella too and remembered the correspondence Grenville had been so loath to give him, neglected in a pocket.

'How did you know it was me?' he asked as Isabella and he travelled home alone. The carriage would return for Lady Rochester, who had business with the Countess.

'That was easy, Sebastian,' she replied. 'Before you came in, I asked Twoshrews, "Is my Hunter also my true love?" My foolish Piskie thought a moment and then answered: "He is your truest love, indeed."'

28 – THE RUNE-CLOAKED SERPENT

Exeter's Letter

To Colonel J. Fairweather Esquire

Dear James,

Think on this:

Suppose there is but one soul in the world whose temper and disposition fits your own, whose handsomeness and status are a complement to yours, and who desires you as much as you do them. Suppose you do not then recognise this attraction and let it fall beyond your life's path…?

I write because I have undertaken further investigation on the matter to which you recently brought my attention, regarding your friend, Lady Isabella Stanton and the wilful and wanton way that her reputation has been sullied by the uncommon gossip you have overheard.

As you know, at our last meeting I confided in you that I had discovered a letter in a most unlikely hiding place and was much perplexed by it. Here, I extend a little more detail of its contents. It purported to be addressed to me and was signed by Isabella Cavendish, as she then was in her maidenhood, and it made mention of her devotion to me for the service I had previously rendered her father, Lord Lisle, which we need not go into here, and also the deep affection that she held for me.

Although I have scarce any experience in such matters, it is clear to me that this was a love letter, delicately disguised, but its motive was surely to convince me of her devotions and willingness to enter into a courtship with me. It was dated two years prior to my discovery of it, addressed from Laycester Manor, where we had both attended a ball, danced on no less than three occasions, and, I think, began to suspect that we suited each other very well. The letter must have been delivered on the night immediately after the ball while we both stayed at the Manor.

It pains me now to relate that this letter never reached me, and I was quite ignorant of the fierceness of her affection, for surely it is uncommon rare for a maiden of seventeen or eighteen to trust so intently in a gentleman's honesty and honour to expose her feelings to him openly. Even without sight of the letter, I would still have pursued her for I had known her and her family for many years and had already recognised in Lord Lisle's youngest daughter someone whose quick wits, considered opinions and liveliness would make for my ideal companion. Had I opened that letter then and found that this feeling was mutual, I daresay I would have spoken straightway to my father and her own and asked for her hand.

But that next morning, someone I shall not name here -- as I am sure they acted from good-hearted motives -- took me to one-side and warned me that my intentions towards Isabella were misplaced and that she was pretending to show me favour as a prank devised with her cousin -- Connie Cavendish most like -- as she wished to wound my pride. Perhaps, still, I would not have rushed to judgement except that Muscari then told me she had taken the trouble to seek out news of Twoshrews in the Other Realm. She was informed that he was an infamous gossip and had spread word that 'Bella', for so he calls his ally, was quite indifferent to me, only showing politeness because her father demanded it, due to the favours I had done him, and that 'his Bella' viewed me with repugnance.

I had thought Isabella received my attentions with pleasure, so, as you can well imagine, I believed then that I had enjoyed a narrow escape and scolded myself that my heart had been too easily touched by her seeming sweetness and consideration. I was, if anything, more desirous of her, but quite determined nevermore to show her the slightest suggestion of warm feeling or good regard.

When, that next morning, I observed Isabella in lively lighthearted discussion with her cousins, I heard not happiness or any expression of her good disposition, but evidence of her cruelty and wickedness.

From that day, I made sure my coldness to her was quite apparent and no glance or unnecessary word was wasted in her direction.

I confess that when you told me there was liberal gossip in certain circles saying Lady Isabella had been too promiscuous with her affections for me and that, in her general expectation of marriage, had let herself be corrupted by me, my first selfish thought was anger at the disregard done to mine own honour. I was also confounded that any could think me such a libertine, as after my heart had so betrayed me -- for so I reasoned it -- I had approached the companionship of women in society with such care and cautious detachment that many think me reserved and slow to friendship.

When you concluded that these slanders extended to a belief that Isabella's reputation was so ruined by my advances and her unchasteness, that her father had been forced to accept the first marriage proposal that came her way, even though it was offered by someone whose situation was far below his own and who would have been thought a most unhappy connection, it gave me pause to consider that my first thought flew beyond fairness.

In the intervening two months since we spoke, I have made it my duty to discover more. Lord Lisle granted me an audience and assured me that he had known nothing about any attractions his daughter may have held for me. Furthermore, he never urged either of his daughters to show special politeness to anyone at any gathering, trusting them to behave as befitted gentlewomen of good breeding without their father's interference.

He did impart that she had become unusually subdued and listless some two years ago. So much so, that Lady Lisle had spoken to Isabella's cousin, Connie, for information about what might be wrong. Connie told her that Isabella had developed an immense affection for a gentleman held in good regard by the family and thought that he and she might conduct a romance. Her sentiments had been made known to the gentleman but had not been returned; indeed, the gentleman had shunned her, and hardly spoken to her again.

Lord Lisle was perplexed to learn that I was likely the gentlemen concerned, and more so that I professed myself quite ignorant of the fact at the time. He admitted that when he learned of his daughter's close acquaintance with the politician Stanton during her visits to London, he did not approve, and vowed he could give no consent to such a union. But, on then observing Isabella showing a small portion of her old spirit and accepting that Stanton had an easy charm about him and a reputation for capability and good horsemanship, Lord Lisle had reluctantly been persuaded to approve their marriage.

So, dear friend, I find myself utterly bereft on every count. I now realise that my reluctance to find a woman that I can develop a partiality for, is due to Isabella displaying every charm and sensibility I desired and none since being her match in this. I prefer her to any other woman in the country, but she is forever lost to me.

I find also that I have done her and her esteemed family much disservice, so that rather than making a good attachment that all would have approved of, she is matched to a fellow who, I'm told, her peers consider below her in wit and status and to have married into considerably reduced circumstances. Lord Lisle also confided that several of Isabella's former friends and acquaintances have dropped her from their circle since the marriage. I know little of the man Stanton. Lisle says that he is the son of a steward but brought up a gentleman, and that his

Umbra is ill-favoured and rarely attends him. Stanton has Pitt's blessing, though that may be down to the connections of his marriage.

Additionally, Isabella is exposed to these vile rumours that you say do neither of us good service – I am painted a rake and she a woman of mislaid virtue. I am also at a loss to explain how I was so easily misled with regard to her true feelings for me. Muscari believes that Isabella's Umbra, Twoshrews, is jealous and capable of more malice than his innocent expression allows, and I can conjure no other explanation. Has he some outlandish magick trick unknown to his mistress? Perhaps he could have seen the letter delivered and somehow secreted it away before I discovered it. Though, this does not explain how it could have then found its way to me.

I have heaped injustice upon this poor woman, only to find I am besotted with her and it is too late.

It seems my life's intended design has been thwarted by a rune-cloaked serpent. Though, in truth, it was I who let pride win out against my heart and instincts. I have denied myself my true love.

More importantly, I have inadvertently ruined this young woman's reputation and status and condemned her to an unworthy marriage. I am honour bound to put matters to rights but have not the slightest comprehension of how I can do so.

Please treat this with every confidence and advise, if you can, when next we meet, should any solution suggest itself to you.

Yours very respectfully, your devoted friend

Robert Huskin,
Viscount of Exeter

29 – A SUMMONS TO THE MINISTRY

Arthur

Two more of the would-be assailants crumple before the warrior's argentium sword. He remembers that argentium expels Greynhym from their borrowed bodies. Are these Greynhym then?

The rest of the group are edging away from the warrior. One trips over his useless leg and gurgles its fear at him from the sand. He is only aware that another two have gone down from their curtailed howls. The rest blunder backwards, discarding broken and unbloodied spears.

The fallen gurgler fumbles for a club but the warrior's dagger flies through the air, embedding itself in the creature's thigh. At the touch of the bright blade, the Greynhym is restored to a state of unlife. He twists around to watch as the warrior harries any who try to flee back up the beach. Leaderless, they stray too close to the tide in their mindless terror and the surf surges forward applying carnage at ankle height, its touch every bit as toxic as the sword. They fall before it.

Fifteen scream-seared moments later, the final creature crumples; its blue-lipped mouth agape in a desolate cry that expires as the empty carcass slips new-dead into the hungry frothing water. The sword is wiped and sheathed.

Lying there, injured, he has the strangest feeling, satisfaction mingling with relief, as if some wild gamble has paid off.

◆ ◆ ◆

Arthur woke but did not open his eyes or stir, trying to make sense of this continuing nightmare. When, at last, he did flicker open his eyelids it was to see Amorrie, sitting on his chest before him, too close to focus on, dark eyes blazing into his.

'You steal my dreams?' She was all suspicion and had a readiness for anger he recognised from his youth. 'They are hard-won and not to be pilfered.'

'Are they just dreams, then?'

'What else?'

'Last night you put into my head the likeness of Cassie, so that I might paint her.'

'Was it not well done?'

'But that was a remembrance, not a dream.'

'That was given freely, but my dreams are mine own, my remembrances more so.'

'There is no profit in it being in my head,' said Arthur. 'And if that was truly a memory then neither of us would be here to speak of it.'

'Good, for I have little intention of doing so.' She dropped from the counterpane into shadow and was gone.

◆ ◆ ◆

Miss Pikestaff was ever cordial company, but Arthur was never in a position to explore further whether she was merely polite, or if she might feel the same special warmth towards him that he felt towards her. After nearly a week in her company, he had yet to learn her Christian name.

Every time they found themselves alone, whether by luck or design; either in a room, on a walk, or standing in front of his canvases, some young Gracegirdle would appear with enquiries for one or both of them. Often Nouhou would be in their wake and would quickly adhere to Arthur or Miss Pikestaff, as the child had a fondness for both.

Their conversation flowed naturally but any company made

it impossible to recapture the delicate moment when they had talked about corresponding and he had found her hand in his.

'I am all a wonder, Mr Tenebris, at your talent and cleverness in depicting Cassandra so true to life (if that is an apt expression), for Mrs Gracegirdle assures me it is her daughter's likeness exactly.'

'No-one is more amazed than me, my dear Miss Pikestaff, for I never saw any depiction of her, but I think Amorrie brought her to me in a dream. The illustration seems to have caused as much tears as happiness.'

'Love is such a complex emotion. Even when it wells up inside me, I find it hard to capture the words to express what is in my heart, but –'

And here were Tabitha and Nouhou racing along the path arriving in a bustle of words and claiming a hand each of the governess and artist, to prevent them walking so closely together.

So, the conversation shifted. 'Galt saw something of Cassandra's spirit I think,' said Miss Pikestaff. 'He reported glimpses of things he could not explain in reflections from ornaments or glass. His conviction was that the manor was haunted. I became exceeding nervous when left alone in it.'

'I am careful now to undress behind the screen in my room, madam, for I would have no notion if Cassie was present with me, though surely a well brought-up young girl would respect a gentlemen's bed-chamber, even after death. She is around constantly, or so Amorrie believes.'

'Amorrie is such an intense creature. How does she fare in the Other Realm?'

'Badly, I fear. She has many enemies.'

'One being the Elven King, I understand.'

'Oh, that is grievous. Who told you so?'

'It must have been Galt. Elves are no friends to Goblins. Take care, Mr Tenebris, for that King avenges any slight.'

◆ ◆ ◆

Even when the children were at dinner, the pair's walks would yet be interrupted by some commotion. One evening an eel appeared writhing towards them on the path, only to be discovered dead on inspection by Miss Pikestaff (Arthur having run some paces back) and its 'wriggling' revealed as a trick of the light.

Before any new disturbance presented itself, Miss Pikestaff took Arthur firmly by the arm and led him off the path. She called for Galt and the combative blue Umbra appeared with three strikes of flint. His heathery scent followed. 'Watch the path,' she told him. 'Warn us if any come.'

The Goblin hopped to the ground and took his club to hand.

'What is it?' Arthur's nerves were already jagged, torn by the appearance of the eel – a species he now despised.

'There is much I would say to you, but time is short. You already know, I think, that you have become dear to me and I believe it is not safe for you here. You must return to London before the weather breaks and the causeway becomes impassable.'

'Not safe?'

'The Elven King must know of Amorrie's presence here. Galt would never say, but others' Umbra may have returned to their realm with stories of her triumph over the Banshee, or...'

'Or what, pray?'

'This long-haired ruffian you spoke of.'

'Mr Hurting?'

'He has sent one killer up here for you.'

'For me?' Arthur felt dizzied by the urgency of her speech as much as the words. 'I thought that...'

'He sent you with a warning about the girls, yes, but what if what was a façade? A lie to place you off your guard. Who else knew you were coming here?'

'The Countess, Hurting, my mother... I told no other.'

'Exactly. Hurting dispatched that murderous charlatan here, ahead of you. You were meant to die on his blade.'

'Why would he want to kill me?'

'Not you, but Amorrie. He may work for the Elven King. It makes more sense than to kill innocent young girls who have no Umbra and not an enemy in the world. And you are friend to the quality in London, no, don't deny it. Perhaps you have imbibed some secret.'

Arthur could think of nothing, then: 'Scampion's true breed? That I know he is not a Piskie – could it be so small a thing?' It seemed ridiculous.

'The Countess?' said Miss Pikestaff in amazement, then recovering, 'Of course, it was she who sent you here. Does she know of Amorrie? No, do not tell me… it is dangerous enough that you know.'

'I must surely be safer here.'

'This is not London, Mr Tenebris, Larkenfen lies close by the muzzle of the wolf and at night you can feel its breath rank with the creep of pestilence.'

Galt raced up to her and half-leapt, half climbed to her shoulder to whisper.

'The girls are coming,' said Miss Pikestaff. 'Say nothing to them. I wish no more worries put upon the Gracegirdles.'

'But Hurting is in London.'

'But he thinks you are here. There were several visiting strangers in Reedston at the Eel Fayre. I heard they were asking questions about you. Having failed once, he will send another against you. We cannot protect you here, but among the throngs of London you are safer. Hush now, let us speak later…'

◆ ◆ ◆

The next day Naomi arrived with a message. The penny-post boy was at the gate to the grounds and would come no further. He was asking for Mr Tenebris.

Arthur thought on Miss Pikestaff's warning as he walked to the gate. He had no wish to leave. He was enjoying his duties. He had the highest opinion of all the Gracegirdles – even Lavinia, in whose esteem he had risen a little – and he imagined Miss Pikestaff to be the perfect companion. Surely, she would consent to wed him, if he but found the time and courage to ask. It reflected well on her modesty that she had not pursued too discernible an affection for him. He well understood that women must feign disinterest until they were sure of a man's intentions, but her concern for his safety, her appreciation of his talent, her realisation that he moved among the noblest of ladies and gentlemen, all these suggested she would receive such a request with favour. She was only a governess, but she would earn no reproach from him on that score.

'Are you one of these Tenebrises, mister?' A shout broke into his thoughts. A head peeked out, half hidden behind the gatepost.

'I am the only Mr Tenebris,' Arthur asserted. There were no gates. The estate set itself apart by a wall, somewhat fallen into disrepair, but still restraining the spread of alder, birch and willow that grew inside the boundary. Beyond the wall, the raised track to Reedston marked a boundary, dividing contrasting landscapes, reed and rush ruled the fenland side, while crops were harvested in the rich black soil to the south.

'Folk say you are a man made of the scraps left over from a murderous fellow and as like to blow away when he is hanging like a mouldy pear on the gallows,' said the head. It was now attached to a boy.

'You can come inside the gate,' said Arthur. 'I hear you have had run-ins with Miss Lavinia, but she is back in the house.'

'No, sir, it is not that. Livvi Gracegirdle is a confounded flagabout but my mam says she will turn out well, and I am not to mind her antics, n' behave gen'lemanly.'

He stepped into the gateway, but his eyes skittered around as Arthur approached.

'You know this place be haunted, sir.'

'I have seen no ghosts,' said Arthur with care.

'Talk in the village 'as it that Mistress Cassie has not yet found her way across. That's why the bells in Eely Bridge toll for her, calling her to join her new kin.'

'Really?' Arthur further understood the gloom that had settled on the carriage on the way back from Reedston.

'Also, that ther's a small black witch now lives at Larkenfen. She has purchased a spell at the fayre and will be all eagerness to use it, even on an honest post boy.'

'She's not a she,' began Arthur, 'I mean, she's not a witch either, and is in fact a young boy, like you.'

'No sir, t'was the talk of the Eel Fayre, how she struck terror into Dob Carter's mare. They do say that the fine weather is her curse and that if it bides long, the Lark will dry and the plague-carriers will cross it in the other world.'

They were suspicious folk, thought Arthur, but living so close to pestilence, they had every right to be. 'What message do you bring, boy?'

'I have word from the constable. You are to come to Reedston tomorrow morning, early mind.' He handed Arthur an official looking document. 'Then 'e will take you to Cambridge.'

Arthur read the document as his faltering steps took him back. 'It was a summons on official-looking paper, addressed to 'The artist, Master Tenebris, whether he be half or whole.'

The seal was already broken and the paper grubby and besmirched by the prints of many fingers. 'Sir, you will be taken to the Cambridge Constable, on receipt of this summons and be escorted from that learned city to London. Once there, you will present yourself at the Ministry for Umbra Affairs in Westminster. There to disclose what took you to Fenland and the home of the Gracegirdles, what foul acts you intended there and what profit you sought. If, though, you be of kindly and cowardly nature, have a care not to worry, for we will consider you the lesser villain in the piece, and may seek means to reunite you with your other half, for the goodliness of both.'

It was signed on behalf of Minister Stanton.

Arthur felt himself kindly, knew himself cowardly, but was altogether filled with worry by this baffling document.

He showed it to Mr Gracegirdle, who felt sure something had been misrepresented in the report of Arnold's attack on his daughters and wrote a letter of explanation for Arthur to take with him.

Arthur said his goodbyes at the supper table. He would take his work with him and finish the portraits in his studio. Nouhou was in tears and it was agreed that he would stay a little longer, perhaps until Arthur made a return. Miss Pikestaff caught Arthur's eye across the table but neither of them felt able to say anything.

As he made his way to bed, Arthur found a folded note had been slipped under his door. He read it. It was unsigned but surely from Miss Pikestaff and she had taken the trouble to disguise her hand, writing in the simplest capitals, in case another found the note.

'Come to the boardwalk at 11 o'clock tonight. Bring Amorrie.'

It was immodest but events had forced her to act. Arthur remained dressed, bottled his excitement and listened to the chime of the clock downstairs. At eleven he took his coat and a lamp and made his way – softly – out into the garden. He had decided not to share his tryst with Amorrie.

He reached the start of the boardwalk and turned around. The night was thick with the chatter of the fen. If it was wind, it was one that never hunted during the day but arrived to chase maniacally through the reeds and rushes from dusk to dawn.

Coercive clouds harried the moonlight, corralling it into scuttling splashes. In one such he saw a dark shape a little off the path. His lamp revealed it to be the body of Rushie, the house cat, her head at an unnatural angle. All Arthur's thrill at this illicit rendezvous had flown. He didn't know if Miss Pikestaff was ahead of him on the boardwalk or still to emerge from the house. Her conviction that he was in danger in this place, became palpable now. In the frisking of the wind he imagined every kind of Fenland ghoul creeping up on him.

Even the thought of Cassie's lost spirit sneaking close filled him with unease.

'Miss Pikestaff,' he called but his quailing voice was whipped away from his lips.

Moonlight daubed the house, and there at a first-floor window he saw the watching figure of a woman. It was Miss Pikestaff, still in her nightclothes, her expression unreadable. He took a half-step back toward the house but petrified as something low and malevolent caught at the edge of his imagination, scurrying between moonlit bushes close to the path. Half-remembered stories of a fiendish hound haunting the eastern marshes, assaulted him from childhood.

The next roaming of moonlight over the house revealed the same first floor window empty. He held his lamp out in front of him. Its light crawled forward reluctantly, scampering back at every quiver of its flame. 'Is anyone there?'

He spun around, thinking steps were coming from the boardwalk. Nothing, and back towards the house, to see a pale spectre dashing towards him. It was Miss Pikestaff, dressed only in her night-gown and still fastening a cloak around her neck. She barely slowed her steps before reaching him, though the wind now declared itself against her. It flayed at her loose hair and a mighty blow tore her cloak away from her, hurling it, bested, back to the house.

Her night-gown was buffeted against her. Arthur could not think where he should look, though his gaze needed no instruction.

'What are you thinking?' her hand grabbed at his frock-coat. 'Did I not warn of danger.' Her eyes flashed beyond him into the wooded fen, probing the crowding bushes.

'Your message?' he stammered.

'Galt, where are you?' She had both hands on Arthur's lapels, but her gaze was everywhere but towards him. 'Galt, now.'

Despite the racing wind, Arthur heard the ting of clashing flints. The blue Goblin materialised on her shoulder in a dance of sparks. 'Galt, is she here?'

Galt lifted a small shiny shield he had taken to carrying. He whirled it around him, staring into it before replying to his ally.

'Back to the house and be quick.' She pulled Arthur about and pushed him before her.

Scolded by her tone, Arthur ran to the door. The wind's violence quelled. He bent to rescue her cloak in a heap by the step. He would have entered, cowed by her fierce temper, but she held him outside a moment. Galt's stare still raked the garden behind her.

'You put a message under my door.' Arthur lifted his gaze a little. He held the lamp and her sand-brown hair, usually wrenched tightly back, flourished in its light, falling upon her barely covered shoulders. With her hair not trussed so severely, Arthur wondered at her revealed handsomeness, even wondered if he recognised her from a time before he had ever heard of Larkenfen.

'I put a mess…?' She questioned his gaze, then more certainly, 'I did, but it was badly done. I overslept and my anger was aimed at myself for putting you in danger.'

'I thought…'

'We must be quiet. Put out your light, for I am only in my night-shift.'

He did so. She reached past him to push open the door. He had not, because he wanted the moment to last. In the darkness she touched his face. He tasted the smoky scent of her, beneath the drift of wild heather.

'You leave early tomorrow,' she had found some gentleness at last, 'so this must be goodbye until, perhaps, we meet again, back here or in London.'

'I could write.'

'Do so. Promise me you will avoid this Hurting villain, but write if he finds you.' Arthur nodded to both demands. 'Go in first now. I will wait awhile as we must not be seen together – not like this.'

Arthur made it back to his bed. He knew he should be bewildered by what had just happened. Instead he was engulfed by melancholy at his parting from Miss Pikestaff and the words that neither had found a way to say.

30 – BAYNARD CASTLE'S SONGBIRD

Stanton

'Is it your Mr Tenebris, Izzy?' Stanton turned to his wife. They were both standing behind a table in the Keeper's rooms at the notorious Baynard Castle House of Correction. At the furthest end of the room stood a tall sorrowful gentleman in manacles between the gaol's enormous Keeper and a grizzled unkempt guard.

The prisoner's garments were of quality but stained and bloodied, one stocking leg particularly so, and he limped, favouring the other leg. He was unshaven, unwashed, unhappy and much bruised about the face.

Mr Larkwing sat behind the desk with his polished boots upon it. The letter of introduction from the Earl of Grenville had won passes for Isabella, Larkwing and Stanton at the gate of the gaol.

Stanton had asked Isabella to join him at the gaol, much to the Keeper's stupefaction and Larkwing's amusement. The pretext was that she would be able to recognise this artistic Bendith – if such it was – having met Mr Tenebris at Lady Rochester's home before he left for the Fens and supposedly split in two. A truer reason was that Stanton was partly anxious that a threat against his wife had been whispered in his ear at the ball on Saturday night, and yet more fearful that Viscount Exeter had designs on Isabella and would act upon them. The

Viscount's letter, which he had read after the ball, had revealed a desperation to put right the 'unworthy marriage' that had resulted from the sabotage of Exeter's and Isabella's curtailed romance. How, Stanton couldn't imagine, but knew it must end ruinously for all.

There was no way for Stanton to respond to this letter. It was knowledge he had promised not to divulge or use for personal reasons and, even if he had not given Grenville his word, he could see no benefit to Isabella in informing her of the Viscount's account.

So, here they were at the gaol that housed many of London's worst felons and debtors. Baynard Castle made a poor gaol and, it was said, a poor castle before that. The old house was built on land reclaimed from the Thames and stood close to where the River Fleet emptied into it at Blackfriars. It was preserved from the Great Fire 126 years before, only by the alertness of its owner's Umbra.

Isabella, was astonished to be asked if she would help Stanton in his work, intrigued when she learnt of their destination, determined when she heard that the painter, Mr Tenebris, was incarcerated in the gaol and vexed when she saw Larkwing waiting for them at the gates.

'It is not he,' she told Stanton.

'You are sure?'

'This fellow bears no relation to Mr Tenebris at all. He is broader, taller, fairer of hair and older by eight or more years. He is altogether a rougher caste than the artist I met.'

The man, who had initially appeared cowed and confused, bowed deeply, 'Arnold Tenebris, at your service. Perhaps you have met my brother, madam. I confess, he is the better artist.' It sounded like the last trill of a caged and broken bird.

'They are not brothers,' said Isabella. 'He is lying.'

'Are you perhaps two sides of the same coin,' asked Stanton. 'Are you the Bendith?'

Confusion returned to the man's expression.

'Where is your Umbra?' Larkwing asked from behind his

boots.

'It has been made clear to me,' the man pointed at his bruises, 'that she is not welcome. She upsets the other Umbra for she is unhappy here and reduced to screaming. We are all in too close a proximity, the bedding straw swarms with vermin, spiders scuttle everywhere, and we are in irons. Other prisoners have the comfort of visits from their Umbra allies, not I. Now, all beat and threaten me when she arrives. This lodging house encourages screaming.'

'Did John Howard's reforms not reach this gaol?' Isabella asked the Keeper.

The Keeper, a vast ball of a man shrugged. He had sat upon a sturdy stool since entering the room. Ignoring Isabella he spoke to Larkwing, who he assumed was captain of this siege of visitors. 'He'll be going to a worse place, sir. 'Tis the Tyburn tree for him.'

'Let us not prejudge the matter,' said Larkwing, who was reading a note from the Cambridge Constable.

'What took you to Larkenfen?' asked Stanton.

'Loot, sir. I knew my brother Tenebris was expected there and felt I could impersonate him afore he arrived and make-off with some silver.'

'Did you threaten the family there, Gracegirdle's young daughters?'

The man laughed, 'Quite the reverse, sir, those girls are wild creatures. All carry blades, and one did stick me in my calf.'

'Tell us about your Umbra,' said Larkwing, earning a stare from Isabella.

'She is a delicate thing, easily alarmed. From Hibernia, she tells me.'

'A Banshee; a female of fearsome complexion' said Stanton, who had consulted W.H. Bradby's book '*Enquiry into the Nature and Characteristics of Umbra*' at the Ministry, 'with a scream that invokes death.'

'She screamed several times in this gaol when we arrived; none have died,' said the prisoner.

'None have died *here*,' the Keeper had awoken abruptly, eyes widening in his fat cheeks, 'but a wife murderer, a lady arsonist and a pickpocket were all taken to the gallows from here yesterday. All three would have felt those screams, which, though invisible to human ears, set our old bricks and mildewed air ashiver.'

'A lady arsonist,' said Larkwing, as much impressed as he had been by the description of the Banshee. 'That is a thing.'

'Your comments, man, do not tally with the accounts of the constables,' said Stanton. 'Speak truly or it will go worse for you.'

'Worse than the gallows? Worse than being returned to that hellspit of a dungeon where all hate and abuse me?'

'I daresay there are many worse ways to die than the gallows,' said Larkwing, 'and worse chambers can be found in this old castle, with worse ways to entertain you.'

'You cannot mean to have him tortured, Sebastian,' said Isabella.

'No, of course not, my dear,' said Stanton. 'It would never be sanctioned.'

'Remember what is at stake here, Stanton,' said Larkwing. 'It is time for you to take your good lady home. She has been valiant in attending this place and done her duty, but this is not for a woman's ears.'

'Because they are too full of delicate fancies, no doubt,' said Isabella. 'If this prisoner's story is important, we should stay and hear it.'

'I fear we will not hear the truth without inducements, madam. And without the truth we may see murder done.'

'Murder?' Isabella spun to her husband.

'You, Tenebris,' said Stanton, 'what will happen when you are returned to the company of your felons and your Banshee visits you again, as she must?'

'Why, sir, I think they will be after ripping me to shreds afore she can open her mouth.'

'Will you answer our questions truthfully if another cell,

more solitary, can be found for you?'

'You may promise, sir, but I doubt we have anything suitable in the castle,' said the Keeper shuffling awkwardly on his stool.

'A room in one of the tenements outside, then,' said Stanton; 'he is manacled, after all. My Ministry will pay for a cellar and a guard, to buy him some peace.'

The keeper glanced at his guard. 'Yes, mayhap, we have another troublesome prisoner here that we would wish to be housed away from Baynard Castle. If it is close and you can arrange guards, we can keep all fed.'

'Please, my dear Stanton,' Larkwing took his feet from the table. 'This is more my Ministry's area of expertise than yours. This fellow will say anything to win such a reward. How will we know if it is true unless we test his mettle?'

'There is a way,' Stanton said, adding, 'Isabella, can you summon Twoshrews to you?'

She gave him an uncomprehending stare but did so.

The Piskie arrived, his charming boyish features clouded as his eyes took in the surroundings and situation.

'Listen to Sebastian, Twoshrews,' said Isabella. 'He has a task for you. It is a most important one.'

'It is quite the nonsense,' Larkwing clapped and chuckled. 'I apologise for it, Keeper, but more serious matters will begin soon enough.'

Stanton began, 'Twoshrews, I will ask that man there some questions. You must tell Bella whether he answers them truthfully or not.'

The Umbra leapt from Isabella's shoulder, his rune-decorated cape billowing behind him, and landed upon the desk as nimbly as a falcon settling upon a pole. He nodded to Stanton but nothing about him suggested any confidence.

'Sebastian, I am not sure Twoshrews has managed two consecutive true statements in all his time with me,' Isabella hissed.

Larkwing's smile widened and he shook his head.

'Is Arnold Tenebris your true name?' Stanton addressed the

prisoner.

'No.'

Twoshrews shrugged and nodded.

'It's Carnaby O'Brien.'

Twoshrews nodded again.

'Captain O'Brien, late of Arran's Regiment of Cuirassiers.'

Twoshrews and Isabella conferred. 'Not true,' said Isabella.

'Just testing your wee man there,' O'Brien's accent slipped into an Irish lilt. 'He's roight, it was Lieutenant, but I was with the Earl of Arran.'

'No more testing if you wish to be found an empty room rather than a quarrelsome cell,' said Stanton, secretly thankful that, so far, Maraziel had been right in her claims for Twoshrews' truth-telling ability.

'What is your Umbra called?'

'She is Dearbhla, not beloved by all, and a torment at times.'

Stanton was watching Twoshrews. The gallant's mouth fell open at the name and he pulled his cape closer around him before remembering his role and nodding.

'They can all be a torment at times,' said Stanton. 'Was it the Queen's Sprig that you hunted for at Larkenfen?

'Yes.'

'What made you think it was there?'

'Such were my orders. I was told to wait and wait in Cambridge, like, until I found opportunity to go to Larkenfen. I received a message from the Fens that an artist – Tenebris – was expected at the house and I might beat him by a day or so.'

'Who told you?'

'A messenger from Reedston. My master has a network of associates. He has investigations for me to undertake. He never tells me what they relate to, but pays well for my handiwork.'

'How could you impersonate Mr Tenebris successfully?' asked Isabella.

'None there knew him, and I had investigated this artist before on a like matter, followed him, so knew him by sight, knew what he carried for his work.'

'What were you to do if you found the Sprig?' asked Larkwing, caught up in the story.

'If I was quite certain, to kill the girl who had it; if I could not find it, to kill them all, but this was by no means a certain outcome and I had me misgivings, which were discussed.'

Stanton's gaze flicked to Twoshrews, but he nodded still.

'Why kill her?' Larkwing again, the questions came thick and fast.

The man gave a shake of the head, 'Because of who she might be, I must imagine.'

'Who?' All three asked.

'I was never told, like, but have a guess, sirs.'

'Oh dear, another royal bastard; I have little doubt,' said Larkwing.

'Or someone who is destined to ally to an Umbra of great import in the Other Realm, when she is of age.' Stanton thought of all the powerful Umbra he had been told about, who still had no English allies.

'Yes, this Elven King perhaps?' said Isabella. 'Or, could she have a link to the Queen, perchance be one of her descendants?' She ended in a rush of wild incredulity.

'Our imaginations are galloping away,' said Larkwing, 'and in quite the wrong direction.'

'Whoever she is, if she has the Sprig, many will believe she can grow to wield the power of the Queen,' said Stanton. 'If any of this rumour becomes known, crowds will scramble to Fenland to find out.'

'We are losing sight of other matters,' said Larkwing. 'I'll wager you have little loyalty to King George, O'Brien?'

'The Crown harvests precious little support where I come from, sir.'

'I thought as much. May I remind everyone that this man is a miscreant, in the employ of some greater felon. Your Umbra, on your own account, madam, has no great affiliation to the truth and we have put all our faith in him.'

'This man, O'Brien, is broken, sir,' said Isabella. 'He has tried lying and it served him badly. What has he to lose by telling the truth?'

'Thanks to your husband's cavalier ploy, O'Brien has everything to gain, by making us think he tells the truth. The more fantastical, the more we are seduced.'

'If word of my singing like a songbird reaches certain ears, I will be silenced, m'lady, no matter where you hide me,' said O'Brien.

Twoshrews quailed a little at this, but nodded.

'O'Brien is right,' said Larkwing. 'The reason we gave Grenville for coming to this hell-hole – begging your pardon Keeper – is to learn about this fellow's Umbra. Our cause is a secret known only to a few and none of them Umbra. I cannot proceed with the important questions while your jack-a-napes there, is present.'

'Sebastian, I appeal to you. We must discover more about these Gracegirdles.'

'Mr Larkwing is right, Izzy. There is a pressing reason I was given these passes. I have allowed myself too many digressions. Also, no word of what has passed here can leave this room. For my part, I think Twoshrews has done us commendable service, Izzy. I have one final task for him to adjudicate and then I must take you from this place. I hope your father never gets to hear of your visit here.'

'I am inclined to dismiss Twoshrews from his service now. It seems to me he has been misused.'

'One question, Izzy.'

She shook her head, but Stanton took it as exasperation overlaying acquiescence. He turned to O'Brien. 'Who is your master in this malfeasance?'

'I've no name. He's after remaining anonymous, sir.'

'There is more,' said Isabella, after listening to Twoshrews.

'What do you know of him?' asked Stanton.

'I think, like myself, he is just a pawn in this game. But a few months back I followed him and discovered him to be a gentleman's gentleman.'

'Which gentleman?'

'A grand one, Lord Strathearn.'

Larkwing rubbed his hands together, laughing, 'First Viscount Exeter and now a Lord of the Realm; the more you poke this with your stick, Stanton, the more hornets you set buzzing. Grenville will not thank you for it.'

'If it is worth anything,' said Isabella, standing and mis-buttoning her coat in her quiet anger, 'I met Lord Strathearn's man briefly the other night. He is one Quartermain Hurting.'

31 – AMBUSHED AT THE WINDOW

Arthur

The warrior turns slowly from the twice dead creatures he has vanquished, to the live one he has rescued. He stares and a sly smile can be seen behind his heavy silvered helm.

'You have bested them, though they were fifteen,' says a bare whisper; a voice that is both familiar and unsettling. It is female and yet, in his dream, he knows he is the one that spoke. An arm appears in his vision, a female arm, without any sleeve and wiry with strength. He realises this recurrent dream has placed his mind in another's body, a young female body.

'If you have secrets to spill, you must speak louder,' says her rescuer.

His grey eyes stare at her leg on the sand. It is naked. It is almost certainly broken. The warrior's eyes are drawn to nearby rocks and one of them is bloody. His shake of the head suggests that anyone who has broken their own leg and put themselves on such a beach, in such danger, doesn't deserve saving.

'Careless, Mor,' he says.

He takes his helm in both hands and removes it, shaking out his blond hair. The face there is familiar. It is a face made recognisable by The Book of Five Hundred.

It is…

◆ ◆ ◆

Arthur is pounded awake by tiny fists on his chest.

'No, do not plunder my dreams,' Amorrie's head lifts up and the anger there makes him fearful that she will stride across his chest and pound the sleep from his face.

'Was that..?' begins Arthur.

'I knew it. You pry into my things that are no part of your life, or your world.'

'...Charon the Borderer?'

'What of it? I may dream of who I wish.'

'They were Greynhym, he saved you from the Greynhym. He called you Mor.'

'I shall talk of it no more.'

'Amorrie..!' but she was gone.

◆ ◆ ◆

Arthur rose, said his goodbyes to the Gracegirdles and promised to inform them when the paintings were finished. He hoped to say farewell to Miss Pikestaff but she had already left the house, 'for a walk, at dawn,' said Lavinia as she shook Arthur's hand. He received warm handshakes also from Mr and Mrs Gracegirdle, a shy hug from Naomi and a longer one from Tabitha.

Conscious of the 'early' in the summons, George Gracegirdle drove him into Reedston in the carriage and the constable was already waiting for him there with a sturdier rougher carriage. He professed ignorance to Arthur's questions and they left straight away for Cambridge, the weather on the route darkening to match Arthur's sorrowful and anxious mood.

Their entrance to Cambridge saw slow progress as the market was busy and Arthur watched as the crowds hustled between stalls. His eye travelled over the throng and seized on a familiar head of sandy brown hair. It moved listlessly through the press of people.

'Miss Pikestaff,' Arthur pushed his head through the carriage door window to shout to the governess, causing the constable to leap up and restrain him, in case he harboured plans to jump out.

'Over here, Miss Pikestaff,' he called as he was pulled back into the interior but she showed no sign of hearing him and soon melted into the bobbing hubbub of the crowd. If she had risen at dawn and paid the Carter to drive her into Cambridge, she would have beaten Arthur here, but she must be busy on other matters.

Arthur was handed over to the Cambridge constables, one of whom accompanied him on the Mail Coach to London, which had waited for Arthur. Fast as it was, the journey took the rest of the day and it was only at the constable's insistence that it continued all the way into the city, arriving just after dusk. Arthur wondered at the importance of the mysterious summons, that it had interfered with the running of the Mail.

It was too late to deliver Arthur to the Ministry of Umbra Affairs and the constable was keen to return to Cambridge at first light. He considered Arthur to have little disobedience in his person, so made him promise to report to the Ministry next morning and told Arthur he may spend the night at his studio.

Arthur hailed a hackney coach to transfer himself and his artist's materials to his studio. Rather than go home to alarm his mother and Gwennie with news of this summons, he elected to stay in his studio for the night. He had not been there long when there came a rap upon the door. Arthur picked up his keys but rather than go down to the door, he doused the light, and went to the window, from where he could look upon the street. A tall black circular hat waited below him. Quartermain Hurting; the same man Arthur had promised Miss Pikestaff he would not go near.

He was about to close the window as quietly as he might, when he noticed a pine resin scent. A pale one-horned shadow leapt towards him. Arthur shouted and nearly fell out on top of his visitor. Regaining his balance he stumbled back into the room. He saw the distinctive silhouette of a broken-horned Umbra, watching him from the open casement. It turned and leapt from the window, out into the night. Even as Arthur rose, he heard a key turning in the door. A quick glance around suggested that they were his keys.

The door downstairs was closed and relocked. Soft steps on the stairs had Arthur searching for hiding places. He gave up as the door opened and Hurting entered, with his hat in his hands and Brughe on his shoulder.

'Good to see you back and unharmed, Mr Tenebris,' said Hurting. 'Brughe borrowed your keys,' he placed them on a table, 'I hope you don't mind, but we did not wish to inconvenience you over much.'

'I do mind. And now is quite inconvenient.'

'Then I will be quick. I know you have just returned and I wished to discover how you fared in your travels to Larkenfen.'

Brughe climbed down onto a table and sat there, watching Arthur closely; probably trying to see if Amorrie was present.

'Amorrie is not with me.'

'You told us that last time,' said Hurting. 'So, how are the Gracegirdles?'

'The three remaining daughters are fit and healthy, despite your best efforts.'

'My best efforts?'

'A man was already at Larkenfen when I arrived. He was claiming to be me and had purchased artist materials in order to give credence to his falsehood. He was threatening the girls and tried to kill me and Amorrie. Only you and the Countess knew of my trip to Larkenfen. I suspect this villain of being your accomplice.'

'Not so. Surely the Gracegirdles and their associates also knew of your commission.'

'But it was these very same he was deceiving.'

'Is your commission complete?'

'No, I had to return on a summons from the Ministry for Umbra Affairs.' Arthur pulled the document from his jacket pocket as proof that he would be missed if he did not appear at the Ministry next morning.

Hurting claimed it from his hand and read it. 'Reunite you with your other half?' He was all puzzlement.

Brughe spoke from the table and Hurting's confusion increased. 'Can it be that they suspect you of being the Bendith?'

'The which?'

Brughe spoke again and Hurting turned to Arthur, 'Brughe has heard a rumour that the Bendith has been resurrected and set forth upon an assassination. Sit, Mr Tenebris; I will fetch you some water. You must tell me all that befell, particularly where I should now look for your "other half".'

Arthur protested but he could see that Hurting was determined and feared a beating might be administered if he did not speak.

When he had finished his tale – leaving out Amorrie's part in it – and repeatedly insisting that the other Mr Tenebris bore him no resemblance, Hurting paced the room.

'So it is Lavinia. She has the courage and aptitude for combat,' Hurting spoke mostly to himself.

'And obstinacy,' said Arthur, 'and rebelliousness.'

Brughe leapt to his ally's shoulder and the two conversed in whispers. Hurting turned, 'Perhaps someone at the Ministry heard the rumour of the Bendith's resurrection and wondered if you and this imposter were its manifestation. They quite misunderstand its nature, but then the Bendith's visits are rare. I have one more question, Mr Tenebris, before I leave you to your slumbers.'

Arthur wondered which of the many events he had spoken of, had caught Hurting's interest.

'This woman in Cambridge you saw, who resembled Miss Pikestaff, should she have heard your call?'

'I would say so and I am sure it was her, but she must have been on some urgent mission for she did not so much as turn her head.'

'Perhaps,' said Hurting, '... or maybe... Yes, go, Brughe, continue your hunt. I must make haste if I am to get there before harm is done.' The Umbra disappeared and Hurting picked up his hat.

'Goodbye, Mr Tenebris, and good luck at the Ministry. When you see Miss Amorrie next, please inform her Brughe has questions for her.'

'What questions? Where do you go to in such haste?'

'I fear the danger is not over at Larkenfen. What you have witnessed may only be the start. Goodbye Mr Tenebris.'

32 – HE INTENDS TO KILL PIKESTAFF

Stanton

'How can this be explained?' Isabella brandished two Umbra Abominables in Stanton's face. 'This is the self-same scandal sheet that you bought the other evening, but with a different story about the attack on Charon.'

'Editions change, Izzy, there are updates.'

'To even such a low publication as this? I find it hard to credit, Sebastian.'

Since they had returned from Baynard Castle on the Monday, having secured promises from Larkwing and the Keeper that the prisoner O'Brien would suffer no bodily torture, Isabella had determined to find out all she could about the affair. Stanton would tell her little, so it had become a dispute between them. Isabella knew few details except that it involved murder and that her husband suspected Muscari among others. She had read widely about the murder of Charon.

She was suspicious of the reports of this 'Umbra betrayer' reported in the scandal-sheet Stanton had purchased.

As for Lieutenant O'Brien, Stanton had provided funds for a secure room to house him close to Baynard Castle and Larkwing had agreed to provide guards for the prisoner from the Ministry for Retaliation. In private, Larkwing continued to question the former Lieutenant of the Cuirassiers (more officially, Arran's Fourth Royal Irish Dragoons) and his Umbra

Banshee, Dearbhla, on the rare occasions she visited.

Yesterday, Larkwing had sought out Stanton on his way home from work to say that O'Brien was not, after all, involved with the French, but Dearbhla had heard that Muscari was searching for Hannah Lightfoot. The Ministry of Retaliation had not been able to trace this Quartermain Hurting.

'He has probably left London,' said Larkwing.

◆ ◆ ◆

When Stanton arrived home in Marksfayre, that evening, Midden greeted him at the door. A well-polished glass was a warning of what was to come. She told him that her mistress was very low. The maid, herself, looked haunted and Keeper Claw even more grim and grey than usual.

'Is it to do with that mysterious gent in the scullery, sir,' Midden plucked at his sleeve, 'Oh please say it isn't.'

'I hope not, Midden, but it is entirely possible. Please take me to Lady Stanton.'

She showed Stanton to the parlour where Isabella sat, red-eyed in misery.

'What is it Izzy? I pray it is not further upset over this affair with O'Brien or the death of Charon.'

'No Sebastian, other matters have intruded. I had tea with friends and they warned me of rumours of a great scandal. It seems this particular report has gathered credence and popularity since the Countess of Harrington's ball.'

Stanton's heart toppled as he guessed that Desi Fitzroy's cruel gossip about Isabella's supposed affair with Exeter, had reached the ears of his wife. 'Does it involve your family, Izzy?' was all he could come up with, for he could not find any way to inform her he had already heard the rumour.

'I can speak to you of it no more, Sebastian. I am overwrought now but I will move past it. There is scarce a whit of truth in any of it and if it should ever reach your ears and find purchase there, it would truly be the death of me.'

'Can you give me the generalities if not the particulars.'

'The usual, Sebastian, a rakish gentleman has sought to varnish his own reputation by sullying that of a young woman's. I think him the lowest kind of blackguard. Please do not ask me to repeat it.'

He didn't, of course, for he had no need.

Isabella rallied for a spot of dinner. She had news from her enquiries she said. 'I take no joy in it any more, Sebastian, and will now retire from my investigations, but this you should know. I made examination this morning among the troop of poor children who distribute and sell the newspapers each evening.'

'You did what?'

'Goldry was with me, I was in no danger of being robbed.'

'Why did you...?'

'Hear me out. I showed them the Umbra scandal sheet you brought home. They can barely read of course but they knew it was not the one they sold last week. I asked to speak to the person who sold that paper in our area. I was introduced to a young fellow – not the girl you described – who was affronted at the thought of a woman selling in Marksfayre, saying, "no blowse would work his patch, not ever".'

'I believe you, Izzy. I cannot explain what you say and I have not the heart to investigate. The important thing is that you regain some of your cheer and spirit. Nothing else matters to me.'

That, at least, was true; Miss Fitzroy's rumour and Exeter's confession had grown into a dark fanged beast. It was the thing he could speak of to no-one and every night it visited and devoured his thoughts, spitting out bitter pips of reproach. Even the plot to kill Hannah Lightfoot could find no room or purchase in his mind.

◆ ◆ ◆

'There is a visitor for you, Minister, should you still wish to see him.'

'Remind me.'

'A Mr Tenebris,' Cotteridge was preparing Stanton's papers for the day. 'I believe he is an artist. We summoned him from the Fens.'

'Ah,' Stanton remembered, 'the other half of this supposed Bendith. However, since we sent for him, I have learnt several things which have forced me to conclude that he is not such a creature. The Chancellor considers it unlikely these horrors can now visit our realm. Mr Tenebris will be a waste of our time.'

'But we have brought him with alacrity from the Fens, Minister. He is likely anxious.'

'Yes, you are right, I should see him – quickly mind – not least to satisfy my curiosity regarding his likeness to Mr O'Brien, and to hear more about the Gracegirdles.'

Shortly after, Cotteridge showed a dishevelled man in a patched and creased frock coat into the office and bade him sit. He cut a disquieted figure, every bit as haunted as O'Brien. Stanton wondered at the ordeal inflicted by these Gracegirdles upon those who visited them. He was more amazed to learn from Tenebris that the Gracegirdle girls were all twelve years of age or younger, and, although their reputation had them wholly wild and barbaric, that they were quite delightful in their way.

'They are nieces of the Countess of Harrington,' said Tenebris, 'destined to be among the finest young ladies in society when they come to London, as they surely will. The Countess will want them out, for they will charm all who meet them.'

'Really,' Stanton laughed at his description. 'This imposter O'Brien, had it that they kidnapped their governess's Umbra, terrorised all messengers to the house, that they carried blades and attacked him, stabbing him most savagely. He was lying to me after all.'

The artist wrung his hands. 'No, no, they do all that too.'

'But O'Brien is a trained soldier. Just how many girls are there?'

'Four, no only three.'

'You don't seem very sure.'

'Three now, one daughter – a rare beauty – was taken by plague at Eely Bridge after the incursion there last year.'

'Ah yes, I know of it. And tell me, Tenebris, did you see any evidence of mistletoe while you were there – the old Queen's Sprig?'

'It is everywhere at Larkenfen, Minister, for it is the sigil of the Gracegirdle family and has decorated their house and family crest since the 13th Century.'

There was an indulgence to Stanton's chuckle, 'So that is it. No wonder Lieutenant O'Brien had a notion it would be a likely place to search for the Queen's infamous treasure. Tell me, sir, this O'Brien admitted to following you, in London before your encounter in the Fens; do you know why he would do so?'

'No, sir, but he is not alone. Others follow me. I caught a young child from the Africas, who had been paid a penny to dog my trail.'

'Strange indeed. Well, sir, I am satisfied you bear no resemblance to this other villain. I am sorry to have interrupted your visit to the Gracegirdles. You are free to go.'

'May I be permitted a question?'

'Of course, it is the least we owe you.'

'What is a Bendith?'

'What can you know of such a creature?'

'Nothing sir, I do assure you.' said the artist. 'Another I consulted understood from your summons that you suspected me of being one.'

'It was a false report. The constable thought you a magical cast-off from the man who stole your name and place. The Bendith is a creature from the Other Realm. There, it is summoned to life from... I know not where, and sent to our world to commit murder upon someone of import. This it does by taking over the body and spirit of an Englishm– no, in fact, it must be an Englishwoman; one who can get close to the intended victim.

'The Bendith, as I understand it, splits its host into two. One half has all the vitality and is controlled by the creature. The other half is left intact but little more than a shell, capable of only mundane errands, barely able to talk. That, my dear sir, is the Bendith.'

'By the gods, he thinks her the Bendith.' The artist leapt up, alarming Cotteridge and scattering papers.

'Calm yourself, Mr Tenebris. We know you cannot be one now. This O'Brien is hardly your twin and this Bendith seems only to split apart and inhabit women – more able to get close to their victims perhaps? I no longer believe that this Bendith was ever in England.'

'You may not, Minister, but another does believe the Bendith has come, and that it is now inhabiting a woman of my acquaintance. He has gone to kill her. I am sure of it.'

Cotteridge and Stanton shared a look, wondering if guards should be called, but Mr Tenebris seemed such a callow, faint-hearted and feeble man, he did indeed resemble the Bendith's discarded shell.

'Kill who?' Stanton spoke into the silence.

'Miss Pikestaff, a wonderful lady. I see now that he suspects the woman I saw resembling her at Cambridge to be the Bendith's cast-off. He will go to Larkenfen and murder Miss Pikestaff.'

'The devil he will. Who is it you speak of?'

'Quartermain Hurting.'

33 – OVER THE RIVER

Larkenfen

'It is from Nouhou,' Naomi handed over the small lapwing skull on a thread, which she often wore, 'well, sort of.'

'From Nouhou?' Cassie took the proffered necklace. 'Why would he give me your lapwing skull? I have had nothing to do with him. I can't say I like him still being here, for you all must take such care not to talk to me when he is around.'

'We have not been careful enough. He has overheard us several times; not least by the Lark last week. He is a quiet little thing, but clever, and seeing Mr Tenebris's painting of you, he has worked it out. He heard me say you could hold dead things, and said I should give my necklace to you. Do you not think it is sweet of him?'

'I think it 'ceeding strange.'

'He believes you must be sad to be dead. I told him you were not dead, just lost.'

'And you a scientist, Naomi. In a way, I am neither one thing or yet another. I fear death. It is a shadow-winged bird, silent and watchful. There is space in its nest for me and it may kill others if I do not come.'

'Your death is the smallest part of you.'

'Hush, I still have tears at my disposal.'

'Nouhou said should you ever need his help, you could use the skull to tell him.'

Cassie shook her head. She did not feel it safe to wear the skull openly, so hid it in a hidey-hole in a tree and thought about it no more…

... until that evening. She had taken to walking the boardwalk to the river as soon as her sisters prepared for bed. She sat upon the jetty as the sun dropped, watching her new family, as she supposed they must be; a congregation of grey sisters and brothers. They assembled, heads above and insubstantial bodies between, the reeds on the far bank. Their eyes turned to her and she detected a heightened hunger, or a growing desperation, in their gaze.

The thin girl with the broken arm and disfiguring marks of pestilence had pushed her way to the edge of the bank opposite the jetty. The horde was so closely confined against each-other, Cassie feared the girl would be buffeted into the Lark. Again the girl beckoned to Cassie, but with more urgency than before. Others took up the gesture.

To her horror, Cassie recognised one. A second glance confirmed that Miss Bell – the governess before Miss Pikestaff – languished among the multitude. She stood several ranks back, watching her former favourite with yearning dark eyes. Cassie held up a timid hand to acknowledge her but no gesture came back from the dead governess, her mind had already succumbed to the horde.

Miss Bell, who Cassie had loved, and who was taken by pestilence after the same incursion at Eely Bridge that had turned Cassie into a spirit. How had she found her way to the right side of the river? Cassie's growing fear was that her continued existence in Larkenfen, the wrongness of her being there, cursed her family in some way. She shrugged her helplessness to the throng. 'I am trapped here, there is no way for me to cross the river to your side. I know I should be with you but what can I do?'

Arms gestured, and even the reeds took up the coaxing wave. The breeze sped over the Lark to press their insistence upon her. As it blew through her, she felt the press of their thousand wills. 'Come,' they urged.

She turned and ran back to the house, her feet silent on the boardwalk. She stopped at the tree and reached in for the lapwing skull. The house was silent when she arrived, the only light left on flowed from Miss Pikestaff's window.

Cassie pushed the small skull through an open window before brushing through the door and regathering it. Up the stairs she went to the room that had been lent to the African child. She had not been in there for reasons of propriety, but also he had bought some feathered and shell monstrosity back from the Eel Fayre that she found repulsed her.

Tonight it was not in evidence. She entered, tapped the skull upon the cupboard by his sleeping head and saw the white eyes spring open. It was not yet full dark but thick clouds had gathered to obscure the moon. His gaze alighted on the skull and she pulled it across the surface towards her, then put it around her neck.

She had imagined the small child would be scared to see the skull move and hang in the empty air but instead his bedclothes were thrown aside and she saw the former page boy was still dressed, needing only to restore his shoes. Once these were tied, she led the way to the door. He opened it and, using the skull as his guide, he followed her outside and to the jetty. She jumped down into the small tethered boat. Nouhou watched, his eyes never leaving the tiny dry bird skull.

Cassie placed the skull upon the boat's seat, bill facing towards the jetty, then very deliberately turned it around to face the far bank. Nouhou nodded and unloosed some of the boat's rope. He jumped in and reached for the oars.

It was as if he had been brought to the Fens to help her find her rest, her place among the grey brethren. Cassie had no need for breath but the habit had not left her. She took her deepest breath. She had no use for tears either but they slipped down her cheeks, one tumbling off her chin and hitting the planks of the boat, where it left no stain.

The two oars were cumbersome for the small child. Lavinia and Tabitha could row this boat but Naomi barely managed and Nouhou was smaller than she. After checking the oars' weight, the child untied a shorter rope that kept it tight to the jetty and left the boat. Nouhou assessed the second rope's length and concluded there was more than enough to see the boat to the far bank. Then he let the boat travel a little way out into a current and disappeared.

Just as Cassie was wondering if he had given up, she heard his tiny shoes racing across the jetty. He leapt off it and landed in the stern of the boat, driving it down into the water. The impact drove the craft out into the main run of the water. The Lark was low and the current was light so the boat was propelled beyond halfway before the current could impose itself.

Nouhou could only manage one oar but dug at the water with it. The waif had no skill but more strength than Cassie had imagined and as the craft arced around, she realised that his clumsy efforts would bring it to rest on a low strand, extended by tangled branches, on the far side further downstream.

A glance to the bank showed the plague-girl had also realised this and was pushing her way through the horde to meet with Cassie there. As the boat caught on the outermost branches, almost at the end of the rope, Nouhou dropped the oar and leapt up, using the branches to pull them to shore.

Cassie watched the dull eyes and broken bodies of those among whom she must spend her afterlife. It was not an agreeable prospect. All were dead, with all manner of injuries and darker blotches of illness, often the disfiguring buboes of plague. Many were dimmed, perhaps by the longevity of their decease. She imagined her bright clothes, spice hair and pale freckled features would quickly grey after she joined this brethren. Cassie's gaze stumbled over one, both crippled and with rope burns around his neck, a fugitive from some long past torture and execution. All were human. Perhaps the same space in the Other Realm was reserved for dead Umbra.

Nouhou had brought the boat as close to the other bank as he was able. The child would surely not have undertaken the journey if he could see what spectres formed their welcoming committee. Instead he watched the skull, checking to see when it left the boat.

The one-armed plague-girl was here now, pushing aside those closest and most curious. No other had reached out to Cassie. As Cassie rose and made to step onto the bank, the girl motioned for her to put out her hand. Then she dropped something negligible into Cassie's palm. Cassie felt its presence rather than its weight. The girl used her good arm to mime putting the thing in her ear.

Cassie did so. 'What is it?'

'My lord fashioned it from the last breath of a will-o-wisp and the first dance of a bat at moondark.' The girl's voice was a sough, meagre and haggard; barely more than the susurration of the reeds. 'It lets the likes of you hear my kind.'

'Am I not your kind?'

'You are a thing between. T'will work three times only.'

'Is this how you talk to each other?'

The girl's grin fought against her marred face. 'What 'as we to talk 'bout.'

Cassie made to step off the boat.

'You cannot come.' The girl pushed out a warding hand. 'You are not for here, not yet. What are your injuries? Where is your body?'

'In Eely Bridge I must imagine.' Cassie sobbed her shame, 'I died when the first signs of plague appeared on the villagers. None dare return for me. All know your pestilence lurks there still. You ring the bells each dusk.'

'Not I.'

'Can I not come over?'

'You needs find your body first.'

'Then why did you summon me?'

'Because I bear you a message from our Lord.'

Cassie shuddered at the thought of who would be lord of these grey souls. 'Is he here? How would he know of me?'

'Our Lord labours in many places. He says go back. Your tasks are not done. One has come who carries evil in their heart, death stains their hands. You must thwart them if you can.'

'I can't. I'm spent. I have been on the wrong side for too long.'

Cassie made to leave the boat, but those on the bank pushed close and made no room for her.

'You have no side. Go back, save your sisters.'

'How?'

The girl indicated Nouhou with her good hand, 'The creature will take you if you outwit it.'

Save my sisters. Cassie sat back in the boat. She picked up the lapwing skull and moved it to the side of the boat. Nouhou watched it go. She handed it to the girl, who handed it to others, who carried it up the bank. As soon as it disappeared from sight, Nouhou sighed and busied himself with the rope. He looped any spare rope around a cleat, used the oar to free and turn the craft and then hauled the boat back towards the jetty. Before the boat left, the lapwing skull was smuggled back to Cassie and she held it out of sight beyond the boat's side.

Nouhou's slight frame was fighting the mainstream current but still he hauled away at the rope and the craft reached the jetty. The child was exhausted but eventually climbed onto the structure and made the boat fast. After he left, Cassie followed his light steps along the boardwalk, hiding the lapwing skull on her way.

As she reached the garden she found Nouhou hiding behind the hydrangea bush. Looking to the house, she saw a dark shadow gliding around it. The figure peered in windows to study the interiors. As it reached the back door, she saw it glance up to Miss Pikestaff's window above. It was now open but the candle had been snuffed.

Cassie walked silently past Nouhou towards the figure, which was about to try the door to the back-garden that the child had left open. Cassie could see no Umbra with the man, so believed she would not be seen. Close up, the man was lean and dressed in black with a tall circular hat that tasted of London, although the long rat-tails of black hair escaping below it, added a seasoning of back stairs and alleyways. That was enough for Cassie to make her guess at their visitor; no wonder Nouhou was hiding. One has come who carries evil in their heart, while death stains their hands.

The man had a practised quiet about him, but he still made some sound on the stony shingle of the path and it had not gone unnoticed. Cassie saw – though the man had not – a dark shadow move away from Miss Pikestaff's window. The governess had perhaps been lying awake and the sound of soft steps at the back of the house, had been enough to alert her.

Unlike her sisters, Cassie had respect for Miss Pikestaff's blend of brittle polish and flinty efficiency. Since the incident with the larcenous counterfeit artist, Cassie knew her to be deceitful and a danger to her sisters. However, Miss Pikestaff was wary of acting openly and displaying her true colours. This midnight interloper likely shared no such reluctance. It was the London ruffian Mr Tenebris had spoken of. The one who knew too much about the planned attack on her sisters and who was thought a threat to Nouhou.

Cassie felt thankful it was Miss Pikestaff who had awoken. She judged the governess to be the person most capable of dealing with the danger approaching the house.

The figure stiffened, perhaps at the soft pattering steps of Nouhou, who was racing away, back down the boardwalk, or, some sense touched by Cassie's presence. The clouds parted and a lone shaft of moonlight framed the man searching his pockets. He brought out a short stubby weapon of some kind and then a polished disk of glass that plucked eagerly at the returning moonlight. Cassie did not fear the first but some instinct warned her against the latter. She ran and hid.

The man held the glass to his eye and began a slow circle of enquiry around the garden. Cassie remained hidden and undiscovered. Still suspicious, the man approached the back door, tried it and found it unlocked. With a final stare at the night, he entered. The key turned; he meant to keep anything lurking in the garden from entering.

Cassie put her head to the door and heard soft steps creep through the hall. Why hadn't Miss Pikestaff raised the house against the intruder?

34 – AN UNFLEDGED GIRL

Stanton

Even as Mr Tenebris was being ushered out of the Minister's office, Stanton was pulling open a desk drawer and reaching for the garish cravat.

Cotteridge returned to find it round Stanton's neck and the Minister shrugging into his outdoor coat. 'Oh, dear, Minister, are things really that bad?'

'Yes, Cotteridge, this Hurting is a man we must apprehend. I have been informed by a source, most reliable, that he is behind the recent attack on young gentlewomen in the Fens. He ordered O'Brien to impersonate Mr Tenebris there. Now Mr Tenebris thinks Hurting travels to the Fens himself to complete O'Brien's mission. My cravat is a signal to an agent from the Ministry of Retaliation.'

'Or we could send a memorandum between departments, sir. Our system is old but well tested and worked long before we heard of utilising detestable neckwear.'

◆ ◆ ◆

Stanton roamed the roads between Whitehall and the Strand, as far as St Clement Danes Church, then down to the river near Blackfriars. He thought he saw Larkwing's child duck away from sight at one point but no-one approached.

He knocked at the door of the house he had requisitioned

for Larkwing to imprison O'Brien, and some other disruptive fellow the Keeper wanted out of Baynard Castle Prison, but received no answer; only some scuffling from inside. Stanton visited the nearby prison and saw the Keeper, who asked if the Minister had a key as the temporary prison was locked and neither Larkwing nor his guard were there at present. Stanton said he had one at his home. The prisoners needed feeding, said the Keeper.

On his return to the Ministry, Stanton saw the dark-skinned urchin, against a railing close to The Embankment. 'Where is your master, child? I must speak with him hastily.'

In reply he was handed a scrawled message: 'My dearest Stanton, our prey is out-manoeuvring us. Dearbhla believes Muscari is closing in on "the People's Queen". I need hardly remind you what follows if Hannah Lightfoot is murdered; our own dear King will be taken from us.

'Worse news follows: as we know these Frenchie agents are well-connected with Lord Strathearn and Viscount Exeter among their number. I can no longer trust mine own Ministry, so have been forced to go to ground. Please resolve things with the prison Keeper. Arrest Exeter if you are able.

'Pray take a flame to this message.'

Stanton looked down but the child had already gone.

Back at the Ministry, Stanton organised for constables to be sent to the Fens after Mr Hurting and to urgently safeguard the Gracegirdles' governess, Miss Pikestaff, whose life was believed to be in danger from this man.

This done he asked Cotteridge to organise a messenger to go to his home in Marksfayre and request the servants to discover the spare key to O'Brien's temporary lodgings, from inside his study desk, and to bring it to the Ministry. Finally he ordered that Cotteridge arrange an audience with the First Lord Pitt the Younger, at the earliest opportunity.

'He will ask what you wish to see him about, Minister.'

'Let him know that a French plot has been uncovered that threatens King George's life and that the assassin is an Umbra.

Also that several important personages may need to be questioned.'

'Good lord, we will have to inform the Earl of Grenville and his Ministry if it involves the French.'

'Yes, yes, Grenville is already aware. He, too, should be at the meeting. And, Cotteridge, prepare a warrant for the arrest of Viscount Exeter. I wish to discuss it with Pitt.'

Word came back later that Pitt and Grenville would meet Stanton at 3 o'clock in St Stephen's Chapel and that Jenny Moonshine would be present as it 'touched deeply upon the notoriety and trustworthiness of her kind'. She wished for Agnieszka and Maraziel to attend also. Stanton was exhorted to keep the King from being assassinated over the luncheon.

'I tell him the King's life is in danger and he says it will wait until 3 o'clock?' Stanton was anxious about the meeting for he had barely met with the First Lord since he had been put in post.

'Pitt will wish to consult first, sir. It is ever his way.'

'With who?'

'With Miss Moonshine for one, sir. She keeps particular hours.' Cotteridge consulted a chart. 'And the moon does not rise until 2.35 today. In the meantime I have news from the Other Realm.'

'What now?'

'My Umbra, Meg Mantis, has discovered Keeper Claw. She did not know him before but sought him out. He guards a gate at the Citadel.'

'As I was informed by his ally. Thank Meg for her diligence, Cotteridge.'

'I will, sir, but she says you must speak with Keeper Claw at the earliest opportunity.'

As Stanton puzzled over what Meg might have discovered about Midden's brooding Umbra, an under-clerk entered to say the key to O'Brien's temporary gaol, which Stanton had sent for, had arrived. He added that the messenger needed to see the Minister.

'Why so?'

'News from home.'

Stanton looked up to see Isabella entering his office, brandishing the key. 'Here is your key, Sebastian. Mr Cotteridge, could you spare us a moment, I have business with my husband.'

Cotteridge stood and invited Lady Stanton to take his seat at the Minister's desk.

'Whatever can it be that brings you here, Izzy?'

'I had to search your desk for the key, Sebastian, and I discovered something else quite by chance.'

It was the swirling hairs escaping their tie, the mis-buttoning of the blouse beneath her redingote, the careless fragility of the woman sitting across from his desk that made Stanton's thoughts race until they hit a certainty and shattered into shards he didn't know how to piece back together.

'The letter,' his voice broke the silence she had cultivated. 'You read it.'

'I had not intended to, but I saw my name upon it and, being near driven mad by the rumours being spread about me, I could not then put it down.'

'Rumours being spread about you.' The words were all he could scrape together from the splinters left to him. They didn't even form themselves into a question.

'I think you know full well the rumours. I think back to your face when I told you last night that I was distraught about some gossip. I realise how naively disingenuous it was for you to ask about my family when I so clearly had to be talking of myself. I think you knew of it regardless of the letter in your desk.'

Stanton could not turn his gaze to find her glistening eyes. 'I had gleaned a little of it before the letter came to me, it is true, Izzy, but –'

'I dare not ask by what means you find yourself in possession of a very private letter meant for another, Sebastian. Did you have to pay a very great sum to steal it? Was it offered up as a blackmail item perhaps? Or did you intend to blackmail the Viscount with it, as seems more likely?'

'No, it is to do with another matter.'

'I cannot think what. What I find most disturbing is that you kept this letter from me. I prefer to think of myself as a woman of spirit and perseverance. But you know, better than any, how broken I was after my encounter with the Viscount, for it was you that put me back together again, piece by brittle piece.

'Of course you cannot imagine what it is to be an unfledged girl of seventeen, confidence only just emerging, drinking in the world and letting dreams take wing and then, after one night of imagined romance, to risk all on an appeal to a man who I deemed both interested in me and in accord with my spirit and desires.'

'I have exper –'

'What then to have the heart I laid at his feet in my letter, not gently broken, not returned, but callously ignored as if it had never been. It felt trampled underfoot, so that I must grow a new one sheathed in tougher hide. I spent nights crying against my pillow, pondering what I had got so wrong, wondering at my madness to plead for love from a man who so plainly hated me.

'And in your hands, who I thought adored me, I find the antidote to all this, but never administered, kept hidden away, lest I forget the state in which you found me.'

'Izzy, I never meant, I did not know...'

'You withheld the proof that my instincts had not played me false, that this man did feel himself my soulmate and want me for his own wife. The proof that my own note was not the imprudent act of a misguided girl, but contained feelings that would have been reciprocated – if not for the scheming of a jealous Umbra.'

'What says Twoshrews?'

'There is much that you have given me, Sebastian, but I think I shall come to prize above all, the knowledge that Twoshrews, when asked a direct question, must give back the truth. I asked him if he was involved in this foul design and he had to admit he was. Twoshrews is banished. He will visit me, for he must, but no more will I acknowledge him or listen when he speaks to me. He will be sent immediately back to his realm.'

Isabella made to get up and, perhaps realising that she would walk out of his life forever, Stanton could only admire her steadiness of speech, the postponement of her tears. He thought he could never love her more than in this moment.

She paused, eyes alighting on a piece of paper on the table. 'And what is this? A warrant for the arrest of the author of the letter. Are you so jealous, Sebastian, that you would condemn an innocent man whose only crime was to admire your wife and who had the grace to keep that knowledge secret... but for a letter that fell into the hands of a miscreant?'

In a flash she was up and swept away in a bustle of petticoats, quick steps and shushing door.

35 – THE DECEASED DUCK

Larkenfen

Lavinia was unsure what had awoken her but she had barely opened her eyes before Cassie brushed through her door intent on rousing her.

'Oh it's you, Cassie. I awoke and felt something was wrong.'

'We have an intruder in the house. I am sure he is the London scoundrel Mr Tenebris warned us of. The one who means Nouhou harm. He is armed. I have been warned that he may be capable of murder.'

'Warned by who?' Lavinia was busily dressing.

'Does it matter? You must wake father.'

'I would not involve Papa in rough and tumble with an armed London ruffian. See where he goes and come back to me. Let us learn what we can before he suspects we are awake.'

Moments later, Lavinia met Cassie on the stair. 'He is in the schoolroom. There is little moonlight so he has lit a candle.'

'There are few valuables there.'

'Some candlesticks only, but he is looking through Miss Pikestaff's lesson plans and studying father's pictures. He has some kind of scrying glass.'

'Could we lock him in?'

'He would hear you approach and grab you before you closed the door.'

'We need a distraction.'

'That can be arranged, Livvi. You get the keys.'

Lavinia slipped to Papa's study for a set of house keys and removed the one to the schoolroom (marked 'parlour'). Cassie emerged from the kitchen carrying tomorrow's dinner. Lavinia smiled and nodded and Cassie raced ahead of her twin into the schoolroom. The duck was half-plucked, which probably made it still more effective as it burst into the room and made a poor impression of flying at the intruder, who stumbled back, nearly tripped and lost his tall hat.

He and the duck glared at each other as the fowl stood on Miss Pikestaff's desk. The intruder bent to retrieve his hat at the same moment the door clicked closed and the key turned.

Cassie brushed through the door, duck-less. She reported that the man had been trying to reach for his glass. The twins grinned at each-other and would have hugged if they could.

'Now sir,' Lavinia spoke quietly against the door as she saw the handle turn ineffectually. 'Tell me what you do here before I raise the house and send for the constable.'

'I judge from your voice that you are one of the formidable Miss Gracegirdles that my associate Mr Tenebris has told me of. I admit you have bested me and I know not how you managed it. You exceed your reputation.'

'You live up to yours, sir. We were warned a visitor would arrive, who...' Cassie repeated her description, ' carried evil in their heart and death on their hands.'

'It is a warning that you should hold to be true, Miss Gracegirdle, but it does not apply to me.'

'You enter our house at midnight without invitation, sir, you skulk around our possessions, study us with some scrying glass and you carry a weapon. This is not the occupation of an honest man.'

There was a dark chuckle from behind the door. 'Yet I was no match for your deceased duck. Put that way, I bow to your argument and I must apologise for my poor judgement in arriving at Larkenfen after dark. Mr Tenebris led me to believe you were in danger, hence my haste.'

'We can defend ourselves, sir.'

'You have proved it.'

'Where have you come from?'

'Cambridge by horse this evening but just yester-eve I met with Mr Tenebris in his studio in London.'

'Here then, is my suggestion, sir. You are to drop out your weapon and glass from the window, which we will keep.' Protests began behind the door so Lavinia added, '...for now. You are to take horse back to Reedston, find quarters there if you can. Tomorrow at 10 o'clock you may present yourself back here, ring the bell and tell us your business. That is the gentlemanly way to conduct affairs.'

'True, but I would prefer to keep my trinkets. There is little to stop me just climbing out the window and escaping to my horse?'

'Except the schoolroom windows are tall but narrow and you, sir, are lofty and angular. I shall await you outside with kitchen and garden implements and do what damage I can to your person as you struggle out. Meantime, my sister will untie your horse and set it a-gallop away into the fen.'

'How?' Cassie laughed and Lavinia needlessly shushed her.

'You win, Miss Gracegirdle. My implements will be left in your safekeeping, hostage against my return tomorrow and good behaviour. Do I have your word that you will restore them to me if I satisfy you as to my intentions?'

'My word as a Gracegirdle. I swear upon my family's crest. What are these implements, pray?'

'Things brought from London to find the kind of demon your... sister was it?... warned you of. A Selkie glass will reveal the Umbra nature of a thing when it is viewed through it. The weapon is venerable and valuable, it is a Faun's horn. It... well it... is to do with creatures in the Other Realm.'

'And its effect on an Englishwoman..?'

'A deep and nasty scratch, I would think.'

'When you return, sir,' said Lavinia, 'you must tie up your hair or my mother will not grant you admittance.'

Cassie laughed.

The deal was agreed upon. First, the Umbra items accommodated in a thin goatskin bag were dropped outside to be recovered by Lavinia, who was much surprised to find Nouhou waiting for her upon the darkened doorstep and sent the child upstairs to his room. Next, the man made his awkward exit through the window and away to his horse.

◆ ◆ ◆

The sisters gathered at the entrance to Larkenfen at 10 o'clock. Naomi and Lavinia carried blades. The Selkie glass and Faun's horn, if such they were, were hidden in the schoolroom.

Their parents had not been told of the visitor. Lavinia argued that they may let slip about Nouhou's presence there. Mother had taken the carriage, father was in his studio, Miss Pikestaff, unusually, had not stirred from her room. Nouhou had been warned to stay hidden.

Cassie asked her sisters that, from now on, Nouhou be told that she had disappeared.

'Why so?' asked Tabitha, who had appointed herself the waif's guardian.

'Because too many people know of me since Mr Tenebris added me to his painting,' said Cassie. 'Galt is always busy peering into his little mirror, father asks Hellekin about me. I intend to be here only for you three.'

The man arrived, dismounted, tied his horse to the remains of the gatepost, took off his hat, bowed low and introduced himself as Mr Hurting. His greased black hair was tied back but otherwise he was still attired like a sliver of night.

'What is your business with us, sir?' Lavinia led the way to the house.

'To satisfy myself on your safety. To pay my compliments to your father, to study his paintings if I may, and to introduce myself to your governess.'

'Then why would you bring a strange glass and your outlandishly carved horn?' asked Tabitha, who had been most taken with the treasures. 'What are we to make of these?'

'The Selkie glass is useful for seeing things that are Umbra in nature. I have a fondness for horns and this one has been especially marked with certain elemental runes in the Other Realm. I am told it has magick properties, but have never had occasion to use it.'

'You believe in magicks, sir?' asked Naomi.

'Believe rather than practice. However, I think Miss Lavinia is more able to answer to magicks than I. Last night she conjured a duck to attack me, even though I later discovered it to be dead.'

They reached the house laughing.

Lavinia sent Tabitha to ask maid for juice, fresh scones and beer, while she escorted Mr Hurting into the schoolroom. She noted that Miss Pikestaff's papers had been removed. So, the governess was awake.

Mr Hurting made a study of their father's paintings. 'These are the Other Realm I imagine.'

'They are Papa's dreams and visions. They may be related to Umbra.'

'Where is your Umbra, sir?' asked Tabitha.

'Brughe is in the Other Realm. He is searching for someone. It is too urgent for him to attend me and meet with you.'

This short speech brought Mr Hurting to the painting titled, 'The Ace of Moons'.

'This is extraordinary. I have seen this creature. She is an Umbra. When was it painted?'

'We have seen her likeness, too,' Naomi spoke before Lavinia could stop her.

'Mr Tenebris's Umbra, of course you have. Was she much present when he stayed with you?'

'She was only in evidence when he first arrived, sir,' said Lavinia, 'but this painting was completed two years ago and comes wholly from my father's imagination, like all his work. It is a coincidence, that is all. What do you wish to discuss with our governess, Miss Pikestaff?'

'That is between me and Miss Pikestaff,' Mr Hurting supped his beer. 'She made an impression on Mr Tenebris and he sends his compliments to her. He thought he saw her in Cambridge when he travelled through it on his return to London.'

The girls were puzzled. 'That is unlikely, sir,' said Tabitha, 'she was absent for much of the day but how would she get there?'

'Tabby,' said Lavinia, keen to move things along, 'could you go up to Miss Pikestaff's room and say she has a gentleman caller. Warn her that it is a Mr Hurting and ask whether she will attend him.'

Tabitha did so and returned shortly to say that Miss Pikestaff would meet Mr Hurting on the boardwalk in due course but requested that Lavinia did not return the trinkets to the visitor until after this rendezvous, to ensure his good conduct, for she was a single woman. She said that after this meeting, Mr Hurting should be asked to leave as he was not a fit acquaintance for refined young ladies.

Lavinia offered their guest a scone. 'Let us speak plainly, Mr Hurting. You are here to do harm to someone. I am not yet sure whether it is one of us, our governess, or another. You are not a friend to Mr Tenebris, who is afraid of you. You told Mr Tenebris of an attack upon us, before it happened. What is afoot that concerns us and is of such interest to you that you arrive at night from London?'

Mr Hurting choked on a morsel of scone and studied the three young girls at length while he recovered. 'There is much afoot, Miss Gracegirdle, in truth I do not know how much of it concerns you three... or are you four?' His stare flared about the room.

'Our beloved sister, Cassie, is dead, Mr Hurting,' said Naomi.

'Perhaps so, and yet I saw her illustration only the other night. My answer begins with a question: do you know the origins of your family crest?'

'The Old Queen, sir,' said Naomi, 'she was from the Fens and passed her crest on to our ancestors.'

'And her sigil was also her treasure,' said Hurting, 'The Mistletoe Sprig brooch. Some believe it was the source of her power and many people have wasted their time on Earth in trying to rediscover it. In bygone times, Larkenfen was naturally a place they would look to, but nothing was ever found and your home has fallen from prominence.'

'The false artist, who preceded Mr Tenebris, claimed to be searching for this Sprig,' said Naomi.

'He thought to find it secreted in our undergarments?' Tabitha blushed deeply as soon as this escaped her. Mr Hurting also seemed discomfited at the suggestion. 'He had been ordered to kill whichever of us hid it. How would that help his cause?'

'He is directed by a cruel master, I think,' said Hurting.

'And who is your master Mr Hurting?' asked Lavinia.

'I have many, but I have come to Larkenfen at mine own behest.'

Naomi had been thinking quietly. 'Why is this happening now? Why the sudden activity around three girls, too young to have their Umbra? Why would Larkenfen now attract those who seek the Sprig, after centuries when we were forgotten.'

'Because, Miss Gracegirdle, it is around five hundred years since the Queen 'Neath the Hedge first entered history, becoming of an age to be allied with an Umbra. Many, both Umbra and Englishmen, think this anniversary will be significant. It is making them desperate.'

Cassie, who had been out of the room, returned. 'This grows too comfortable. Let us not forget I was told that this man has death on his hands. I have just looked in on Nouhou's room. He has vanished, gone into hiding I think. Hurting knows more than he tells us.'

'Desperate to do what?' Tabitha's ire had been forged in Cassie's report on Nouhou. 'It hardly explains why Arnold was ordered to kill us, or how you knew of it.'

'I am...'

'You are evasive, sir. You know how we are connected to

this.' Lavinia felt for the blade wrapped in her petticoats. 'You should either tell us all and prove our friend, or you should leave.'

The maid knocked and entered. 'Beggin' pardon, young misses, but Governess Pikestaff is on the boardwalk and says she will not tarry long. If your visitor wants to see her, he must go alone there, now.'

Mr Hurting rose and bowed as he retreated to the door. 'I have kept things from you. Things I have no certainty about and would not cause you to worry over needlessly. I intend to tell your father.'

'You will not have the opportunity, Mr Hurting. We have risked your company long enough.'

He hesitated. 'You are right. I realise now you need to know and are resourceful enough to use the information wisely. I will say more after my visit with Miss Pikestaff. Tell me, though, have you noticed her much changed, say, in the last few weeks?'

'Yes, sir; she had never before conspired to rob or kill us.'

'Ah, then, could I perhaps have my –'

'Your items will be returned to you after you meet our governess,' Lavinia pointed to the door, 'providing you survive the encounter.'

36 – ST STEPHEN'S CHAPEL

Stanton

Stanton arrived at St Stephen's Chapel, burdened by the turbulent wake of Isabella's visit and a much put-out tousle-haired Umbra who blamed him for politicking during a scheduled nap time.

'Hush, I had not wished you here, blame your compatriot Jenny M, it was her insistence. Please try not to fall asleep or embarrass me in front of Pitt, who I know you do not admire, and do not be rude to Agnieszka. In truth, I wish that we both stay quiet unless asked a question.'

'Grenville's watery wench and Pitt in the same meeting,' Maraziel stirred into consciousness, 'Jenny does not want for wet companions. I suspect she does it for sport, do you not think?'

'I am not in the mood for your drollery. I am beset by worries. My agent is missing, gone into hiding. The cell I set up for the Irishman and his Banshee, is locked and too quiet. Isabella has taken offence. I am of the opinion that I should not have called this meeting; it is ill-timed.'

They were kept waiting for several minutes before being shown into a room. The Earl of Grenville and William Pitt (the Younger and First Lord of Parliament) ceased talking as they entered. Agnieszka back in her hunting outfit with accompanying bow and Jenny Moonshine, were also in conversation, which subsided a moment later, though Stanton could not have heard what they said.

Pitt was thirty-three and had been in power for nine years. He was at the peak of his political might, having extended his majority two years before. His rival, Charles Fox, leader of the Whigs, found his party split on the subject of a war with revolutionary France.

Jenny M, as she was known to the country, was a formidable Parliamentarian in her own right, mustering her version of the cabinet and advising Pitt of its views. She was smaller than Agnieszka but from the same willowy stock. Her skin glowed silvery and was much on show as her matching gowns were ever in retreat from her shoulders. Strange markings waxed and waned upon her face, neck, shoulders and back. Meetings were oft delayed while these signs were consulted.

Her afflicted grey hair was a match for Maraziel's in strangeness, always bound up within a thicket of thin grey sticks.

Stanton was ushered into a seat. Pitt turned to him. 'Grenville has given me a little of your suspicions, Stanton, but I would hear more from your own lips.'

'The background of this is known to you, sir, so, because time is short, let me get straight to the particulars. We have come into knowledge that King George III's life is in danger. The means of the assassination will be for an Umbra to kill Hannah Lightfoot in the Other Realm.'

'Extraordinary, and Grenville tells me you have arrived at a suspect.'

'I discovered little more than the name of two Umbra thought capable of plotting to kill their own to serve an agenda, but one of the agents from the Earl's own ministry, who is already known to you, sir, investigated further and believes Viscount Exeter's Umbra, Muscari, to be our villainess and that she is on Hannah's tracks now.'

The silence, accompanied by a stern glare from Jenny M, was enough to set Stanton talking again, though he had not intended to. 'I have drawn up a warrant for the arrest of the Viscount. We must force him to summon Muscari to our world.

She must be questioned about this matter and her possible links to France.'

Maraziel was climbing down his sleeve to join the other Umbra on the table top and he saw her pause in her descent at his assertion.

'I am ever cautious when informed "we must", Stanton,' said Pitt. 'Ministers, admirals and generals alike insist on things that *must* be done. I find necessity to be the resort of those who are not entirely sure of their arguments. What set you on this investigation? What led you to believe the King's life is under threat?'

'The information from Grenville's agent was that the Ministry for Retaliation had uncovered the plot of this French Umbra. But it is also logical; for is it not the most devastating blow the French could strike against us.'

'This agent has taken a lot upon himself and has not sought to share his suspicions with me.' Grenville's mood had soured further since last he and Stanton spoke.

'And yet,' said Pitt, 'we know that radicals are speaking against the monarchy, admittedly less to support France than to make Britain a republic. Losing George III would propel the Prince Regent to the throne and he is deeply unpopular with the people, due to his profligacy and wantonness.'

'Killing the King would be a good strategy and encourage the coffeehouse radicals,' Stanton responded to the First Lord's support.

'But why would the French approach Exeter, a man renowned for his impeccable conduct and loyalty. Surely they would seek to use the Umbra of a radical supporter of their rebellion? Is it possible Exeter does not know his Umbra has been corrupted?'

'*If* she has been corrupted,' Grenville said. 'I believe Stanton sails close to the wind with these suspicions. They suit other events in his life.'

'Hush please, William, if a man is to be condemned, it should be by his own mouth not words that others imagine are there,' Pitt gestured for Stanton to answer.

'It is possible, yes, but we felt someone of influence would be the most useful target for the French, and this Umbra was turned while Louis the XVI sat on the throne. At that time France would have had no appeal to radicals.'

'What evidence is there that any such campaign exists?'

'There have been more deaths due to events in the Other Realm in recent years, my lord, including more among The Five Hundred. The last being the Countess of Alnwick, due to the murder of her Umbra, Charon, possibly by Muscari. In addition, I am told that many noted soldiers and bureaucrats have been taken. Archbishop Feargood Chislett claims senior clergy were likewise killed prior to his appointment, and the Umbra of religious men are usually pious and rarely inclined to warfare.'

'Truly? That does suggest radicalism. We know the French revolutionaries began with a campaign against the wealth of the church. Did you know of this William?'

'We have no time to note deaths among the Clergy. My Ministry is stretched by the coming war and the scourge of radicalism that France's Republic has encouraged at home.'

'The problem is not that the radicals are wrong.' said Pitt. Grenville gave a snort at this, but Pitt continued, 'It is that to put the world to rights would require too much breakage, suffering and death. I have sympathy with radicalism, but we need only set our sights across the Channel to see the misery that accompanies change when pursued too swiftly. We must plot a different path. And that path means persuading radicals to change at a gentler pace.'

'It means stretching their necks if they support France, my lord.'

'Can we be sure we identify the activist, and not the theorist, among them?'

'Better to kill hundred innocents than let a single French agent consummate his plots.'

'Take care, William. There has always been radicalism, but now there are also newspapers. Extreme views allied to the means to spread them are a recipe for every kind of trouble.' Pitt swung back to Stanton, 'So, to be clear, an Umbra is recruited to France's side and is killing the best of us. You have sources in the Other Realm that have named Muscari.'

'In a nutshell, my lord.'

'Well, we have another source, here. When you mentioned Muscari at Whites the other day, Agnieszka informed the Earl that she experienced a premonition that Muscari would kill a British man before the moon turns full, which is –' he waited for Jenny M's contribution – 'in three night's time. It seems we must investigate further.'

Stanton swam in relief.

The three Umbra – even Maraziel – had been following the conversation. Now Jenny M was invited to speak. Maraziel and Agnieszka repeated her words to their allies.

'Jenny refuses to believe any Umbra would support the French. It is a base lie. She seems to agree with mine own opinion that Pitt is a fool,' Maraziel told Stanton. Although he could not see her laugh, he could imagine it from the way her bare brown bony shoulders shook. 'She is telling him so. It is admirable. I am glad now that you woke me. Jenny's main concern is that he has treated your balderdash as credible. Were Muscari to kill the King's Umbra it would be an unpardonable breach of the Queen's Treaty, she says. She has a point.'

Stanton's jaw fell. 'But it was you who first alerted me to Muscari as one who might kill for the French.'

The small silvery Umbra heard this and walked across the tabletop to where Maraziel squatted among a meadow of skirts, and began to quarrel with the witch.

Jenny gave vent to her thoughts, stray twigs evacuating her hair while she did so.

Agnieszka's commentary on this discussion was conveyed to Grenville. 'What is this? Was all begun by Stanton's loose cannon of a sea hag, then?'

All heads swung in her direction. Maraziel lurched unsteadily to her feet to make answer.

'While this is all commendably diverting, I propose some order before we proceed. Let me say this to all. My Englishman asked if I knew of any Umbra who would kill to order, or for a cause. I named him two Umbra, who I knew had done this and thought likely to do so again. I know Muscari could not have killed Charon, and never was any mention made to me of the French.'

Eyes turned to Stanton, who pointed at Grenville. '...because his agent insisted that no Umbra could be made aware of his Ministry's secret.'

Maraziel spoke again with her compatriots relaying her words. 'Please tell the Earl that if he ever sees a true sea hag he will know it because she will claim one of his eyes for the privilege. I find it enchanting that British innocence extends to believing that war with France and the assassination of a King to be the biggest threats to your kingdom and way of life...'

Jenny's hand flew to the witch's shoulder and she gave a clear warning to Maraziel to speak no further. Stanton saw an arrow nocked in Agnieszka's bow.

'...but let us assume for a moment they are,' Maraziel continued as if such had always been her intention. 'Muscari is, by reputation: proud, headstrong, capable of murder when in tempest and without strong affiliations – save one: she is passionately loyal to her ally, Exeter.'

Maraziel waited while her words were relayed (with Jenny M's nodded confirmation as she spoke them to Pitt), then went on: 'Muscari's bond to Exeter goes beyond devotion. She will do all in her power to keep Exeter prospering and to keep him to herself alone. She would kill… to defend him. I know because, unlike Mr Stanton, I have a faithfully truthful source.' Stanton imagined she meant Twoshrews and wondered if that had been a wink beneath her swarm of hair. He was unsure he was going to come out of this well.

'Neither King or Clergy are, I surmise, a threat to the Viscount, so all comes back to Stanton's constant source, Grenville's agent. Now I am exhausted and suggest you begin from here, while I take rest.'

Pitt listened then responded. 'Your Umbra poses a pertinent question, Stanton, who is this Ministry of Retaliation agent I'm supposed to have met with?'

'Mr Larkwing, sir; he claims his briefing to you regarding the French agent, caused you to create the Ministry of Umbra Affairs and put me in post.

'I cannot recall any such meeting.'

'We have no agent called Larkwing and never have,' said Grenville.

'It's an alias, Earl. He more or less told me as much,' said Stanton. 'He goes by many names. Lady Rochester knows him by another, she calls him... oh, what is it?'

'Lampwick?' Grenville guessed.

'That is it.'

'Lampwick is not my agent, he is a villain, sir,' said Grenville. 'He is worse than a radical, for he adopts causes that are not his own. He applied to our Ministry a few years ago and we took an interest in him, for his spoken French is flawless, but he was quite mad. He advocated that we should employ ragamuffins from the streets. Can you imagine? They would testify to anything for a penny and most likely rob those they were sent to spy upon.'

'But he had letters bearing seals from your office, his messenger arrived in a Ministry of Retaliation curricle...' Stanton's conviction withered as he spoke.

'We do not have any such carriage. As for Lampwick, I said mad, sir, not stupid. He was capable of scheming even before we trained him. His more imaginative intrigues surrounded Lady R. He was intoxicated with her; spread rumours about her, placed her behind every plot we investigated, set urchins to follow her.'

'None of which explains this affair with the King,' Stanton felt the weakness of his protest.

'Lampwick was born to a minor English gentleman, but spent his childhood in France, so, of course,' Grenville's eyes found

Agnieszka's, and there was a hint of something more than pride in them, 'the man has no Umbra.'

Stanton turned to Pitt, 'But, my lord, if you received no briefing from Grenville's agent, why did you set up my Ministry?'

Pitt lowered his voice. 'I owed a favour to Lord Lisle, Stanton. Although, I admit I was also tempted to see how you coped. You come from a different stock and belong to a different species to most of us. As for this Lampwick, where is he now?'

'In rooms I requisitioned by Baynard Castle Gaol,' said Stanton. 'He's questioning a prisoner I had brought back from the Fens, a former Irish Dragoon whose Umbra is a Banshee. He had tried to kill some young girls up there.'

'Questioning him about what?' asked Pitt.

'Initially I wanted to find out if he was the Bendith?' Stanton's voice trailed off to an apology. 'We had reports from Cambridge.'

'The what?' Grenville was dumbfounded.

Maraziel laughed, while Agnieszka and Jenny M exchanged glances.

'It is of no matter; the Irishman was not such a creature. Then Larkwi... Lampwick wished to question the Irishman further on other matters.'

'Relating to Lady R is my guess?' said Grenville.

'No, my lord,' Stanton hesitated and corrected himself, 'or well, perhaps, yes, for the man's Fenland conspiracy seems to lead back to Lady Rochester's stepson, your political opponent, Lord Strathearn.'

'My head is ringing,' said Pitt. 'Let me have clarity on two things: firstly, that we no longer believe Muscari is plotting to kill the King?'

'It seems not, my lord,' said Stanton, while Grenville gave an exasperated laugh.

'Secondly, that we no longer believe there to be any French agent and that the Borderer Charon was merely killed by the Greynhym, just as everyone supposed, before your accusations.'

'I must agree with your conclusion, my lord.' Stanton just wished to leave St Stephen's, rush back to Marksfayre and discover what Isabella proposed to do. Above all, he wished for an end to these proceedings.

'This has been a farce from start to end,' said Grenville, 'and I apologise to you, First Lord, for my part in it.'

'I will shut down the operation, and tender my resignation forthwith,' said Stanton. 'If Charon was killed by the Greynhym, there is no murdering Umbra for my Ministry to find.'

'Your resignation is correctly offered, Stanton,' said Pitt, 'let me think on it.'

Maraziel spoke closely to Jenny M, who spoke to Pitt.

'Yes, I will hear her, if I must.'

'Much as I have been intrigued by your arguments and, despite my wish to return to my bed, I feel someone should point out the considerable and likely fatal flaws in your conclusions.' Maraziel's words were repeated for Pitt and Grenville.

'What flaws, madam?' said Grenville. 'It was you who damned your ally here, and you cannot save him now.'

'I am indifferent to how my Englishman earns his potage,' said Maraziel, 'but he is right; Charon was not killed by the Greynhym – he was killed by an Umbra.'

'Who?' The question came from all sides.

'By the one known as The Mor. She has no connection to France.' Maraziel paused for Jenny M and Agnieszka to take this in and pass it on. 'Secondly, there is a French agent, and it is Stanton who has unearthed him.'

'Who?' this, from Grenville.

'The creature your Ministry invented and trained, Earl. The French agent is Lampwick and I suspect his plan to kill Britain's King is now gathering speed.'

'How so, pray?' asked Pitt.

'From all I have heard this afternoon, I believe he has achieved what he set out to; the means to coerce an Umbra to kill Hannah Lightfoot.'

37 – THE BOATHOUSE WALK

Larkenfen

Cassie sped across the garden. The sisters had taken a moment to study Miss Pikestaff and Mr Hurting through the Selkie glass but did not know what signs they were looking for. If anything, Mr Hurting looked darker and Miss Pikestaff prettier.

The governess was waiting at the start of the boardwalk. Mr Hurting strode towards her. At the last moment she turned around and Mr Hurting stopped mid-step.

'You?'

Even from behind, Cassie registered the man's astonishment.

'Mr Hurting,' Miss Pikestaff could not entirely hide her satisfaction at the man's bewilderment.

'I had expected someone, or something, to be masquerading as the Gracegirdles' governess. I never thought it would be you, madam. Do they not suspect?'

'How could they? The parents both abhor *The Book* for different reasons. Only Tabitha has any interest in The Five Hundred and she has only seen my restricted copy. In truth, I never thought to spend six months as a governess but these are desperate times, as I heard you telling my charges. Let us walk to the River Lark, sir. Take care what you say.'

'I am ever careful around you, madam.'

'I mean take care what names you use. You don't know who may be listening. '

'I understand. I brought some artefacts with me, but nothing that will reveal the aura of any deceased who linger – at least not to our eyes.'

'No indeed, you arrived with a Selkie glass that exposes the Umbra essence behind any fabrication and a horn scrawled with the elemental runes for the Bendith. Really, Mr Hurting, am I grown so old that you think me resurrected as the Bendith after some five hundred years?'

'No more, madam. It was truly you Mr Tenebris saw in Cambridge the other day. I surmised he had seen Miss Pikestaff's cast-off shell.'

'It was me, sir. I had to relay a message that lay beyond Galt's uncompromisingly pithy discourse, so went in person to Cambridge. It seems I have cost you a wasted journey.'

She prompted Mr Hurting along the old boardwalk to the boathouse, it led downstream of the jetty to a deep pool around another bend of the Lark. Cassie and her sisters knew its route but were strictly forbidden to use this section of the boardwalk. The walkway was so dilapidated it was barred by a crisscross barrier of stakes. Even Lavinia had yet to break the taboo.

'Not wasted,' Hurting led the way on the narrower weaker boards, 'for it gave me a chance to encounter the Miss Gracegirdles.'

'And be humbled by them.'

'True, I was no match for Lavinia. She relieved me of my toys.'

'It is well you do not need them. Would your make-shift horn work do you think?'

'It is not a thing you can ever practise. There are surer ways to dispatch the Bendith. I assume you have some defences against such creatures here with you?'

'I have charms that should warn me of such a presence. I did not bring any means to dispatch her.'

Cassie saw the shambolic stake and reed construction that normally prevented access to this route; it was half sunk in a nearby pool, a little way off the structure and partly hidden by clumps of sedge. Miss Pikestaff must have removed and hidden it beforehand.

'What do you make of my pupils? I am curious.'

'Before I met them, I considered it unlikely these particular young ladies would be involved. I always felt if she returned it would be as someone none of us could suspect. The Gracegirdles are of an age, true, but it seemed too obvious a place to look. I knew some would search here still, so sent a warning.

'And now?' Miss Pikestaff encouraged him on. 'This walk ends in a charming boathouse – no longer in use – we can turn back after that.'

'And now I find you lying in wait. You would not be here without cause. The girls all have something about them. I wonder… it could be any of the three.'

'Or none of them… or perhaps the fourth girl.'

'Who died before you came?'

'Yes, and not at my hand. How goes the ditty?

"They seek her in the morning-o; they seek her in the evening-o; in dale, on hill, by fen;

They hunt for her in England-o; and look for her in Highlands-o; through Powys and back again;

They think she be a maiden-o; or perhaps an Umbra-o; they hunt; they kill, they fear;

They say she is returning-o; with plague and war and burning-o; after so many a year;" or some such.'

'Your version has a different last line, to the one I know. I thought you'd prefer: "She appears virtuous, but will out-do the devil."'

Cassie trailed them, but her mind had raced ahead to a conviction; Pikestaff was walking Mr Hurting into a trap. He adopted the guise of a villain, so she'd assumed the ghostly plague girl's warning referred to him. But could she have meant Pikestaff. There was no way to warn him and no time to run back to hail her sisters. Perhaps Larkenfen would be better off without either of these plotters.

'Then she must be Tabitha.'

'I understand that you did not know which of them to kill,

but I'm perplexed as to why you did not kill all of them and have done. That would be more your style, I think.'

'As I told the Irish lieutenant, I have no wish to kill any of them. I was sent here to watch and search, reporting only if I discovered the Mistletoe Sprig... until my orders change.'

'But you are happy for another to undertake the murder. This sham Tenebris, appears to have had very different orders. I assume he was sent at the behest of the El –'

'He wasn't. He is in the employ of another. I saw a small opportunity and had to find an accomplice swiftly. The soldier was already in Cambridge, knew something of the matter, he had an Umbra with a rare gift and a cruel disposition. His master's interests aligned with my master's own up to a point. These times lead us to unlikely bedfellows. Oh take care, Mr Hurting, a board is missing there.'

'The lieutenant was all for killing.'

'Naturally, he used to be a dragoon.'

Mr Hurting turned to face Miss Pikestaff on the narrow boarding. It creaked and bent forcing bubbles of marsh gas up to dimple the surface of the ponds. 'Do you deny, madam, that your master wants her dead?'

'He is hardly alone in that. Do you deny you wish to bring her back from the dead?'

Cassie could make little sense of it and wondered if they spoke of her. She used the flurry of argument to ease between them and run further down the boardwalk. Something tickled her senses, causing her to pause: the scent of wild heather.

Hurting turned to continue his progress. 'I am probably alone in that.'

'I know you think the worst of me, but I am not inclined to bloody my hands wantonly. I give you my promise, Mr Hurting. I will not kill any of the girls – on Galt's life I swear it – not even Lavinia.'

'She would take some killing, I think.' Cassie heard Mr Hurting stop and turn again. 'You think it is Miss Lavinia. If word gets out, you won't have to kill her. Others will rush here to do the job for you. No matter, I am here to defend them now.'

'Oh word is out. I will tell you more at the boathouse. Perhaps we can find some solution that works to both our ends, sir. My master wishes mostly to uncover the Queen's infamous treasure.'

Cassie knelt down and bent over to peer under the boardwalk. It was raised about a foot and a half above the water-level, and the sight of her pigtails sliding unimpeded into the pool caused her to stare a moment. She saw that most of the board supports on one side had been cut away. The posts were left in but sharpened to points. Glancing to the pool beside the walk, Cassie noticed more lethal stakes driven in and waiting, with murderous intent, below the surface of the water. This was not the work of a few hours, this trap had been laid for some time – months judging by the weeds that colonised the spikes below the water. Perhaps it had been laid for Lavinia.

Mr Hurting's tread on the boards would cause them to give way, pitching him onto the stakes. Her gaze ran on to find Galt waiting beneath the structure, just before the trap. He gripped his club. The blue Goblin was looking up and behind him to where the creaking boards gave away Mr Hurting's approach. Cassie saw the glint of the charm chain brooch threaded through some bent rushes beside Galt. The trap may have been prepared long ago but it was primed this morning and Miss Pikestaff was ready to set it off.

'Who knows about Miss Lavinia?' Mr Hurting's voice sounded closer.

'The Irish soldier works for eminent people. Their influence will help him escape, or win access to him at the least. They will be aware. I would think the Elven King has heard by now.'

'We know the King's anger was directed at another. He has had one attempt at assassination, which failed. Brughe heard the King had resurrected the Bendith to finish the job, so when I heard from Tenebris that the Parliament believed her to be in the Fens, and that the weather was set unseasonably fair, I wondered if she had been deflected. Revenge is a powerful motivation and five hundred years is a long time for it to stew. It could easily win precedence over her other mission.'

'The Parliament, sir; how...?'

'They had this confusion of Tenebrises for the Bendith. You know the fool is quite smitten with your charms.'

Lavinia, Kings, Bendiths – whatever they were – the bewildering conversation quite addled Cassie's mind, hampering her judgement. She decided that Mr Hurting was the lesser enemy and should be saved if possible. But she was at a loss as to how to warn him of the cruel trap just steps away. She cast around for anything dead, anything she could grasp. Her eyes ran the surface of the pond but stopped as she found herself eye-to-eye with the Goblin, who was gaping at her reflection. She had once grasped Galt she remembered.

'I so rarely use my charms, Quartermain, I have not the least notion if they still work or not,' Cassie barely registered the governess's words.

'They are as effective as ever, madam.' Mr Hurting made more comments but Cassie could not take them in. His foot came down and the structure bowed. She reached towards Galt, but his club was lashing out towards her temple. Cassie had no idea if he could hit, or hurt her but instinctively pulled her head away and back up.

The club thumped into the boardwalk's last viable support and the structure shuddered.

'What the..?'

Cassie saw Hurting leap back. Miss Pikestaff gave him a firm push before he could regain his balance. He was lost to the boards, but some instinct made him throw himself to one side. A mighty splash welcomed him into the pools. Cassie's hand went to her mouth. She realised Galt's role was to use his club to make doubly sure the boardwalk collapsed.

Miss Pikestaff bent close and lifted Galt's brooch from the reed. Her Umbra leapt onto her sleeve, spilling tales of Cassie, no doubt. Mr Hurting thrashed in the water, desperate to right himself. Cassie smelt blood ripen the water. One or more of the stakes must have caught him at least. However, Miss Pikestaff judged he was far from finished and marched swiftly back the way they had come. As Cassie watched her go, an amphibious hand, covered in mud and weed, caught on the broken edge of the boardwalk. After a few moments Mr Hurting's drenched torso emerged and hung there. A rip showed in his jacket and upper arm. Cassie saw more blood ooze from his leg.

'Cassie,' the man said.

She started. How did he know?

'If you are close, get after her. Do not let her spin too many lies before I can follow.'

She was up and running. She heard Mr Hurting drag himself onto the boards behind her and pull himself upright with a brittle groan.

She saw Pikestaff making speedy progress ahead of her, about to rejoin the main boardwalk. As Cassie gained on her, a breeze reared up from nowhere. It stirred the branches of nearby alders, then lashed at them with savage ferocity. A hail of spent black cones ricocheted off the boardwalk. They burst through Cassie causing her to bend low and cover her face. The wind must have been conjured it was so at odds with the day. It whipped through her, angry at her advance. It would have dismembered her if it could, flung her in scraps to the ends of the fens, but it could gain no purchase on her.

Behind her came a grunt as it buffeted against the wounded Mr Hurting.

Cassie realised she could overcome the wind. Its possession of her had snagged her memories, not her insubstantial body. She stood tall, shook free her mind, and walked determinedly through it.

When she emerged in the garden, it was to find Miss Pikestaff in conversation with three gentlemen who were all armed. One she recognised as the Reedston constable.

Miss Pikestaff was pointing back down the boardwalk. 'There is the ruffian, who attacked me, sirs. He little thought how fiercely I would protect my virtue,' she pointed behind Cassie to where a drenched, wounded and bedraggled Hurting dripped upon the boardwalk.

'You be Mr Hurting of London, I take it, sir?' one addressed him.

The accused man continued his difficult progress towards them. 'I am, good constables, but you should hear my side of this story, before we go further.'

'What have you done with Nouhou, you villain?' It was Tabitha who shouted, and Cassie saw her sisters by the back door to the house, held by the maid's arms, to keep them from running out.

'Cor blast me, sir, you 'ave caused such a stir, here-abouts,' the Reedston constable stepped forward.

'We have a general warrant for your arrest, Hurting,' said another constable. 'Some London folk want a word with 'ee. Hands forward now.'

'This woman attacked me. If you plan to take me before a magistrate, you should take her also. I have been hoodwinked. She is a... she is capable of great harm here.'

'Tha's talking a load'a old squit.' The Reedston constable applied manacles to Mr Hurting's outstretched arms.

'We must search for Nouhou,' Naomi called from under the maid's restraint. 'It may yet be murder.'

'What's that?' said Mr Hurting, looking to the three Gracegirdles. 'Tenebris's African child is here with you?'

Cassie ran to her sisters and did her best to set out what had occurred on the boardwalk and who was to blame.

By the time they had heard all, a still dripping Mr Hurting was being marched around the house to a waiting carriage in manacles. The girls ran to the front door, which the maid had locked, and then to the schoolroom window. Lavinia opened it and shouted as Mr Hurting stepped into the carriage.

'What is this man arrested for?'

'Word from London is that Hurting sent that soldier scoundrel here to do you harm and came himself when his murderous plan was thwarted, Miss Gracegirdle,' said the constable with the London accent. 'He has to provide answers for it to the Parliament.'

The sisters consulted, before Lavinia shouted again to the departing carriage. 'Do you want your Umbra artefacts, Mr Hurting?'

'No, you keep them, Miss Gracegirdle. You have the greater need. Use them.'

38 – THE HUMMING BUCKET

Stanton

≡

Umbra of note
Nixie and her human ally Jonah (also know as Grumm)

≡

The Keeper of Baynard Castle Gaol would not attend them at first. Only at Grenville's threatening insistence did his spherical silhouette appear at the gates, blocking out any internal lights. Nor was he keen to let a guard attend the room that Stanton had requisitioned for the incarceration of Lieutenant O'Brien plus one other prisoner that the Keeper had been anxious to move beyond the gaol walls.

'Sirs, it is after dark. I beg you, come back on the morrow. We will have everything prepared and can escort you to the room,' he said.

'It will not wait, sir,' Grenville's temper had not improved on the journey from Westminster to Blackfriars. Having to share the hackney carriage with two hastily found soldiers, did not prevent the Earl from berating Stanton for a gullible imbecile. The soldiers carried muskets, Grenville had his gentleman's sword, Stanton bore his newly sharpened wretchedness.

Their Umbra had returned to the Other Realm. Stanton had left St Stephen's with Pitt and Jenny M in debate over his future.

'You will be in deep water if we don't have a guard who knows the room, here this minute, Keeper. I'll have you shackled to your own castle walls,' said Grenville.

'You complained this morning that the prisoners had not had food this day,' Stanton said. 'You sent me away for a key.'

'Yes, sir, but I did not expect you back after dark. But you will have your guard, my lord,' said the Keeper with an eye for Grenville's temper.

'Where is Mr Larkwing?' Stanton asked as the guard was fetched.

'He has not been here today and the guard he brought daily to do this duty has not been seen either. We were left no key to the door and the prisoners are likely manacled against the walls and in a poor state.'

'Is it possible the guard is in there three sheets to the wind?' asked Grenville.

'No, my lord, he would not stay overnight; not for all the Old Tom in London.'

The Keeper gave his man firm instructions but would not stir himself. His guard had a long sturdy club, so they were five that went the one hundred and fifty yards to the door of O'Brien's new lodgings. No light came from within the room and Stanton struggled with the unfamiliar key in the lock.

'Are you there, Lieutenant O'Brien?' Stanton called as the lock turned. 'Stand away from the door, man.'

The door opened to darkness, a bloated stench, which made a poor attempt at escape, and the sound of a splash. The guard they had been lent held a torch and entered hesitantly with the two soldiers clipping his heels.

'There is only one prisoner here, my lord. He is safely manacled,' one soldier said as a wall sconce was lit and Stanton followed Grenville in.

The manacled man was splayed against the wall. He was thick-set, much stained and not O'Brien. Stanton had brought a jug of ale from the prison and squatted at arms length from him. 'You are Mr Grumm, I think,' he said. 'Sit up, man, and try to hold this jug.'

'We're not Grumm,' the man's voice was a hollow rasp and reeked of portents. He heaved himself into a more upright position and reached for the jug. The chains were heavy and crudely bolted to the wall.

Stanton shook his head to Grenville. 'It's not O'Brien.'

'Who the devil are you then, man?' said Grenville. 'You look like a Grumm to me. More pertinently where is the man you shared this cell with? Where are the men that guarded him?'

'My lord,' one of the two soldiers interrupted, 'there's something in this 'ere bucket.'

He nudged a large metal container with the toe of his boot.

'You may be sure, soldier, that they won't be in there.'

'For yuzzown zakes, zirs, Keeper zays do not go near tha' bucket,' the prison guard was hastily dressed, his clothes no better than the prisoner's. He had been slow to enter and quick to edge back to the door.

'It's a piss-pot, man, we need no such instruction,' Grenville said.

'Something moved in there, sir, something alive.'

The prisoner put down the jug of beer and wiped his chin with one chained hand, 'We're Jonah,' he said, 'and not to be disturbed after dark. Out, all of you.'

'Forget your name. Answer me, where is your fellow prisoner? Give him a kick for his impudence, Stanton.'

'The night's our time. Leave, come back to us in t'morning.' Some of the prisoner's stupor had left him now.

'If you want to see morning, villain, you will answer me.'

'Be-ez you quick, zirs,' the guard had one hand on the door jamb.

'Did you 'ear that?' said the second soldier.

'What did you hear?' asked Stanton. This bare room, to which he had condemned O'Brien, felt more baleful than the deepest, dankest dungeon to him.

'Humming, sir, crooning, a tune like.'

'I hear nothing,' Grenville, alone, was unaffected by the general unease.

'Youz laddy, youz bes' cumz out'.

'Go now. This is 'er time.'

'It's no piss-pot,' the first soldier had taken off his hat and was bending by the bucket. 'It's full, mind. Got a stink on it, but it ain't piss.'

'Leave the blasted bucket.'

'There, it moved again.'

'You must 'ear it, sirs, so sweet a melody.'

'Cumz youz out. Cumz youz out.'

'Go you fools. Before she stirs.'

'Out zirs, I begs you.'

'It's all swirly, like the water's full of a maid's tresses.'

'Sweeter'n honey.'

A raucous splash. Stanton stared to see one soldier's head buried in the bucket. He heard the guard's frantic steps running in the street.

Grenville was swearing. He rushed to the soldier.

'Too late. Leave 'im to 'er. Go.'

'Get that other idiot out of here, Stanton.'

Stanton tugged at the second soldier, then heaved, hauling him to the door. He could hear it now, a soft melodic murmur. The soldier was not for moving. His fellow was holding firm in the bucket, for all Grenville's heaving at his shoulders.

'Too late, too late, she has 'im now,' came Grumm's airy rasp. 'Which of ee be next?'

Stanton pushed his soldier beyond the door so violently that they both sprawled onto the wet street. The crooning call was quieter outside. Stanton sprang back to his feet and stared within. Grenville was striving to tip over the bucket, but the soldier's strangely rigid body weighted it in place.

'Ee's gone.'

'Leave him, Grenville. Get to the door, man.'

The Earl's head turned in an addled stare. He lurched to his feet then reeled. Stanton shook the lulling song from his ears, ran in, seized the befuddled Grenville and hauled him out after him.

He closed the door and locked it, just hearing: 'What 'ave you done now, Nixie? Old Jonah'll be in for a kicking tomorrow.'

The guard and the Keeper stood in the drizzle back by the Castle gates. Stanton wondered if they had been hoping that Grenville did not make it out.

He waved to the hackney and supported Grenville until it reached them. 'We'll return tomorrow, Earl. At first light.'

◆ ◆ ◆

A pall hung over Marksfayre, so that Stanton knew before he entered that Isabella would not be found inside. In tears Midden informed him that Isabella had arrived home, packed a bag and departed, with few words, except to tell cook and Midden that their master would be dining alone for several days.

'Oh, sir, her eyes were so red. Mercy on me; I fear it is my doing. '

Stanton gently removed a brightly gleaming glass from Midden's hands and assured her it wasn't.

'But that man, sir.'

'What man?'

'That gentleman in black, parading like an ebony peacock in our scullery. He set all in motion.'

'Not this.'

He noticed Keeper Claw over Midden's shoulder upon a shelf. The carmine-capped Umbra was staring intently at Stanton and saying something. Stanton realised that the words were being mouthed only and aimed at him. Midden apparently heard nothing.

'Mistress was so distressed, she didn't even hail a carriage,' said the maid, still making polishing motions, though there was nothing in her cloth.

Stanton went to his desk. There was no trace of Exeter's letter. He asked Midden if Isabella had burnt it. She said no, but her mistress had stuffed just such a letter into her bag at the last.

Stanton grabbed his coat and ran across Marksfayre Square to the home of Lady Rochester and her step-son Lord Strathearn. Lady R received him five minutes later in her drawing room. Capu was not present, nor any staff. Stanton reflected that he was alone – again – with probably the most sought-after and beautiful paramour in Europe.

Her smile contrived to hint at opportunity. 'You are not come with news from France, I think, Minister?'

'Hardly, madam, I am here to claim news from you; news of my wife.'

'Isabella; yes, I will give you news. In return you must give me a solemn promise that you will not act on it tonight but let things run their course for a day or two.'

'You ask the impossible, madam.'

'I negotiate from strength, Minister Stanton. Should you wish to hear more, you have my price.'

Stanton hesitated. 'Is she here?'

'No longer, sir… but I have seen her. I will tell you all if I have your word you will give her some time in the country with her thoughts, remaining in London with me, rather than chasing after her.'

'You have no fears there, madam. I have vital business to attend to tomorrow; lives depend on it. I am tied to London. I give you my word. I only want what is right for Isabella.'

She sighed. 'You are young to lose a wife, sir, but old enough I fear to fail one. I think you mean well, but your judgement on what is best for your wife is flawed. While Isabella is away, I should perhaps tutor you on the things women deem to be in their best interests. Desi Fitzroy being not among them.'

'Madam, I beg you, tease me no more. Where is Isabella?'

'She has taken my coach. She has an item you borrowed to return to a gentleman.'

'Exeter.'

'She feels it incumbent upon her to also warn him of his imminent arrest and that there may be threats to come against

Muscari.'

'Madam, stop, these are things that pertain to government business and the impending war against France. Things you should not know.'

'I will do my utmost to forget them. You should remember, sir, that this war is not against France, a country I hold as dear as Britain, but against the revolutionary Jacobins who have usurped my family's throne. In that struggle, you enjoy my sincerest support.'

'My lady, you were right about Mr Lampwick, as I learn is his true name. At the ball you spoke of French infiltration and said I must look closer to home. Who should I suspect, Twoshrews?'

'Why, sir, Twoshrews is as much of an innocent in these matters, as I,' her girlish laugh lit up the room. 'No, here is an example of the best reason why a gentleman should bed his maid. To discover what is really brewing in his house.'

'Midden.' Stanton regained his feet and bowed. 'Please do not repeat anything that Izzy told you, Lady R. I thank you for your information and hope that you will remind her of my love, should she return first to you.'

◆ ◆ ◆

Back in his own home, Stanton called on Maraziel to attend him and together they went to the scullery to find Midden and Keeper Claw.

'Midden, I wish Maraziel to speak to Keeper Claw. I ask that you let them converse here for they do not know each-other in their realm.'

'Mercy on me, sir, Claw is not himself, with our mistress gone. Will it not wait?'

'No, I fear I may have misjudged Keeper Claw and would like to know him better. Maraziel.' He lowered the hand that cradled the witch and she stepped onto the chopping block where Claw was studying a board of cheeses and meats. The pale-blue-skinned creature switched his attention to Maraziel. His nod suggested he understood the reason for the meeting, but Midden paced back and forth in such a flap that Stanton became only more anxious to hear Claw's thoughts.

Maraziel began: 'Keeper Claw, it seems I am remiss in not better acquainting myself with you sooner. I assumed your duties in the Citadel of False Sorrows, kept you too busy for idle chatter. It is rare I discover fault in myself, but believe that once I have remedied this, my ally will permit me to return to my bed. I intend to be blunt. What secrets does your Englishwoman keep from her master?'

Claw seemed to breathe a sigh of relief and spoke at length to Maraziel. Her wild swarm of hair vibrated with several nods and a couple of chuckles even escaped. Claw's answer drove Midden into such a flurry of 'Mercies', dramatic flopping and frantic polishing activity that Stanton sat her upon a stool, fearing she might swoon.

At length, Maraziel turned to Stanton, 'This admission is pertinent to events. According to the admirable Claw, Midden's references and appearance at your door, was not as a result of Isabella's enquiries, instead she received her instruction from the black-clad fellow who then claimed your eager trust thanks, in part, to Midden's ministrations.'

'Lampwick,' said Stanton, causing Midden's bosom to heave and gawkish clucking sounds to slither from her throat. Claw climbed onto her lap and permitted himself to be polished by the motions of her hand on his tabard.

'As we have come to know him,' said Maraziel. 'Claw says she perceived her obligations to the gentleman to be light. In return for good references, she had only to give him a sheet of your Ministry notepaper and once he had written his message upon it, to seal it with wax and imprint it with the stamp from your own desk. She presented it to your wife as having come from an impressive messenger.'

'An M.o.R. curricle drawn by two,' Stanton laughed at the memory. 'I should have realised all when I heard that absurdity.' Midden slumped further on the stool and Stanton found that Claw was patting one of her hands and he the other.

'Do not be too severe on yourself,' said Maraziel to Stanton. 'You have been played by two masters of their craft. Claw has tried, frequently, to persuade Midden to admit all to you – not least because it plagues her so. He fears you do not own sufficient cutlery and glassware for her to polish away her remorse. He is most anxious that you do not dismiss her as no place can be found for her at the Citadel of False Sorrows – presumably because hers are all too real.' Maraziel permitted herself a small flutter of amusement at this.

'Rather, he recommends a sound whipping, which he is in a position to administer if you will but hold her still, followed by a slight increase in her rations as she is thinner than he likes.'

'Maraziel, could you part your hair for a moment.'

'Why?' but she did so.

He took no little delight that her impish expression was exactly as he had imagined it would be, but then floundered into her violet eyes. Her horns were hidden by her lifted hair and the rootish growths around her jawline no longer offended him as much as they had. Today she had out-thought Britain's First Lord, almost got Stanton sacked, then somehow made him the hero of the hour and here managed to enchant him, when he should be beyond any cheer. And all between naps.

'That is enough,' she said, letting the hair spring back. 'You are becoming mawkish.'

'Pitt should accept my resignation, Maraziel. Grenville is right, I'm too unworldly for all this.'

'You will stay in post until you have provided me with Peter of Langtoft's account of the signing of the Queen's Treaty,' she said. And then, less harshly, 'Jenny M recognises your worth, she will not let Pitt dispose of you lightly.'

'Recognises your worth, you mean.'

'Summon me when you have Langtoft. I must leave you to administer your whipping. I would go easy on Midden. This disloyalty did not come naturally to her and she has suffered much for her part in it.'

◆ ◆ ◆

Grenville awaited him outside Baynard Castle walls. Only one soldier was with him, a different fellow from the previous night. Also there was the dishevelled gaol guard. Grenville handed over two small pellets of wool. 'To preserve your ears from enchantments. The guard swears there is no danger in daylight, but he has not won my trust.'

'The Keeper?'

'On his rounds. I'd string him up by his balls, if I thought they could be found amidst all that blubber... or could lay hand on rigging robust enough.

'What news of the King?

'None. Pitt will not tell him, unless he must. His Majesty is not long free of his particular illness and Pitt fears this threat against Hannah could tip him again into madness. A particular enquiry yesterday, determined that the King has no knowledge of Miss Lightfoot's whereabouts in the Other Realm.'

The guard had the key and opened the door. He also had food for the prisoner, a crust of bread and jar of ale. The soldier held a lamp and entered first, warily.

The first soldier from the previous evening was there. His dead body was slumped beside the bucket. His head was free of the water and tinged bruise blue, greening in the yellow lamplight. His mouth and eyes were open, the latter full of endless nothingness, staring into air as if it was a forgotten element.

'Welcome back, sirs,' said the prisoner from his wall. 'I fear your comrade drowned in the night.'

Grenville addressed the soldier, 'If aught stirs in that bucket, shoot it promptly.'

'You have nothin' to fear during the day. She is a creature of night, only attendin' Grumm after dark.'

'You are Grumm this time,' Stanton handed him the ale jug

and removed Grenville's woollen pellets from his ears, 'not Jonah.'

'Aye, sirs, I'm Grumm, a seafarer. Jonah is my night-time sobriquet, what me shipmates named me when they realised that too many of their brethren were slipping over the ship's rail.'

'She sings to them?'

'Calls to 'em, sirs, drowns 'em, then shows their spirits 'er world, 'neath moonlit waves, drifting between the tides. While I was at sea, she did not call so many, for she could commune with others of her kind, but she finds the bucket dreadful lonesome. I can find little blame for 'er, as we must all do what is in our nature.'

'What of O'Brien?'

'Ee could not answer 'er call for ee was chained to the wall. It drove him near mad every night.'

'I can imagine. Does it not affect you, Grumm?'

'No, sir, I do not hear her as others do. As a seafarer, I should have no Umbra at all and the one I do have behaves in a quite contrary fashion.'

'And O'Brien?'

'In the day, ee spoke of all the sights she would promise him: indomitable breachin' leviathans and porpoys; sea-birds slashing into rough water under cliffs, how small pools would brim with life of every kind when the tide slipped in.'

'Is she a mermaid?'

Grumm laughed, 'No sirs, a rougher sort, but Nixie spoke to him of her sisters' beauty.'

'How is it a sea-farer has an Umbra?' asked Grenville.

'Press-ganged as a lad, sirs, but brought back too early, too close to British shores, methinks.'

'What has happened to O'Brien?'

'Ee would do anything to get out of 'ere. That man in black, cut 'im a deal. If'n O'Brien's terrible Umbra would consent to find another in her world, he would not 'ave to spend 'nother night in 'ere with Nixie. If she would then kill this other, ee would go free. If she would not, ee could stay 'ere and they would both be driven mad.'

'Hannah Lightfoot?'

'Tha' be the one they wanted dead. O'Brien did not want to do it. Told them straight, but ee didn't hold out long. My Nixie be a torment if'n yer not used to 'er. He agreed n' they took 'im out, the dusk before this last.'

◆ ◆ ◆

'I must tell Pitt what has come to pass. Lampwick has the tide now, Stanton. It will be hard to catch him. I am sure he will have taken O'Brien to some subterranean hidey-hole. I cannot see how we can catch this ghastly Umbra of his. It may be we can get word to Hannah, through the King; warn her of the danger.'

'I armed Lampwick with this weapon. I am to blame.'

'You'll have no argument from me on that.'

'And, you should know I have lost the letter from Exeter you gave me. Isabella found it and has determined to return it to its writer.'

The Earl nodded as if he had expected such a thing. 'You cannot tell Exeter, when he asks – and he will – where you came by this copy of his letter.'

'I know.'

'And, you had best look to your duelling skills.'

'I have none.'

'You are an execrable excuse for a Minister, Stanton. Pitt said you would sink or swim. Instead you would drown us all. Furthermore, you had the effrontery to save me from a watery death last night. That is the thing I will never forgive you for. So what now?'

'We have two courses I think.'

'Go on, man.'

Stanton turned to the prison guard. 'Did Larkwing, the man put in charge here, have a small child from the Africas visit him often?'

'Aye zirs, that he did. Little fellow came creepin' roun' many times during the day, when your man was 'ere.'

'If we can find that child and follow it, there is a chance we will be led to Lampwick, and so to O'Brien.'

'Then find it we must. What else?'

'One man has bested O'Brien and his fearful Umbra. An unlikely fellow but he helped to prevent him, and her, from inflicting harm on some girls in the Fens.'

'He may at least know something. Who is he?'

'Arthur Tenebris.'

39 – A FIERCE YELLOW WEASEL

Arthur

The helmet is placed on the sand. Beneath it is Charon.

Arthur recognises the face of the murdered Borderer from many depictions in The Book of Five Hundred. *The artists have done him justice in their illustrations: usually in fighting stance on a tableau in front of the late Countess Alnwick, sunlight glinting off his celebrated invulnerable armour plate and helm, spent Greynhym imagined and sketched in around his boots. They have caught the muscles rippling down his forearms, cording around his neck, the sunlight in his blond curls and the grey eyes – eyes whose irises, the Countess had famously claimed, were flecked with the countless desperate souls Charon had freed on his sword's edge.*

But the artists couldn't capture the physical intimidation of the Borderer as Arthur sees him through Amorrie's eyes, the brutish size of the warrior when confronted by him on his own scale. He looms over Amorrie in the dreamscape.

'You've taken some tracking down, Mor,' says Charon. 'I'd all but given up until I followed the Greynhym. They had scent of your blood.'

The artists hadn't caught the cruelty in those eyes.

'Careless to be bloodied, weaponless and naked in Greynhym country,' he wipes the dead creatures' ichor from his argentium sword but doesn't sheathe it. 'It's as if you know it's your time.'

'I haven't given up,' Amorrie's voice issues from his dream mouth.

Arthur barely recognises it.

'Your buzzing is the faint thrum of rebellion, little fly. Hellico-nian and the Elven King wish you swatted. Some even say you are the Queen-to-come, Mor,' Charon steps towards her. 'Are you?'

Arthur feels his shoulders shrug.

'You may as well confess before I despatch you. For when you are dead, I will search every shred of your naked body for the tell-tale mark.' Amused eyes run over the body Arthur and Amorrie share in this dream. 'Which will not take long. Will I find the Mistletoe Sprig on your nakedness?' His sword reaches for her throat.

Amorrie's voice is faint. It must be withered by the same fear Arthur feels sluicing through him. Surely now is when he should wake. Surely he should not dream her death – his death?

'They do not know what I am.'

'What's that? I barely hear you, little Hag. Air your secret. You do not want to join Shait'n with it unsaid.'

Another distant voice rings in her head. It's... it's Arthur's voice: 'Amorrie, come now. Upon the instant.'

The sword-tip lowers to her naked chest as Charon bends his ear close. It is almost a mocking gesture.

'Amorrie!'

◆ ◆ ◆

'Enough.'

Arthur awoke to find Amorrie pacing his chest. Tremors wracked his body. His forehead swam with the residue of fever.

'That was...'

'That is enough. Your dream is a nightfrit, that is all.'

'Be assured, I know it for truth. It was the evening of Lord Strathearn's party. What I cannot fathom is how you escaped so grievous a situation. Was it my summons? That was Charon. Why did he hunt you?'

'You are too full of questions and it is light. I must go.'

'You cannot go back there, Amorrie. I have indulged you too much. Do you not realise how close you brought us to death.'

'Death would have been the least of the indignities I would have had to suffer at Charon's hands. If I do not leave at first light, we will be in danger again soon.'

'Why say you so?'

'The hunt for me goes on. Hurting's one-horned creature is upon my trail. It has more wit than Charon. I have a curlew to meet but I do not fly to escape. I need a plan to kill him.'

'Can your disposition be so bad? I have yet to use up this day's summons; I could order you back and keep you with me.'

'You do not want me with you,' she reminded him. 'You have a meeting with Scampion's ally.'

'Oh gracious, the Countess of Harrington. I pray she never hears of our roles in this affair. Our death would be a blessing compared to that. Yes, go then, but we speak on your return.'

◆ ◆ ◆

'I never saw such a thing, Mr Tenebris. You look utterly neglected, quite dissolute. Can it be that my nieces administered so many privations and mischiefs upon you,' the Countess of Harrington was enjoying herself.

Too much, thought Arthur, 'No, madam, I assure you; they charmed me utterly. You are to be congratulated on the fine choice of governess you have provided and they are a credit to her. It's just that there were all kinds of calamities at Larkenfen. A villain had visited afore me, claiming to be me, and intending theft and harm upon your relatives.'

'My sister wrote me of it. Nothing about that place surprises me, Mr Tenebris. Your little Hag must have been quite at home, I daresay.' She shared a glance with Scampion who sat beside her on the chaise. The Umbra grinned back.

'So, you didn't complete your commission?'

'No, madam, but I have the studies I need to finish their portraits in London. I have brought the paintings with me to get your thoughts, before I conclude them. Unfortunately, the misunderstanding with the imposter led to me being recalled to London to answer to the Minister for Umbra Affairs.'

'Ah, Minister Stanton, not long in post and not impressing, I hear.'

'I hope he does impress, madam, as I fear for your governess's life and must rely on the Minister to send her help.'

'But, Miss Pikestaff is a treasure. Who could wish her ill?'

'I fear it is a misunderstanding, and pray that all will be well.'

'I hope so, governesses are a delicate breed. One proven not to flourish in the Fens. You best show me your illustrations.'

Arthur went to the large table and arranged his studies and sketches with the portrait of the four girls in pride of place. The Countess approached.

'Oh they are indeed charming, as you say, or have you flattered them too much?'

'On the contrary, my lady, I have barely done them justice.'

'Well, take care this little one does not look too studious when you finish. This other is a delight, like a miniature princess. I fear this older one may appear a bit too spirited. You will have to tone her down, remember they will be in want of husbands, and men do not admire too much boldness in a wife in case they venture beyond their salons.'

'I think she has inherited some of your spirit, madam.'

She studied him. 'You are trying to play me, Mr Tenebris. You may go far, after all. Well perhaps I can find someone military who can bridle her. This fourth is a true beauty and you have captured a certain serenity within her, almost an air of melancholy. Gallants will be queuing to St Paul's to ask for her hand.'

'That is Cassie, my lady.'

'I look forward to meeting her in the flesh. I cannot wait to arrange their affairs in London. In my day we wed who we must. This new fashion for marrying for love seems fraught with danger. I daresay it will not last, but it promises to be fun while it does.'

A doorman entered with a tray. It held a communication and he spoke to the Countess about it, until dismissed.

'Well this is as unexpected as it is unwelcome. I cannot imagine what brings this gentleman hither.'

Arthur saw Minister Stanton enter from the door to the hall, his attire and demeanour every bit as dishevelled and haunted as Arthur's own.

'To what do I owe this honour, Minister Stanton. How is your dear lady?' It was as if the Countess had stumbled over the word 'wife'.

'She is… no matter. My lady, could you indulge me with a moment's conversation with your guest?'

'My guest? Mr Tenebris? Really, Mr Stanton, you presume too far. My salon is not a meeting room for the convenience of Parliament. You must wait outside, sir.'

'It will not wait.'

Arthur's hand flew to his mouth at this audacity.

'You forget yourself, Minister, I will brook no obstinacy in –'

'I'm sorry for it madam, but it is a matter of life and death.'

'Whose life could be more important than the sanctity of a lady's salon?'

'The King's.'

'Oh,' she sat down with a bump on the chaise, Scampion barely escaping a squishing. A handkerchief appeared in her hand and it fluttered towards Arthur.

Stanton turned to the dumbstruck Arthur. 'Mr Tenebris, you recall our conversation two mornings since?'

'Yes, sir, does this bear upon Miss Pikestaff's welfare?'

'No, on that I have no further news. I have tracked you here because Lieutenant O'Brien, your imitator, has escaped gaol.'

'By all the Saints. Does he intend to return to Larkenfen to pursue the Countess's nieces?' Arthur gestured to the pictures strewn on the table.

'No, he is engaged upon another victim. I must ask you to tell me all you learnt of this fellow in your contest against him, and particularly about his Umbra.'

'Dearbhla,' Arthur shuddered, and saw Scampion doing likewise.

'Yes, the Banshee.'

'She was a blood-curdling sight, all pale hair and claws. Her scream afflicted any who heard it. My Umbra and the Irish scoundrel were both incapacitated by it.'

'How was she undone?'

'Amorrie, found a way through her defences.' Arthur's eyes were on the Countess as he spoke and saw her exchange knowing nods with Scampion.

'Your Umbra bested a Banshee?'

'I told her not to,' Arthur was embarrassed to admit to such a thing in front of the Countess.

The Minister studied the paintings as he spoke. 'These are fine. Could you perhaps draw me an illustration of the Banshee?'

'Not here, but back in my studio, yes. What is this concerning.'

'The Banshee has been persuaded to murder another Umbra in the Other Realm, thereby causing the death of their British ally. We have to find and tame her urgently.'

'The King's Umbra?' the Countess sat forward.

'Hannah Lightfoot?' Arthur moved to the table and, from his case, he produced the card he had purchased for a penny at the Eel Fayre.

'Yes,' Stanton answered them both. Taking the card from Arthur's hands. He stared at it. Then it quivered in his hands as he stared harder. He spoke as if in a trance: 'She had a picture of herself with a crown, a fierce creature like a yellow weasel and a horned steed.'

'Who does, Minister?' asked the Countess.

'She calls herself "the Mad Queen",' Stanton turned the card so both could see it. 'Hannah has this card.'

'I do not begin to understand.'

'An Umbra described to me this very picture of Hannah, with a unicorn and a lion upon it. She has somehow smuggled a copy of this card into the Other Realm. Where did you get it, man?'

'At a fayre in the Fens, but they are common enough. Does it help?'

'Yes. We need to discover Miss Lightfoot urgently in the Other Realm and furnish her with guards. I now know of someone who can help us find her. Come, Tenebris, let us start on a picture of this Dearbhla.'

'Stop. Minister, Mr Tenebris and I have unfinished business. I will not be so interrupted. You act beyond your station. How is any of this to do with my nieces or the threat to their governess? I insist on hearing.'

The Minister hesitated, 'Can we trust your Umbra, madam?'

'Of course we can, you impudent man, Scampion is a High Piskie.'

Arthur did not dare intervene, but determined he would tell the Minister later that Scampion was but a common Hedge Imp.

'The link is not clear to me,' said Stanton, 'but I feel connections running everywhere. O'Brien was engaged on something that relates back to the Old Queen.'

'The Queen 'Neath the Hedge?'

'The same. He was searching Larkenfen for her treasure, the Mistletoe Sprig.'

'It is not her treasure he seeks,' Arthur was surprised to find he had spoken; more so, that others had heard him.

'What is it you know, sir?' asked Stanton.

'The sprig he searches for isn't the treasure, but a mark or sign upon the skin, I believe. It denotes something about the one that bears it.'

'Why would he search my nieces? Is the disgrace of their existence at Larkenfen not enough, that they should be submitted to this new discourtesy.'

'That, I do not know, Countess, but I am quite sure such a search goes on – both in this realm and the other,' said Arthur.

'I believe you, Tenebris,' said Stanton. 'We are all entangled in some conspiracy, about which we know nothing. It pertains to your nieces, madam, to the Church, to the Old Queen, to her Treaty, to all Umbra, it seems. I trip upon its tentacles everywhere, having begun merely to uncover the killer of Charon, the Borderer.'

'The Greynhym, surely,' said the Countess.

'No, madam, an Umbra. One they call the Mor.'

◆ ◆ ◆

Arthur waited until nightfall before he summoned Amorrie. He was back in his studio, working, from memory, on the portrait of the Banshee, Dearbhla. The Minister, Stanton, had gone back to his offices. He said he would visit Arthur in his studio soon, but for now he had to arrange to send word to the ally of another Umbra, Twoshrews.

'Is that not your wife Lady Stanton's Umbra, Minister?' Arthur had asked and found the man greatly discomfited to admit that it was but that she was currently 'with friends' in the country.

Amorrie slipped in covertly among the shadows of his pots and brushes. She appeared tired and meagre of temper.

'Is all safe?' Arthur asked.

'For you perhaps. Not for me.'

'That is nonsense. It is hardly safe here, Amorrie. I am involved again with the Ministry for Umbra Affairs. They are trying to discover who killed Charon. They know it was not the Greynhym, but an Umbra. They know this Umbra to be called the Mor.'

'They do not know that she is I, or I, she.'

'Hurting does, his one-horned creature told him so when we were at Lord Strathearn's party.'

'The hornéd devil hunts me down. I can evade it no longer. It will soon cease to be a problem. Tomorrow, either I will kill it, or it will kill me.'

'You insist on putting us both in danger.'

'I killed Charon, did I not. You saw my trap. The Borderer was well-armed and well-armoured. He was a brutal slayer.'

'I thought, from your dream, he was more certain to kill you.'

'He had been sent to do so. I had espied him close, but the Greynhym closer. I needed to get him to drop his guard, so I went naked upon the beach, without concealed weapons, my leg broken and at the mercy of the Greynhym. I gambled all.'

'Oh, Amorrie. Do you not consider me at all in this?'

'I am here, aren't I. My plan was to borrow a Greynhym blade to kill him but the Borderer himself furnished me with a weapon when he threw his argentium knife into the Greynhym closest to me. I secreted it while he was busy slaying.'

'Had Charon just left you to the Greynhym, we would both be dead.'

'He should have done so. He worried, perhaps, that they would butcher me too much for him to search my body for a sign.'

'He would kill you because others thought you had the Old Queen's mark, a sprig of mistletoe, upon you.'

'Mainly because they think I inspire dissent, but some say I have the mark, 'tis true.'

'Why would they think you have that mark?'

'They search everywhere for it. Any who show spirit fall under suspicion – near all of them innocent – human as well as Umbra. They will kill any they suspect.'

'Including the Gracegirdle girls.'

Amorrie nodded.

'Hurting's Pooka, Brughe, suspects it too?'

Amorrie shrugged.

'Tell me, do you have such a blemish upon you?'

Amorrie scowled.

40 – THE QUEEN'S SPRIG

Stanton

Stanton had rushed back to the Ministry. His note to Isabella was honestly worded, but limited in its information. He told her of his need to speak urgently to Twoshrews, and that it was related to the affair with Lieutenant O'Brien, his Banshee Umbra and a plan to kill the King. He had a wish to see her on his own part, but this affair, whilst unconnected to that, was the most urgent. He asked her to keep it to herself.

He sent the note by messenger to Exeter's country home, addressed to Isabella and marked most confidential.

It being a Sunday, Whitehall was broodingly quiet. A note sent by the Earl of Grenville informed him that King George was having a further episode of his particular malady, refusing to meet with Pitt and no longer recognising Queen Charlotte. His surgeons reported that he could not be disturbed but he had been visited by his Umbra, Hannah Lightfoot. Grenville would see Stanton on the morrow to discuss the search for the African child.

◆ ◆ ◆

Monday began with a visit from the nervous fair-haired curate from All Hallows and a sealed message from the Archbishop of Canterbury. It carefully informed Stanton that Feargod Chislett now had possession of a manuscript in London.

The Archbishop and the manuscript would be waiting for the Minister in the Crypt at St Etheldreda's in Bleeding Heart Yard, 'hopefully today or on the morrow'. He hoped the Minister would bring news of 'the matter close to both their hearts'.

'Be aware, sir,' Chislett had written, 'that the work is long, and, being written in Anglo-Norman and Middle English, will take some study to be sure of its contents.'

The famous old crypt was close to Smoothfield Market, where Tenebris had his studio. Stanton would have to arrange for Cotteridge to be with him and to summon Maraziel.

First he had to attend the meeting with Grenville at the Ministry for Retaliation.

'We are turning London over hunting for a small urchin from the Africas,' the Earl said. 'Eight of the most dependable officers in our armies have been found for the task. As of this morning we have no sightings. Are you sure he is in London, still? Perhaps he has gone to ground in whatever hole contains Lampwick and O'Brien.'

'Why use officers?'

'We breed good British musketeers to fire their fusillade across the bows of any French cavalry, but I doubt they would deliver me an African ragamuffin in one piece and sensible should they run one down. With officers from good families there is more likelihood that the urchin might survive long enough for us to question it. I hope you bring better news.'

'Perhaps; from my conversation with the artist, Tenebris, I have discovered that Twoshrews may know the whereabouts of Hannah Lightfoot in the Other Realm.'

'Then let us surround her with Umbra guards if we can.'

'There is a problem, still; Isabella is not home at present,' Stanton said. 'She is with Exeter, I believe.'

Grenville's anger flared, 'Can you not keep your wife on a shorter leash, sir. This infatuation is doubly inconvenient. I have my own plans for Exeter.'

'She attends him, merely to return his letter, is all. I have dispatched the fastest messenger after her.'

There was a knock on the door and, at Grenville's shout, his secretary entered to report that one Quartermain Hurting had arrived at Stanton's Ministry under guard and ready for questioning.

Grenville knew of Hurting by reputation and, although he did not know to what this related, asked to be present at the prisoner's questioning.

◆ ◆ ◆

Hurting arrived freshly washed, at Cotteridge's insistence, having been delivered with the stink of the fen upon him. An armed soldier also attended.

The fall of damp black hair, his growth of beard and several contusions gave credence to the accusation that Hurting was an evil-hearted ruffian.

'Do you give orders to one Lieutenant O'Brien,' Stanton asked when Hurting was seated opposite him.

'I do not.'

'Does Lord Strathearn do so?' Stanton asked, earning a glance from Grenville.

'Not to my knowledge but I only worked for his Lordship for the one party. He will confirm this.'

Stanton studied a report he had been handed. 'You attacked a gentlewoman in the Fens, I understand, Hurting; a governess of all things. It was well I was warned of your intentions. It seems the constables arrived barely in time.'

'So the governess gave report to your constable, sirs, but she gave a false account of our rendezvous. It was she who had set a trap for me. I barely escaped with my life.' He pointed to various injuries.

'Death by governess?' This came from Grenville, who was now reading the report. 'A gentle soul employed by the Countess of Harrington, no less, tasked with turning her nieces into young ladies. You think us so gullible, sir.'

'She was no governess when I knew her before, sirs.'

'No matter,' said Stanton. 'We had been alerted to your intentions by the artist, Tenebris. He believed this good lady to be in peril from your hands. The constables confirm this.'

'They would not listen to my story.'

'What, then, was your intention that you rushed pell-mell to the Fens.'

'In truth, sirs, it was to challenge the governess for I know you are searching for the Bendith and I believed the woman might be that creature.'

Grenville gave a growl of disgust. 'Not this nonsense again. Why would you suspect such a creature, not seen in England for five hundred years, to have appeared now and in the Fenlands?'

'There is only one reason for the Bendith to be resurrected, sirs; to kill.'

'Ah, here he shows his true colours. Do you confess, sir, to be involved in a plot to shed royal blood?'

Hurting's startled glance ran from one minister to the other, as if weighing them up. 'I confess that I am aware of such a plot, sirs. But it is not mine.'

'Who's behind it then? One of your employers, perhaps. Who is involved in this cabal?'

'Easier to ask who is not, sir.'

Grenville gave a guffaw. 'From whom do you take orders in this matter?'

Stanton suspected that Grenville and Hurting were now at cross-purposes, but felt powerless to intervene.

'In this matter, I am my own man.'

'I knew it, you villain. You would rid our Kingdom of a much-loved monarch and give succour to our enemies.'

'Not so, sirs. If anything, the opposite is true. May I enquire what you know and what you do not, that I may offer better assistance.'

Grenville rose and leaned across. 'You would do better to enquire how many lashes you have just earned for your impudence. You are here to answer what questions we determine, before you are hung for a French traitor.'

Hurting rose more slowly to his feet, to stare Grenville in the eye. Behind him the soldier raised the butt of his musket, ready to strike the prisoner down. Stanton's hands lifted to persuade the soldier to desist.

'What care I for your petty squabbles with the French?' Hurting's head inched towards Grenville's. 'While you set out your tin soldiers and sail your two-deckers in and out of port so all may be saluted, I toil to preserve Britain's future.'

Grenville nodded, the rifle butt thudded between Hurting's shoulders and sent him sprawling onto the table.

'One under your republican masters, no doubt,' said Grenville.

Hurting drew himself painfully upright again in his chair. 'Which royal do you refer to?'

'The King, you fool.'

'More fool you, sir, if you do not realise that there is a far more important struggle for Britain then any involving King George.'

'You, villain, are a known molester of women, a would-be regicide and far worse, a radical.' Grenville, caught the soldier's eye, 'Take him to a dungeon until he is ready to confess.'

'I have more questions,' Stanton felt a bystander at his own interrogation.

'Well, take care you do not let this one escape, Stanton.' Grenville turned to the soldier as he left, 'Do not lose sight of him, Savage. He is as callous and barefaced a blackguard as I have met.'

When the Earl had left, Stanton ordered water and food and directed the soldier to a chair, before continuing. 'You must forgive the Earl, we are all beset by troubles that may or may not relate to you, Hurting.'

Hurting was silent, so Stanton proceeded, 'You asked what we know and I would wish us to be frank with each-other for I believe that you spoke of the Queen 'Neath the Hedge in your replies to the Earl.'

Again, no answer.

'Mr Tenebris believes that men, and Umbra, are hunting for someone with a mark upon their body; a sign, in the shape of the Old Queen's Mistletoe Sprig. Is he right?'

'He is.'

'I would summon my Umbra to attend our conversation. You are at liberty to call upon your own ally.'

'My Umbra is engaged, sir, but feel free to summon Miss Maraziel.'

Somewhat taken aback that Hurting knew her name, Stanton did so.

'There will be subjects that your Umbra is unwilling to go into,' said Hurting. 'Perhaps, question for question would be fairest.'

'Mr Hurting has the look of a well-sucked delicacy,' said Maraziel, viewing the prisoner on her arrival. 'Some of his sweet shiny sombreness has worn through, leaving us with just his grim menace.'

'You have met before?' Stanton asked Maraziel.

'I have watched him before, across a room or two; we have nodded to each-other. I knew Hurting by reputation only. You were never introduced because... well, you have never before shown interest in the truly significant people.'

'I am changing, Maraziel.'

'That may not be the best course? Let me say before we begin, that this is not your fight, Sebastian. It is rather one I have taken care to keep you away from. It touches on things no Umbra can speak of.'

'The fight has come to me. Help me find questions so I understand all, Maraziel.'

'You are on your own... for now.'

'Very well.' Stanton looked to Hurting, 'What does the sprig birthmark, if such it is, denote?'

'Your guess?'

'The person's connection to the Queen 'Neath the Hedge.'

'It indicates the Old Queen, but in embryo, so to speak,' Hurting said. 'The Queen in waiting to return before she grows into her powers, therefore, her "sprig". They have searched for this sign since she departed the three realms.'

'*Three* realms?'

'If we count the land of the dead,' Maraziel salved his ignorance.

'Why now?'

Hurting laughed. 'This is not new Minister, they have been killing "sprigs" for generations before we were born.'

'But not the right ones, then?'

'Some must have been right, I suppose, for they have kept her at bay, 'til now. With each passing century, they convince themselves her time is closer. I do not know why the five hundred-year anniversary of her coming into her powers is considered decisive, but it makes them more desperate. My turn. What is your involvement in this, Minister?'

'I began investigating the killer of Charon, believing it was an Umbra working for the French. I was tricked, but my investigations into them and their realm, led me to here. Do you know why the Borderer was murdered?'

'He was ordered to kill another Umbra, one who has upset certain lords and ladies in the Other Realm. There was also a suggestion his victim bore the Queen's sprig mark. Somehow, she turned the tables on Charon. Why did you think Mr Tenebris the Bendith?'

'A report from the Fens, which proved unfounded. It was a villain masquerading as Tenebris, that was all. I have since been informed by the Chancellor of Balliol College that Bendiths are no longer possible in our realm.'

'The Chancellor tells you what Dawn Withheld allows,' said Maraziel. 'Ask Hurting why he travelled to confront the governess?'

He did.

'Firstly, Miss Pikestaff is no governess, but another commissioned to search out the Mistletoe Sprig – both the bearer of the mark and the Old Queen's treasure. I did not know that until I met with, and recognised, her. Secondly, because the Gracegirdle girls will attract attention as the Old Queen had a connection to Larkenfen. I thought this too obvious a hiding place for the sprig, but now... I am not so sure.

'Thirdly, my Umbra informed me the Bendith was supposedly summoned after Charon failed in his quest. The Bendith was sent after this rebellious spirit.'

'The Mor?'

Hurting stared at Stanton, 'You are assiduous, Minister. Yes, the Mor. She is chaotic, with no temperament for leading a rebellion, but it was felt her open ferment might inspire others. Using Charon was heavy-handed, but all expected his assignment would be an end to her. It back-fired, as our American cousins would have it.'

'I know the term. How so?'

'She killed him. I cannot think how. The thought of invincible Charon leading an army against them inevitably kept many in the Other Realm in order. Those who feigned support for Charon's lord's faction, will feel freer to agitate a little more openly. And the Greynhym have reacted, albeit slowly. Most of the creatures enjoy little wit beyond a raw cunning borne of desperation, but if there is a crack in Umbra defences, Shait'n's legions will find it.'

'The Greynhym can never get back that which they have lost; no more can they ever stop striving to do so,' said Maraziel.

'So you were wrong about the Bendith being after the Gracegirdles?' said Stanton.

'I'll admit this concern has plagued me. I doubt it is the governess...' Hurting thought a moment. 'But there are too many coincidences. The days have been unseasonably fine in the Fens, and were still when I left. Yet, clouds rush in to cloak the moon at night. I was also beset by a ferocious wind there. Why do you laugh, Minister?'

'Because we get those in London; in Bedford Square, no less. A devil wind there was brought on by a man in a coat of bees, if I recall correctly.' Stanton chuckled again.

'A devil wind? That was exactly what the child called it.'

'What child?'

'Nouhou, an African child, a page boy who had been thrown out of his master's London house. He witnessed Tenebris attacked by "a devil wind". The boy followed Mr Tenebris to the Fens and is there still, despite the artist's return.'

'That is impossible. I know the child you mean. We currently search for this urchin all across London. She is a messenger to the man who plans to kill the King. She cannot be in the Fens, Hurting; I have seen her too recently in London.'

'Why do you say, "she"?'

'I thought her a boy, but Lady Rochester said the child's mother had made the girl pretend to be a boy as their London family would value an African boy but not a girl. Believing this, the family made her into their page boy, but when her mother died, the truth was revealed and the girl thrown out to forage on the streets.'

'This child messenger, what was her demeanour?'

'Taciturn, no emotion beyond mournfulness. I never heard her speak.'

'By all the souls of Shait'n.' Hurting leapt to his feet. 'Here is our Bendith. This one in London is the creature's shell. The one in Larkenfen is the assassin. Miss Pikestaff swore to me she would not kill any of the sisters. She did so secure in the knowledge that she already had her killer, the Bendith, primed and ready to murder. Pikestaff may have her own reasons for preserving the Bendith's original target, and must have convinced it that a chance to avenge a past failure lay among the Gracegirdles.

'Minister, I must return to the Fens.'

The soldier was upon his feet as quickly and aiming his musket at Hurting.

Maraziel said, 'Someone should go.'

'He cannot,' Stanton pointed at Hurting. 'He is under arrest. Grenville would have us both shot if I freed him. I cannot if I am to save King George.'

'You are condemning one of those sweet girls to death,' said Hurting. 'You are condemning the Other Realm to misrule; you be may be condemning all Britain.'

'But, to what?'

41 – NOTHING IS AT IS SEEMS

Larkenfen

'They spoke of something called a Bendith,' Cassie was giving her sisters details of the conversation she had overheard between Hurting and Miss Pikestaff. 'It comes from the Other Realm, but is here in the Fens, we must suppose, and it is an assassin.'

They turned to Tabitha, who had most interest in the Other Realm, but she shook her head. 'I have never heard of it.'

'Hurting thought Miss Pikestaff could be one and that is why he bought a Selkie glass to spy her out. And the horn, I think, is meant to hurt it.'

'We must find out what it is,' said Lavinia, 'especially if Miss Pikestaff may be one.'

'How? Tabitha knows more about the Other Realm's peoples and creatures than either mother or Papa,' Naomi was thinking aloud. Her sisters knew the signs and knew better than to interrupt. 'We have to ask an Umbra, but we would need their ally to relate their answer to us.

'Hellekin, is the one I would trust most, but Papa will not understand, quickly lose interest and, he tells us, Hellekin is hazy and likely to drift off topic.'

'She will only tell us that, "Everything is fluxed, and nothing is as it seems,"' Tabitha said.

'Mother's Woodbastick spends so little time here and that

Gnome Grimstone is barely intelligible according to maid,' said Lavinia. 'The post boy has a new Umbra. If we could capture him...?'

Tabitha and Naomi both giggled.

'This is serious,' Cassie had not mentioned that Hurting believed Lavinia the most likely to be killed. 'Hellekin must be our source. Papa always says she observes things in the Other Realm many Umbra would miss. We need to find a way to talk with her.'

'Questioning her is easy. She understands us perfectly well and Papa invariably naps after his luncheon,' said Naomi. 'The problem comes in hearing her answers.'

'I have something that may help with that. Here comes Nouhou, so I will go. Miss Pikestaff and Galt know I am here still, but they may not have confided in Nouhou.'

'Nouhou spends little time with her since Mr Tenebris left,' said Tabitha. 'They have fallen out. Perhaps Pikestaff's connection to Hurting has made the child mistrustful.'

'What did you find out about Hurting, Livvi?'

'Only that the constables proceeded with him at haste to Cambridge and there to London.'

'Perhaps, he thinks Pikestaff will do harm to Nouhou, if he cannot. We must make sure that she is not left alone with the little darling.'

◆ ◆ ◆

After lunch on the Monday afternoon, they gathered outside father's studio.

'Cassie, you can go silently without opening the door to check if Papa is asleep,' said Lavinia. 'If he is, we will creep in.'

Cassie eased into the studio and saw her father asleep. Hellekin lay across his head, seeming to murmur into his ear. She pulled away at the same moment, her eyes frisking the room. She wore an elaborate head-dress that Cassie had not observed on her before. It looked like a slender upturned claw. By the time the other three sisters had been called in by Cassie, Hellekin was sat upon a table, at the limit of their father's aura, awaiting them. The head-dress had gone.

Lavinia put her finger to her lips and they crept close to the table. 'We need to ask you some questions, Hellekin. Can you answer quietly.'

The Umbra pulled her loosely-woven black shawl over her shoulders and studied the three in turn. Her mouth formed words.

'Oh,' said Cassie, 'I had forgotten.' She pulled out the dead plague girl's gift from a pocket and pushed the nebulous pellet of vapour into her ear. 'Ask her to repeat it, Livvi.'

'The fourth sist-kin is here too, I knows,' Hellekin twitched as she spoke, 'though I sees her neverwhere.'

'It does work. And she knows I'm here,' said Cassie.

'Cassie is here, Hellekin. She can hear you,' said Naomi.

'Howso?' Hellekin crouched down on all fours, eyes boggling.

'Quickly, Livvi, she's going to bolt,' said Tabitha.

'Hellekin, we are in danger. You must help us. What is a Bendith?'

'A thing conjured in my realm forto kill in this one. It forces 'isself insides a person and splits'em in two.' Hellekin grimaced and her claw hands wrested an invisible thing apart. Cassie passed her words on.

'Two?'

'Each part looks wholesome. One part has the body but no spirits and fewer wits. The other part has all the potency. She is full of malices and deviousness. The one who's here, she is that part.'

'There's one here, at Larkenfen,' said Cassie, 'It's a "she".'

'She?'

'Evers and always a "she".'

'Is it Pikestaff?'

'Who s'a?'

'Will these help?' Lavinia pulled the Selkie glass and sharpened prong of horn out of the bag and placed them on the table.

Hellekin leapt back, then crept hesitantly forward, pushing a tentative finger at the items placed on the table. 'Selkies' glass,' she said eventually, then smiled, 'shows things that are not what they seems.' She tapped two of the runes carved into the horn. 'This is for Bendith,' she made a stabbing gesture, 'to kill it – to sends it back into its other half.'

'Why is the Bendith here?'

'To kill.' A bent finger pointed slowly at each of the three sisters in turn, then slowly searched the studio for the fourth.

'We could get Papa to fire Miss Pikestaff,' said Tabitha. 'He doesn't like her.'

'Bendiths cannot leave until they'sa made a kill,' said Hellekin. 'And 'member, nothing is as it seems.'

'Get father to sack Pikestaff and we lose our chance to stab her with the horn,' said Lavinia.

◆ ◆ ◆

The sisters decided if it must be female, it could not be mother or maid but must be Miss Pikestaff. But they had viewed her through the Selkie glass with Mr Hurting and could detect nothing untoward. Cassie and Naomi insisted they could not stab Pikestaff unless they were quite sure it was her.

'Mr Hurting spied through the glass on the first night he came. Perhaps it only works on the Bendith after dark,' said Cassie.

'But we seldom see Miss Pikestaff after dark, except for teatime,' said Tabitha.

'She is often awake until late,' said Cassie. 'While you three would be seen prowling around outside, I could spy on her when she comes to her window.'

They hid the Selkie glass beneath a hydrangea bush after checking that the back of Larkenfen Manor could be seen from there. The glass was secured by pliers from the tool shed. Looking through it the other way, gave a view of the boardwalk. Lavinia hid the Faun's horn in Cassie's hidey hole in the tree, alongside her skull necklace.

By Monday night, everything was ready and Cassie settled down to wait beneath the hydrangea bush for a view of Miss Pikestaff.

42 – THE HUNT FOR NOUHOU

Stanton

Stanton promised to send yet another constable to the home of the Gracegirdles. Hurting's protestations that help would arrive too late unless he be allowed to take horse this night, went unheard. Hurting travelled instead to a Whitehall basement cell. Maraziel returned to the Other Realm, asking to be summoned to see Langtoft's Chronicle at the first opportunity.

The Archbishop had left St Etheldreda's by the time Stanton reached there, so he returned home to a tear-stained, but unwhipped, Midden and a sullen Goldry, who was missing his mistress.

◆ ◆ ◆

The next morning Stanton travelled to the Ministry, intending to take Cotteridge to St Etheldreda's. On his arrival, he found his clerk inside the office examining a pile of reports.

'Minister, your Umbra was right to investigate the magicks. There is a pattern. I have also studied all the Bills of Mortality, since the very first in 1592.'

Stanton wondered at this flicker of animation in the usually understated Cotteridge. 'A pattern?'

'In the reports of magicks, sir. We did as Miss Maraziel suggested and investigated further a sample of the reports we received of Umbra magicks in various parishes.'

Cotteridge handed over the papers for Stanton to read.

'The church congregation of St Ethelborow's in Hemingford Fae are attacked weekly by various tall trees that line their route. Balls of the Old Queen's herb are thrown down upon them both toing and froing.'

'Mistletoe is the sigil of the Old Queen, sir,' Cotteridge said, 'take note.'

'Sheet two: Our emissary to Queensbridge reports back that the strange circumstance of the Bolt Head rock being sculpted by forces unknown and unseen, is without any doubt a great craggy likeness of the Old Queen. Ravens and Choughs sit there and attack any men or women who wander too close.'

'The Queen, again.'

'A linguist from London, who makes a study of old and Medieval language, was sent to meet a fusilier in the village of Bickerton. The fusilier is followed everywhere by songbirds and stood many a round of drinks in the village tavern, so sweet is their singing. The linguist was much puzzled by the man's guttural speech but the Umbra of the two men conferred and were in no doubt that his language is "old Hedge".'

'The Queen's language.'

Stanton turned to the next. 'Ah the good gentleman of Bettws Asrai who is haunted by a chess piece...'

'A black queen, sir.'

'Cleeve Abbey wardens report that the "wooden angels" carved in the roof do nightly discuss the return of the Queen 'Neath the Hedge and the efforts of many in both realms to prevent such an occurrence.'

Stanton set aside the sheaf of papers. 'I see the pattern.'

'Indeed, Minister, and you have there another ten. Miss Maraziel told you they would be of a kind. All we investigated, save one, relate to the Old Queen in some way.'

'What was the exception?'

'The gentleman attacked in Bedford Square. No-one else experienced such a wind that day and no-one witnessed anyone dressed "in a coat of bees".'

'The man was Mr Tenebris, Cotteridge, and the child who reported a figure dressed in a coat of bees, was not a child, but the Bendith, I think. That same creature from the Other Realm we suspected Mr Tenebris of being. I believe the creature invented the "bees coat" man to place suspicion elsewhere and so cover his attack. I think this incident also relates to the Queen.'

Cotteridge hovered at his desk. 'But why would the Bendith attack Mr Tenebris and follow him to the Fens, there to attack him again?'

'That is a fine question, Cotteridge.' Stanton stared into space as events began to fall into place inside his head, 'Unless it is to do with Mr Tenebris's Umbra. Gods preserve us, Hurting said the governess tried to save the Bendith's original target. We must speak to Mr Tenebris again. I start to believe he may be at the centre of all. What's this?'

Cotteridge held another sheet of paper. 'The last few years' annual Bills of Mortality; they reveal another pattern.'

Stanton knew the Bills of Mortality as a weekly publication recorded reliably every year since 1603 and kept by the Ministry of Guardianship. It was a record of deaths in the four-score and seventeen parishes within the walls of London, and such other parishes without, as could be got information on. Most particularly it was created to keep a record of plague victims.

Whenever he chanced to see a copy, it left him puzzling over some aspect of the record that defied interpretation or some new disease or condition he had not been aware of. Among the seventy-or-so reasons recorded – the 'Bit by mad dog's, 'Dead in the street's, 'French Pox's and 'Executed and prest to Death's – Cotteridge had ringed two lines. The first read 'Plague, 126'; the second 'Affray, etc. in the Other Realm, 1,388'.

'I have seen these already,' said Stanton, 'deaths caused in the Other Realm are increasing I know.'

'It follows a formula, ' Cotteridge waited a beat, 'for over the last hundred years.'

'How do we know some of these others: Lethargy, Lunatiques, or Suddenly, for example; were not also due to influence from that Kingdom?'

'We do not, Minister and this is not all deaths, listing only burials and births of Anglican faith. Any individual case may be argued over, but I surmise that deaths dealt from the Other Realm – plague deaths, due to Greynhym incursions; and deaths here that are attributed to events there – ebb and flow in a consistent way, which has gone unnoticed.'

'How so?'

'They always fill the gap between deaths from other means and births.'

'Keeping the population of London at a level?'

'We only record London. I wager they keep all Britain level.'

'France's population is surmised to be four times our own. They grow, while we stagnate. You think this is due to the Umbra?'

'I do wonder, sir. What if the Great Greynhym outbreak in 1665, was a manufactured correction. It brought near 70,000 plague deaths to London alone. Someone thought we had grown too many. Since then the population has grown little.'

'Another thing is clear, Cotteridge. This tally gives the lie to the notion that the connection to our Umbra's life force, prevents death or causes us to live longer. I daresay the same proportion of Englishmen die each year now, as before the Queen's Treaty.'

'Quite so, sir. Our longevity is a myth.'

'And what does your theory propose?'

Before Cotteridge could utter more, word came from without that Isabella had arrived at the Ministry to attend an appointment.

Cotteridge left Stanton to speak to his wife alone. On entering his office Isabella sat and asked primly how went his pursuit of Exeter and Muscari, and whether either they or Lieutenant O'Brien had yet killed Hannah Lightfoot or the King.

'Please do not judge me too harshly, Izzy. I felt my duty was to the Parliament and the welfare of King George, however, I now know that Mr Larkwing, whose real name is as Lady R had it –'

'Lampwick,' Isabella gave a small show of vindication.

'The same. His name was not the only thing that was specious about him. He played me for a buffoon and has now spirited away Lieutenant O'Brien, having persuaded the man's Umbra, Dearbhla, to kill the People's Queen.'

Isabella's shock took a moment to subside. 'Poor Hannah Lightfoot, she is the innocent in all this. Is it always we women who suffer for the sake or position of men?'

'It is of Hannah we must talk. Do you remember when we questioned Twoshrews about the Other Realm, he spoke of a lady there, a friend who called herself "The Mad Queen".'

'Yes, though we took little notice of him.'

'Twoshrews said this Umbra had shown him a picture of herself wearing a crown, attended by a fierce creature like a yellow weasel and a horned steed.' Stanton handed across the card he had borrowed from Mr Tenebris.

Isabella gave a gasp. 'Twoshrews knows Hannah Lightfoot in the Other Realm.'

'We must discover where she is and warn her of the threat, for the King is again thought out of his wits. If possible, we must find other Umbra, who are loyal and willing to guard Miss Lightfoot.'

'Guard her from the Lieutenant's Banshee? So, Exeter and Muscari are no longer thought to be traitors to Britain and the Crown?'

'No, I believed I was pursuing an Umbra, who worked for the French and killed to their orders. That it was he – or she – who killed Charon. It seems the only French agent is Lampwick. You have a fool for a husband, Isabella.'

'A fool who acted from the best intentions and has discovered much about Umbra that was not known.'

'More than you know, far more. I was much helped by Maraziel, who I have misjudged and previously maligned as altogether unserious. The Government and Pitt's Office saw her value where I could not. How stand things with Exeter?'

'Strangely. Let us not talk of that gentleman now. However,

Muscari we must talk of. She has reacted with fury to the news and letter I brought. She particularly feels Exeter's reputation and her own are sullied by any suggestion of disloyalty to King George and is vowing to take revenge on any involved. She intends to hunt them down in the Other Realm. Exeter claims she will not rest until she is avenged on those concerned.'

'Surely not Twoshrews?'

'No, he would not allow that. I spoke of Lieutenant O'Brien in her presence. She knows where to find Dearbhla, and may begin enquiries there. I fear the Banshee may put an end to her and to Exeter.'

'I think not. If Exeter knows I am to blame. She will go after Maraziel?'

'Oh no. But Maraziel is not involved?'

'Maraziel is involved; both in putting Muscari in my thoughts and subsequently in clearing her of being the French agent, but Muscari will not know that.'

It occurred to Stanton how well events could play out for Exeter. Not only had his letter fallen into Isabella's hands, revealing the Viscount's deep and abiding feeling for her, but Stanton had inadvertently given Muscari, the perfect excuse to avenge herself on Maraziel, ridding Exeter of the inconvenience of Isabella's husband. He remembered Agnieszka's prophecy; that Muscari would kill a British man. He had not expected it would be him.

That was how it should be, he reflected, surely it was what destiny had intended for Isabella, marriage to one equal in status. A fate only thwarted by the jealousy of an Umbra. Twoshrews had somehow found a way to keep her and Exeter apart. The Piskie had also unwittingly revealed that Exeter was Isabella's true love… and Twoshrews always answered a direct question with what he had heard to be truth.

The Umbra in question arrived. Isabella had summoned him for the meeting.

'Twoshrews,' she began, when he was sat upon the table, 'I know we are friends no more for the disservice you did me, but it is Sebastian who asks: do you know this Umbra?'

Stanton saw him nod at the card.

'What can you tell us about her? Where she is to be found, perhaps; could you get a warning to her?'

Twoshrews returned an answer, which Isabella relayed to Stanton. 'He says he knows where she lives and it is less than a day from him. He also says that Muscari asked him the same question yesterday.'

'Why so?'

Twoshrews, through Isabella, answered. 'When we received word at Exeter's home that you wished to speak to Twoshrews in London, Muscari asked him why and Twoshrews guessed it would be to do with his "Mad Queen".'

'Does she mean Hannah harm?'

Stanton saw Twoshrews shrug. 'He says that Muscari is all a ferment. When roused to a tempest she is a force. He cannot withstand or deny her, he never could.'

'Can he get a message to Hannah?'

'Not quickly.'

'Are there any who can; any who may help guard her?'

'Perhaps, if they have contact with birds, he says.'

'Does Muscari?'

'Yes, a jackdaw.'

'I will ask Maraziel,' said Stanton, 'although I cannot see her acting as guard.'

Twoshrews was dismissed, having been asked to travel to Hannah, warn her to go into hiding and stay close to her. 'Not so close as you bring harm to yourself or Isabella,' was Stanton's last command.

'What now, Izzy?'

'I must return a coach to Exeter, if you have no further use for me.'

'Are you willing to help, further?' asked Stanton, hoping his anxiety was kept from his voice. 'We are hunting for an urchin, the African child you saw in Pickadills.'

'You hunt her, Sebastian?'

'Not to cause her harm, but in the hope that she will lead us to Lampwick and O'Brien. She is Lampwick's messenger. There are soldiers turning London over – good officers –'

'Officers will not find her. They do not see the London she inhabits. If you want her found and tracked, you should speak to her fellows – the guttersnipes and ragamuffins who share her world.'

'The more beggarly they look, the more invisible they are to gentry,' remembered Stanton. 'You are right of course, Izzy.'

She stood, 'Then let us go quickly. I know some we can speak to.'

'This is a dangerous venture, Izzy.'

'Then it should not be undertaken alone by one who considers himself foolish. Or would you rather I returned to Exeter?'

'You know that is the last thing I wish. Let us go. There is another, here, who knows things we do not about this child. He should come with us, if he pledges to me he will not escape.'

'Who?'

'Quartermain Hurting.'

◆ ◆ ◆

Cotteridge was forthwith dispatched to St Etheldreda's Crypt and Hurting brought forth from his prison cell. With the prisoner and his zealous guard, Sergeant Savage, in tow, they took a landau carriage to Marksfayre. Isabella called for the carriage to stop on a corner of Jermyn Street and jumped out. She had seen two of the urchins that had helped in her quest for the seller of the Umbra Abominable. The pair returned to the carriage with her, suspicions eased by the bright pennies Isabella had pressed into their palms.

'Do you know the small African child who is out on these streets?' asked Stanton.

'Nouhou,' said one.

Hurting nodded to Stanton, 'That is he, or rather, she.'

'Has she been seen these last two days?' asked Stanton.

'She skulks aroun' Mista'. Workin' for that spruce fellow in black, spyin' n' such. She's dogged your tail more'n once.

'Where is she now?'

'Damfino.'

'He doesn't know,' interpreted Hurting.

'Could you and your fellows find her?'

'If there's a penny for all of us tha's looking, mister, n' a shiny shilling for those who finds 'er.'

Hurting pulled Stanton and Isabella back inside the carriage. He spoke in hushed tones, 'If the African child is as I suspect, she will be unable to speak and barely sensible.'

'A shell,' Stanton said.

Hurting nodded, while Isabella looked shocked and the soldier bemused.

'I will explain as we go, Izzy,' said Stanton. 'What do you suggest, Mr Hurting?'

'That it may be better for these street children to spy upon her, rather than bring her to us, then send word of whichever buildings she visits.'

Stanton agreed and returned to the carriage door, to find both children's heads, pressed against it.

'We was earwiggin' Mista,' said one. 'I reckon we could follow 'er, without 'er knowin'. Mebbe, not as she was, but nowadays she's 'ardly wiv it at all. An' yer man's right, she ain't 'xactly a church bell.'

'She doesn't speak much,' Hurting said.

Pennies were dispensed and it was arranged that they would meet back on Jermyn Street when St Sepulchre-Without struck noon.

Stanton directed the carriage to Smoothfield. Inside, he and Hurting explained what they knew of the Bendith and some of what Hurting knew about Mr Tenebris. Isabella gained more knowledge of affairs. Sergeant Savage spent much of the journey yawning and posturing threateningly with his musket.

◆ ◆ ◆

Stanton allowed Mr Hurting to call up to the studio, while he and Isabella waited by the door and the soldier lounged by the carriage.

'It's Hurting, Mr Tenebris.'

The window opened and Tenebris peeked out, confused and frightened. 'You villain. Have you been to the Fens? What about Miss Pikestaff? What do you... oh is that you Minister? And... by the Gods, Lady Stanton?' He disappeared and opened the door a moment later.

The three visitors refused tea and joined Mr Tenebris in his studio where there were but two chairs. The soldier waited without.

'Are you here to give me news of Miss Pikestaff?'

'No, Tenebris, nothing beyond that she is well. And the Gracegirdles too, to my knowledge. Have you finished your commission for me?'

'I have, Minister.' Mr Tenebris took a painting from his easel and placed it before Stanton. A fearful female peered from the canvas, a sweep of grey-black hair, contained in a lattice that reminded Stanton of Jenny M's twig construction. The artist had captured a hunger in her wild eyes, sketched ferocious talons and given her a demon's grin. 'Behold Dearbhla.'

'I have no experience of Banshees,' said Hurting, 'but this matches descriptions I have been given.'

'This is O'Brien's Umbra?' Isabella studied the illustration, 'She looks deadly enough even without her screams.'

'I assure you it is a capable likeness,' said Mr Tenebris.

'Yet your Umbra subdued her,' said Hurting. It wasn't a question.

'Can you summon your Umbra here?' asked Stanton.

'No, sir, she meets with a curlew.'

'She does what?'

'Amorrie is being hunted by Mr Hurting's Umbra. I fear one

will kill the other before the day is out.' Mr Tenebris fixed Hurting with an angry glance.

Stanton turned in astonishment, 'Is this true, Hurting? Why did you not say on the way here?'

'It is true that Brughe is chasing Miss Amorrie. I know nothing about a curlew but now fear that its long bill might be primed for Brughe. I very much hope that neither one will kill the other,' Hurting waited a moment, 'for all our sakes.'

'Well, call your Umbra here, Mr Hurting,' said Isabella, 'and tell him to desist. Mr Tenebris is a very fine artist and while I have not met Amorrie, she sounds both spirited and inclined to the right cause in a fight, no matter the odds.'

'I am reluctant to do so, my lady; for Brughe has questions for Miss Amorrie. His quest to find her has been a long one, and I understood they were close last night.'

'I would not wish to lose either one of you to this combat, Hurting, but I judge Tenebris and Amorrie, the greater loss. If you want my help in gaining your freedom, you will call Brughe off.'

'Brughe does not answer to me, Minister. Do you order Miss Maraziel around so? Do you order your wife?'

'No I do not, but neither of them are villains, intent on hunting anyone down.'

'Very well, Minister, but if you think Brughe the villain here, you are much mistaken.' Hurting went to a far corner of the room to make his summons.

Stanton turned to the artist. 'Tenebris, do you think Amorrie could best Dearbhla a second time?'

'I confess I do not. Amorrie is brave – nay foolish; reckless of her life and my own – but Dearbhla has only to scream and Amorrie's blood will congeal. In the feud in the Fens, she had the aid of Galt, a sturdy Goblin with a huge club, and Miss Gracegirdle stabbed O'Brien at a fatefully opportune time.'

Isabella clapped, 'Bravo, I would love to meet these Gracegirdles.'

Mr Tenebris beckoned her to study a table where more pictures were laid out. 'You may meet them here, my dear lady, let me introduce you.'

'Oh they look as glamorous as they sound courageous. No French lancer would be able to withstand them. If he got past their blades, he would lose his heart to their beauty. I know you to be a fine artist, Mr Tenebris, but this work is exemplary.'

'You are ever gracious, madam, but in this you speak true. It is my favourite commission. Here is Naomi, a lady scientist...'

'Oh, what a fabulous notion.'

'This is Tabitha, perhaps the prettiest but also ardent and kind. Here Lavinia, who has the spirit of a lion.'

'She is especial, indeed, madam;' Hurting had returned from his conference. 'I confess that she outwitted me utterly, disarmed me and made me her prisoner.'

Isabella gave him a reproachful stare, so he added, 'We parted on more friendly terms.'

'And this last? Of all of them, her beauty is most haunting.'

Hurting and Mr Tenebris shared a glance that seemed to dispel some of their anger towards each-other. 'That is Cassie, good lady,' said Mr Tenebris. 'Sadly, she was taken from us by the pestilence.'

'She is deceased?'

'Perhaps,' said Hurting. 'I fear, my lady, that these girls are in danger and all may end up dead too. My time would be better spent riding forthwith to their rescue.'

'What danger?'

'The Bendith we spoke of in the carriage.'

'Miss Pikestaff is not a Bendith,' Mr Tenebris showed rare temper.

'I know, she is something else entirely. The Bendith, Mr Tenebris, is Nouhou.'

Mr Tenebris's stunned gaze trawled the company. 'Nouhou is an eight-year-old pageboy of sweet temperament.'

'Nouhou is a young girl, who masqueraded as a pageboy. This was discovered by her master's family after her mother's death and Nouhou was thrown out onto the streets,' said Stanton.

Hurting took up the particulars: 'As you were travelling to an appointment, Mr Tenebris, the Bendith – a clever determined killer, who has power over the element of wind – chose Nouhou's form to carry out her orders, most like because the child was, at that moment, the closest human female to you.'

'The devil wind,' Tenebris sat. 'That was Nouhou? Not the man in a coat of bees?'

'A fiction, I think,' said Hurting. 'It is likely the Bendith had been conjured to assassinate Amorrie in this realm – she failed because Amorrie was not with you that morning. The creature had then to stay in that form and close to you until Amorrie presented her with better opportunity.'

'Why Amorrie?' asked Stanton.

Mr Tenebris spoke quickly, as if this secret must spill from him, 'Because she is rebellious; because some believe she carries the mark of the Old Queen upon her, in the shape of a sprig.'

'The urgency is not with Miss Amorrie, who is out of the Bendith's reach, but with the Gracegirdle girls,' said Hurting. 'The assassin has been persuaded one of them is a more tempting target than Amorrie.'

'Persuaded by who?'

'Er...mmm, that does not matter, Tenebris.'

'Why do people want to kill these girls?' asked Tenebris.

Isabella answered, her words growing in certainty: 'Because whoever carries the Queen's Sprig will mature into a new Queen 'Neath the Hedge. One of the Gracegirdles will grow to become Queen.'

'It is a possibility,' said Hurting, 'no more.'

'One of them; not Amorrie?' Tenebris's question was tinged with guilty relief.

'Which one?' Stanton spoke to Hurting.

'Lavinia,' said Tenebris.

'Such is my suspicion,' Hurting admitted, 'and I am sure the Bendith will be drawn to that sister. That is why I must go.'

'You cannot. Sergeant Savage will not allow it even if I would.

You have a cause, Hurting, and some of your deeds are honourable, but you have scant regard for the law.'

'The law is no help to the Miss Gracegirdles. At least one of them will be killed. Let us pray it chooses the wrong sister.'

'Their father is with them. Constables have been dispatched, and will arrive upon the morrow.'

'Constables are no match for the Bendith,' said Hurting.

'Then we must hope those Gracegirdle girls are,' said Isabella.

43 – BATTLE ON THE BOARDWALK

Larkenfen

Cassie waited all night without sight of Miss Pikestaff.

'It was as if she knew our plan,' she told her sisters next morning.

Miss Pikestaff was due to visit around Reedston with their mother that day but had left lessons for the girls to do in the morning. If they wished they could help maid with her baking in the afternoon.

Lavinia prowled the morning, angry that Pikestaff had eluded them. Naomi finished her lessons quickly and pulled out some private studies on the natural world. Tabitha helped Nouhou with his letters. Because Nouhou was present, Cassie kept her distance.

A while after lunch, Cassie went to see whether they might ask more of Hellekin if their father was asleep. He was soundly snoring but Hellekin was not there.

◆ ◆ ◆

She returned to find her sisters in discussion with Nouhou outside the kitchen. Naomi broke away and took Cassie out of sight of the little African.

'Tabitha said there has been something wrong with Nouhou all day. She asked him what worried him and he said he had heard Miss Pikestaff plotting with Galt to come back early this afternoon.'

'So?'

'She plans to make excuses to come back ahead of mother and while Papa is still asleep. Nouhou is fearful that she means harm, whether to one of us or to him, is unclear.'

'I can keep watch and warn you of her coming,' said Cassie.

'There is more. It is quite the longest speech any of us have heard him make. When Miss P and Nouhou were on better terms, he discovered that she has something quite secret that she keeps at Larkenfen.'

'What?'

'He does not know, but is certain she hides it in the old boathouse.'

'The boardwalk is broken there, where Mr Hurting fell in.'

'Yes, but he thinks it only a short stretch and one of the board supports remains. It can be reached, although Livvi is so determined she would risk wading through the fen itself to get there.'

'She would sink to her waist and stink to the rafters.' From their first memories they had been forbidden to set foot in the carr, halfway between woodland and swamp, where alders battled up only to drop and rot where they fell.

Growing up, their father had shown them a thick straight branch, protruding only a hand's height above the mud but when he lifted it, the branch rose high over his head without its other end ever leaving the gloop. The whole thing fled back down as soon as he let it go. Lavinia christened it 'the stinky stick', for the foul bubbling gasses that percolated forth every time it was lifted. The demonstration made sure none of the girls left the boardwalk.

'Well, it should not be necessary,' said Naomi. 'Nouhou says we can get over the support beam.'

'Is the boathouse not locked?'

'Nouhou thinks the lock is old and Pikestaff has bent it out of shape. He dare not go in on his own.'

'What can I do?'

'Just warn us if Pikestaff returns. Both Livvi and I have our blades. Nouhou has a small hatchet from the tool-shed, in case the lock proves awkward.'

'I do not like it, Naomi.'

'We cannot let this chance go.'

Cassie set off towards the entrance of the estate. The afternoon sun found passage through the trees to scatter its wares before her on the path. As she passed the studio, she saw Hellekin, now returned, at a window.

She ran over and slipped through the door. Hellekin visibly started as Cassie entered. Cassie found her ear-piece pellet and put it in.

'... ing news, fourth sist-kin? Wheres'a your sisters?'

This is useless thought Cassie, she can't hear me. Her father's snores reverberated through the room.

Hellekin was staring around the studio, as if for some sign. She started sniffing. 'Finds them, warn them. The Bendith is the little one. Do you hear fourth sist-kin? Danger. I will try to wake Gracegirdle. Fly, look through the Selkies' glass, take Bendith stabber.'

Cassie left the studio and ran back. She heard her sisters' distant shouts. They were chuckling and boisterous. Then one of her ears caught something altogether diabolic. It was a laugh of pure malicious triumph and she could not imagine where it had come from. She fingered her ear touching the little bundle of thickened vapour the dead lord had gifted to her.

She only saw her sisters and Nouhou running along the sunladen boardwalk. In a moment they would be out of sight. She dived under the hydrangea bush and contorted to find an angle that let her watch them through the Selkie glass.

There were her sisters, awash with exhilaration and adventure, but with them was a malevolent impish thing she did not recognise... only it had the height of Nouhou and wore his clothes. It laughed and the sound of evil pulsed again in her ear. The repulsive thing was female, if anything. She pulled away from the glass and stared and there was Nouhou again.

'One has come who carries evil in their heart, while death stains their hands,' she remembered. It could only be the Bendith. It wasn't Pikestaff; it was Nouhou. He (she?) turned round and stared back at her.

They had been tricked. Cassie hoped Hellekin could raise her father, for she had no way to make herself heard to him. Instead, she leapt up and began running after her sisters shouting. A breeze whisked up and whirled her words away.

Running faster on the boardwalk, Cassie found herself running into air so dense it physically repulsed her. It halted all progress. If she could have been sick she would have been. Confounded, she stared around and finally saw the source of the impediment hanging behind a screen of branches above the boardwalk – the abhorrent doll thing that Nouhou had bought at the Eel Fayre.

Naomi had jokingly told her that it was a ward against dead spirits and they had both laughed at the absurdity. Yet here it hung, blunt reed-stem limbs and spume of feathers catching in the breeze. Its blood-stained eyes glinted balefully down upon her, mocking her helplessness. Either side of the boardwalk lay stretches of marshy water that she could not cross. She had no way to move past the abhorrent charm. Nouhou – no, the Bendith – had her sisters at its mercy.

Heavy steps came stumbling along the boardwalk behind her. Cassie spun to see her father, with Hellekin on his shoulder racing towards her. The Umbra's black shawl was attached to both his ears. As he ran straight through her, she saw Hellekin almost reining him in: 'Theres'a somethin', aboves us now. The killer has left a hateful portent. You must tears it down.'

Her father grunted, jumped up and snatched at the damnable doll, trying to dislodge it from its mooring in the trees. On his third jump, he grasped it, scrunched it up and threw it into the water. On, he ran.

'Swift, be swift, Gracegirdle; it is nots a child, it is an assassins,' Hellekin whipped him forward. She again wore the tall claw-like headdress. 'Everything is fluxed.'

George Gracegirdle needed no further prompting. Cassie could not remember the last time Papa had moved so fast. She sped after him. Only stopping at the tree to find the Faun's horn stabber. She pulled it out. Thank goodness, the Faun must be dead, for she could lift and wield it.

They ran past the warning on the spur of the boardwalk that led to the boathouse. The ramshackle barrier was still in the swamp The breeze strengthened now, as it had when Cassie pursued Miss Pikestaff on the Saturday. It became a gale, whipping about her, forcing her back.

''Tis a malevolents wind,' Hellekin screamed above the thrashing of the trees. 'Do not think it a natural blow, it is the creature's. It is hell-born.'

'Nothing is as it seems,' roared George Gracegirdle, ahead of Cassie, as he bent low and laboured forward against it.

It took all Cassie's conviction to remind herself that she was beyond winds; they could no longer dictate to her. Fixing this thought in her mind, she ploughed forward. She had not gone a dozen steps, when she saw her father blown past her, on his back, Hellekin clinging desperately to his chest.

The Bendith's wind was too fierce for him. It was down to Cassie. She reached the part of the boardwalk destroyed by Galt's trap and Hurting's fall. There, the heart she'd thought she no longer owned leapt and lodged in her throat.

The last board support that she remembered being there, which she had planned to tiptoe over, had been hewn away. Nouhou had a hatchet; she remembered Naomi telling her as if it was some trifling thing. The creature was cunning indeed. Its plan was well-hatched and well-executed. Low pools of water flooded the ground around her on all sides. The carr was all brown iris leaves, drowning branches, broken reeds, bent bull-rushes, stunted stems of alder and no way through. Cassie and water did not mix. She could not walk, nor swim nor jump to the other side.

On the boards beyond this place, she saw a blade – Lavinia's – lying on the boardwalk; another smaller blade lay further on.

Her sisters had been disarmed. Still the ferocious wind whistled about her, plucking Cassie's last hopes away with it.

A fiendish laugh sung within it.

'Save your sisters,' had been the plague girl's command. She could not.

She stared down at the horned weapon Mr Hurting had left them. It would be of no use. She imagined the fell imp she had seen in the Selkie glass, threatening Lavinia with the hatchet, using its elemental powers to drive her sisters back against the boathouse wall. Would he kill all three? Would they be reduced to shades wandering Larkenfen as she was?

She listened, hoping against hope not to hear what seemed inevitable...

And then it came and it tore what was left of her spirit away...

A high-pitched scream.

44 – THE UMBRA PACT

Stanton

'Brughe will answer my summons,' said Hurting. 'He was most reluctant, as the Mor was in sight.'

'The Mor?' Stanton's astonishment was immediately followed by a realisation that he should already have arrived at this conclusion. 'Amorrie is the Mor? Of course, she is.'

Mr Tenebris just hung his head and slumped into a vacant chair. 'She was never known as such to me, sir. Not 'til I overheard Mr Hurting refer to her so.'

'What of it?' asked Isabella.

'The Mor is the Umbra who started all of this, Izzy. All began when she killed Charon.'

'It is true, Minister. She is my most grievous affliction. I will make no excuses for her on my part. She set a foolhardy trap for Charon before, I believe, killing him with his own knife. I am only recently made aware of it and do not know all the particulars.'

'It wasn't the Greynhym?' Isabella looked as if certainties crumbled all about her.

'Maraziel told Pitt and me so on Saturday. I was partly right; it was not a troop of the dead, but an Umbra.' Stanton pointed at Mr Tenebris, 'His Umbra.'

'She killed Charon and defeated a Banshee,' Isabella said in no small wonderment.

'For Amorrie's defence, I should say that Charon had been sent to kill her,' said Hurting.

At that moment a small grey ball of mist formed close to Hurting and a one-horned Umbra with a bow upon his back and a sword at his belt stepped out. It took in the people in the room and bowed, lower and a moment longer, than necessary.

'Brughe has arrived,' said Hurting. 'Can you confirm to Minister Stanton, there, that you do not mean harm to Miss Am... to the Mor, Brughe, a nod will have to suffice.'

The goat-faced creature bobbed a deliberate nod.

'That is a start,' said Stanton. 'I confess, Brughe is not as I expected.'

'A Pooka, Minister, a rarity; indeed, the last of his kind.'

'He is... a he?!'

'We have no time for explanations of that.'

'No, I daresay we do not. Tenebris, I insist you call Amorrie to us. My dear, perhaps you could ask Twoshrews to attend, to explain where Hannah Lightfoot can be found.'

Amorrie took the most coaxing but soon a trio of Umbra were in the studio, all eyeing each-other with suspicion.

Stanton addressed them, 'Gentlemen and women, the King of Britain is in grave danger. I believe we, in this room, represent the best chance of preserving him. I would ask that we put aside our own quarrels to accomplish it.'

Amorrie, who appeared small in Umbra terms, and little older than the Gracegirdles in human ones, was determinedly disdainful of his speech. She stared vehemence at Brughe through darkly clouded black eyes while twisting a swirl of jet hair around one tiny finger. She had materialised in Tenebris's shadow, knife-drawn, expecting a trap.

'Brughe will need to know how, Minister.'

'The means of the murder is to kill the King's own Umbra in your realm, Brughe. King George's ally is Hannah Lightfoot, perhaps known to you as the Mad Queen.'

Brughe shook his head and Amorrie stared blankly back.

'The would-be assassin is Dearbhla, a Banshee, who you have

already fought, Amorrie, and who, I can see, you others have heard of by reputation.'

Amorrie spoke.

Tenebris relayed her words, 'She says Dearbhla is in Hibernia.'

'That sounds good,' although Stanton had no way of knowing if it was, as he had no idea where Hannah resided and only a vague memory of Hibernia on the Umbra charts.

'She also asks if Brughe speaks true and that another assassin is at Larkenfen?'

'Possibly so, the Bendith we spoke of.'

'Amorrie thinks it will kill the angry Gracegirdle; she means –'

'Yes,' said Stanton, 'but constables have been sent. For now, it must be a matter for them. Twoshrews, can you explain where Hannah is to be found in your realm.'

Twoshrews did so nervously and a long debate followed, none of which Stanton could hear. Hurting followed it but Tenebris just stared miserably down, wrapped up in his own thoughts.

Eventually, Brughe had the final word and Hurting relayed it. 'They know the Dee marshes that Twoshrews describes. There is no easy way to get there quickly without birds. Brughe and Amorrie can call mounts and take bird to the marshes, as it does not involve crossing over Greynhym lands or through any Spriggan wars. Dearbhla is a fierce warrior, even without her portentous scream, and as demented as any in their realm. So the two have agreed that they must work together to thwart the Banshee. They will warn Hannah, and stay with her until the morrow.'

'What then?'

Hurting gave an apologetic smile, 'They both have business to attend to in their Realm. Brughe will use the intervening time to ask Amorrie some questions, she will stick him with her blade if any cause offence.'

'What if Dearbhla still hasn't come for Hannah after tomorrow?'

Amorrie spoke and Mr Tenebris revived sufficiently to pass it on, 'They will assume she is still in the wilds of Hibernia.'

Stanton was about to object but Hurting shook his head, 'It will have to suffice, Minister. We have other plans afoot here and we will do well to reach the West End before St Sepulchre's strikes noon.'

First Amorrie and then Brughe, departed.

'Mr Tenebris,' Stanton said, 'it will be crowded in our landau, but you must join us in case of news.'

◆ ◆ ◆

'We 'ave sight of 'er, Mista,' said the taller urchin. 'She 'as been at two addresses. The first in ol' Convent Garden, not near the well-to-dos, mind. The second is just souff of Penton's Land, near St James's – all night-gals n' robber gangs it is there. We should've asked for more coin.'

'Give both addresses to the coachman.'

'We ain't so good at addresses, Mista.'

'One of you ride up top then, and you'll get your shilling if we find Nouhou or the men we are looking for. The Convent Garden address is first.'

The coach stopped at the grubby end of Rose Street. The urchin jumped down. He whistled and waited.

'You won't find this address in 'arris's List, Mista.'

Hurting answered Stanton's confusion with, 'Harris's List of Convent Garden Ladies. You probably haven't read it, Minister.'

Another youth of about twelve slunk out of the shadows. They conferred before the tall urchin returned to the carriage. 'Nouhou left 'ere straightways after coming. She 'ad the black-suited gent with 'er. 'E won't have much use for a Convent Garden nun; reckon he's a Molly.'

'Really,' said Stanton, feeling he was starting to get to grips with the urchins' slang.

'Rickets 'ere,' he nodded to the twelve-year-old, 'put a fagger under a windo,' (or perhaps he wasn't) 'but the place's empty since they left.'

'Well done, Rickets,' said Stanton, handing over a few pence. 'What's your name?' he asked the tall urchin.

'Jem, if it please ya, Mista.'

'Well, onto Penton's Land, Jem.'

It was three-quarters of a mile and the coach arrived without incident. Jem suggested the driver stop at the end of a short alley and whistled. Again, it was answered by an urchin, this time a small girl with brown curls peeking out from a dirty white bonnet. She was chilled by the morning's drizzle and clad in a thin grey dress and apron.

Jem turned. 'The Molly's gone off on some ovver errand, but Nouhou came 'ere, wen' in and is still in there. Freckles, 'ere, reckons she ain't alone but she ain't seen anyone else enter.'

'Good work, Jem, and you, Freckles,' said Stanton. 'Izzy, you and Mr Tenebris, stay in the carriage with the driver. Will you attend with me, Mr Hurting? And we'll need you too, Sergeant Savage. Is your musket loaded?'

Both men nodded. Jem pointed to a small door.

The door was recessed in a two story house. The window beside it had the look of a large, slightly bowed, former shop window but the inside was secreted behind old papers, dust and cobwebs. Two tiny windows in the floor above showed no sign of life. Stanton saw one of them was broken and wished he'd had the foresight to bring a fagger (whatever that was) with him to get them inside. The building had a disused look.

Freckles, who had appeared at his elbow, reached up and motioned his head down towards her and closer to the window. 'D'yer hear, mister?'

Stanton followed her lead and heard voices inside, one had an Irish lilt – O'Brien; the other was London but woven with a touch of something more exotic. It wasn't Lampwick; perhaps, the guard then.

Hurting squatted by Freckles, 'Is Nouhou definitely a girl?'

'Yessir, I did check; 'cos o' the way she was dressed, like.' The girl clutched at the front of her apron, 'In't nuffin' there, no gingamobs.'

'There's two in there, men I mean,' Stanton added, realising his comment could be misconstrued. Two adults at least. One is O'Brien, whose situation I am unsure of; the other is his guard, who may be armed. Our aim is to break-in and get them to surrender. If we kill O'Brien, we end the affair, but I would rather we took him alive and persuaded him to do what is right.'

'They have light in there,' whispered Hurting. 'We passed a chestnut seller back-aways. If we buy his coal bucket off him, I will throw it through the window. You can threaten the guard through the hole with your musket, Savage; persuade him to the door to unlock it. Even if he refuses, he will be covered as we break in.'

Sergeant Savage was peeved at being ordered around by his prisoner, who he decidedly disliked. 'Yous'll be in trouble for any window-breaking,' he said.

'But you won't be, Savage,' said Stanton. 'You'll just be doing your duty for King George. If all goes well, I'll recommend you for a medal.'

A few minutes later, Hurting hurled the weighted coal-bucket at the window. Glass, wood and paper gave little resistance and a large part of the window followed the bucket into the interior.

Savage thrust his musket barrel in while shouts of alarm still echoed from inside. 'Stands where yous be, or'n I'll fire.'

Stanton stood behind him and peered in. It was gloomy inside but he could make out one figure standing and one squatting against a wall. 'Is that you, O'Brien? Are you alright, man?'

'Minister? No thanks to your fellow, Larkwing, who subjected me to nights of watery torture,' the Lieutenant's voice emerged from the dust. A choking laugh followed, 'Isn't it time you English learnt to use doors?'

'Tell your guard to throw out the key to me. We have the place surrounded.'

'Do you though?' said a new voice. 'There's a little mouse in here with us; petit, un innocent. I have a knife at her throat.'

'Kill her and you'll swing,' Hurting spoke by the door.

'I'll swing anyway. '

'More's the pity to die slow for the sake of a street rat, then,' said Hurting.

Stanton gave Savage a long wink, before he shouted. 'Shoot him, you men, but have a care not to kill him. If he hurts the girl, we'll cut off his... gingamobs.'

There was a shout and the sound of a scuffle inside. Stanton leapt, following the bucket's path through the window, and landed sprawled painfully on a floor of splinters and glass shards. He bounded to his feet and saw that O'Brien held another man. The Irish Lieutenant's manacles chain was wound tight around his guard's throat. A knife lay on the floor and Nouhou cowered by a wall.

Stanton grabbed up the knife. 'You have him, O'Brien. Keys?'

'In Granger's pocket. If you cut them out, feel free to nick his gingamobs'

'I'll get 'em,' Granger said, a quick hoarse wheeze. 'The girl's unharmed.'

He pulled out the keys and threw them to Stanton, who opened the door to Savage's musket and Hurting's darkness.

'Where is Lar... Lampwick?' asked Stanton, brushing debris off his hands, noting cuts on his wrists and fingers.

'Lampwick, is it,' said O'Brien. 'He's no been this day. Did you guess his cause, sir?'

'To make you order your Umbra, Dearbhla, to murder Hannah Lightfoot.'

'You have it. And Granger, here, and Larkwitch or whatever his name is, put me through such a nightly torment, we agreed to their demands.' He gave the chain around Granger's neck a wrench backwards as he spoke.

'Summon Dearbhla here, now. Call her off.'

'I will, sir, but it is hardly necessary. These eejits, being half-French, understand nothing of the Other Realm. Dearbhla's home is among the whins and quickens of Hibernia. She is a wild sea away from this Hannah creature, and has no means of getting to her. I lied when I said she could.'

'Thank God.'

'It would have gone worse for me if your wife's wee man had been present. They would've known I was lying.'

'Where's Nouhou?' said Hurting, looking around.

'Slipped outside,' Savage was torn between covering Hurting, Granger or O'Brien with his musket.

Hurting made a dash for the door.

'No yous don't,' Savage swung around.

'Leave h –'

There was a cry from outside – Isabella. Stanton beat Savage to the open door. He saw Hurting, running, closing on the African girl.

'It's Lampwick, Sebastian.' Isabella was halfway from the coach, pointing beyond Nouhou to a familiar black-caped figure; who was observing the scene. The fake agent ran.

Stanton started after him, 'Quick, Savage. They're getting away.'

Then, fast as he ran, he watched in slow motion, as events unfolded in a terrible way that he never had intended.

He half turned to check on Savage.

Saw the soldier raise his musket to his shoulder.

Wondered, in the moment, which of the two men he meant to shoot?

He stumbled, looking to Isabella as he fell.

A shot rang out.

There was a long, horrible gut-wringing scream. Shot and scream echoed off the buildings, the two sounds locking together in his head, in his heart, in their inevitable cause and effect.

It sounded like more than one death.

Could you hear an Umbra dying in the Other Realm, wondered Stanton? Did it leak in through the conduit of their ally?'

But Lampwick didn't have an Umbra.

A click-clunk intruded. Stanton turned to see Savage in 'make ready', pulling the lock to full cock.

'Wait,' Stanton shouted.

Steps came on his other side. Isabella was running to him.

'Stay back. I'm not hit.'

'I know,' she said.

'Which did he shoot?'

She spoke.

But the noise of another shot meant he did not hear properly.

He watched her lips.

They hadn't said, 'Lampwick'. They had said, 'dead'.

Stanton raised himself to his elbows. 'Stand down, Savage. Let him go, man.'

Savage was by his side now, lifting him. 'Yous alright, sir? I fear 'e got away.'

'Never mind,' said Stanton.

He looked now. He saw Freckles and Jem crouching by a body in the street.

Then Freckles screamed. And they both leapt up and ran. Ran, not waiting for their shilling.

The sprawled body was small. They moved towards it in the empty street.

'Always the innocent,' said Isabella.

'I dunno how I hit 'er, sir,' said Savage. 'I weren't aiming for her, but him. She just leapt in the way.'

'Not your fault, Savage.'

'The Earl will have me hung for letting him get away.'

'We've saved the King, man. Think on that.'

They reached Nouhou's tiny form, lying face down on the cobbles.

In death, her figure seemed plainly a girl, not a boy.

Stanton reached out and turned her over.

They, all three, recoiled. 'Great heavens.'

The body was Nouhou's, the head was Nouhou's, the horrible grimacing rictus belonged to something else entirely; a grotesque manic imp. Then, as they watched, the rictus relaxed and it became again the face of a small dead innocent child.

Stanton put a kerchief over the features, picked her up and

carried her back to the carriage.

Mr Tenebris gasped in horror as Stanton laid her form in the landau. 'It's Nouhou, poor little Nouhou. The child was here, all the time, how?'

'I do not fully understand it, Tenebris.'

'If he... she is here, then what is in the Fens?'

'I sincerely hope, as of now, nothing is.'

◆ ◆ ◆

Savage had made the prisoner, Granger, fast. He had found the keys to O'Brien's irons but elected to keep him in them.

Mr Tenebris refused to go near O'Brien and left to hail another carriage. Before leaving, he said that Amorrie had come to report that Brughe had departed a few moments ago. There was no sign of Dearbhla. 'Amorrie is fed-up and she is leaving.'

'She was right, Mr Tenebris,' Stanton said, 'Dearbhla was in Hibernia. Hannah was not in danger. She may go.'

'Will she be arrested for killing Charon, sir? For killing the Countess of Alnwick? Must she hang?'

'I do not know, Tenebris. I am not inclined to tell anyone. Hurting cannot say, for he must now be on the run.'

'I promise, we will not tell a soul, Mr Tenebris,' said Isabella.

'Neither Grenville or Pitt, know who the Mor is, or who she is allied to,' said Stanton.

'No-one will hang, Mr Tenebris,' said Isabella, 'which is fair, because Amorrie acted to defend herself.'

Isabella bound Stanton's cuts. She reminded him that she still had Exeter's carriage and must return it to him, and that he had made her promise to do so, no matter what befell in London.

'What then, Izzy? I know I have been preoccupied and see now, I should have shared more with you, especially the secrets that belonged to you. This episode reflects badly on many men, both in the Government and those nearer the gutter.

'I confess, I have never been more impressed with the female of the species, though: the Gracegirdles, Maraziel, Amorrie...' he laughed, 'the unfathomable Miss Pikestaff, who has claimed Tenebris's heart; little Nouhou, who was blameless and loyal. Especially you, and your convictions, and judgements. Tell me this realisation comes not too late.'

'I have much to think on, Sebastian. There are many that I must decide upon, whether or not I forgive them – you among them. I need time. Before I go, there are some things I should tell you.'

'Pray do.'

'Firstly, Twoshrews just came to me unsummoned, he told me that previously, in Mr Tenebris's studio, the two other Umbra had agreed a pact between them. Brughe did not have a bird. They could never have got to Hannah in time, who they believed too far away and in no danger.'

'What then?'

'Twoshrews said that Amorrie proposed, instead, to warn someone about your Bendith. It was another Umbra, Hellekin or some-such. Amorrie said she lived close by. Amorrie said she had no love of Gracegirdles, but the angry one had saved her life. Twoshrews was warned not to speak of it but, after they had left, I think he saw it as a way to win back some of my forgiveness. Mr Tenebris was too distracted to listen to their plots, I think, but Hurting would have heard and sanctioned it.'

'It is well we did not need their intervention. What else?'

'I am not entirely sure of it but feel I should ask. Would Hurting have reason to throw Nouhou into the path of a bullet?'

◆ ◆ ◆

Mr Tenebris returned with a hackney cab. It was dispatched with Mr Tenebris and Isabella: Tenebris to his studio; Isabella back to the beguiling country estate of her 'true love'.

Stanton took the original landau back to Westminster with Savage, Granger, O'Brien and the dead body of Nouhou – a guilty burden for all inside the carriage.

Sergeant Savage explained that Hurting had run off after the first shot. He had not noticed anyone else dressed in black.

'You must tell us where to find Lampwick, Granger, if you expect any clemency,' said Stanton.

'I expect none.'

'What of this other fellow?' asked O'Brien, 'Hurting was it?'

'Grenville will hunt him down. You did not know him? He did not give you orders?'

'Never clapped eyes on him before. My orders came from Lord Strathearn's man… though now I think on't, I believe he may have been taken.'

'Misadventure in the Other Realm?' Stanton felt weary to the bone with it all.

'Yes, Minister, I believe it was. Do you think my efforts in saving the King will count in my favour?'

'I'll speak true on all that occurred, but your crimes, I suspect, are many, O'Brien.'

'That they are, sir. But… I know what is happening, you do not. Your Parliament does not, although many would be shamed by my revelations. I know some of those involved. Most are gentry who will not wish to be named, sir. What is my chance of a fair trial, do you think?'

'Your best chance is to share those names with me, now, O'Brien, before I hand you over. We can make those names known around. That will be your insurance.'

The Lieutenant considered, then, 'Right you are, Minister. I know you are close to guessing a part, but it is the smallest part of what is happening to the country you govern. What do you know of the true nature of *The Book of Fi–*'

His question ended in a gasp. His manacled hands flew to his head. His face crumpled up, so that it resembled the one lying in the bottom of their carriage.

'What is it? O'Brien, what's –'

The carriage hit a loose cobble and shook as if gunpowder exploded beneath it. The air within seemed to come alive, affecting everyone, although nothing could be heard. Then came the scream from O'Brien and it came from deep. It seemed not entirely the Irishman's voice.

Stanton imagined himself transported to the 'whins and quickens of Hibernia'. For the second time that afternoon, he felt the Other Realm reach through into his and consume the sensibilities of whatever it found there.

Across the carriage O'Brien slumped in his seat. He was white and he was quite dead.

EPILOGUE – LANGTOFT'S CHRONICLE

Stanton

Stanton left word in the Ministry that Hannah was threatened no longer and the King was saved. Savage was to escort Granger to a cell and tell his superiors that the hunt for Nouhou could be called off.

The bodies of Nouhou and O'Brien would be sent to the matrons of the Parish of Westminster to record the deaths and set down cause.

Stanton kept the landau for his next appointment.

Archbishop Feargod Chislett awaited Stanton above the Crypt of St Etheldreda's.

Stanton was surprised the clergyman had waited. Were it possible he looked even older, more gaunt and more frail than when they had last met. He leaned heavily upon a stick but shook off the attentions of his gaunt young curate when Stanton arrived.

'Your clerk, Cotteridge, is buried deep within Peter of Langtoft's Chronicle, Minister. I have kept my side of the bargain.'

'I thank you, Archbishop. Why are we met here? St Etheldreda's is a Catholic Church, surely.'

'It is both apt and private, Minister; a cryptic crypt. It means none of my fellows will catch me sharing a chronicle we are forbidden to show to any – let alone any in power or among the laity – a stricture that we have adhered to for nearly five hundred years.'

'But you are Archbishop; you set the rules, there is no higher authority.'

'Let us hope there is one.

'Meeting you here with this chronicle is a sin, for which I do expect forgiveness. I have a fondness for my Catholic brethren. But for one unholy Queen, we would all be Catholics still. St Etheldreda's is their oldest church. It dates from Longshanks's time and it is a wonder her infernal majesty did not lay waste to it as she did to so many of its kind… and my kind. It is ancient, survives when it should not, and is out of keeping with the times. Scant wonder I feel at home here.'

'Where is the chronicle?'

'Out of sight, below. Where is your reciprocation? What can you tell me of assassins in the Other Realm?'

'We have seen one dispatched this very afternoon, no two in truth.'

'Truly, Minister; should I rejoice?'

'No, one was bent on murder in our realm. The other had been tasked with an execution in hers that she could not carry out. Their human equivalents are dead too, and must be on my conscience. I do not think either responsible for the murders that have decimated your clergy.'

'So Wissendene must sleep still with one eye open.' Chislett glowered at Stanton, his milky eye watering in rheumy irony.

'My work is not done, but I can tell you much of what I have discovered, more of what I suspect and still more, I believe, when we have discovered Langtoft's secrets.'

'Down into the crypt with you then. I'll join you when I may.'

Cotteridge was bent over scrolls on a big table close to a large stained glass window. A spray of lanterns blossomed close by. Stanton summoned Maraziel and the three of them studied the immaculately-penned documents, which looked damp but smelt dry.

'What news on the King, Minister?' asked Cotteridge.

'Safe.'

Maraziel studied the roughly bound and bloodied cuts on Stanton's wrists and hands. 'What revels has Pitt involved you in?'

'I accidentally oversaw the death of the Bendith.'

'Before it had committed its murder?'

'I have not yet heard. There was such a horrible scream, I fear…' he didn't know what he feared.

'Any more delicacies to impart?'

'I witnessed the death of a Banshee, I think.'

'Which?'

'Dearbhla.'

'I have not had the dubious pleasure. How was it accomplished?'

'I do not rightly know. I set two Umbra the task of killing her but neither did. It may be they were on the wrong side of the Hibernian Sea.'

'Yet you know she is dead?'

'Yes, her ally, a robust young man died in front of me, from no cause I could see. I'm sure I heard her scream echo through him into this world. Could an Umbra kill a Banshee?'

'I doubt any of us can best a Banshee.'

Stanton remembered Agnieszka's prophecy. 'Muscari?'

'She is one of the few who would try. You would have to make her very angry…'

'I see.'

'… which is not difficult.'

'She believed she and Exeter had been shockingly slandered.'

'That would do it.'

'She may have thought she could save their reputation by preventing the death of King George.'

'It sounds unlikely.'

'Which side of the Hibernian Sea is Muscari to be found?'

'The wrong side; that is to say, the one with Banshees on it.'

'Then that might explain Dearbhla's death.'

'Was my name mentioned at all, in relation to this slandering?'

'You should take precautions.'

'You do well to warn me, as no good comes to you if Muscari discovers me. I daresay you realise this, human nature being so closely, but ineffectually, aligned to self preservation. I shall huddle down in Cernyw and prescribe sleep.'

'Would you be safer here, with me?'

'You seem much mired in murders and Bendiths. Cernyw is quite barbarous, and bristles with conflicts, but it is not as dangerous as your realm.'

'Cotteridge has discovered a shape to this explosion of magicks. The common element is the Queen 'Neath the Hedge.'

'The magicks are unimportant in themselves; only a sign that our worlds are on the cusp of change.'

'And there are ever more deaths here, caused by events in your realm.'

'Never mind, you'll catch up when your armies toddle off to France.'

'Perhaps so. There is yet more evidence of plague returning.'

'Yes, the dead are hemmed in too tight. They have to go somewhere. They are forced by weight of numbers to break their bounds – to become Greynhym.'

'The Greynhym are forced out of what? Hell?'

Cotteridge had been listening to just one side of this discussion and biding his time.

The clerk coughed for attention. 'If I may interrupt, Minister?'

'Let us hear him,' said Maraziel.

'The Chronicle is too large and arcane for quick translation Minister, said Cotteridge. 'I have given the Archbishop a solemn promise to only view and translate the two chapters relating to the Treaty signing and whether the Lords of the Dead, Gorgomon and Shait'n, attended it.

'The Archbishop told me their copy of Langtoft has long been under lock and key and the Church has passed down instructions, for generations, for it to remain hidden away; for it not to be read.'

'That is surely unnatural. It is the best record of the most important Treaty in Britain's history. A Treaty that binds us, still, and which no one alive can find, let alone view or read.'

'I doubt Langtoft was privy to all the particulars of the Treaty, for I doubt he understood the language of Hedge, but his role was to record its clauses for Longshanks, so he gained more insight than any other man.'

'Enough to warrant his death,' said Stanton.

'Before that, we must suppose, he gave a copy of his chronicle to Archbishop Winchelsey for safekeeping. I suspect Winchelsey took one look at what it contained and buried it in the deepest catacomb he could find. There must have been other copies but I wonder if they have not been destroyed or hidden since.'

'You have our attention, Cotteridge. Please tell all.'

'Are you sure, Minister. When it is known we have read it, there will be many who want to silence us... as Peter of Langtoft was silenced.'

'I've come this far, Cotteridge. You should not bear the burden alone.'

'So be it. First, Shait'n, Captain of the Greynhym, he was party to the Treaty. The Dead Lord Gorgomon would not attend, so Shait'n was the sole representa...'

'Soul representative,' a chuckle that Maraziel stopped quickly. 'This is noteworthy. If Gorgomon was not at the signing, much is clearer to me.'

'Shait'n was the only Dead Lord present. He agreed to restrict the dead, only for 350 years, to the area prescribed in the Treaty. Gorgomon's instruction, notes Langtoft, was that there was already no room to keep all the dead within their proposed lands. Around 140 years ago, the Umbra lords were supposed to cede more land to the dead.'

'It never happened,' said Maraziel, 'that part of the Treaty was er... nibbled.'

'By wolf's head moth caterpillars?'

'They were blamed.'

Cotteridge returned to his notes. 'The Queen drafted the Treaty so that the Umbra had to nominate one of their kind to ally with each adult Briton, as you know. Her aim was to reduce the number of dead, to lessen the strain on the Other Realm.'

'To cut the number of Greynhym, presumably?' Stanton asked Maraziel.

'Hardly in Shait'n's interest.'

Cotteridge said, 'We can summon our Umbra once a day and they must obey. A daily dose of their boundless life-force preserves us. She hoped death from old age would be unknown.'

'It didn't work,' said Maraziel. 'You humans find too many ways to die.'

'In this, I am sure, we are aided.'

'Most of us still age. Look at the Archbishop,' said Stanton.

'Many low-spirited Umbra are chosen for Englishmen and women. They resent giving their vigour away, so hold some back,' said Maraziel. 'There are exceptions. I can name five hundred.'

They turned at a tapping on the stairs as Archbishop Chislett limped towards them on his stick.

'Carry on, Cotteridge.' Stanton said, catching the Archbishop's glare towards Maraziel.

'This next, is more devastating, sir. The Treaty has a cessation date. It ends.'

'The blazes it does. How was this not known?' Stanton's confusion swung from Cotteridge to Maraziel. 'Did you know?'

'There are things you Englishmen must discover without help from me.'

'The end of Umbra,' Chislett spoke softly as if he had discovered God anew, 'thank the Lord.'

'When? What is its end date?' Stanton turned back to Cotteridge.

'Exactly five hundred years after the Queen took up her powers. That is, when she came of age.'

'Her puberty?'

'Yes.'

'Is that year recorded?'

'Not by Langtoft but we may estimate it from records of her age in later documents.'

'Tell me. When does it end, Cotteridge?'

'Any time now.'

'What happens then?' asked Chislett.

'Umbra no longer keep to their peace, I would think,' said Cotteridge. 'Their wars and rivalries are played out in our lands as in theirs; the dead will again be free to roam, to renew war on the Umbra, pestilence returns to its historic levels. Both Britains are likely restored to their state before the Queen came.'

'A more natural, Godly state,' said Chislett.

'What can we do?' The enormity of this knowledge had landed too quickly after Stanton's death-filled day.

'Pray,' said Chislett.

'Or, we could do what everyone else is doing – at least in my realm,' said Maraziel.

'Search for the returning Queen,' said Stanton.

'Langtoft has recorded her words here,' said Cotteridge. '"When Britain hath need of my power hence, you must look to my Sprig to return it to you." But he writes it is by no means certain she meant to return or can return. She will try if she believes her Treaty has not fulfilled its remit; if it is irredeemably broken. He speculates that most Umbra will work against it.'

'She returns?' the Archbishop hurled his stick to the flagstones, almost falling. Stanton secured him. 'Hell's whore is coming back?'

'Does Langtoft say how she comes back?'

'Trailing death and idolatry,' gobbets of spittle frothed from Chislett's mouth.

'There is a clue,' said Cotteridge.

'Let me guess: for her embryo to be known by her sigil; a blemish or birthmark in the shape of the Mistletoe Sprig?'

Cotteridge studied his Minister. 'Just so.'

'She will destroy us all. She will resume her war against God.' Chislett's mouth dropped open at a realisation, 'Oh, she already has.'

'This is why all this is happening now. The conspiracy that ranges as far as the Fens and endangers the Gracegirdles. The conspiracy that Lieutenant O'Brien said related to *The Book of Five Hundred*.'

Maraziel now stood on the document. 'Over the centuries, some men and women have always known of it,' she said. 'There is a song.'

Cotteridge reached for scribbled notes. 'An old folk rhyme.' He read out:

'The seek her in the morning-o; they seek her in the evening-o;

'In dale, on hill, by fen;

'They hunt for her in England-o; and look for her in Highlands-o;

'Through Powys and back again.

'They think she be a maiden-o; or perhaps an Umbra-o;

'They hunt, they kill, they scheme;

'They say she is returning-o; with war and plague and burning-o;

'They don't say where she's been.'

Maraziel applauded slowly, 'That's one version.'

Stanton slumped into a settle. The implications of what he had heard overwhelmed him. 'If the Treaty is allowed to end, it will pitch all Britain into the Dark Ages.'

'But, if she comes back, it's "War and plague and burning-o",' Chislett waved his reclaimed stick. 'She will plunge us all into Hell.'

If you think **The Mortality of Queens** deserves a bigger audience we'd love you to review it on Amazon or other review or sales sites. To follow the story as it develops, please go to **www.amorrie.com**.

Acknowledgements

Thanks to **Agnieszka Ryling** for beta reading, making suggestions, improving my blurbs and imbuing me with her enthusiasm for the story. She even became an Umbra when required.

More thanks to the talented writers of the **Cottered Writers Group** who suffered some chapters at a time when I still hadn't found the thread of the story; and the **Curtis Brown** Creative Writing school of 2019, particularly tutor **Simon Wroe** and fellow students **Julian Dobbin**, **Anwyn Kya Hayward**, **Alex Chai**, **Emma McDonagh** and **Peter Taylor-Gooby**, all terrific writers, who helped improve the early chapters.

If you enjoyed this story and want to find out how it continues, look out for book number two in The Umbra series: **A Conspiracy of Queens**. You can keep up to date with the series and help develop Umbra for future books at **www.interactpublishing.com**.

Here's a preview of Chapter One of that novel.

A Conspiracy of Queens

Chapter 1: The Mist-hung Nymph

The three new passengers huddled into the coach seats. Arthur's coach had picked them up from beside their overturned carriage two miles beyond Swanage. To Arthur's inexpert eye it looked as though their carriage had stumbled off the contorted rolling road in a thicker swirl of mist and thrown a wheel. It canted at an awkward angle and blurred shapes of mist-men were working on it.

Even upended and smoked with the sea fret, the carriage reeked of money.

Arthur's own journey had begun four days ago from London on a crowded stage coach. This last day from a coaching inn at Lytchett Minster to Swanage had been slow progress on corrugated roads, slicked by frost. At Swanage Arthur had reminded the driver of his need to go onto Netherwyck. The man's face set as bitter as the weather, but his employers had an agreement with Lord Lisle to ferry guests the four miles beyond Swanage to his estate when need arose. It was an agreement made for summer, not for fading afternoons of frost, fret and scant visibility, but Lord Lisle had not taken his household to London this winter. The driver and his guard had been looking forward to an early start in the ale-houses of Swanage and made their discontent known.

They had come upon the overturned carriage on a lonely stretch of road beyond Langton Maltravers. Branches of spectral beech trees overhung the road, their trunks fading in and out of view with the churn and coil of the mist. The calls of lost birds wished an end to the afternoon.

They picked up four in all: two young women, disguised in borrowed great coats that looked to have been lent by portly Russian generals, and one gentleman, in a frock coat and thick breeches. His clothes spoke of quality, even down to the scarf he had wrapped around his features to keep out the cold. The fourth, a man, presumably a servant, had climbed on top of the coach.

'We are very pleased to find you on this road, sir.' One of the women addressed him through upturned collars and chattering teeth. She sounded young but confident. 'We did not expect any others to be travelling to Netherwyck on such an afternoon. We must save introductions until we are safe there and sat before a fire.'

The coach returned to its lurching journey. Arthur thought the woman spoke to her Umbra as she whispered into the lapel of her coat. When he lip-read her 'go', before she hugged the coat closer, he imagined her Umbra had been released to return to the Other Realm.

A half-mile or so further on, there came a cry from beyond the coach.

'Hold.'

It was followed by a loud retort and the scuffle of activity on the carriage roof.

The gentleman jumped to his feet and fell again almost immediately as the coach stumbled to a halt. The two women shared a glance as horses whinnied and stamped skittering hooves on the road outside.

Arthur peeked out and caught movement in the mist – a rider on a horse. A voice came from the coach's left-hand side. 'Out this way if you please, sirs. My companion has a pistol trained on the other side to dissuade you from vacating that way.'

'Highwaymen,' said the gentleman. 'Let me go first.'

The gentleman opened the door and spoke to the indistinct shape he found there, 'There are ladies inside. I demand they be spared any ordeal.'

'I have no interest in your ladies, but all must leave the carriage so that we may search it.'

The four occupants stumbled out and lined up on the road beside the carriage. The servant climbed down and joined them, while the driver tended to his shot comrade on the road some yards away.

The highwayman had dismounted. His face was disguised by a kerchief, his tricorn hat pulled low. He levelled two horse pistols at them. What could be made out from the man's horse and thick coat suggested he prospered. A sword pushed at the confines of his riding cape.

'On your knees.'

As they complied, the gentleman spoke again, 'You are wasting your time, man. We four have been forced to leave our luggage behind and, as for this other poor unfortunate, you can see by his coat and hat, he is unlikely to have anything worthy of your trouble.'

'It is not your trinkets or purses I require. You sir, remove your scarf.'

The gentleman did so. 'If it's ransom you're after, then I am the one you seek. You may let these others go. I am Viscount Ex –'

'Yes, I daresay you'd fetch a good ransom, Exeter, but you are of no interest to me.'

'You know who –'

'Stay down and stay quiet, my lord.' The highwayman stepped close, one pistol levelled at Exeter's forehead.

Arthur could make out a tiny figure, five or six inches tall, wreathed in mist, standing on the Highwayman's shoulder – his Umbra. She was likely a Nymph, dressed in an insubstantial belted costume with a gauzy brown shawl wrapping her shoulders and drawn above her head. Her arms were bare with bracelets at each wrist. She was not dressed for this climate but for the weather in her own world, the unknowable Other Realm.

She spoke to the highwayman and her words drew his attention away from the Viscount to the other end of the kneeling line.

'You two there, I require your names. One of you has travelled from London, I think.'

'Do not give it,' warned Exeter. 'One is my servant, sir, and of little interest to you I'm sure. This other passenger is of no consequence and will furnish you with neither ransom or coin.'

'Not another word, Exeter, or I will shoot one of your two fillies in her commodity.'

Both ladies uttered something at this: one a small cry, the other what sounded like a gasp of amused astonishment.

He bent low and spoke with his Umbra, 'Yes, we must be sure. I think it the shorter fellow, but her scent will be on him if so. Can you sniff her out?'

Arthur watched as the Nymph slipped from the highwayman's shoulder, to elbow and then, with a spry hop to the ground, she moved towards Arthur and climbed up his coat, although he felt neither her weight or her presence. She pushed her nose close to his cheek and inhaled. Arthur tucked his chin in to observe her nod of confirmation to the highwayman. Looking up, he saw the pistol straighten in his direction.

Before the flintlock could be fired, the Nymph's eyes widened in horror just as a tiny hand came from beneath his lapel. It pulled her head hard against his coat material. A blade appeared at the Nymph's throat.

A yelp escaped Arthur, 'No, Amorrie, do not –'

But the blade had done its work. The Nymph's head dropped back as blood sprayed out. Her body gave a final shudder and vanished, taking most of the blood with it.

There was a cry of: 'Rozella, get you –'

Looking up, he saw the crouching highwayman drop his pistols to claw at his own throat. A smothered gurgle escaped as the man keeled over onto the road.

It took a moment before the turn of events dawned on any of the kneeling travellers, then Viscount Exeter was on his feet. He rushed across to the highwayman's body.

'Who is this villain? No common scamp, I'll wager.'

Exeter's servant, who had run to take down one of the coach's three lamps, brought it over, holding it above the stricken highwayman.

The kerchief was removed and Exeter swore. 'By the heavens,

I know him. It's Wycherley, Thomas Wycherley, he's one of The Five Hundred. He is no highwayman.'

'No, he's the son of a banker,' said one of the ladies, brushing frost from the front of her coat. 'I have refused him dances afore now.'

'He will not ask again,' said her young companion but found no levity in it.

'Amorrie,' Arthur appealed to the small dark girl, who sat in the crook of his arm, cleaning her blade on a corner of handkerchief she had teased from his coat pocket.

Her raven hair glistened wet in the light from the lamp. He hoped it was not from blood. Her fierce eyes peered at him through damp tendrils of hair, 'Do not dare scold me. I had to. You know it so.'

'Could you not, perhaps, have incapacitated her somehow.'

'Her incapacity would have ended when that masked devil shot you. It was her life or ours.'

'You are always too violent,' he struggled to regain his feet.

'Nymphs are no great loss to the world; either world – yours or mine.' She stood, stepped off his arm and dissolved into a shadowed fissure in the air, taking only her blade, her rich-earth scent and an over-curious wisp of mist with her.

Exeter had reached him and clamped a gloved hand beneath his elbow. 'I needs ask. Who are you, sir? Why would Wycherley want you dead?'

'Tenebris, Arthur Tenebris, my lord.' Arthur, still half crouching, attempted a bow. In a small voice he added, 'An artist. We met before Christmas at Lady Rochester's party in Marksfayre.'

'Truly? I have no recollection of it. And what of Wycherley?'

'I have never met him before today.'

≈

End of Chapter one of **A Conspiracy of Queens**.

Discover more about it at **www.amorrie.com**

◆ ◆ ◆

You can also check out my **The Doll with a Bruise** novel, in the crime thriller genre on Amazon and at the website:

www.interactpublishing.com

J.L. Dawn

Printed in Great Britain
by Amazon

74960574R00214